LOST ANGEL

Kitty Neale was raised in South London and this working class area became the inspiration for her novels. In the 1980s she moved to Surrey with her husband and two children, but in 1998 there was a catalyst in her life when her son died, aged just 27. After joining other bereaved parents in a support group, Kitty was inspired to take up writing and her books have been *Sunday Times* bestsellers.

Kitty now lives in Spain with her husband and is working on her new novel for Avon, due to be published in summer 2010.

To find out more about Kitty go to
www.kittyneale.co.uk

By the same author:

KITTY NEALE

Lost Angel

AVON

A division of HarperCollins*Publishers*
77–85 Fulham Palace Road,
London W6 8JB

www.harpercollins.co.uk

A Paperback Original 2009
1

First published in Great Britain by
HarperCollins*Publishers* 2009

Copyright © Kitty Neale 2009

Kitty Neale asserts the moral right to
be identified as the author of this work

A catalogue record for this book is
available from the British Library

ISBN-13: 978-1-84756-097-1

Set in Minion by
Palimpsest Book Production Limited
Grangemouth, Stirlingshire

Printed and bound in Great Britain by
Clays Ltd, St Ives plc

My thanks as always to my wonderful husband, Jim and daughter, Samantha, along with my agent, Judith Murdoch, and the wonderful team at Avon/HarperCollins.

For Shelley Blofeld.

Thank you, darling, for giving me two beautiful great-grandchildren and for making my grandson so happy. I hope your marriage will go from strength to strength, and though distant, you will always be able to see us as a part of your family.

1

Battersea, South London, September 1940

Nine-year-old Ellen Stone woke to the incessant wail of the air raid siren. Neighbourhood dogs were already howling and Ellen's stomach churned with fear as she flung back the blankets.

'Come on, get a move on,' her mother, Hilda, shouted, 'and don't forget your gas mask.'

Ellen's thin legs wobbled as she reached out in total darkness to fumble for the light switch. With the blackout in force, and the windows covered to prevent even a chink of light escaping, her bedroom looked gloomy in the dim glow of a bare lightbulb. Ellen pushed her shoulder-length dark hair aside as she thrust bare feet into her shoes, and then, grabbing the hated gas mask, she ran downstairs.

'Hurry up,' her mum urged.

They stumbled down the garden to the Anderson shelter, but could already hear the heavy, uneven throb of bombers flying across London.

'Oh, Mum,' cried Ellen.

'I know, love, I know,' she consoled, closing the shelter door behind them. 'Don't worry. They're probably going for the Surrey Docks again. Now hold the torch so I can light the oil lamp.'

With hands shaking, Ellen did as she was told, and though her mum was a tiny woman, less than five foot tall, she leaned on her strength. With light brown hair, small dark eyes and a thin face that ended in a pointed chin, her mother was like a pretty mouse in appearance, yet there was nothing meek in her demeanour. She could be soft and kind, but woe betide anyone who crossed her.

'There, that's better,' Hilda said in the glow from the oil lamp.

They sat on the camp bed, but Ellen jumped as a loud barrage of gunfire sounded, relieved when her mum put an arm around her shoulder, saying, 'They're ours, love. It's those huge banks of anti-aircraft guns they've set up in Battersea Park.'

'I . . . I'm still scared, Mum.'

'I know, and this can't go on. We need to get you out of London, but I don't fancy this evacuation lark where you'd be sent off to strangers. I've sent a letter to my old friend Gertie, asking if you can stay with her for a while.'

'But . . . but what about you? I don't want to go without you.'

'Your gran and granddad won't shift and I can't

2

leave them. You'll be fine with Gertie and you'll love it on her smallholding. She's even got chickens.'

There was the sudden shriek of stick bombs falling, along with the clatter of incendiaries as they landed on roofs and pavements. This was followed almost immediately by a loud boom, and another, so many that Ellen lost count as the ground shook beneath them. She was deafened by the noise, terrified, her mum now hunched over her like a shield.

All sense of time was lost, but then came a strange stillness, a hush before more noise – this time the dull thud of walls collapsing. 'Mum, I can smell burning.'

They sat up to hear the crackle of flames and swiftly her mum moved to douse the oil lamp, a tremor in her voice. 'The . . . the gas mains may have been hit, but it's all right, we're safe here. I think it's over now, but we'll have to wait for the all-clear. I can't light the Primus so we'll just have a drop of water.'

Fumbling in the dim light, her mum poured water from a bottle into tin mugs and, throat parched, Ellen drank it greedily. 'Thanks, Mum.'

They sat, ears alert, dreading another wave of bombers until at last, after what felt like another hour, the all-clear tone from the siren sounded.

Tentatively they left the shelter, only to stand

almost paralysed with shock at the sight that greeted them. Their house, along with every other in the street, had been destroyed, crushed, and all that remained were piles of rubble.

'Oh, no, no,' Hilda gasped.

The landscape appeared vast, alien, and at first beyond Ellen's comprehension, but then she realised why. It wasn't just their street that had been hit; it was the next one and the one beyond that, the area now a huge open mass of destruction. Dust was thick in the air, along with the smell of gas and smoke. Fires burned and Ellen was dimly aware of the distant sound of bells clanging as fire engines rushed to the scene. Yet still she and her mother stood, dazed and unmoving.

Gradually more people appeared, covered in dust like them, and it was only then that Ellen's mother seemed to come to life.

'Mum! Dad,' she cried, grabbing Ellen's hand to drag her forward. They stumbled over rubble, disorientated, both soon coated in filth, until at last Ellen thought they might be in what had once been the next street. Even though she knew what to expect, a sob caught in her throat. It was gone, like theirs . . . her grandparents' house was gone.

'Mum! Dad!' Hilda yelled, falling to her knees as she frantically dug at the rubble. Ellen ran to help, their hands and fingers soon bleeding, yet still they dug.

4

'I told them,' Hilda sobbed. 'I told them to use their shelter, but they just wouldn't listen and preferred to crawl under the table. Mum! Dad! Can you hear me?'

For a moment they paused, listening, praying to hear voices, but there was nothing. They began to pull at the rubble again, but then hands reached out to drag them away.

'Come on, you've got to stand back,' an ARP warden said. 'It's too dangerous and the heavy rescue teams are here now.'

Exhausted, they were led from the devastation and not long after a mobile canteen arrived. They were given cups of tea, a woman saying sympathetically, 'Are you all right?'

'My parents, they're under that lot. I've got to help,' Hilda gasped, about to move forward again.

'You won't be allowed past the cordon. Leave it to the rescue teams. They know how to assess the risks, how to find people buried under rubble; it's best if you stay out of the way.'

The vast area was a hive of activity now, firemen, policemen, ambulances, heavy rescue teams, ARP wardens, but all Ellen could think about was her beloved gran and granddad. She was aware of other people around them, women and children crying, but she felt strange, remote, the sounds coming as though from a distance. She swayed, a rushing sound in her ears, and then, as her knees caved beneath her, Ellen knew no more.

Hilda was reeling with grief. It had been a dreadful twenty-four hours and she was almost on the point of collapse, yet she had to hold herself together for her daughter's sake. Her only relief was that Ellen wasn't hurt; the fainting fit a combination of shock and nervous exhaustion. She was still whey-faced, her blue eyes bruised with pain; her daughter, like her, was grieving.

It had been hours before her parents were pulled from the rubble, both dead, and for the rest of her life Hilda knew she would never forget the nightmarish sight of their broken bodies. Now she had the funeral to arrange, and even though her friend, Mabel Johnson – whose house was outside the bombed area and untouched – had taken them in, Hilda felt so alone. If only Doug was here; but at the outset of the war her husband had enlisted in the navy. He was on a ship, somewhere at sea, and, with so many naval losses being reported, she feared for his safety.

'Here, get that down you,' Mabel said, her kind, round face soft with concern as she handed Hilda a cup of tea.

'Mabel, I've lost everything. My home, furniture and, until you all rallied round, we only had the filthy clothes we stood in.'

'You'll be found somewhere else to live, but in the meantime didn't you mention once that your mum had a sister? I expect you'll want to go to her.'

'She died years ago, Mabel, and after that her husband and son moved away. They didn't bother to keep in touch with us and I've no idea where they are.'

'Until you're re-housed you're welcome to stay here,' Mabel said soothingly. 'With my Jack away fighting in this bloody war and both my boys evacuated to Devon, I've got plenty of room.'

'Thanks, it's good of you.'

'Don't be daft. We've been mates since we were nippers and I know you'd do the same for me.'

'I still can't believe my parents have gone. All I've got left of them is this necklace, Mum's chain and crucifix. She always wore it, swore by it, but . . . but a lot of good that did her,' Hilda said, once again overwhelmed by grief.

Mabel let her cry for a while, but then said, 'I knew your mum well, although . . . I didn't know she was religious.'

'She wasn't really, well, not a churchgoer. The necklace was my grandmother's, passed on to Mum when she died. For some reason she used to say that wearing it made her feel as though Gran was watching over her.'

'Who knows? Maybe she was.'

'She's dead, Mabel. My dad too. What was the point of believing in a daft cross and chain?'

'From what you've been told, they didn't suffer.'

Hilda nodded and, though thankful for that, she still felt lost, bereft. She clutched the chain, her mother's face still so clear in her mind, and then slowly fastened it around her neck.

'That's it, girl. Sometimes we all need something to cling to, something that gives us a bit of hope.'

'I don't think this necklace has some sort of mysterious power. I'm only wearing it because . . . because it was hers . . .' And with those words Hilda broke down again. She was a grown woman, a wife and a mother, yet now her parents were gone she felt lost. They had always been there for her to run to – had always loved her unconditionally. Now, without them, she felt so alone.

2

Bombs continued to rain down on London, and Hilda soon lost count of the number of times they had to flee to Mabel's air raid shelter. The funeral had been dreadful and she'd barely managed to get through it. So many of her parents' friends had been there, people like them who had lived in this neighbourhood all their lives. Now they were watching it crumbling around them as more and more houses were destroyed. Those whose homes remained refused to leave the area, stoically saying that the Luftwaffe weren't going to chase them out, but Hilda had found it hard to listen to. If her parents had left Battersea, they'd still be alive. She had to get Ellen to safety and was still waiting to hear from Gertie, but the thought of parting with her daughter was almost more than she could bear. With her parents gone and Doug away, Ellen was all she had left.

Hilda stood in the queue now, there to beg for

accommodation again, and when it came to her turn she said, 'Please, you must have something?'

'We're doing our best, Mrs Stone. We've got so many families to re-house and at least you've got temporary accommodation with Mrs Johnson.'

'My daughter's in a dreadful state. Her nerves have gone and she needs the stability of her own home again.'

'She should be evacuated.'

'Don't you think I know that?' Hilda snapped. 'I'm waiting to hear from a friend and if she'll take her in, my daughter will be sent to Somerset.'

'Perhaps you should go with her.'

Hilda stared at the woman, mouth agape, yet as her words sunk in, they gave her food for thought.

'If you ask me, it would be the ideal solution,' the woman continued, 'or you could try some private landlords. I'm afraid you aren't a high priority, Mrs Stone, but if anything becomes available, we'll let you know. Next, please!'

Dismissed, Hilda moved aside, her place quickly taken by the next person in the queue. It was hopeless, she thought, dejected as she made her way back to Mabel's.

'How did you get on?' Mabel asked when Hilda returned, footsore and downcast.

'It was a waste of time. I think you'd have to be

kipping on the street before they'd help. Oh, I shouldn't moan, Mabel. I know there's worse off than me.'

'Yeah, you're right. Pat Randle got re-housed – not that it was much, just a couple of rooms – but within a week she was bombed out again. It's terrible, Hilda, and I live in dread of this place being hit.'

Hilda didn't say it, but she too lived with the same fear. It broke her heart to pass through the streets where she and her parents once lived, the area a vast, ugly bombsite now, and Mabel was right, the same thing could happen to this house, to this street, and they'd be homeless again. Was it any wonder that they were all so jumpy and Ellen a bundle of nerves?

'You're miles away, Hilda.'

'Sorry, I was thinking about Ellen. If I don't hear from Gertie soon, I'll have to think about having her evacuated.'

'It'd be for the best. I know your mum used to take you to play with Gertie, but after what came out later I wouldn't fancy sending my kids to her.'

'Don't be daft. Gertie wouldn't hurt Ellen, she loves children, and I'd rather she went there than to strangers. Mind you, something the housing officer said has set me thinking.'

'About what?'

'She suggested that I go to Somerset too.'

'What! But you're a Londoner. You'd go mad living in the sticks.'

'At one time I might have, but now I'm not so sure. The thought of being away from these bombing raids, of a bit of peace and quiet, is more than tempting.'

'When this war started everyone said it'd be over in five minutes, but they were wrong. Families have been torn apart, mine included. Jack's away fighting, my kids are miles from me and . . . and now you're going too.'

Hilda was shocked to see tears in Mabel's eyes. She wasn't usually an emotional woman; more the take what life throws at you and get on with it type.

'I'm only thinking about it, Mabel. I haven't made my mind up yet.'

The air raid siren suddenly wailed and Mabel jumped to her feet. 'Oh, sod it, not again.'

They hurried to the shelter, Hilda's forehead creased with worry. 'I hope Ellen's all right. I wish I'd kept her at home now.'

'She had to go back to school sometime, and, if you ask me, it'll do her good to play with her friends again. Stop worrying. She'll be fine.'

They sat down, Hilda's heart racing with fear and her hand clutching the crucifix. Whenever she was frightened or deep in thought it was something she seemed to do automatically now and impatiently she let it go. It couldn't help her, just as it hadn't helped her mother, and she was just being silly.

Tense, they listened for the sound of bombers, but heard nothing and less than an hour later looked at each other with relief when the all-clear sounded. Back in the house Mabel immediately put the kettle on the gas.

'I don't know about you, mate, but false alarm or not, I could murder a cup of tea.'

'I hate it being rationed. How are we doing?'

'We've got enough and, anyway, I use the same tea leaves twice to stretch them out.'

'Yes, I know. Sometimes I can see through the tea to the bottom of my cup.'

'You cheeky mare. Still, it's nice to hear you sounding a bit lighthearted again.'

'I don't feel lighthearted, Mabel. When I wake up in the morning the first thing I think about is my parents, and they seem to remain constantly on my mind.'

'It's early days yet, but it'll get easier, you'll see.'

They sat drinking their tea, Hilda trying to keep up with Mabel's chatter while her mind kept drifting elsewhere – to Gertie and Somerset.

It was an hour later when the door opened and Ellen walked in.

'Hello, pet. Did you have a nice day at school?'

'It . . . it was all right,' Ellen said, the stammer she'd developed evident. 'I . . . I was frightened when th . . . the siren went off an . . . and we all had to go down to the basement again.'

'It was a false alarm and nothing to worry about.'

'M . . . Mr Green said th . . . the school will be closing. He gave us letters to . . . to bring home.'

Hilda took it, but after what Ellen had just said, she wasn't surprised by the contents. It was a general letter, addressed to all the parents, saying that the school would be closing at the end of the month. As others had before him, the headmaster also urged that any children still in London should be evacuated. Hilda looked at Mabel, dreaded telling her, but the letter had sealed her decision.

'I've got to get Ellen away from here, Mabel. If Gertie had got my last letter I'm sure she'd have replied by now. I'm going to write to her again.'

'N . . . no, Mum. I don't want to go away. I . . . I want to stay with you.'

'Don't fret, love. This time I'm going to ask Gertie if we can both stay with her.' Smiling sadly at her friend, Hilda added, 'I'm sorry, Mabel.'

'It's all right, I understand, but I'm gonna miss you,' she said, a choke in her voice.

'I'll miss you too, and doing this blows any chance I've got of getting re-housed. I'm beginning to feel like a gypsy with no fixed abode, travelling from one place to another. I just hope it won't be for long, that it'll be over soon and we can come back to where we belong.'

'Yes, mate, you'll be back,' Mabel said with a show of bravery now. 'Once a Londoner, always a Londoner.'

Hilda knew she was putting on a brave front and smiled gratefully. If Mabel broke down she would too, but more tears were the last thing Ellen needed to see. Yes, Gertie would take them in, she was sure of it, and a little time in the country was just what Ellen needed.

It would be hard to leave her friends, especially Mabel, but in Somerset they'd be safe, Gertie's home providing a haven until soon, she was sure, this dreadful war would be over.

3

Ellen was shaken awake when the train pulled into Crewkerne station and climbed bleary-eyed out of the carriage. It was three in the afternoon as she and her mother stood on the platform, a bitter cold wind cutting through their clothes. Only moments later a tall, big-boned woman appeared and Ellen was amazed to see that she was wearing scruffy, brown, corduroy trousers that were tucked into wellington boots, along with a dirty navy duffel coat. Not only that, she was wearing a brown flat cap with her dark blonde hair tucked up beneath it.

'Hilda,' the woman cried, her dark brown eyes warm as she strode up to them and her strong features softened by a wide smile.

'Hello, Gertie,' smiled Hilda.

'You look exhausted. Come on, let's get you home,' Gertrude Forbes said as she grabbed both suitcases. 'My goodness, is that Ellen? I can't believe it.'

'Of course it's Ellen. It was her birthday last month and she's ten now.'

'She's so pretty – but has it been that long since I've seen you?'

'Yes, nearly seven years and you've been in Somerset for six of them.'

'Where does the time go? Come on, follow me,' said Gertie, striding ahead of them now.

'Blimey, is that yours?' Hilda asked when she saw a small horse and cart.

'Yes. Ned's the only transport I have and I'd be lost without him.'

Hilda eyed the horse warily, but Gertie urged them to climb onto a bench-like seat at the front of the flat cart. She then stowed their cases in the back before heaving herself up beside them.

'Right, we're off,' she said, taking the reins, and with a gentle click of her tongue, the horse moved forward.

Ellen had never been on a horse and cart before and found it strange: the gentle sway, the clip, clop of hooves as they rode along a narrow street. Soon they were passing through a small town and she listened as her mother spoke with Gertie.

'Thanks for this. Thanks for taking us in.'

'It's nothing and I'm sorry it took so long to answer your letters. I don't get post delivered, and rarely go to the village. It was quite a surprise to find two waiting for me, but awful to hear about your parents. I should have kept in touch with your mother, but when it all came out I wasn't sure she'd want anything to do with me.'

'She was shocked, but you know my mum, she never had a bad word to say about anyone. Oh, Gertie, I still can't believe she's gone, that they're both gone.'

'I'm so sorry, Hilda, so very sorry.'

Ellen leaned against her mother, shivering, her teeth beginning to chatter. 'Mum . . . I . . . I'm cold.'

'Here,' Gertie said as a tarpaulin-like cover was thrown over them. 'Tuck that around you and it'll keep you both warm.'

'How far is it to your place?' Hilda asked.

'It's a fair trot, and don't expect too much. By the time we get there you'll find yourself in the middle of nowhere, and as for those daft shoes, forget it. Like me, you'll need boots and the same goes for Ellen.'

'Gertie, I can't believe how different you look. In London you always looked so smart, if a bit severe, and I never thought I'd see the day when you'd wear trousers and wellies.'

'Needs must,' Gertie said dismissively, 'and anyway, I prefer them.'

'You said in your letters that you're fine, but it's been years since Susan left. Have you found anyone else?'

'No, and I don't want to.'

'Aren't you lonely?'

'Not really. I have my animals, and – unlike people – they don't let you down.'

'You sound so bitter, Gertie.'

'What do you expect?' she replied, eyes flashing. 'I lost everything for Susan, my reputation, my career, then after moving here she left me.'

'You could have returned to London.'

'At first I wanted to lick my wounds in private, then, as time passed, I became used to the seclusion. I love it now. I'm self-sufficient and I doubt I'll ever leave.'

'At the moment you're better off here. London is hell. Since September we've had bombing raids day and night, but mostly at night now.'

'You'll be safe here.'

'Have you heard from your father?' Hilda asked. 'Is he still in London?'

'I expect so, but I haven't heard from him and doubt I ever will. You know what happened when he found out. He almost had an apoplectic fit and said I'd disgraced the family name. He'll never forgive me.'

Ellen was at a loss to understand this strange conversation. Forgive Gertie for what? She spoke of licking wounds, and what on earth was an apothingy fit? Ellen wanted to ask, but knew better than to interrupt her mother when she was talking.

She'd learned that if she kept quiet, sometimes adults would forget she was there, but one sound, one word, and they'd either stop speaking or chase her out.

They had left the town behind; the countryside they were passing through wintry and bleak. It was so quiet, so peaceful and warm beneath the cover that Ellen closed her eyes. She felt the sway of the cart and found the voices drifting, growing distant.

Hilda saw that Ellen had fallen asleep again and held her close. She sighed heavily, the tension in her neck easing. Gertie had welcomed them and at last they were away from the bombings. Surely in the peace of the countryside Ellen's nerves would heal?

'It's lovely to have you here, Hilda, and yonks since I've seen you. Just how long have we been friends?'

'I'll have a go at working it out. I was about eight years old when my mum started work as a domestic in your father's house and you were the same age. I think we saw each other occasionally, though at that time I'd hardly call us friends.'

Gertie chuckled. 'Yes, I remember now, and my goodness I was such a stuck-up little bitch.'

'Don't remind me,' Hilda said ruefully.

'When my mother died and I was sent to boarding school, it was a rude awakening. I missed her so much and hated it, yet it was worse when I came home during school holidays. My father had changed so much and, other than religious instruction, he ignored me. If it hadn't been for your mother's kindness, my life would have been very bleak.'

'Mum was a good woman, but even then you and I rarely saw each other. I think it all changed when you were expelled and by then we must have been close to twelve years old.'

'I wasn't sorry to be expelled; in fact, I think I pushed for it by behaving so badly, yet I came unstuck. It was worse being tutored at home and I was so bloody lonely. My father was wrapped up in his work, the church, and was hardly ever home. After lessons I just rattled around in that huge house, with only your mother and the cook for company.'

'That was when Mum started dragging me to your house every weekend and during school holidays.'

'She dragged you! Was it that bad?'

'Gertie, I hate to say it, but it was at first. I hardly knew you, and, let's face it, you were a lot different from my usual friends. To me you sounded posh, upper class, and in fact, you still do.'

'It certainly didn't rub off on you though,' Gertie said, but the sting was taken out of her words by her warm smile. 'You've never mentioned it, but you must have resented having to come to Kensington, especially when my father would only allow you to play with me if you joined us in religious instruction.'

'I must admit I didn't like all that stuff from the Old Testament.'

'Oh, yes, he loved to talk about God's wrath, of fire and brimstone.'

'It frightened the life out of me, but Mum still made me join you. It was years later before I found out why. She thought a lot of you, Gertie, and knew that I'd have to keep it up or be banned from the house. I think in some ways she came to see you as her second daughter.'

'Did she? I thought your mother was being kind because she felt sorry for me. In fact, I envied you your family – the closeness you shared.'

'I don't know why. Compared to mine, your home was like a palace.'

'My life was so restricted that it was more like a prison. Thank goodness you came along and we became more than just friends. I wish I'd known that your mother saw me as a daughter, because to me you were like a sister, one who stood by me through thick and thin.'

'Now don't exaggerate,' Hilda protested. 'As adults we went our separate ways. You for teacher training, and me, well, until I met Doug, I only worked in a local shop.'

'Yes, but we always stayed in touch, and unlike everyone else you didn't judge me, or ostracise me.'

'Why should I? You're still the same person and a good one at that. Take now for instance. If it wasn't for you I'd have been forced to have Ellen evacuated to strangers.'

'When I read your first letter, asking if Ellen could come to stay with me, I can't tell you how much it meant to me. When the school found out, they couldn't get rid of me quickly enough. I was treated like a monster, a bad influence and unsafe to be around children. My father was the worst, saying I was an abomination in God's eyes.'

'That's rubbish. There's nobody I'd trust more with Ellen.'

'Thanks, and it's nice you've arrived just before Christmas. Mind you, I've had enough religion stuffed down my throat to last me a lifetime, but as it was once a pagan festival I won't feel like a hypocrite if we have a bit of a celebration.'

Hilda's throat tightened. She didn't want to think about Christmas – her first one without her parents – yet for Ellen's sake, she'd have to make some kind of effort.

Ellen stirred, sitting up to look around her. 'Are . . . are we there yet?'

It was Gertie who answered. 'Sorry, but we've still got a way to go. Are you hungry?'

Ellen nodded. 'Ye . . . yes.'

'I've left a beef casserole braising in the range and it'll be ready when we arrive.'

'Cor,' Ellen said, fully awake now.

'I'm not much of a cook, but hopefully it'll be all right.'

'How do you get on with rationing?' Hilda asked.

'So far it isn't a problem, and the butcher doesn't even ask for a coupon.'

'You're lucky. In London we only get our rationed amounts and there's talk of it getting worse.'

Soon a tiny village loomed in front of them, but Gertie just drove through it and out the other side. On and on they went, the light dimming and no sign of any other habitations, until at last Gertie eased the horse and cart left into a narrow lane. At the end she finally pulled on the reins, saying as the horse drew to a halt and she hopped down, 'I'll just open the gates.'

Ellen could see little as her eyes tried to pierce the gloom. Gertie didn't get onto the cart again; instead she gripped the bridle to lead the horse through. Ellen could now see a small cottage, and as Gertie tethered the animal she watched her mother climb down from the cart, her feet sinking into thick, heavy mud.

'Yeah, I can see what you mean about boots,'

her mum complained then held up her arms. 'Come on, Ellen.'

Ellen felt the ooze as her feet touched the ground, then the sucking sensation as she lifted one foot.

'Come on, this way,' Gertie said as she grabbed their cases, 'but watch your step.'

Tentatively they squelched to the front door, both taking off their mud-caked shoes before stepping inside. It was dark, but they felt a welcome blast of warm air, along with a low growl.

'Oh Gawd, what's that?' Hilda gasped.

'It's only Bertie,' said Gertie as she lit an oil lamp.

'Bertie?' she yelped as the growls turned to sharp yaps.

'He won't hurt you,' Gertie assured and, as light pierced the gloom, a small white dog with a blaze of black on his face came into view.

The dog ran up to Ellen, yapping and jumping around her with excitement. She smiled, crouching down to stroke him. 'He . . . he's so sweet.'

'He's a Jack Russell terrier and perfect for ratting.'

'Rats,' her mother squeaked. 'Oh, blimey.'

'There are rats in London – in fact, probably more than around here. Now take your things off and make yourself at home while I see to the horse. I expect you're dying for a cup of tea so you can put the kettle on the range to boil.'

'Why the oil lamps? Ain't you got electricity?'

'No, but at least I've got running water.'

The journey had seemed to go on for ever, and now unable to hold it any longer, Ellen said, 'I . . . I need the toilet.'

'Go through the scullery and you'll find it outside the back door,' Gertie told her.

Ellen barely took in the deep sink and draining board as she passed through the scullery. The wooden door to the outside toilet squeaked, but there was no light so she left it open, managing in the gloom as she perched on such a funny seat.

It was strange here, so quiet, but sort of nice too, and Ellen thought she might like living in the country.

When Gertie marched outside again, the dog at her heels, Hilda took a look around the room. The ceiling was low, crossed with heavy, dark beams, the room dominated by a huge, black cooking range. A small, scruffy wooden table stood in the centre, and on each side of the range she saw wing-back chairs, one with horsehair stuffing poking through the upholstery. Other than that there was a dresser, the shelves packed with a mishmash of china.

Gertie was right, this place wasn't much, but nevertheless Hilda was charmed by the cosy atmos-phere. Gertie had done her best, the tiny, deep-set, lead-paned window dressed with chintz curtains, the wide sill sporting a jug of dried flowers. Hilda found herself sniffing the air, her mouth salivating at the rich aroma of beef casserole.

'It . . . it's a funny toilet,' Ellen said as she came back inside. 'There isn't a . . . a proper seat, just a long wooden bench with . . . with a hole in it.'

'I never thought I'd see the day when I thought our little house was luxurious, but compared to this . . .' Hilda had to pause, a lump in her throat. There was no house now, her home just a pile of rubble. Hilda managed to swallow her emotions. They were here now, safe, and that was the most important thing. 'We'll be eating soon, but in the meantime I'll make us all a drink.'

'Why . . . why does Gertie wear men's clothes?'

Hilda paused as she wondered how to answer her daughter's question. Ellen was too young to understand so, grasping, she said, 'I expect it's because it's sensible to wear trousers when you're working outdoors, and warmer too.'

'Can . . . can I wear trousers?'

'Well, yes, I suppose so, but I don't know how we'll get hold of any.'

'Get hold of what?' Gertie asked, catching the tail end of the conversation as she stepped inside.

'Like you, Ellen wants to wear trousers.'

'That won't be a problem. I've got an old sewing

27

machine and we can soon knock her up a couple of pairs. You'll need some too, Hilda.'

'Me! No, I don't think so.'

'We'll see. Now then, have you put the kettle on the range?' she asked brusquely.

'I was just about to do it.'

'Get a move on, and you, Ellen, can lay the table for dinner.'

'Gertie, you haven't changed and sound as bossy as ever,' Hilda said, giggling as she added, 'Talk about a school mistress. What next? If we don't behave, will you give us the cane?'

Gertie at first looked shocked, but then she too began to laugh. 'Oh, Hilda, I really am glad you're here.'

'Can . . . can we have our dinner now?' a small voice said.

'Yes, all right,' Gertie agreed, 'and tomorrow I'll show you how to collect eggs for our breakfast.'

'Where's your dog?'

'He's been cooped up in here while I went to fetch you, but once we've eaten you can call him in again. I've a cat too, but Wilfred's a tom and is mostly off roaming.'

'Wh . . . what else have you got?' Ellen asked eagerly.

'Two pigs and a goat.'

Hilda saw her daughter's delight and smiled. It was going to be all right, and she was sure that bringing Ellen here had been the right decision. Ellen would recover and enjoy exploring the countryside. And I'll be fine too, Hilda decided, yet there was no way that Gertie was going to get her into trousers.

4

During the next five months Hilda saw a huge change in her daughter. Ellen's stammer disappeared, and, though they were both still grieving, the horrors of living in London during the Blitz soon seemed far away. Instead of an air raid siren, they now woke up to the sound of birdsong and Gertie's cockerel.

The only school was on the other side of the village and, as it was a long way to go, Gertie was tutoring Ellen at home. At first she had missed the company of other children, but once spring had arrived and the skeletal trees burst into new growth, Ellen had become totally enamoured with the countryside. When not having lessons or helping out on the smallholding, she spent hours roaming the woods, bringing home all sorts of things – bugs, bluebells and other wildflowers – all of which Gertie would identify for her. Gertie also showed her how to press the flowers and leaves before carefully placing them in albums, and, for Ellen, a love of nature was born. Hilda's smile was wry when she thought about her daughter's new passion. She couldn't feel the same. Yes, it was safe here, but she hated living in such total isolation. Gertie didn't have a wireless, so the only news they got was when they made the hour-long trip to the village. She kept in touch by letter with Mabel and had received shocking news. Mabel's house had been structurally damaged during a bombing raid, but thankfully she hadn't been hurt. Mabel had then had a stroke of luck when, through the grapevine, she'd found a private landlord who offered her a flat in Clapham. It seemed that Mabel loved it there, and, not only that, it was an area that so far had been barely touched by bombs.

It made Hilda realise how lucky they were to have left Battersea, though she still wasn't keen on working outdoors. Thankfully Gertie always mucked out the pigs, though that still left the back-breaking work of digging for spring planting. If she had news of Doug it would be something, but though she'd sent him a letter with her new address, so far there had been no reply. God, she missed him so much, prayed he was safe, and for a moment tears stung her eyes. Britain had lost so many vessels, so many seamen, and Hilda lived in constant fear of hearing that his ship had been sunk. Inadvertently her hand rose to clutch the crucifix.

'Hilda, I know you only wear that thing because it belonged to your mother, but when you're miles away you always seem to hold it,' commented Gertie. 'I thought that, like me, you'd had enough religion rammed down your throat.'

'I have, especially after the way your father turned on you. What happened to all that stuff he used to spout about not judging others lest you be judged?'

'Try telling him that.'

Hilda shuddered, remembering her childhood fear and awe of Gertie's father. The man had been almost maniacal in his preaching, and it had been enough to turn her off going to church for life.

'Gertie, can we go to the village today?'

'There's no need to go every week and I'd rather get the rest of the potatoes in, along with cabbage and carrots. There's the salad crop too and tomatoes to bring on in the greenhouse.'

'For goodness' sake, Gertie, give it a break. I'm worried about Doug and there might be a letter.'

'This is a busy time of year and if I don't plant, I don't eat. I know I've preserved fruit from last year, made jam and pickles, but I need to sell produce to buy flour, meat, and anything else I can't grow.'

'It still seems strange to think of you making jam.'

'I hate it, hate any kind of cooking, but needs must.'

'Before we came I had no idea how much land you had. How on earth have you managed on your own?'

'I had a lad of fourteen working for me, but once conscription started labour became short. He found a job earning more than I could possibly pay him, and since then it's been impossible to find hired help. I had to cut down on planting, but now you've arrived we've managed to start a lot more off.'

'Yeah, and I've done my best to muck in, but I'm really worried about Doug. I haven't heard from him yet, and if you take me to the village I promise I'll really get stuck in again when we get back.'

'If you'd only learn to handle Ned you could go on your own.'

'He hates me.'

'Hilda, he's a horse and just needs firm hands on the reins.'

'I was firm, but the sod wouldn't move.'

Gertie shook her head with obvious disgust, but Hilda tried a winning smile. It was all right for Gertie. She was happy living like a virtual recluse, but for Hilda it was becoming more and more difficult. She missed her friends, the bustle of London, and if only the Luftwaffe would stop dropping bombs she'd go back like a shot.

'Please, Gertie.'

'Oh, all right. I need to see the butcher so might as well do that, but I'm not hanging about while you waste time gossiping with the locals again.'

Hilda smiled with delight as she went to the bottom of the stairs to call Ellen. They shared a bedroom under the eaves, snuggled up in a huge, lumpy, iron-framed bed.

'Ellen, Ellen, come on, get up.'

'Another one,' Ellen said when she finally appeared, her hands cupped around a catch.

Hilda shuddered as she backed away. That was another thing she hated, the huge spiders that regularly appeared in their bedroom and the rest of the cottage.

'Is it one of them whoppers?'

'Yes, a tree spider,' Ellen said as she walked over to the back door.

'Hurry up! Get it out of here before you drop it.'

'Honestly, Hilda,' said Gertie, 'anyone would think you've never seen a spider before. You should be used to them by now and there are plenty of spiders in London.'

'Yes, but not those bloody great hairy things.'

'They won't hurt you,' Gertie said as she opened the back door for Ellen and the spider was dispatched.

Hilda's cheeks puffed with relief, the insect soon forgotten as she began to boil eggs for their breakfast. She was anxious to go and as soon as they'd eaten she chivvied Ellen to get ready, while Gertie went to get the horse from the small field.

Just getting the horse and cart harnessed took ages and it drove Hilda mad but, knowing better than to complain, she just smiled gratefully at Gertie when at last they set off. It was a nice morning with hardly a cloud in the sky and just a slight nip in the air. 'Oh, Gertie, I hope there's a letter.'

'Stop worrying. If anything had happened to Doug you'd have heard.'

'I haven't got a clue where he is, what ocean, where he's headed. I think he tried to tell me in his last letter, but it was so heavily censored with line after line blacked out that it was unreadable.'

'How did he end up in the navy?'

'As soon as the war started he couldn't wait to get to a recruitment office. He said he didn't fancy the army with all the foot slogging, so volunteered for the navy.'

'What does he do?'

'He's a stoker and I've been allotted most of his pay, but I don't know why the silly bugger was so quick to enlist.'

'Mum, you sweared,' Ellen protested.

'Swore,' Gertie corrected.

Hilda smiled ruefully as she ruffled her daughter's hair. 'Yeah, well, this war is enough to make a saint swear – not that I want to hear you using bad language.'

Ellen leaned against her. Hilda's mind was full of her husband. When they met she had fallen for his tall, dark good looks and twinkling blue eyes. Doug had been a milkman before the war, up at the crack of dawn, out in all weathers, but nothing had seemed to get him down and he always had a ready smile. Ellen took after him, and every time Hilda looked at her daughter she could see her husband. She longed to see him, and though Hilda knew that she and Doug looked odd together – him six foot tall and her under five – she didn't care. She loved Doug, missed him so much and cursed this bloody war. His letters had been fairly regular until now, but then this gap had come and she was worried sick.

At last the village came into view and, pulling on the reins, Gertie said, 'Whoa, Ned,' as she brought the horse to a stop outside the general store-cum-post office.

Gertie had hardly tethered Ned before Hilda was hurrying inside, thankful to find she was the only customer.

'Is there any mail for me?' she asked eagerly.

'No, I'm sorry, there's nothing,' Mrs Brandon, the elderly postmistress said.

Hilda sagged with disappointment, but as Ellen rushed into the shop she managed to hide her feelings.

'Is there a letter, Mum?'

'No, pet, but don't worry. Your dad's sure to write soon.'

'Can I have some sweets?'

'I suppose so and I might as well get a few things in.'

There was still no evidence of food shortages as Hilda pulled out their ration books, glad that at least she had always taken these, along with their birth certificates and marriage lines to the shelter. She asked for butter, sugar, flour, yeast, along with a newspaper, while Ellen chose a gobstopper and some barley sugar.

Mrs Brandon was totting up the bill when Gertie stepped inside. 'Come on, Hilda, get a move on,' she chided.

'Morning, Miss Forbes,' the postmistress said pointedly.

'Good morning, Mrs Brandon,' Gertie replied, her tone clipped.

'I was only saying to Mrs Cook earlier that it must be nice for you having a friend to stay.'

Gertie didn't answer the woman, only saying to Hilda as she marched out of the shop again, 'I'll wait for you outside.'

Mrs Brandon's neck stretched with indignation as she puffed, 'Well, I never.'

'Sorry,' Hilda said as she hurriedly paid for her goods before leaving the shop.

'Look, I've got a gobstopper,' Ellen said as she ran to Gertie's side.

'That'll keep you quiet for all of five minutes.'

'Gertie, you were a bit short with Mrs Brandon,' Hilda complained.

'She was just after gossip and I won't give her, or anyone else in the village, the satisfaction of knowing my business. Now let's get to the butcher's and then we can go home.'

Hilda sighed. Unlike Gertie, she missed chatting to people – all right, gossiping if that's what Gertie wanted to call it – but nowadays she didn't get the chance. 'While we're there I'll get some sausages and a bit of bacon, but why do you need to talk to him?'

'Until I get new crops to sell money will be a bit tight, so at this time of year I take him one of my pigs for slaughter.'

'No! No!' Ellen yelped.

'Oh, darn, I shouldn't have said anything in front of her.'

'It's a bit late now,' Hilda snapped as Ellen flung herself against her.

Gertie crouched down. 'Listen, Ellen, you like eating roast pork, sausages, and bacon, don't you? I raise pigs for food, not as pets – but I'm sorry, I should have warned you.'

'Wh . . . what about the other one?'

'She'll be having a litter soon, and once weaned

38

I'll sell all the piglets but one which I'll fatten up for next year. I know it all sounds awful to you, but it's the way of life on farms and smallholdings.'

Ellen wasn't mollified, but just then they were all distracted by the roar of an engine as a motorbike drove into the village. At first Hilda thought the driver was going to pass straight through, but then he suddenly braked. The man lifted his goggles, turned to look at her, and Hilda blinked, unable to believe her eyes.

The bag of shopping left her hand in shock and groceries spilled onto the pavement, unheeded as Hilda dashed forward. 'Doug! Ohh . . . Doug,' she cried, her face alight with joy.

5

Ellen couldn't stop smiling. Her dad was here, staying in the cottage, and almost immediately she saw a change in her mother. She was wearing make-up again, even when working outside, and instead of wrapping her hair in a turban, she wore it softly curled around her face.

Working side by side, they got on with the planting, but now her mother's voice often rose in song as they put in row after row of vegetables. Ellen didn't understand why she had to sleep with Gertie now. She'd rather have squashed in between her parents, especially as Gertie snored so loudly, but for some reason they wanted to be on their own. There were times too when her parents went off on the motorbike, leaving her feeling excluded, but then they'd come back, her mum rosy-cheeked and smiling, and her dad lifting her in the air, calling her his pumpkin again.

One morning, over a week later, the sun was shining, and Ellen was bashing the top of her egg as her parents chatted.

'Travelling by train is murder now, Doug. Thank Gawd that bloke lent you his motorbike. It was good of him.'

'Yeah, he's a good mate, on board ship and off.'

'I wish you hadn't joined the navy. I hate it that you're at sea with the constant danger from those German U-boats.'

'I'd have been in just as much danger in the army.'

'What's a U-boat?' Ellen asked.

'It's a German submarine. But enough talk about the war. I've only got another five days' leave, so let's make the most of it.'

'I think you're right,' Gertie said, 'and as we've done so much planting, why don't the three of you go out on your own for a while?'

'That isn't a bad idea,' Doug said.

'You can take Bertie with you. I want to go into the village, but tomorrow we need to make a start on the salad crops.'

'Some leave this is,' joked Doug, 'and there was I, expecting you women to spoil me for fourteen days. Come on, Ellen, get dressed and then we can explore the woods.'

Ellen rose eagerly to her feet, but as she did so she noticed a look pass between her mother

and Gertie. She frowned. They looked secretive
. . . but why?

As soon as the three of them left the cottage,
Doug's arm around Hilda's shoulder and Ellen
clinging happily to his other hand, the false smile
Gertie had put on for their benefit left her face.
It had been pre-arranged that while they got Ellen
out of the way, she would take the pig for slaughter
– but that wasn't why Gertie had to put on a false
front.

As a child she had thought her feelings for Hilda
were sisterly, but that had all changed at puberty.
While Gertie had battled with her confused feelings, Hilda had been attracted to boys. Ashamed
and bewildered, Gertie had pretended interest in
them too, but all the time she had grown more
and more enamoured with Hilda.

They'd always been such a complete contrast,
she tall, big-boned, whereas Hilda was tiny, petite
and feminine. Gertie had longed to hold her, to
kiss her, but knew it was unnatural – that if Hilda,
or anyone else, found out, they'd be disgusted. She
had hated her feelings, wanted to be normal, but
the thought of being touched, held, or kissed by
a man repelled her.

Somehow Gertie had kept up the pretence, but,
in the end, fearing she would no longer be able
to contain her feelings for Hilda, it had been a

relief when they went their separate ways. To her utter amazement, once out in the world, Gertie discovered that she wasn't a freak – that there were other so-called unnatural women. She had met Susan, found happiness, but the affair had cost her everything. To escape they had moved here to Somerset, and until now she hadn't seen Hilda for many years. When she'd written to ask if both she and Ellen could come to stay, Gertie had hesitated, but then hadn't had the strength of will to refuse. They were in danger and she couldn't bear to think about that, but as soon as she saw Hilda again, Gertie found her feelings rekindled.

It made her feel so guilty, pretending to Hilda that she saw her as a sister, but now that she was here, Gertie couldn't bear the thought of her leaving again. To cope she'd created a fantasy, albeit a celibate one, where they were a family and Ellen their daughter. But then Doug had turned up and one look at Hilda's face when she saw him was enough to shatter Gertie's fragile illusion. Her lips tightened. Hilda was so obviously in love with her husband that it was painful to watch, the two of them barely able to keep their hands off each other.

Five more days – five more days of this purgatory before Doug left, and Gertie couldn't wait to see the back of him. Of course Hilda would never turn to her, Gertie had long accepted that, but at least they'd be a family again. Hilda was bound to stay until the war was over and, with no end in sight, she and Ellen could be with her for years.

Doug smiled at Hilda, his hand now holding hers as they walked along with Ellen and the dog running ahead through the woods.

'Blimey, love, I never thought I'd see the day when you'd be on your knees planting vegetables.'

'Me neither, but we had to get out of London.'

'It was good of Gertie to take you in, but aren't you a bit nervous?'

'What's that supposed to mean?'

'Well, you know. What if she tries it on?'

'Don't be daft. We're like sisters and Gertie would never do that.'

'I wouldn't be so sure. She comes over as a bit bossy to me and sometimes it feels as though she resents me being here.'

'Of course she doesn't, and Gertie's always been a bit bossy. We've been friends since childhood and, as I said, we became like sisters. You've got nothing to worry about and, anyway, Doug, you know me. If she tried anything I'd flatten her – not that she would and I'm sure of that.'

'Yeah, you might be small, but you're a little spitfire,' Doug agreed. 'All right, stay, and at least when I go back I'll know you're safe.'

'It's a shame I can't say the same. When I didn't hear from you for so long I was worried sick.'

'I've told you. I did write, honest.'

'Maybe the bloomin' Luftwaffe bombed the sorting office.'

'Yeah, maybe,' Doug mused.

'Like I said, we lost our place, and . . . and my mum and dad . . .'

Doug turned Hilda round to pull her into his arms, her head resting on his chest. 'I was shocked to the core when I read your letter. It must have been hell for you and I see you're wearing your mum's cross and chain now.'

'I know it sounds daft, but it's all I've got left of her and it sort of brings me a bit of comfort. It . . . it was an awful time, Doug, and to top it all Ellen's nerves went.'

'She seems all right now, though it's a shame you're so far from the village that she hasn't got any friends to play with.'

'I know, but she's grown to love it here, the peace, the quiet, the animals and the woods, yet I can't stand it.'

'It won't be for ever and, now I know I haven't got anything to worry about with Gertie, you're to stay here until the war's over,' Doug ordered, but then as Hilda reared back he knew he'd put his foot in it.

Her shoulders stiff, neck stretched to look up

at him and eyes flashing, she snapped, 'If I want to go back to London I will, and neither you, nor the bloody Germans, are going to stop me.'

'All right, calm down,' Doug placated. Just a moment ago Hilda had seemed so soft and vulnerable, but now she was back on form. His wife might be tiny, but he had long since learned that he couldn't win an argument. If you got Hilda's back up, woe betide you, and he should have known better than to issue an order. He tried a different approach. 'What about Ellen? Surely you don't want to put her at risk again?'

'Of course I don't. Oh, take no notice of me, Doug,' she said, her features softening as their daughter ran up to them. 'It's just that I'm fed up, that's all.'

Doug couldn't get over the change in Ellen. She was so much taller, her nose sprinkled with freckles and her complexion glowing with health. Life in the country suited her and, in fact, Doug had found he liked it, too, enjoyed working the land – the digging, the planting – and when the war was over he'd love to live out of London. Of course, Hilda would take some persuading, but surely he'd be able to talk her round?

'Come on, Mum, come on, Dad,' Ellen urged.

'Yeah, all right, but slow down,' Hilda called as Ellen dashed off again, Bertie at her heels, yapping with excitement.

'It's a shame we've only managed the one child,' Doug mused.

'I know, but after having so much trouble falling pregnant, Ellen still seems like a miracle. My mum was the same, and her sister, all of us only managing one child.'

'You never know, you might fall again one day.'

'Don't bank on it, Doug.'

'I'm not,' he said, with a cheeky smile and a wink as he added, 'though if you ask me nicely, I'll give it another go tonight.'

Ellen had become used to playing alone. She loved exploring, finding things, and had turned the woods into her own magic kingdom. This time, instead of roaming alone, it felt strange to be out with her parents and so far, amongst other things, they had seen a squirrel that was thankfully in a tree and safe from Bertie. Ellen led her dad to one of her favourite places, a pretty glade where if she sat quietly rabbits would emerge from their burrows, noses sniffing, but there was no sign of them today.

'Come on, Ellen, it's time to go back to the cottage.'

'Oh, Dad, do we have to?' Ellen appealed. 'There are so many things I want to show you.'

'I'm afraid so, but we'll come here again another day.'

Ellen nodded, looking forward to that, but sadly aware that her dad would be leaving again soon. She still found that if she kept quiet, her parents would sometimes forget she was there and it was then that she found things out – like at breakfast, when they had been talking about U-boats. Ellen was still worried about the danger she'd heard her dad was in and asked now, 'Dad, what's a submarine?'

'Well, I suppose the easiest way to describe one is to say that it's a kind of boat, but one that submerges and spends most of the time underwater.'

'Have you been on one?'

'No, and I don't want to.'

'Why did Mum say you're in danger?'

A look passed between her parents and Ellen saw the small shake of her mum's head before her dad replied, 'You know what a worryguts your mum is, but there's no need. I'm not in danger, pumpkin, and she's worried about nothing.'

Ellen wasn't convinced, but her dad refused to talk about the war again and soon they were back at the cottage. Once again Ellen saw a strange look pass between Gertie and her mother, a sort of half-nod from Gertie that puzzled her.

'Why did you have to go to the village?' Ellen asked, sure that the trip held the answer.

'I went to get a few things in. Now let's grab some lunch and then it's back to work.'

'Slave driver,' Hilda groaned.

While her mother began to make sandwiches, Ellen wandered outside with Bertie, the dog running to his bowl to slurp water. There was something going on, Ellen was sure of it, but if she kept really quiet during lunch they might let something slip. Why did grown ups have to be so secretive? She wasn't a baby now, she was nearly ten and a half years old, but still treated like a little kid. The village – Gertie hated going to the village, so why had she gone that morning? It was only when Ellen thought about their last trip that the penny dropped. Gertie had told her about the pig, but then her dad had turned up and everything else had been forgotten in the excitement.

With her heart thudding, Ellen ran to the sty. There was only one pig now, her belly fat with babies, and, sobbing, Ellen ran back to the cottage.

'Pinkie's gone! You took her to be killed, didn't you?'

'Yes, I'm afraid so.'

'Why didn't you tell me?'

It was her mum who answered. 'Because we knew you'd be upset.'

'I . . . I don't want Pinkie to be killed.'

'Ellen, I told you not to give the pigs names,'

49

said Gertie, 'and warned that you shouldn't get too fond of them. They aren't pets and you know that.'

'You're horrible! I hate you,' Ellen yelled before dashing outside again, but only five minutes later her dad found her.

'You shouldn't have yelled at Gertie like that. She knew you'd be upset, we all did, but Gertie hoped to make you feel better with a special surprise.'

'Don't care. I hate her.'

'Let's see if you feel the same in a minute,' he said, taking her hand to pull her along. 'Come back inside.'

Sullen, Ellen was dragged back to the cottage, but she refused to look at the cardboard box that Gertie held out.

'Come on, Ellen, open it,' her mother urged.

Gertie laid the box on the table. 'It's something for you, Ellen, something all of your own to love.'

'Don't want it.'

'Are you sure?' Gertie asked and opening the box herself she drew out a tiny bundle of black and white fluff.

There was a mewling sound and, unbidden, Ellen rushed forward. A kitten! Gertie had got her a kitten, and, her eyes brimming, Ellen took it from her hands.

'Do you like him?' Gertie asked.

'Oh . . . oh . . . yes, and . . . and thank you.'

'You need to apologise too,' her mum cajoled.

'No, it's all right, Hilda. She was upset, and I understand that. Now then, Ellen, what are you going to call him?'

Ellen looked at the kitten. He was mostly black, but there was a white band at the bottom of both front legs. She grinned. 'I'm gonna call him Socks.'

'Socks,' her dad chuckled. 'Yeah, it kind of suits him.'

Bertie jumped up at her legs and Ellen held the kitten protectively to her chest.

'It's all right,' Gertie said. 'Bertie has had a few scuffles with Wilfred and knows better than to go up against a cat. Just let him smell Socks and he'll be fine.'

Tentatively Ellen crouched down, her fears soon alleviated, but then the kitten burrowed inside her cardigan.

'Right, Ellen, he's your cat and you'll have to look after him. It'll be your job to feed him, and until he can go out you'll have to change his litter box regularly,' her mum said, then puffed out her cheeks. 'I must have been mad to agree to this and heaven knows how we'll get him back to London.'

'London! But I don't want to go back to London.'

'I'm not talking about now, you daft moo, but the war won't last for ever.'

Ellen pulled back her cardigan to look at Socks.

He was almost under her arm, snuggled close, and though she wasn't looking at her father she was aware of his words.

'There isn't an end in sight yet and, who knows, you could be here for years.'

'Doug, I hope you're wrong,' sighed Hilda. 'I'm going potty stuck here in the sticks.'

'Well, thanks,' Gertie snapped.

'I'm not having a go at you, Gertie, and I'm really grateful that you took us in. It's just that I'm not suited to life in the country, that's all.'

'Suited or not, it's where you need to stay,' Doug warned.

'All right, don't go on about it.'

Ellen's emotions were mixed. She was thrilled with the kitten, sad that her dad would be leaving soon, but ecstatic at the thought of staying here with Gertie for a long, long time.

The next five days seemed to fly past, and soon Gertie was hiding her feelings of satisfaction as Doug said his goodbyes. It was irritating to see how Hilda clung to him, tears in her eyes, but touching to see Ellen doing the same.

Gertie shook Doug's hand and then left them to it, pleased to hear the roar of the motorbike only minutes later as he sped away. It might take a few days, but then it would be back to normal, the three of them again living contentedly together.

Both Hilda and Ellen were in pieces when they came indoors, and Gertie did her best to sound sympathetic. 'Oh dear. You poor things.'

'I can't believe how quickly the time went, and . . . and who knows when I'll see him again . . .' Hilda said as she dashed tears from her cheeks.

Ellen ran to pick up Socks, seeking comfort as she held the kitten close, and Gertie was pleased with her idea. Ellen had soon forgotten the pig in her joy at having her own pet, and as the farmer's cat had just had kittens, the timing was perfect. Her own cat, Wilfred, rarely ventured indoors and so far hadn't seen the kitten, but Gertie feared that fur might fly when he did.

'How about a nice cup of tea?' she suggested, deciding that there was time enough later to worry about Wilfred.

'I won't say no.'

Gertie busied herself with putting the kettle on the range and by time it came to the boil, Hilda had at last stopped sniffling. Gertie decided to try a touch of lightness as she poured the tea, saying with a smile, 'I suppose you'll be back to wearing trousers now.'

'I suppose so. I never thought you'd get me to wear them, but must admit they're comfortable. It was murder doing the planting in a skirt.'

'Once summer's here, we'll all be in shorts.'

'Things in London may have eased up by then.

I might be able to go back; to find us somewhere to live, a home for Doug to return to.'

'Don't bank on it,' Gertie said. There was no sign of a let up, the Luftwaffe still bombing the city and, as Doug had said, they could be with her for years. At least she hoped so – the thought of Hilda leaving was more than she could bear.

6

Hilda turned over in bed, hating that it was winter again, and loathing life in Somerset. She had come here expecting the war to be over long before this, but how long had they been here now? Nearly two years, but it felt like ten, and so long, so very long since she'd seen Doug. At least in London she saw people, had friends, heard a bit of music and jollity; but nothing happened here to break the month in, month out of boring routine.

Hilda heaved a sigh. She had stuck it out for Ellen's sake, and Gertie had seemed to sense how she felt, taking her to the village at least once a week now. Though Hilda enjoyed a bit of gossip with the shopkeeper, and one or two other villagers, she felt she had little in common with them. They were nice folks who seemed content with their lot, with their sleepy, tiny community, but even after all this time in Somerset, Hilda knew she'd never feel the same.

Ellen woke beside her and as soon as the sleepiness left her eyes she said, 'It's my birthday.'

'I know. Happy twelfth birthday, but don't expect much,' Hilda warned. This would be Ellen's second birthday in Somerset, but there wasn't a lot on offer in the village store now, though thanks to Mrs Brandon she had a little extra something up her sleeve. It was Monday, and with the shop closed yesterday they'd have to go into the village to pick it up today. It was a special treat and sure to bring a smile to her daughter's face.

'Mum, I feel a bit funny, sticky,' Ellen said as she got out of bed. Her voice then rose to a yelp of fear. 'Mum! Mum, I'm bleeding.'

Oh no, Hilda thought, already? What a thing to happen on her daughter's birthday. 'It's all right. It's nothing to worry about.'

'But what's wrong with me?'

Hilda fought for words as she flung back the blankets. As far as she was concerned, Ellen was far too young to be told the facts of life. Her tone was brusque as she said, 'It's just something that happens to all girls when they get to a certain age.'

'But why?'

'It's just that things are changing in your body, that's all, and this is going to happen every month now.'

Ellen looked appalled. 'Every month!'

'I know it sounds awful, but you'll get used to it.

56

Now come on, let's get you cleaned up,' Hilda said, knowing that Ellen's questions were far from over.

Ellen was still confused by what was happening to her, and felt too queasy to eat her breakfast. She also had little cramps of pain in her tummy, but was distracted now as her mother held out three packages.

'Happy birthday and these are from me,' she said.

Ellen tore one open, loving the blue scarf with matching hat and mittens. She was sure her mum must have unravelled her nice jumper to provide the wool and managed a smile. 'Thanks, they're lovely.'

'I made them in the evenings when you were in bed.'

In the next package Ellen found a new vest, but finally, best of all, she tore open the last one to find a large, beautiful book of plant illustrations. Ellen could see that it wasn't new, but loved it anyway and hugged it to her chest. 'Oh, Mum.'

'I managed to buy it from one of the villagers.'

'Happy birthday,' Gertie said as she came in and handed over a roughly wrapped parcel.

Inside Ellen found tweed trousers that had been cut down, the pains in her tummy forgotten now as she grinned. 'Thanks, Gertie, but weren't these your best ones?'

'Yes, but you've grown out of your others, and will need warm trousers now that winter is here. Here you are,' Gertie said, holding out a paper bag. 'I got these too. I know you love barley sugar.'

Ellen smiled with delight, but then her mother spoke again as she held out another parcel, saying softly, 'I thought I'd save this one till last.'

As soon as Ellen took it, she knew who it was from and ripped it open eagerly. Along with a letter, there was a beautifully carved wooden cat.

'Oh, look,' she said holding it up. 'It's from Dad.'

'I know, darling, and he made it himself.'

Ellen stroked the cat lovingly and then placed it down to pick up the accompanying letter, her eyes filling with tears as she read it. She missed her dad so much, longed to see him again, and said sadly, 'He . . . he doesn't say he's coming home. It's been so long since his last leave and he must be due in port again soon.'

Socks rubbed against her legs and Ellen bent down to pick him up. He was a big cat now, sleek and lovely, but like Wilfred he'd taken to wandering. She looked at the beautifully carved one, her voice a croak. 'Dad must remember Socks and that's why he made me a cat.'

'I'm sure he does, but don't cry, love. It's your birthday and it should be a happy time.'

'Come on, Hilda,' said Gertie brusquely as she rose to her feet. 'You said you wanted to go to the village. We'll wrap up warm and, Ellen, you can wear your new trousers, along with the hat, scarf and mittens.'

Ellen felt uncomfortable as she pulled on her new trousers, hating that it might show. 'I'm ready,' she said returning downstairs.

'Right, I'll harness Ned.'

As Gertie went outside, Ellen saw her mother looking at her before she said, 'I'm sick of seeing you in trousers.'

'You wear them all the time too.'

'Sorry, pet, I didn't mean to snap. It's just that, like you, I'm missing your dad and it's always worse when we've had letters.'

'It'd be lovely if he was here for Christmas.'

'Yes, it would, but come on, it's your birthday and it'll be nice to have a ride into the village.'

'Mum, I feel funny wearing this . . . this rag thing. Does it show?'

'No, you look fine.'

It wasn't long before Gertie called out, saying as they set off, 'As it's your birthday, there'll be no lessons for you today, especially as you did so well with your arithmetic yesterday.'

'Thanks,' Ellen said, but she really didn't mind her lessons with Gertie. In fact, she made learning things fun. With Gertie's way of bringing events to life, even history wasn't boring, though Ellen knew she still struggled with geography.

'It's good of you to teach Ellen so much,' said Hilda, 'but once we're back in London she'll be able to go to a proper school again.'

'That could be years away.'

'Since the beginning of the war and that awful Blitz, there aren't many bombing raids on London now.'

'It still isn't safe,' Gertie warned.

'Mum, you aren't thinking about going back, are you?' Ellen interrupted. 'I don't want to go. I want to stay here.'

'All right, don't go on about it. I didn't say we're leaving.'

They were all quiet then, the mood subdued, and Ellen doubled over as her tummy cramped. Gertie turned her head, her smile sympathetic.

'Your mum told me that you're menstruating. It's a rotten thing to happen on your birthday.'

Ellen said nothing as she tried to get to grips with a new word. Menstruating, so that's what they called it. She hated it – hated that she would have to go through this every month and she still didn't understand why.

'Nearly there, Hilda,' said Gertie as at last they neared the village.

'Good, I'm flaming freezing.'

'It'll get worse before it gets better.'

When they reached the general store, Ellen was about to climb down, but her mum said, 'There's

60

no need for you to come in with me. Stay with Gertie.'

'But . . .'

She was ignored, her mum hurrying into the shop.

'What's going on, Gertie?' Ellen asked.

'Don't ask me, darling.'

It wasn't long before her mum was back and clutching a cardboard box that Gertie leaned down to take from her while she climbed onto the cart.

'Mum, what's that?' Ellen asked curiously.

'Nothing much, a bit of shopping, that's all. Right,' she said, taking the box from Gertie, 'we can go back to the cottage now.'

Ellen was puzzled, wondering how her mother had finished her shopping so quickly. 'Aren't you going to the butcher's?'

'No, now enough questions and let's get home.'

As Gertie eased the horse out into the road a truck tooted from behind. As she pulled over, the sound of singing reached them as the vehicle passed. The tarpaulin was raised at the back, and they saw several women dressed in breeches, with green jerseys visible under open coats, all of them sporting brown felt hats. Some of them waved and Ellen waved back.

'It's the Land Army girls.'

'The Land Army was first set up during the Great War following disastrous attacks on our merchant shipping,' Gertie said, using this opportunity to give Ellen a history lesson. 'We import about sixty percent of our produce, and with so many ships sunk during that war, Britain came close to starvation. The Land Army was formed and the girls carried out vital work in increasing our agricultural output. They were disbanded in 1919, but as we're now in the same position, the government has re-formed the Land Army. Those women are invaluable to farms, either arable or dairy to increase production, and, though it's jolly hard work, it's once again vital.'

'Rather them than me,' Hilda said.

Gertie refrained from saying that both she and Ellen had been working the land for ages on her smallholding, and she didn't know what she would have done without their help. When they left, she'd be lost – but as there was no sign of the war ending, thankfully she didn't have to worry about it yet.

When they got back to the cottage, Hilda safely stowed the cake. Mrs Brandon had kindly offered to make it, insisting that she had enough ingredients hoarded to make it special. And it was, Hilda thought as she peeped inside the box.

'Let me look,' Gertie whispered as she came

alongside, placing an arm casually around Hilda as she leaned forward. 'I told Ellen to go upstairs and change into her old trousers.'

Hilda tensed. When Doug had left seventeen months ago she had missed him so much, and had thought nothing of it when Gertie had comforted her when she cried. The trouble was that since then Gertie still took to throwing an arm around her at every opportunity. Equally casually, Hilda moved away, saying, 'It's lovely, isn't it?'

'Yes, very pretty, and Ellen's going to love it. Is it fruit or sponge?'

'Fruit! You must be joking; dried fruit is getting like gold dust. It's sponge, but Mrs Brandon has sandwiched it with jam.'

'I don't know how she had the patience to make all those tiny little flowers out of icing sugar. I hate doing anything that's fiddly.'

'Gertie, let's face it, you hate anything to do with cooking.'

She grinned. 'Yes, that's true, but thankfully you do it now. It's nice to have you in the kitchen while I'm doing the mucky jobs outside.'

'When it comes to the pigs, rather you than me.'

'They're clean creatures really, but I'd better get on with it,' Gertie said, giving Hilda another quick hug.

Hilda stiffened, but seeing Gertie's open smile she decided that she had to be imagining things. Gertie was just being friendly, that was all. They were as close as sisters, and surely sisters occasionally hugged? Not that she had one to judge by and, like Gertie, she was an only child. Hilda was saddened. History was repeating itself with Ellen, and though she'd hoped to find that she was pregnant when Doug had left, once again her hopes had been dashed.

'Yes, Gertie, you get on while I make a start on our lunch.'

'Righto, but I can't wait to see Ellen's face.'

She's just being nice, Hilda told herself yet again as Gertie hurried off, yet there was still a niggle of doubt . . .

At two o'clock, Hilda called both Gertie and Ellen inside. 'Grub's up, but before both of you sit down, I think a wash is called for.'

'Oh . . . Mum.'

'Don't argue, Ellen.'

'Come on,' Gertie urged. 'We are a bit dirty.'

'A bit! It looks like the two of you have been rolling in mud.'

'You look nice, Hilda,' said Gertie, a soft smile on her face.

'As it's Ellen's birthday lunch I thought I'd make a bit of an effort,' she said, looking down at her skirt. 'You two should do the same.'

'I don't own a skirt,' Gertie said.

'Ellen does, though she's grown so much and I doubt the two she has would fit her now. Go on,' she urged, 'at least make yourself presentable.'

They were soon back, smiling with appreciation at the nicely laid table. 'My, aren't we posh?' Gertie said. 'It's almost like being back in my father's house.'

'Hardly. For one we haven't got silver cutlery, and this table only seats four, not twelve, but for once I've put a nice tablecloth on it.'

'I think it looks lovely,' Ellen said as she took a seat. 'What's for lunch?'

'Vegetable soup.'

They all tucked in, and, once finished, Ellen was about to leave the table. 'Hold on,' Hilda said. 'Stay there.'

'Why?'

'Never you mind.'

Hilda hurried to the scullery and, taking the cake out from under its cover, she lit the candles, but then suddenly, from nowhere, a strange feeling washed over her. No, no, she had to be imagining it, yet the sense of someone standing beside her, a presence, was strong. She wanted to turn her head, wanted to look, but, frozen with fear, she couldn't move a muscle.

'Come on, Hilda,' Gertie called.

In that instant the spell was broken, leaving Hilda shaken and bewildered. At last she was able to move, to turn her head, but saw nobody there. Still trembling, she picked up the cake, and somehow managed to plant a smile on her face as she carried it into the living room. Her voice sounded a bit quivery, but this was a special moment for Ellen and she didn't want to spoil it as she sang, 'Happy birthday to you . . . Happy birthday to you . . .'

Gertie joined in and Hilda saw her daughter's delighted smile. There had been few real treats since the war had started, and suddenly she found her eyes moist with tears. If only Doug were here – if only he hadn't missed his daughter's birthday again. Hilda shivered; the incident in the scullery was still with her and now she almost cried out against the thought that crossed her mind. Of course it hadn't been Doug. She didn't really believe in ghosts, in spirits, so why was she letting it get to her? It was just fear, Hilda told herself, that was all, the day-in, day-out fear for Doug's safety.

'Oh, Mum, it's smashing,' Ellen said, her eyes on the cake that Mrs Brandon had decorated so beautifully with pink and white icing.

'Blow out the candles and make a wish,' Gertie urged.

'I . . . I wish my dad . . .'

'Don't say it out loud,' Gertie warned. 'If you do, it won't come true.'

Ellen closed her eyes, this time making the wish silently, and then opening them she blew out all of the candles in one go. 'There, it'll come true now,' she said, smiling happily.

Hilda fought to pull herself together. She could guess what her daughter had wished for and hoped it would be fulfilled – that Doug would get leave again soon, or, even better, that this rotten war would end and he would come home for good.

7

All Hilda's worries and imaginings left her early in December when she got a letter from Doug. Christmas came, a spartan one, followed by a dismal New Year. There hadn't been any more strange incidents, but sometimes Hilda found herself thinking about the feeling of someone being there, beside her in the scullery, yet she still couldn't come up with an explanation.

One day in early January, Hilda decided to talk to Gertie about it, and said, 'Gertie, do you believe in ghosts?'

'Of course not. Why?'

'You'll think I'm mad, and anyway, it happened over two months ago.'

'What happened?'

Hilda told her and, seeing the expression on Gertie's face, she wished she'd continued to keep her mouth shut. 'All right, I know it sounds potty.'

'Our mind, senses and eyes can play all sorts of

tricks on us, and if you want my opinion, that's all it was. I refuse to believe in any of the mumbo jumbo that people come up with: ectoplasm, speaking to the dead, or, even worse, fairies at the bottom of our gardens.'

'What on earth is ectoplasm?'

'A substance emerges from so-called mediums and is supposed to be spirit, but if you ask me it's just a clever conjuring trick, an illusion.'

'So you don't believe in life after death?'

'I'd like to think there is, but there lies the problem. Scientists have looked into these claims and so far nothing has been proved. Until it is, I'll stick with the scientists who deal with fact, not fiction.'

When Gertie talked about ectoplasm and fairies in the garden, Hilda had to admit it sounded a bit silly, yet she still wasn't convinced. What happened to her had felt so real, yet if investigated she couldn't offer proof. Oh, she was tired. With windows shut and curtains drawn to keep out the cold, she found the room stuffy and yawned widely. 'I think I'll turn in.'

'All right and goodnight, dear.'

Hilda lit a candle to guide her upstairs, nervous as the flames flickered, illuminating some areas while others remained creepily shadowed. It was this old place, having no electricity, along with being stuck in the middle of nowhere. Perhaps

Gertie was right and her mind had played tricks on her. In fact, if she stayed here for much longer, Hilda was beginning to think that it would slowly drive her mad.

Another couple of months passed and at last winter changed to spring again. Ellen loved this time of year when new green shoots emerged on plants and trees. It would be a time of planting again, working outdoors, something she loved.

It was still cold though, and any time spent on the smallholding meant wrapping up well, but digging was a great way to warm up. All three of them worked steadily and, at last, close to the end of March, Ellen's wish came true. The cottage was too remote for visitors, so when there was a knock on the door they all looked at each other in surprise; Ellen was the one to answer it.

'Dad! Oh, Dad!'

Moments later her mum was there. 'Doug! I can't believe it! It's nearly two years since you were last here and I was beginning to despair of you ever getting leave again.'

Ellen moved aside as her father took her mother into his arms and their hug seemed to go on for ever.

'Well, are you going to let me in?' he finally asked.

Smiling with joy, Ellen walked in ahead of them, but Gertie looked less than pleased. 'Doug. How long are you here for?'

'Three weeks.'

'Is that all?' Hilda wailed.

'I know, love, but considering the journey was a bloody nightmare, at least I'm here.'

'Did you come on that motorbike again?'

'No, pumpkin, I had to get a train this time.'

'How did you get here from the station?' asked Gertie.

'I managed to get a lift for part of the way, but had to walk the rest.'

Ellen couldn't take her eyes off her father. He looked so handsome in his navy blue uniform, sailor's hat worn at a jaunty angle and blue eyes shining as he held his arms out to her mum. She ran into them again, the two of them locked in an embrace. 'I've missed you so much,' he murmured.

'I've missed you too, but look at me, in trousers, no make-up, and my hair in a turban.'

'Darlin', to me you'd look great in a sack, in fact, I can't wait to get you into one.'

'Doug! Ellen's listening.'

'Sorry, but how about a kiss?'

Ellen looked away as her parents' lips met and her eyes fell on Gertie. She frowned, puzzled. Gertie looked furious, her face dark with anger.

Yet why? She was about to ask her what was wrong, but then found herself pulled forward, her father's arms enclosing her as well.

'Come here, pumpkin. My God, look at you. You've grown so much.'

'Are you hungry, Doug?'

'Hilda, you know me, I'm always hungry.'

'Yes, like father like daughter,' Hilda said happily. 'Well then, I'd best get you something to eat.'

Gertie had seen Ellen looking at her, the puzzled look on her face, and somehow managed to compose herself. It hadn't been easy. She hated seeing Hilda in Doug's arms, kissing him, and anger, along with jealousy, made her stomach churn. Hilda looked ecstatic as she scurried to make Doug something to eat, and now his attention was focused on Ellen as he sat down, pulling her onto his lap.

'How's my girl, then?' he asked, hugging her close.

Gertie couldn't stand it any more. Doug's arrival was an unwanted intrusion, spoiling everything, and her carefully built-up illusion was being shattered again. When he'd left last time she had picked up the pieces, comforted Hilda, pretending sympathy when she cried, but feeling nothing but joy as she held Hilda's slender body in her arms.

Hilda seemed so fragile, so delicate, but of course that was an illusion too. Hilda was an enigma, appearing frail, yet sometimes as tough as old boots and was it any wonder that she loved this feisty, yet sometimes soft, woman?

Of course it hadn't lasted, Hilda's tears abating, and, with no excuse to wrap her arms around her, Gertie had to be content with just the occasional quick hug. Hilda had been with her for so long now and she'd been sure they were growing closer, dreamed of feeling Hilda's lips on hers, but now Doug was here to come between them again.

'What's up, Gertie? You don't look pleased to see me.'

Startled out of her thoughts, she said, 'Er . . . of course I am, Doug. It's nice for Hilda and Ellen, but such a shame you're only here for three weeks. Anyway, lots to do so I'd best get on.' On that note, Gertie hurried outside. Three weeks! Why couldn't it be three days? Even better, three hours. There was only one crumb of comfort, Gertie decided as she tramped over the smallholding. When Doug left, Hilda would be distraught and would turn to her again for comfort.

It was only when they were in bed that night that Hilda and Doug could talk privately, but as they fell into each other's arms after nearly two years apart, all Doug's worries were put to one side as he made love, first passionately, and then gently, to his wife.

The sheets and blankets were in a tangle, their bodies glistening with perspiration, but now, as Hilda lay with her head on his chest, his worries returned and Doug voiced his thoughts. 'Hilda, what's going on with Gertie? She didn't look too pleased when I arrived.'

'I didn't notice. I was too busy looking at you.'

'I know I asked this last time I was here, but has she, you know, tried it on?'

'Of course she hasn't. I've told you before, we're like sisters.'

'Then how come when I was hugging you she looked jealous?'

'Don't be daft. You're imagining things,' Hilda told him.

'If you say so,' Doug said doubtfully as his eyelids drooped with tiredness. It had been a long day, delay after delay on the trains before he'd finally arrived; his last thought before falling asleep that he'd keep an eye on Gertie while he was here. If his suspicions were right, he wanted his wife and daughter as far away from her as possible.

Hilda lifted her head to see that Doug was asleep, the soft glow of a full, luminous moon shining on his face. She moved gently away to prop herself up on one elbow, gazing at him, heart bursting with love. Every day she had worried about his safety, fearing that his ship would join so many others that had been sunk with horrendous loss of lives. The thought of U-boats terrified her, visions of huge, dark prey, sneaking silently under the seas, torpedoes ready to strike unsuspecting vessels. She had nightmares, seeing Doug's ship hit, of him fighting to get on deck while fire raged all around him. Hilda shuddered, recalling the many times she had awoken in the night, her nightmares so vivid she had thought them real.

She frowned, thinking about what he'd said about Gertie, and, though she had denied them at the time, his concerns echoed her own. Gertie *had* looked annoyed when Doug arrived, and she'd been funny with him all day.

Doug turned in his sleep and as his arm wrapped around her body, Hilda at last lay down. She didn't want to worry about Gertie, didn't want her short time with Doug ruined. She'd continue to deny her concerns and, anyway, Gertie hadn't really tried anything – just an occasional hug that didn't really make her feel threatened in any way. If Doug thought there was more to it, he'd go mad, so she would just have to alleviate his worries somehow.

Hilda snuggled closer, pushing thoughts of Gertie away. For now she could hold Doug – for now he was safe, but already she was dreading the thought of him going back to sea.

8

The dawn chorus woke Ellen, and finding herself in a different room for a moment she was disorientated. Her last memory was of falling asleep on her dad's lap, that thought causing her to sit bolt upright in bed. Her dad! Her dad was here and must have carried her up to bed in Gertie's room.

Excitedly, Ellen flung back the blankets, careless of the cold linoleum underfoot as she scampered to see him. 'Dad!' she cried, jumping onto the bed.

An eye opened, a groan, and then he said, 'Blimey, pumpkin, you're up early. Come on, you're cold. Get in between me and your mum.'

Ellen scrambled into the bed, uncaring that she had woken her mum as her arms wrapped joyfully around her father.

'Ellen, your feet are freezing,' Hilda complained, 'and you're a bit big for getting into bed with us now.'

'Leave her, Hilda. She's all right with us for a while.'

'Doug . . . you . . . you haven't got anything on.'

'Bugger, I forgot about that.'

'Why haven't you got your pyjamas on, Dad? Did you forget to bring them?'

'Er . . . no,' he said, 'but shift over for a minute and I'll put the bottoms on.'

As his arm reached out to grab them from a nearby chair, Ellen was aware that her mother was getting out of bed. She turned over, eyes wide when she saw that her mum was naked. 'Mum, where's your nightdress?'

'Stop looking at me. I forgot to put it on, that's all.'

'Hilda, now that you're up, how about a nice cup of tea for your old man?'

'See what you've done, Ellen,' she complained, shrugging her flannelette nightdress over her head.

'Blimey, talk about a passion killer.'

'Doug, watch what you're saying in front of Ellen.'

'What's passion?' Ellen asked.

'See what I mean?'

'It's just another word for enthusiasm, that's all.'

Ellen still didn't understand, but after wriggling about under the bedclothes her dad managed to get his pyjama bottoms on and she snuggled up to him again.

'You needn't think you can stay there for long, my girl,' her mother warned. 'Now that you've got us up at the crack of dawn you can give me a hand with our breakfast.'

'I'll get up when you fetch Dad his tea.'

'Oh, so now he's to have it in bed, is he?'

'Cor, yes, please, love.'

Though her mum was trying to look cross, Ellen could see that she was happy, her brown eyes bright as she left the room. It was lovely to see her smiling all the time and she said sadly, 'Dad, I wish you didn't have to go back to sea.'

'So do I, but buck up. We've got three lovely weeks together before that happens.'

There was the sound of a miaow and moments later Socks jumped on the bed, lying down on her father's chest. He stroked his head, saying, 'He was only a kitten the last time I saw him. He's a whopper now.'

'Yes, but he isn't around much. He turns up every morning for something to eat and it's my job to feed him, but then he's off again.'

'He should have been neutered.'

'What's that?'

'Er . . . it's something that's done to tomcats to stop them roaming. Now tell me, did you like the carving I sent for your last birthday?'

'Yes, it's lovely and looks a bit like Socks.'

'That's what I was hoping,' he said, but then as Ellen saw her mother walking in with a cup of tea he added, 'Well, Ellen, if it's your job to feed this cat, I think you'd best do it.'

'But . . .'

'No arguments. Now scat,' he said. 'I'll be up soon, but stay downstairs until I am.'

Ellen reluctantly climbed out of bed, Socks jumping down to follow her out of the room. She heard her mum giggle, followed by the sound of the bed creaking, and it was over half an hour later before they appeared again.

Usually Gertie was the first one up, but not today. She forced a cheerful smile, saying as she sat at the table, 'Good morning, Doug. Did you sleep well?'

'Eventually,' Doug said, winking lewdly.

Gertie couldn't hold back a scowl, but hoped to hide it as she picked up the teapot to pour a cup, then adding milk.

'Gertie, that tea's been made for ages. I'll make a fresh one,' Hilda said as she walked through from the outhouse.

'No, this will do me. I've got a lot to do and running late.'

'I'll cook you an egg on toast.'

'No, Hilda,' snapped Doug. 'Ellen's waiting and we're going for a walk. Gertie wasn't up when you were cooking breakfast and, anyway, I'm sure she's perfectly capable of making her own.'

'Yes, I am. Go on, Hilda, you can go for a walk.'

'She doesn't need your permission,' Doug snapped.

'Doug, what's the matter with you?' Hilda asked.

'I just don't think you need Gertie's say so to go out. It's not as if you work here or that Gertie's your boss.'

'Gertie took us in, you seem to be forgetting that.'

'You pay your way *and* work on her small-holding. If you ask me she's got a good deal.'

Hilda seemed to stretch, neck high and face flaming with temper. 'Now you listen to me, Douglas Stone. I choose to do the cooking and, when necessary, outdoor work. Gertie works like a dog and, as her friend, I'm pleased to be able to help.'

'Your friend, yes, but is that *all* she is?'

'What's that supposed to mean?'

'Don't act the innocent again. You know full well what I mean.'

'My God, I can't believe you'd even *think* such a thing.'

'I saw what it was like when I was last here, with you waiting on Gertie hand and foot. She acts more like your husband than your so-called friend.'

'Now you sound jealous.'

'What do you expect! I'm in the navy and there isn't much I haven't seen, between both two men, *and* two women.'

'Well, there's nothing like that going on between Gertie and me,' Hilda said forcefully.

Gertie said nothing as the row raged. She thought she'd hidden her feelings from both of them, but in Doug's case she obviously hadn't been successful. He thought she and Hilda were lovers but, oh, if only that were true. Still, she would have to be careful, to hide her feelings, or Doug might just persuade Hilda to leave.

Doug seemed to slump, his elbows on the table and his hands rubbing his face. 'I'm sorry, love. I don't know what's wrong with me.'

'I should think so too, but it isn't just me who deserves an apology.'

Doug looked up, swallowed, then said, 'Sorry, Gertie.'

'That's all right. You're obviously under a lot of strain, and maybe you just needed to release a bit of anger.'

'It's the things I've seen, ships going down, men drowning before we could pick them up, horrible, terrible things.'

'Oh, Doug,' Hilda cried, running to kneel by his side.

Gertie couldn't watch and quietly she went out of the back door. It's a shame it wasn't Doug's ship that went down, she thought, then was immediately appalled with herself. How could she think like that? It was disgusting, dreadful – but nevertheless the thought wouldn't go away.

9

Hilda didn't have any nightmares while Doug was there, but he did, his sleep often broken as he would suddenly sit bolt upright, crying with horror in the night. She had of course forgiven him for his outburst over Gertie. More so now that she was seeing the evidence of what he had been through and, anyway, maybe he did have reason to be suspicious. Oh, not of her, but of Gertie.

Perhaps it was time to leave Somerset, to go back to London. As soon as Doug left in the morning, she'd put out feelers and write to Mabel to see if it was safe. Of course there'd be the problem of finding somewhere to stay. With so many houses destroyed, accommodation was short, but surely she'd be able to find something, even if it only had one room for now.

Hilda snuggled closer as she lay in Doug's arms, her three weeks of happiness almost over.

'The time has gone so fast and I can't believe you'll be leaving in the morning.'

'I know, but come on, let's make the most of our last night together.'

Hilda gave herself up to his lovemaking, and when it was over they were lying peacefully when she told Doug what was on her mind. 'I'm so fed up here. I hate being in the middle of nowhere and might go back to London.'

'I'm not going to argue with you, but you've got to think about Ellen and whether it's safe.'

'I know that, Doug, and I wouldn't be daft enough to put our daughter at risk.'

'I'd feel better if you stay here.'

'I thought you didn't like us living with Gertie.'

'I don't mind, love. I was mad to think there was anything going on between you.'

'Yes, you were. I don't fancy women, Doug. In fact, I don't fancy other men. There's only you.'

'And you're the only woman for me,' he said, hugging her.

'I thought sailors had a girl in every port.'

'Not me, but I can only speak for myself. I don't know about the rest of the crew.'

'You'd better not be unfaithful,' Hilda warned.

'I wouldn't dare. You'd have my guts for garters,' he said, then yawned widely. 'Let's hope I get a night of unbroken sleep for once.'

'I dunno about that. I might just wake you for another bit of nooky.'

'You're insatiable,' he said, grinning widely. 'Oh, well, there's nothing else for it. I'll just have to wear you out now. That should stop your games.'

'Ooh, yes, please,' she said cheekily, yet as Doug bent to kiss her, Hilda felt another surge of sadness. With Ellen diving in on them every morning, this would probably be the last time they could make love – the last time she would be totally alone with her husband – and now she struggled against tears.

In the early hours of the morning, Gertie was still awake too. She could hear the noise coming from Hilda's room. Every night had been the same, while Gertie lay with her stomach churning, longing for it to stop. At least it was the last night, she thought, and Doug would be gone in the morning.

Maybe, just maybe, now that Doug had planted the seed of the idea, Hilda might actually turn to her; after all, a woman without a man must grow frustrated. You're a fool, an idiot, Gertie told herself as she turned over to thump her pillow. Hilda was normal and would never be attracted to someone of the same sex. But I'm not – I'm not! Gertie cried inwardly. In my mind I'm a man, yet cursed with this body of a woman.

At last, after a restless few hours' sleep, Gertie woke early, pleased to find that Ellen was no longer beside her in bed. She smiled. Good. The girl had probably gone to her parents' room and that would put paid to any more lovemaking.

It was over. Doug was going, and she couldn't wait to see the back of him. Hilda would be upset, devastated, but after that they'd get back to normal – just the three of them, living like a family again.

Ellen could barely eat her breakfast as she sat across from her father. Gertie was the only one who looked cheerful, which made a change because out of sight of her parents, Gertie had been moody and snappy. Ellen had hated sleeping in her bed again, but if it meant her dad could stay, she'd do it for ever.

When her dad stood up, Ellen felt the tears welling and was unable to stifle a sob. She flung back her chair, rushing to him, her arms wrapping tightly around his waist. 'Do you have to go, Dad? Can't you stay?'

'There's nothing I'd like more, but if I don't go back I'd be a deserter.'

'What's a deserter?'

'Someone who runs away, who doesn't go back on duty when their leave's over.'

'You could do that, Dad,' she said excitedly.

'If I did, I'd be named a coward and end up in

prison. Never mind, pumpkin. This war won't go on for ever, and when it's over I'll be home for good.'

'Oh, Dad . . . I still wish you could stay here now.'

He held her close for a moment, stroked her hair, but then gently moved away. 'Me too, but sorry, pumpkin, I've got to pop upstairs to get my kit.'

'I'll come with you,' Ellen cried, unwilling to let him out of her sight.

'No, stay there. I won't be a minute,' he croaked, quickly heading for the stairs.

'Listen, Ellen, I know it's hard, but somehow we've got to be brave for your dad's sake. He's upset, too, so let's see if we can send him off with smiles.'

'I . . . I'll try.'

'That's my girl.'

Her dad appeared again, kitbag slung over his shoulder. 'Right, all set?'

'Ned's harnessed, so let's go,' said Gertie.

'It's good of you to take me to the station.'

'Oh, it's my pleasure.'

'Right then, my lovely girls, time to go.'

'Girl, huh, I wish I was.'

'You'll always be my girl, Hilda, even when you're old and grey.'

'I'd better be,' she warned.

Gertie marched ahead of them out of the door and swung up onto the cart. 'There isn't room for all three of you up here. Perhaps you should sit on the back, Doug.'

'I'm sure we'll manage with Ellen on my lap,' he said.

Ellen thought Gertie looked angry, but then her expression rapidly changed. With a shrug of her shoulders, she said, 'OK, Doug, whatever you say.'

Ellen settled onto her dad's lap, his arms tight around her. As they set off, she wished the journey could go on for ever, that they'd never reach the station; but if anything, Gertie seemed to be urging the horse to a faster pace than usual.

When they arrived in Crewkerne, Hilda fought to keep her composure, but inside she felt as though her heart was breaking. She wanted the train to be late, anything to stop Doug's departure, but when they got to the platform it was already drawing in. She cursed Gertie, wishing the bloody woman hadn't been in such an all-fired hurry to get here. Poor Ned had looked almost on the point of collapse by the time Gertie had drawn the cart to a halt. If the journey had taken longer, Doug would have missed this one and had to wait for the next. It might have taken hours, perhaps giving them time to walk around Crewkerne, to explore the town together; but instead it would be a hurried goodbye.

Steam hissed, engulfing part of the platform, as Doug said, 'Gertie timed that right.'

Few people had got off the train and Hilda could see that the female guard was about to blow her whistle, her arm up and waiting to signal the train's departure.

'Bye, pumpkin,' Doug croaked, quickly hugging Ellen.

Hilda then found herself crushed against him, and fighting tears she said, 'I love you, Doug. I'll always love you.'

The whistle sounded now, Doug's voice strangled in his throat as he let her go to pick up his kitbag. 'I love you too – both of you,' and then he had to dive into the nearest carriage, only able to pull down the window to blow them a kiss before the train pulled away.

Hilda would never know how she managed it, her heart swelling with love for her daughter when she saw that Ellen, too, was somehow smiling as they waved him off.

They remained where they were, both still with fixed smiles on their faces and waving until the train went out of sight. Only then did Ellen turn to fling herself into Hilda's arms.

'Ned needs a bit of a rest,' Gertie said innocently as they at last went outside, 'but wasn't it good that I managed to get Doug here in time to catch that train?'

Hilda was too upset to speak, but this was the final straw. She'd had enough. No matter what, she and Ellen were going back to London.

10

Just a few days after Doug left, Ellen went down with an awful cold that turned to a raging fever, and two days later she passed it on to Gertie.

Hilda was run ragged as she nursed them both, along with seeing to the chickens, pigs and the goat. Bertie was contented once he'd been fed and would lie on Gertie's bed, and the cats were happy and off out as soon as they finished the food in their bowls but Hilda became seriously worried as Ellen and Gertie's temperatures fluctuated – one minute they were hot, the next cold. Tiredly she went into Gertie's room.

'I'm thirsty and my head's splitting,' Gertie moaned.

'Somehow I'm going to have to go into the village. You both need to be seen by a doctor.'

'Waste of time. He's at least eighty,' she said, then bent double with coughing before she croaked, 'See how we are in a couple of days.'

Hilda rubbed her eyes. They'd been like this for over a week now and she was now feeling a bit rough herself. Maybe Gertie was right, maybe there would be an improvement soon. 'All right, but if Ellen gets any worse, no matter what, I want her seen by the doctor.'

'My throat's raw.'

'Here, drink this,' Hilda said as she poured Gertie a glass of water. 'I'll be back soon, but I must see to Ellen now.'

Gertie lay back, closing her eyes, and Hilda quietly left the room. She found Ellen tossing and turning, her hair wet with perspiration and the bedding in a tangle around her. Hilda sorted the bed, bathed her with cool water and for a moment Ellen opened her eyes, but then they closed again. Hilda shook her head in despair. She felt so helpless and the feeling of isolation, of living so many miles from any other human beings, overwhelmed her.

For the rest of the day Hilda kept up her vigil, only leaving Ellen to see to Gertie and the animals. At night she sat in a chair by her daughter, unaware in the early hours of the morning that she had fallen asleep, her upper body and head resting on the bed.

'Mum . . . Mum . . .'

Hilda awoke with a start, her back screaming with pain as she sat up. She groaned, still half asleep at first, but as soon as her eyes settled on her daughter, she was instantly awake. Ellen looked a lot better and, as Hilda reached out to place a hand on her daughter's forehead, for the first time in a week she smiled. 'Your temperature's down. How do you feel?'

'A lot better, and I'm hungry.'

Hilda could have danced with joy but, standing up, she swayed. Her throat was on fire, head thumping, but she fought it off, determined to get her daughter something to eat. 'I'll look in on Gertie, and then make you some breakfast. Hopefully, Gertie's feeling better too.'

'Mum, you look awful.'

'I'm fine,' Hilda lied.

Gertie was still asleep when Hilda peeped in the room, so leaving her for now she went downstairs, clinging to the banister for balance as her head swam. The range would need lighting and, opening the doors, she stuffed in paper and wood, before adding coke, praying she could get it going. Was that a knock on the door? No, surely not? The cottage was so remote and they didn't get visitors. Another knock and, swaying with dizziness, Hilda finally managed to get to the door.

'Mrs Brandon,' she croaked.

'You haven't been to the village for a long time and I was worried about you,' the woman said, but then paled, her hand reaching out. 'My dear, are you all right?'

Mrs Brandon's voice barely reached Hilda as she sank into a pit of darkness.

As Hilda's condition worsened, she lost any sense of time passing, vaguely thinking at one point that she was in some sort of motorised vehicle. She drifted in and out of consciousness, hardly aware of what was going on around her as her temperature raged. When briefly conscious, coughs racked her body, the pain in her chest excruciating before she sank, exhausted, into blackness once again.

Voices reached her again and Hilda forced her eyes open, her first thought for her daughter. 'Ellen . . . Ellen,' she gasped.

'Your daughter's fine,' she heard a gentle voice say, but then Hilda knew nothing once again, unaware until later that day that both her daughter and Gertie were sitting beside her.

'Is she gonna be all right?' Ellen asked a nurse worriedly as she stared at her mother's ashen face.

'There's been some improvement,' said the nurse.

Ellen saw her mother's eyelids flicker, and then they opened, her eyes dazed and confused.

'Wh . . . where am I?'

'You're in hospital, my dear; and, look, your daughter has come to see you.'

'Ellen,' Hilda said, her head turning.

'Oh, Mum . . . Mum.'

Hilda started to cough, the nurse raising her shoulders, and Ellen stared with horror as her mum's chest heaved and she fought for breath.

'I think you should both go now,' the nurse urged.

'Go?!' Gertie said, looking annoyed. 'But we've only just got here.'

'I'm sorry, but maybe Mrs Stone will be more up to visitors tomorrow.'

'I don't want to go,' Ellen cried. 'I don't want to leave her.'

'Your mother needs to rest, my dear,' the nurse said. 'I promise you she's in good hands.'

Ellen looked frantically at her mum as the nurse lowered her gently back onto the pillows. Her eyes were closed again, body limp. 'Mum . . . can you hear me?'

There was no response and, unable to help it, Ellen began to cry. Gertie had told her to be brave, but how could she be brave when her mum looked so ill? 'She . . . she's not going to die, is she?' she sobbed.

'Don't worry,' the nurse said kindly. 'I'm sure your mother is going to be fine.'

'Ellen, you know your mum,' Gertie said. 'She's a fighter and she'll get better, you'll see. Now come on, let her rest and we'll come back tomorrow.'

* * *

Gertie hoped she was right as she took Ellen's hand, gently drawing her away and out of the small ward. They had all been ill, apparently flu, and if it hadn't been for Mrs Brandon taking it upon herself to call, Gertie dreaded to think what would have happened. Gertie had shunned the people in the village, called them nosy busybodies, but now she knew that if it hadn't been for Mrs Brandon, Hilda could have died. The woman had rallied help, and taking it in turns to use an ancient bicycle, two villagers had come in to nurse them all, but then, as she and Ellen recovered, Hilda had worsened, developing what they now knew to be a serious chest infection.

'Oh, Gertie,' sobbed Ellen. 'My mum looked awful.'

'I know, darling, but, as the nurse said, she *is* improving,' Gertie said, trying to reassure Ellen, yet equally worried by what she had seen. Hilda didn't look any better to her, but she had been unable to fob Ellen off any longer and had given in, allowing the child to come with her when she went to the hospital instead of leaving her with Mrs Brandon. It had been a bad decision, one she regretted now. Maybe the nurse was right, maybe they would see an improvement tomorrow, especially as she doubted that she'd be able to keep Ellen away now.

On the way back to the cottage, Gertie stopped

off at the village and, holding out her arms, Ellen jumped off the cart and into them, the two then going into the general store together.

'How is she?' Mrs Brandon asked.

'The nurse said she's improving.'

'Oh, God is good,' the woman said. 'Mrs Stone is such a lovely person and we've all been praying for her. I'll pass on the news and I know that everyone will be delighted.'

'I've already thanked Mrs Levison and Miss Pringle, but my added thanks to you for all you've done and for looking after Ellen while I went to the hospital. I don't think it will be necessary any longer, but it was very kind of you.'

'She's such a lovely girl, no trouble at all. Ellen, I bet you were pleased to see your mum.'

'Yes, but . . . but she looks awful.'

'As she's been so ill, it isn't surprising, but it's lovely to hear that she's getting better. You wait and see; your mummy will be on her feet and home again in no time now.'

Ellen looked a little more cheerful, and after she got a hug from Mrs Brandon, they said their good-byes and left the shop. Gertie helped Ellen onto the cart, and then climbed up beside her, taking the reins.

'Mrs Brandon said that God is good and that they've been praying for my mum. Gertie, do you believe in God?'

'I think I'll have to pass on that one, darling.'

'We used to sing hymns in assembly when I was at school, and one of the teachers used to teach us about things in the Bible. You never do that.'

'I know, and I'm sorry. All I can say is that I can't teach you things that . . . well . . . I'm not sure about,' Gertie said, hating this subject. Her father had turned her away from any leanings she might have had towards religion. Did he really think that she wanted to be this way? That she chose to be this way? With a sigh of exasperation, she signalled Ned to move off, but then had to pull him up again as someone called out to her.

'Miss Forbes . . . Miss Forbes.'

Gertie turned to see Martha Pringle hurrying towards her, a basket clutched in her hands. 'I'm so glad I caught you,' the woman said. 'I know it takes such a long time getting to Crewkerne and back, so I made you this.'

Gertie took the proffered basket, seeing an earthenware dish in the bottom.

'It's a chicken casserole,' Martha Pringle said, 'something for the two of you to have for your dinner.'

'Goodness, how kind,' Gertie said, amazed that these women she had snubbed were still rallying round to help. Yesterday Mrs Levison had given her a lovely rabbit pie, and now this.

'How's Mrs Stone?'

Once again Gertie passed on the news, but, anxious about the animals now, she again thanked Martha Pringle before setting off.

'Give her my kindest regards,' the woman called and once again Gertie was humbled. She'd been a snob, stuck up, afraid that if the villagers found out about her, they'd make her life a misery. She'd lived like a recluse until Hilda arrived, but, unlike her, Hilda had always been friendly to these women when she saw them in the village, taking an interest in their lives. Gertie sighed. The barriers she had put up had been breached now, and though grateful for all their help, Gertie wasn't sure that she wanted any more intrusions into her life.

11

Hilda slowly recovered, but it took a long time. She was left debilitated, but at last allowed home, only to have Gertie fussing over her. At bedtimes, Gertie had wanted to help her undress, but, no matter how weak she felt, Hilda wouldn't stand for that.

So much time had passed since her illness and it was now early June, the weather lovely as, earlier than usual, Hilda climbed out of bed. Gertie was still treating her like an invalid, the physical contact getting worse, the touching, the stroking, and it was turning Hilda's stomach. Not only that, Gertie was even more reluctant to go to the village now, and they had only been once since Hilda had left hospital. She was beginning to feel like a prisoner, though at least that one occasion had given her the chance to post two letters.

Socks made an unusual appearance, jumping up on the bed. 'Leave her alone,' Hilda said as the cat lay on Ellen's chest, his front paws paddling her as he purred loudly. 'I'll feed you today.'

As if he understood her words, the cat jumped down again to follow Hilda. She fed him, then lit the range, hoping that Gertie would take them to the village once again. It didn't help that she was so busy and behind with the planting. Ellen did her best, but no matter how many times Hilda said she felt strong enough, Gertie wouldn't let her help.

Socks licked his paws, and then went out through the cat flap, but only moments later Wilfred pushed through, his round, green eyes looking up at her in appeal.

'All right, I know you want feeding too.'

'You're up early,' came Gertie's voice from behind her.

'So are you.'

'I've got a lot to do.' Laying an arm around Hilda's shoulder, she asked solicitously, 'How are you feeling today?'

'Gertie, how many times have I got to tell you? I'm fine. In fact, if you'll run me to the village after breakfast, I'll make it up to you by giving you a hand with the planting when we get back.'

'I can't spare the time.'

'Gertie, we're low on food and need to stock up.'

'Can't you just knock up some vegetable soup again?'

'I'm sick of the sight of it,' Hilda said, then trying another tactic, 'If you won't take me, fine, I'll walk.'

'Don't be silly.'

'I'm not being silly. Ellen needs more than soup for nourishment, and I can't even make any bread. We've run out of flour, and yeast, let alone not having a scrap of meat.'

'All right, we'll go to the village, but we can't stay long.'

Hilda busied herself with feeding Wilfred. Yes, she had talked Gertie into going, but her feelings of isolation, of being trapped here, were growing ever stronger. Please, please, let there be a reply to her letters, because if she didn't escape soon, Hilda feared she'd go out of her mind.

Ellen was happy as they rode to the village, the sunshine warm on her back, but wished she could say the same about her mum. She was well again now, but so quiet and moody. Gertie was always giving her mum hugs in an attempt to cheer her up, but if anything that just seemed to make it worse.

'Now remember, we can't stay long,' Gertie warned as Ned trotted along. 'I'm not only planting, I'm weaning the piglets.'

'All right, there's no need to nag. I just want some shopping, a newspaper, and to see if there's any mail.'

Ellen wished Gertie hadn't mentioned the pigs. Like last year, and the year before, she knew there'd been a large litter. All but one would be sold again, a part of living on the smallholding Ellen still didn't like.

Gertie took one hand from the reins, leaning across Ellen to lay it on her mum's leg. 'Cheer up, Hilda.'

'I'm fine,' she snapped, impatiently pushing her hand away.

Gertie then patted Ellen's leg, too. 'Your mum might be a bit short-tempered, but it's nice to see her looking so well now.'

Ellen glanced at her mother, but she was staring straight ahead, her lips tight; sensing her mood, Ellen remained quiet for the rest of the journey.

When they arrived at the general store, Gertie made no attempt to climb down, only saying, 'Don't be long, Hilda.'

'I'll be as long as it takes,' she retorted angrily.

Ellen clambered down and inside the shop, Mrs Brandon returned their greetings. 'Hello, and it's nice to see you both. There are two letters for you, Mrs Stone.'

Ellen saw her mum's face light up as she took them. 'This one's from my husband, but as I only wrote to him ten days ago, they must have crossed in the post.'

'What else can I get you?' Mrs Brandon asked.

Hilda passed her a list, chatting to Mrs Brandon as she gathered the goods together, while Ellen ogled the few sweets on offer, thrilled when her mum said they had enough coupons to buy some. The sherbet lemons looked sticky and clung to the jar as they were shaken onto the scales, but Ellen's mouth watered with anticipation.

'There you are, Ellen,' said Mrs Brandon as she passed her the paper bag.

'I'm sorry I can't stay longer to chat,' her mum said, 'but Gertie is anxious to get back to the small-holding.'

'Yes, it's a busy time of year.'

Calling goodbye, they left the shop.

'It's about time,' said Gertie as they returned to the cart.

'I'm going to the butcher's, so you'll just have to wait.'

Ellen didn't like his shop. Sometimes he had whole dead rabbits hanging from hooks and the sight sickened her. 'I'll wait here,' she called as her mum hurried off, and then, climbing up beside Gertie, held out the bag of sherbet lemons. 'Do you want one?'

'No, you eat them. I haven't got a sweet tooth.'

Ellen pried one sticky sweet from another and popped it into her mouth as her eyes roamed the small village. To her it was beautiful, the thatched cottages, the stone walls behind which lay pretty gardens. She loved it here, the countryside, and living on the smallholding. She sighed with happiness, hoping they'd never leave.

When Hilda returned again to the cart, Gertie asked, 'Did you get everything we need?'

'Yes,' Hilda said shortly, and as the horse ambled along she pulled out Doug's letter, anxious to read it. She smiled at first, loving his cheeky innuendoes, but when she got to the second page her expression changed. Doug must be out of his tiny mind, writing about how much he'd enjoyed working on the smallholding and going on to suggest that after the war they move out of London. No way, Hilda thought as she stuffed the letter back into the envelope. She'd had enough of living in the back of beyond with hardly any amenities other than a few village shops. In London you could jump on a bus, a train, or the tube and go anywhere without a problem. Here there wasn't any transport and all they had to rely on was a flaming, cantankerous horse.

'What did Dad say?' Ellen asked again.

'He misses us, he's fine, and he sends you his love.'

'When's he coming home again?'

'I don't know,' Hilda said sadly.

Once outside the village the road became uneven and they bounced as the cart hit an occasional hump, but despite this Hilda managed to scan the newspaper. Her mood lightened. There hadn't been any raids over London, and she dared to hope. She wanted to be away from Gertie, to have her own home again, somewhere to settle and for Doug to return to when this rotten war was over. Keeping her thoughts to herself, Hilda folded the newspaper. She didn't want to talk about her plans in front of Ellen, and, anyway, with the way Gertie was behaving lately, she might kick up a fuss. Hilda wondered yet again if she was imagining things; yet recalling the many times Gertie found any excuse to touch her nowadays, she doubted it. There'd been so many hugs, so many occasions when she'd caught Gertie looking at her with a strange, almost lustful expression.

Hilda shivered. Maybe she was imagining it, maybe not, but, just in case, she wanted to be away from Gertie; the thought of her wanting a love affair nauseating.

Gertie knew that Hilda was fed up with life in the country and there'd been times when she'd talked about going back to London, yet, despite this, she wasn't worried. Hilda was a loving and protective mother who would never put her daughter at risk, their stay with her assured until the war was over. 'I saw you had two letters,' she said. 'Who was the other one from?'

'Mabel. I'll read it when we're back at the cottage.'

'Was there anything interesting in the newspaper?'

'There's no mention of bombing raids on London and, as Hitler has turned his attention to other targets, there's speculation there might not be any more.'

'You said it, speculation, and no guarantee.'

'Look,' Ellen said, pointing to a farmer's field. 'It's full of Land Army girls.'

'Lucky farmer,' Gertie said. 'I wouldn't mind a few of them helping out on my smallholding.'

'I've offered to get stuck in, but you won't let me,' Hilda said curtly.

'Once you're fully recovered, I'll welcome it.'

'I *am* fully recovered, and I'll tell you something else, I'm fed up with you telling me what I can and cannot do.'

'All right, calm down. It's just that you were so ill and I'm worried about you over-exerting yourself.'

'I'm a grown woman, not a child, and if I say I'm up to giving you a hand, then I am.'

'Fair enough,' Gertie said. 'You can start tomorrow.'

'I'll start when I'm good and ready – not when *you* decide to give your permission.'

Gertie shook her head. When Hilda was in this mood there was no pleasing her. Her chest infection had been serious, so bad that Gertie had feared she would lose her. Maybe she had been a bit bossy, over-protective, but it was time to loosen up. They needed to get back to normal, to return to their old routine, and once that was achieved, Hilda was sure to brighten up.

12

When they returned to the cottage, it wasn't long before Gertie and Ellen were working outside again, while Hilda read Mabel's letter, her mind racing. Mabel wrote that South Clapham was still lovely, hardly touched by the Blitz, or any of the infrequent bombing raids that followed. The next bit of the letter was more exciting. By an absolute fluke, Hilda's letter to Mabel had arrived at an opportune time. Apparently the old lady who lived downstairs was unable to look after herself any longer and was going to live with her daughter. Mabel had already spoken to the landlord on Hilda's behalf and he was willing to let her have the place, but to secure it she'd have to travel back to London as soon as possible.

Gertie was sure to kick up a fuss, and Hilda didn't want Ellen to hear what might develop into a row, so going to the back door she called, 'Gertie, can you come in for a minute? I need a hand with something.'

Thankfully Hilda saw that Ellen remained where she was, and as soon as Gertie reached her, she beckoned her inside, saying curtly, 'Gertie, we're going back to London.'

'What! No, Hilda, tell me you don't mean it.'

'Mabel said a flat has come up, and if I go back I've got a strong chance of getting it.'

'You're being selfish. Ellen loves it here, but you're going to drag her back to London where it isn't safe.'

'It is safe and I am *not* selfish.'

Gertie's stance became rigid, her lips set in a tight line. 'You're not going. Despite what you say, London is too dangerous. I insist you stay here.'

Anger flared in Hilda and she yelled, 'Who are you to tell me what to do? If I want to go back, I will. In fact, we're going right now!'

'And how do you think you're going to get to the station? I'm not taking you.'

Hilda fumed. It was miles to the village, let alone Crewkerne, but even if it took many hours, somehow she'd get there. 'And you call *me* selfish. It won't work though, Gertie. You can't keep me a prisoner and if you won't take us, fine. We'll walk to the village and I'm sure someone there will give us a lift to Crewkerne.'

As Hilda stomped outside, Gertie almost doubled over in anguish. She'd said all the wrong things, been too forceful, and her stupid threat that she wouldn't take them to the station had rebounded. She'd wanted to delay Hilda, to have time to talk some sense into her, but instead it had made Hilda even more determined to leave. Gertie wanted to chase after her, to beg her to stay, but Hilda was now so angry that there'd be no getting round her.

Poor Ellen, she'd be so upset, but that thought gave Gertie a smidgeon of hope. Seeing her daughter's distress might be enough to sway Hilda, and Gertie now hurried back outside, hearing Ellen's voice high in appeal as she drew closer.

'No, Mum! I don't want to go.'

'It's safe in London now and we've no reason to stay here. Now get a move on. We've got packing to do.'

'No,' Ellen said mutinously.

'You'll do as I say, my girl.'

'I want to stay here!'

Gertie laid a hand on Hilda's arm. 'Please, at least leave Ellen with me.'

'No!' Hilda spat, pushing a protesting Ellen ahead of her to the cottage.

Gertie knew she had lost and, heartsick, she stood unmoving, watching them go. Before they'd arrived she had become used to living on her own, adapted to the loneliness by burying herself in working the smallholding. She'd found a contentment of sorts, but their arrival had changed all that; her way of living, of thinking, had been transformed and Gertie knew she couldn't face the life of a recluse again.

She had loved teaching Ellen, had seen how she enjoyed the lessons, her mind absorbing so much. Gertie knew she was a talented teacher, a wasted talent now, and with that thought came a yearning to teach again. With her past record she doubted it would be possible and for the first time in years Gertie felt tears flooding her eyes. She wasn't an emotional woman, but Gertie cried now, cried at the thought of losing Hilda, of losing Ellen, and for the loss of her career.

Sobs racked Gertie's body and she folded at the waist, clutching both arms around her stomach. *Oh Hilda, Hilda, please don't leave me,* her mind screamed, until her knees gave way and she sank onto the ground.

Ellen didn't want to leave, couldn't bear the thought of going back to London, but her mother was so angry that she found herself almost shoved upstairs and into the bedroom.

'Do . . . do we have to go?'

'Yes, and I can't believe that selfish bitch. We've worked like bloody dogs since we've been here, outside in all weathers, and what thanks do we get? None! She won't even take us to the station.'

'I . . . I didn't mind doing the planting, Mum. I like seeing things grow.'

Ellen was ignored, her mum opening drawers and stuffing things into a case, but she tried again nevertheless. 'Mum. I . . . I'm scared. Ger . . . Gertie said there still might be bombing raids in London.'

At last her mum's face softened as she beckoned Ellen to her. 'Now listen, I wouldn't take you back to London if I didn't think it was safe, and not only that, we won't be living in Battersea. We're going to Clapham. From what Mabel told me, it's a nice house. She lives upstairs, and we'll be downstairs. You'll love it there, and it's close to the Common with a nice school too.'

'I . . . I'd rather stay here.'

'I know you would, but it's time you went to a proper school and mixed with girls of your own age again.'

'I could go to the one in the village,' Ellen suggested in a desperate attempt to change her mother's mind.

'You know it's too far away. Now come on, buck up. We've a train to catch and a long walk ahead of us to the village. To start with, grab that carving your dad made for you from the windowsill.'

Ellen did as she was told, but as she picked up the cat and looked down onto the smallholding, she frowned. 'Mum, what's wrong with Gertie?'

'What do you mean?'

'Look,' she urged.

'Oh Gawd,' her mother said when she saw Gertie on her knees, the dog frantically scrambling all over her and trying to lick her face. 'Stay here and take over the packing.'

Ellen didn't do as she was told, but remained at the window, watching as her mum rushed outside. She couldn't hear what they were saying, but moments later Gertie was on her feet, reaching out to drag her mum into her arms.

Hilda had been worried about Gertie, but was now more worried about herself as she fought the vice-like embrace.

'Gertie, leave off. I know you're upset, but let me go.'

'Don't leave me, Hilda. Please don't go.'

'Stop it!' she yelled, writhing with panic as Gertie's lips sought hers. With her arms clamped, Hilda did the only thing possible and stamped hard on Gertie's foot. 'Don't you dare! Don't you dare kiss me!'

At last she was free, sickened by what had happened as she stared at Gertie in disgust. 'And you wonder why I'm leaving!'

'Hilda, please, I'm sorry, it . . . it's just that you haven't objected when I've touched you, and . . . and I was beginning to think . . .'

'Well, you thought wrong! I took it as just friendly affection, a sort of sisterly affection, so of course I didn't object.'

'Oh, Hilda, what I feel for you is more than that. I . . . I love you . . . I've always loved you and can't bear the thought of losing you.'

Hilda stood rigidly in shock and indignation. 'Losing me! You never blinking well had me. I'm a married woman – married to a man! I don't fancy women and you know that!'

'Of course I know and I was stupid, mad, to hope. Honestly, it was just a moment of madness, that's all. If you stay I promise it'll never happen again.'

'Too bloody right it won't. The sooner I get out of here the better.'

Gertie seemed to deflate before Hilda's eyes, her tone desolate when she spoke. 'All right, I understand, but don't leave like this. Can't we at least part as friends?'

Ellen came running out of the back door, white-faced and calling, 'Mum, what's wrong? Why are you fighting? Why did you stamp on Gertie's foot?'

Hilda drew in a deep breath, fighting for composure. 'We're not fighting. It's just a bit of a misunderstanding, that's all.'

Ellen didn't look convinced, but then Gertie knelt down and beckoned her over. 'It was my fault, Ellen. I wasn't very nice, so no wonder your mother stamped on my foot.'

'Does it hurt?'

Gertie's laugh sounded forced as she said ruefully, 'Yes, a bit, but I forgive her and I hope she forgives me. Don't worry, we're friends again now. Isn't that right, Hilda?'

Hilda paused before answering, yet saw the concern in her daughter's eyes and knew she'd have to go along with it. 'Yes, but come on, Ellen, we've still got packing to do.'

'What about Socks? We can't leave Socks.'

'Sod it, I forgot about the cat. With our luggage, I don't know how we're going to manage him too.'

'Don't worry,' said Gertie. 'I've got a basket somewhere and he'll be fine in that. You won't have to walk. I'll take you to the station.'

Hilda knew that Ellen would kick up a fuss if they left without the cat so it wasn't practical to refuse the offer. Her thanks were begrudging as she urged Ellen inside and she dreaded the long ride to town. At least Ellen would be with them so they wouldn't be alone, but if Gertie laid another finger on her, bigger in stature or not, she'd flatten the unnatural cow.

With a spurt of energy, Hilda threw their things into the cases. She had used every excuse in her mind to return to London: the need for her own home, to find some sort of work that would help the war effort, along with Ellen's education. Mabel said it was safe, so she'd chosen to ignore Gertie's warnings of more air raids. Now, after what had just happened, she no longer had to find excuses to leave – her conscience was at last clear.

Gertie reluctantly harnessed the horse, her emotions in turmoil as they set off. Hilda wouldn't look her in the eye, her expression implacable as they left the smallholding. She cursed her own lack of control. If she'd kept her hands to herself, maybe Hilda wouldn't be so intent on leaving, yet, even as this thought crossed her mind, Gertie knew that it wouldn't have made any difference. Hilda hated it in Somerset, and though living with her for well over two years, she'd never adapted to country life.

Sadly, Gertie glanced at Ellen and saw she was close to tears. Ellen had come to Somerset a pale, stammering, nervous wreck, but now she had blossomed, glowed with health and had been a pleasure to teach.

'Ellen, did you pack your books?'

'I wanted to, but Mum said they'd make my case too heavy. Will . . . will you look after them for me?'

'I'll do my best, but as I too might be leaving, perhaps I should parcel up our favourites and post them to you.'

Hilda's head shot around. 'Leaving! What do you mean? I hope you're not going to follow me back to London.'

'No, Hilda, but I feel it's time for me to wake up, join the world again. I'm thinking about enlisting in one of the armed forces.'

'Yeah, well, the uniform would suit you,' Hilda said derisively. 'Mind you, I'm not sure that as a *woman,* you'd be allowed to wear trousers.'

'Hilda, don't be like this. I'd kept away from you for years, and you seem to be forgetting that it was *you* who asked to stay with me. I wasn't sure how I'd cope, but knowing you were in danger, how could I refuse?'

'I asked to stay with you because I saw you as a sister. I trusted you!'

'I know, and I'm sorry. It shouldn't have happened, *wouldn't* have happened if I hadn't been in such a state. I just couldn't bear the thought of you leaving and lost control.'

'That's enough! Ellen shouldn't be hearing any of this. All I'll say is that you shouldn't have tried it on, and now just shut up about it.'

'What did you try on, Gertie? Was it one of Mummy's dresses?'

Gertie floundered for a moment, but then said, 'Yes, my dear, I'm afraid I did try on your mother's best dress and she wasn't very happy about it.'

'Why? Did you tear it?'

'Well, darling, look at the size of me compared to your mother.'

Ellen giggled, and it was followed by a chuckle

from Hilda before she said, 'I suppose in a way I should be flattered, but I wasn't, Gertie. I was just disgusted and in future, don't you dare do that again.'

'Don't worry, I won't. Your friendship means too much to me and I won't risk losing it. We are still friends, aren't we?'

'I suppose so, but only friends and no more.'

'I'm happy with that,' Gertie assured her. She'd been mad to want more – mad to expect that Hilda would feel the same, and though Gertie doubted her feelings would ever change, at least she had the compensation of Hilda's continued friendship.

'Are you really going to join up?'

'Yes, I think so.'

'Will you sell the smallholding?'

'It wouldn't be practical to keep it. Unattended it would just go to rack and ruin and I have to think about the animals too.'

'What about Bertie?' asked Ellen.

'I'll have to find a new home for him.'

'And Wilfred?'

'Him too.'

'Mum, can we have Bertie?' Ellen appealed.

'We can't, love. We've already got Socks.'

'Socks won't mind. He likes Bertie.'

'I'm not sure the landlord will allow one pet, let alone two. As it is, if we get the flat, we may have to sneak the cat in.'

'But, Mum . . .'

'That's enough,' Hilda snapped, her patience obviously wearing thin and her mood changing again.

'Your mother's right, Ellen, and anyway, I doubt Bertie would be happy living in London. Don't worry, I'll find him a good home locally,' Gertie assured her as they neared the village. 'Hilda, if you want to catch the train, we won't be able to stop. If we do it'll mean getting a later one.'

'No, I don't want to do that, but do me a favour, Gertie. Will you say goodbye to everyone for me, and . . . and tell them that I'll never forget them, or their kindness?'

'Of course I will.'

They passed through without seeing anyone, and Gertie knew that when they finally reached the station she would somehow have to hold herself together. To do that she'd have to leave quickly, the thought of saying goodbye was almost tearing her heart in two.

She straightened her back, hands tight on the reins as she forced her thoughts to the future. Yes, she would join the armed forces, but first she had to find a buyer for the smallholding.

Hilda was happy as they drew closer to Crewkerne. Soon they'd be on a train and heading for London, and, as Mabel had offered to put them up until they could hopefully move into the downstairs flat, she wondered if her friend would mind taking the cat in too. It would break Ellen's heart if they had to get rid of Socks, and as her daughter was already unhappy about leaving Somerset, that was the last thing Hilda wanted.

For a moment Hilda felt a shiver of doubt. Was she doing the right thing? And was Mabel right about London now being safe? As the station loomed, Hilda pushed her worries to one side. Ellen would go to school, make friends, and though she learned a lot under Gertie's tutelage, it wasn't right that for so long she'd only had adults for company.

Still, it had been good of Gertie to teach her, and that was something she had to thank her for. If only Gertie had kept her hands to herself. If only she hadn't tried to kiss her; but even if she hadn't, Hilda knew that she'd still be heading for home. Doug's last leave had been the catalyst that unsettled her, made her look at Gertie differently, and only her illness had held her up from leaving.

'Here we are,' Gertie said as she reined in the horse in front of the station.

Hilda climbed down. Please, please, let the train be on time, she thought, dreading a prolonged goodbye. With Gertie helping with the luggage, she bought their tickets, relieved to be told that there was only a small delay, and then they moved onto the platform.

'I suppose you'll be staying with Mabel until you get your flat,' Gertie said. 'If you give me her address, I'll post Ellen's books.'

Hilda wasn't sure that she wanted to keep in touch with Gertie. After what had happened, things could never be the same between them, and though she had agreed to remain friends, she wasn't sure it was possible. She hadn't told Gertie that the flat was in the same house, so said, 'It might be better if you wait until we move into our own place. I'll write to you from there.'

'Will you, Hilda?' asked Gertie, her brows rising in scepticism.

'Yes, of course.'

'I'd best get back to the smallholding. Good . . . goodbye Hilda.'

'Don't go yet,' Ellen begged, throwing her arms around Gertie.

'I'm sorry, but I've got to see to the animals.'

'You won't forget to post my books?'

'Of course not, but we'll have to hope I get your new address before I sell up and leave. Goodbye, sweetheart. I'm going to miss you.'

'I . . . I love you, Gertie. I wish we could stay here.'

'And I love you, darling,' she said, her voice sounding strangled.

Despite everything, Hilda was touched by the scene. It was clear to see that Ellen was very fond of Gertie, and that her affection was returned. She pulled a piece of paper out of her handbag, hastily scribbling Mabel's address. 'You'd better have this. If the flat falls through it might take me a while to find another.'

Gertie took the piece of paper, her face taut with emotion as she croaked, 'Thanks.'

'Stay safe when you join up, Gertie, and let me know where you are.'

'Do you mean that, Hilda?'

'Ellen's going to miss you and she'll want us to stay in touch.'

Gertie gave Ellen another hug, and then, her eyes awash with tears, she hurried from the platform and out of sight.

Ellen was crying too and Hilda reached out to put an arm around her. She didn't like seeing her daughter unhappy, yet felt a surge of excitement. It was June 1943, and at last they were going home – going back to London.

13

When they arrived in London, Ellen found it strange, alien now. People, so many people, rushing around, and noise, there was so much noise. In the sky she saw huge, silver barrage balloons and she shivered with fear. All her memories returned. The sound of aircraft engines approaching, the scream of stick bombs as they fell, the fires, the smells, the houses flattened, one on top of her grandparents. She didn't want to be here, she wanted to go back to Somerset and cried, 'Mum, I want to go home.'

'You are home. This is London, and it's where we belong.'

'I don't like it. I want to go back to Gertie's.'

'Well, you can't,' her mother said impatiently.

They were on a bus now, and Ellen wanted to close her eyes against the sights they passed. So many gaping holes where buildings had been, rubble, so much rubble, and instead of greenery, everything looked grey and dull.

'Look at that, a female messenger,' her mother said, as a girl on a motorbike passed the bus. 'The bus driver and the conductor are women too and I've never seen so many in uniforms.'

When the bus pulled up at a stop two elderly ladies got on and sat in front of Ellen and her mother.

'I hate these bleedin' things,' one complained as her gas mask strap slipped off her shoulder.

'Put a sock in it, Ethel. You're always moaning about something,' the other one quipped.

'No more than you. I heard you having a go at that ARP warden last night.'

'He asked for it, Flo, knocking on my door after midnight and telling me I had a light showing.'

'And did you?'

She shrugged. 'I hadn't pulled one of my blackout curtains fully across so there might have been a tiny chink, but that's only because I was using me small torch to come downstairs. Without it I'd be in danger of falling arse over tit and I was desperate for a pee.'

'Well then, it seems apt that you told him to piss off.'

Ellen heard a titter, then a giggle, and turned to see her mother trying to hold it back. She couldn't, and suddenly howled with laughter.

'Are you laughing at us?' the one called Flo asked indignantly as she twisted round in her seat.

'Oh . . . oh, sorry, but I can't help it.'

'We ain't a couple of comedians put on this bus for your entertainment, you know.'

'Please . . . I . . . I'm sorry,' Hilda gasped, obviously fighting for composure. 'It . . . it's just that it's smashing to hear London humour again. We've been away, you see, living in Somerset, and it's so good to be back.'

There was a loud, howling miaow from the basket and the woman asked, 'Gawd, blimey, girl, what have you got in there?'

'My cat,' Ellen told her. 'We've been travelling for ages and he wants to get out.'

'He sounds like a noisy bugger.'

'No more noisy than you, Flo.'

'Shut your face, Ethel,' said Flo before speaking to Hilda again. 'You ain't alone in coming back to London. Lots of people have now, including kids that were evacuated.'

'Yeah, but I think their daft parents should have left them where they were.'

'Ethel, you're only saying that 'cos you don't like kids.'

'I do. Mind you, I couldn't eat a whole one.'

Hilda laughed again, but Ellen didn't join in. She looked out of the window, hating what she saw and wanting only to go back to Somerset.

After several changes, they at last arrived in Clapham, climbing wearily off the bus. Hilda liked what she saw. Clapham Common stretched along one side of the road, and as they plodded along carrying the luggage and cat basket, arms aching, Hilda saw Clapham South underground station. Mabel had written that her house was only a couple of streets away from there. They crossed over the main road, turned a corner, and soon found the right place.

Hilda plonked her case and the basket down, gazing at the house for a moment. There were two front doors, one for the upstairs flat and one for the down, that one having bay windows. It looked nice and Hilda hoped she was in time to secure it, her eyes gritty with tiredness as she knocked on Mabel's door.

Only moments later it was opened, steep stairs visible behind Mabel as she said, 'Hilda, you got here then?'

Hilda picked up the case and basket again. 'Yes, we're here.'

'Come in . . . come in,' Mabel urged and tiredly they followed her upstairs.

Hilda looked around the sitting room, which wasn't a bad size, and then, taking a deep breath, she said, 'Mabel, I hope you don't mind, but we've brought Ellen's cat with us. She'd have been brokenhearted if we left him behind.'

'Of course I don't mind,' Mabel said as her son, Percy, walked into the room.

'I guessed it was you,' he said, 'and I've put the kettle on the gas to boil.'

'You're a good boy,' Mabel said.

'Can . . . can I let Socks out now?' Ellen asked.

'Yes, love,' Mabel said, 'and my goodness, I can't get over how much you've grown. Hilda, take the weight off your feet. I'll make you a cup of tea and then show you your room.'

'Is the downstairs flat still empty?'

'Yeah, and don't worry, you'll get it.'

'I hope so, Mabel, 'cos if not I don't know what we'll do.'

Ellen opened the basket and for a moment Socks looked around warily, but then he slunk out, heading straight for Percy.

'Hello, feller,' he said, crouching down to stroke him.

'Animals seem to like my Percy,' said Mabel, smiling fondly at her son.

'Er . . . er, Mum . . . Socks might need to go to the toilet,' Ellen said, her eyes wide with worry.

'He can't go out yet or he'll stray,' Percy warned. 'I'll find him something to go in, and dig up a bit of soil from the garden.'

'Mabel, I'm sorry, I didn't think,' Hilda said worriedly as Percy left the room. 'He's a tom and it might be a bit smelly.'

'A bit of a whiff won't kill us, and anyway the

129

landlord is due round in the morning. Once you give him the rent money you'll be able to move in downstairs.'

'How can you be so sure?'

Her eyes flicked to make sure that Percy was still in the kitchen, then she said with a wink and a whisper, ''Cos he likes me.'

'Mabel!'

'Don't look so shocked. Nothing's happened and never will, but he doesn't know that and a bit of harmless flirting goes a long way. Mind you, I could be tempted. Unlike you, I haven't seen my husband for over eighteen months.'

'How about this?' Percy said, returning and holding up a roasting tin.

'No, that's me good one,' Mabel protested. 'Come on, I think I've got an old one somewhere and it's about time I made Hilda a drink.'

Socks wandered round the sitting room, sniffing and rubbing against every piece of furniture, while Ellen watched him, her expression morose.

'Cheer up, Ellen,' Hilda urged.

'He's going to hate it here,' she complained.

'He'll be fine, and we will too. The Common is only a spit away, and once you're in school, making friends, you'll soon forget about Somerset.'

'No, I won't. I'll never forget Somerset. Never!'

Percy returned clutching a rusted tin. 'I'll dig up a bit of soil now.'

'Is the garden shared between the two flats?' Hilda asked.

'Yeah, we've got a metal staircase down to it from the kitchen, but despite being told to dig for victory, we hardly use it.'

'What's digging for victory?' Ellen asked.

'With food in short supply, we've been told to grow vegetables and such.'

'We could do that, Mum,' Ellen said eagerly.

'Yeah, well, we certainly know how,' Hilda agreed.

'Mum can't stand gardening,' Percy said, 'but if you want a bit of help, I wouldn't mind giving it a go.'

'Thanks, love, I might take you up on that,' Hilda said.

Percy grinned as he left to go down to the garden. He had grown so much since she had last seen him and would be fourteen this year. The opposite in looks and character to his younger brother, Percy was tall and gangly with brown hair and eyes. He had a soft, caring nature, while his younger brother, Billy, was a little terror, causing his mother nothing but worry.

'Here you are, get that down you first,' Mabel said as she carried in a tray, 'and then you can have a bite to eat. I'm afraid it ain't much, just a bit of corned beef hash.'

'Lovely, and thanks, Mabel. Where's Billy?'

'Gawd knows. The little sod is always off out as soon as my back's turned. I wish he'd been a girl. He's the same age as your Ellen and she doesn't give you a moment's worry.'

'Percy doesn't either.'

'Yeah, he's a good lad,' Mabel said, smiling as her son came in again, the tin now full of earth.

'Where do you want me to put it?' he asked.

'Blimey, I don't know,' Mabel said. 'Stick it behind the sofa for now.'

'Come on, boy,' Percy urged, and Socks didn't need any more bidding. It wasn't long before the pungent smell of tomcat filled the air, all of them wrinkling their noses.

'The poor sod must have been bursting,' Percy observed, 'but I'd better empty this straightaway.'

'I'll do it,' Ellen offered.

'No, you eat your grub,' he said.

Hilda wasn't sure she fancied it now, what with the smell lingering and pervading the room.

Mabel hurried to throw open a window. 'I hate to say this, but I'll be glad when you get that cat out of here in the morning.'

'I can't blame you for that, and can't wait to have my own place again. Oh no!' she exclaimed, her eyes rounding. 'I wasn't expecting to move in so quickly. What about furniture? I can't move into an empty flat.'

'The daughter didn't want any of the old girl's

stuff, so it's still there. All she took were a few bits and pieces. The landlord was going to clear it out, but I asked him to leave it.'

'Mabel, you're a treasure,' Hilda said, smiling widely.

'You may not say that when you see it. Most of the stuff's ancient.'

'I don't care, and, anyway, once I'm in I can start replacing it.'

'All you'll get nowadays is utility furniture. It's as plain as a pikestaff.'

'Mabel, I'm home, I'm back in London, and that's all that matters,' Hilda told her friend and she meant it. Ellen might look miserable, but once she made friends she'd soon snap out of it. Somerset and Gertie would become a distant memory.

14

Ellen sat looking out of the window after break-fast. It was a Sunday morning in July now, but she was still miserable, despite making friends with Lucy Price, the girl who lived next door. Lucy was pretty, with lovely blonde hair and blue eyes, the image of her mother. They went to the same school, one that had strangely been renamed The South West Emergency Secondary. She didn't mind it there, but Socks had gone missing on his first foray outside. She and Lucy had become inseparable, combing the streets at every opportunity in the hope of finding him, but as the weeks passed with no sign of him, Ellen was desolate.

'Are you still mooning about that cat?' she heard her mother ask.

'Lucy said she'd pray to Jesus to bring Socks back, but it hasn't worked.'

'I could have told you that.'

'What if he's hurt? What if he's laying some-where, injured?'

'Ellen, he's a tom and has probably gone off after a female in heat.'

'In heat! What's that?'

'Me and my big mouth,' she complained. 'Look, it's just that tomcats like to roam and he's prob-ably as happy as a lark with a lady friend, that's all. You never know, he might come home again one day.'

Ellen hoped her mum was right, that Socks was happy, but she missed him so much. Not only Socks, her dad too. 'I wish Dad would come home.'

'So do I, darling.'

There was the sound of the back door opening and Mabel came in, carrying something on a small plate.

Ellen saw her mother looking at it warily as she said, 'Watcha, and what have you got there?'

'Harry just came round with it. I've cut a bit off for us and thought you might like the rest for your dinner.'

Harry lived at the end of the street, a cheeky, furtive-looking chap with a bit of a gammy leg who was always getting hold of stuff that was almost impossible to get now.

'Spiv or not, bless Harry's heart,' Hilda said. 'Mind you, it's funny-looking meat. Is it beef?'

'No, it's horsemeat, but he said it's very tasty.'

'Horsemeat! No, Mabel, I don't think I could eat that. I'd be wondering if the poor animal has just raced in the 3.20 at Kempton Park.'

Mabel chuckled. 'You daft moo.'

'No, I mean it. You know what Harry's like and I wouldn't put it past him.'

'Leave it out. He might be a bit of a tea leaf, but even he wouldn't nick a flippin' racehorse.'

'Why did you call Harry a tea leaf?' Ellen asked.

'Tea leaf – rhymes with thief,' Mabel told her, 'but one with a heart of gold.'

Hilda snorted. 'Oh, did he give it to you for nothing then?'

'Well, no, but he only wanted a tanner for it.'

'Sixpence for that! You were robbed.'

'Fine, please yourself,' Mabel said, beginning to look annoyed. 'If you don't want it I'll offer it to Dora.'

Ellen was relieved that her mum had turned it down, though she didn't think Lucy's mum, Dora, would want to eat horsemeat either. She pictured Ned, Gertie's horse, and gulped, the thought of eating him awful.

'Are you all right, Hilda?' asked Mabel. 'You've gone a bit pale.'

'I feel a bit queasy.'

'In your condition, it ain't surprising.'

Ellen saw her mother give a warning shake of

her head before she said, 'Ellen, why don't you go and play with Lucy?'

'She's gone to church with her parents. She won't be back yet.'

'Well, go and play in the garden for a while, there's a good girl.'

'Why?'

'Because I said so. Now do as you're told.'

Ellen felt shut out again. She wasn't silly; she had heard her mother and Mabel whispering. There was something going on, something her mother hadn't told her, and as she ambled through the kitchen on the way to the back door, she paused. Instead of going outside, she opened the door and closed it loudly, then sneaked back to listen to her mother and Mabel talking. A recipe. All Mabel was talking about was a recipe for something called Wooten Pie that was made with vegetables.

'It sounds all right, Mabel, but I'm too worn out to bother much with cooking. I don't know why it's taken me like this.'

'Do you remember Lily Baxter?'

'I think so. Didn't she live on the end of your street in Battersea?'

'Yeah, that's her, and if I remember rightly she was the same as you, sick a lot and worn out.'

'I feel so rough, Mabel. It could be because I've been ill, going down with the flu and a chest infection in Somerset. In fact, when I didn't have a show for a couple of months, I just put it down to that.'

'When are you gonna tell Ellen?'

'Soon, but I don't know how she's going to take it.'

Ellen went rigid. Was her mum ill again? Something tickled her nose and she tried to hold it back, pinching her nose desperately, but it was no good and the sneeze burst loudly.

'Ellen, is that you?'

Shamefaced, she walked into the living room, her eyes down.

'I told you to go into the garden.'

'Sor . . . sorry,' she stammered, but then desperate to know she blurted out: 'Mum, what's wrong? Are you ill?'

'Oh, I get it. You were eavesdropping.'

Ellen felt tears pricking her eyes, but then her mother beckoned her over. 'Don't look so worried,' she said. 'You shouldn't have been listening, but no, I'm not ill.'

'I heard Mabel say that you've been sick, and then you said you felt rough.'

'Yeah, that's true, but it's got nothing to do with illness. I wasn't going to tell you this until I was safely past three months, but well, I'm having a baby.'

'A baby! How?'

'We'll talk about that when you're a bit older; suffice to say for now that in around six months or so you'll be getting a baby sister or brother.'

'Does Dad know?'

'I wrote to him as soon as I was sure, so I hope so. Now go on, off you go and leave me and Mabel to chat in peace.'

Ellen was still smiling as she went into the garden. A baby sister, she'd love a baby sister, but she didn't know how she'd feel about a brother. Billy came rushing through the back gate, clutching what looked like apples, and seeing her he ground to a halt.

'What have you got there?' Ellen asked.

'None of your business,' he said stuffing them under his shirt, 'and if you say anything to me mum, I'll punch your lights out.'

With that he ran up the metal stairs, leaving Ellen scowling. She liked Mabel's son, Percy, but didn't like Billy. He was the same age as her, and at the same school, but he was always hopping off, him and his gang running wild and nicking things, especially from the market stalls. She kept out of his way as much as possible, and was glad that he'd gone upstairs.

Ellen scanned the garden. With Percy's help she had dug over the soil, but she doubted much would grow. They had come across all sorts of rubbish – rubble, bricks, old bottles – and, unlike Gertie's lush earth in Somerset, Ellen could see that this soil hadn't been fertilised in years.

'I'm back,' Lucy called, her head appearing above the garden wall.

Ellen smiled at her friend, wondering what it would be like to go to church every Sunday. Lucy didn't seem to mind and sometimes talked enthusiastically about it, and when she had been invited round to her house for tea last week, Ellen had thought it strange that they had to pray before starting to eat. What good did praying do anyway? Lucy had prayed for Socks but it hadn't brought him back.

'Hello,' Ellen now said.

'Are you coming out to play?'

'Yes, and guess what? My mum's having a baby.'

'Wow, you're lucky. I wish my mum would get one too.'

'Do you know where they come from?'

'My mum says that children are a gift from God.'

Ellen wondered if her mother knew that God had sent her a present, and decided to ask her later, but for now she said, 'How about a game of hopscotch?'

'Yes, all right.'

'If God sent my mum a present, how do we thank him?'

'That's easy,' Lucy said. 'You just close your eyes and talk to him.'

'What? Like praying?'

Lucy nodded as she bent down to chalk numbers on pavement slabs, while Ellen wondered again what it must be like to go to church every Sunday. There was only one way to find out. She'd have to ask her mum to take her, but somehow, even as this thought crossed Ellen's mind, she doubted her mother would agree. Unlike Lucy's mum, she never talked about God – but surely she'd want to thank him too for the baby?

When Mabel left, Hilda sat, smiling. Yes, she felt tired, drained, but what did it matter? Doug's last leave while they were still in Somerset had resulted in a baby. She was having a baby! It had taken her over two months and they had come back to London before the penny dropped. She'd been overjoyed. They had tried for so long, so many years and she had given up hope, but at last, when she had least expected it – it had happened!

Ellen had looked pleased too, but there would be a huge age gap between them. Her daughter would be thirteen in November, and the baby born a month later. Would it be a boy? Oh, she'd love a boy, a son, and was sure that Doug would too. There hadn't been a reply from him yet, but she could just imagine the look on his face when he read her letter.

'Mum, will you take me to church?' Ellen asked as she came in.

'What for?'

'Lucy said the baby is a gift from God and I think we should go to church to thank him.'

'Lucy's talking rubbish and, no, I'm not taking you to church.'

'Where did it come from then?'

'From under a gooseberry bush and that's all you need to know.'

'But . . .'

'That's enough. Now go and have a wash, you're filthy.'

Ellen had barely left the room when someone knocked on the door. Hilda went to answer it, smiling at Lucy's mum, Dora Price. 'Hello, back from church then?'

'Yes, and it was a lovely sermon,' she said, her eyes flicking around the living room.

Hilda followed her gaze, too happy to care about the shabby, old-fashioned furniture. It had been a shock when she'd first seen the flat and its contents, the clutter, the flowery décor and frills, but she'd cleared a lot of it out and one day, when she had the money, she'd buy stuff that was more to her own taste. Before realising she was having a baby, and a week after returning to London, she'd decided to go for a job in the same factory where Mabel worked, relishing the thought of earning two quid a week. Of course her difficult pregnancy had put paid to that, but new furniture didn't matter. All she cared about was the baby, the things it would need, saying now, 'Sit down, Dora.'

'No, it's all right, I can't stay. I hope you won't take offence, but I'm a bit of a hoarder and I wondered if you need a cot?'

'Oh, so you've heard about the baby?'

'Well, yes, Mabel just came round to offer me some disgusting horsemeat and mentioned it. Wasn't she supposed to tell me?'

'Now that Ellen knows, it's fine, but I was keeping it under wraps until then. As for the cot, I'd love it.'

'I'll get Cyril to get it out of the shed before he goes back tonight.'

'Thanks, it's good of you,' Hilda said, unable to help feeling envious of Dora whose husband was in a reserved occupation. He worked in an aircraft factory out of London, but managed to come home every weekend, sometimes arriving on Friday night or Saturday morning at the latest.

'It's only been used for my Lucy and it's in good condition. I'd have loved another child, but something went wrong when I had Lucy and they told me there'd be no more. I don't know why I held on to the cot, it was daft really, but it's nice to know it'll do you a turn.'

'Dora, I'm so sorry. I didn't know,' Hilda consoled.

'It's all right, I accepted it years ago. I have Lucy;

she's a wonderful daughter, and praise the Lord for giving me such a beautiful gift.'

Hilda didn't know how to respond to that. She wasn't happy that Lucy was filling her daughter's head with the same rubbish, but they were a nice family and she didn't want to upset them, so said only, 'Lucy is certainly beautiful.'

'So is Ellen. In fact, I was wondering if you'd mind if I invited her to church next week?'

'No, I'm afraid I've no time for religion.'

'I'm sorry to hear that, but surely you shouldn't force your lack of belief onto your daughter? At least think about it,' Dora urged. 'Ellen might enjoy church and I know Lucy would love her to go.'

Hilda's back was starting to ache. 'All right, I'll think about it,' she said, pleased when that seemed to satisfy Dora and she left. She had housework to do, dinner to make . . . but didn't have the energy and sat down again. Maybe Dora was right, maybe she should let Ellen go to church, decide for herself, but she didn't want her to be frightened by the sort of things she herself had been forced to listen to. Gertie's father had talked about God's wrath, of plagues and pestilence, and she didn't want Ellen frightened. Yet Lucy seemed fine, happy and well balanced, so perhaps the things she was being taught were different.

Hilda fidgeted, her back still aching. If only Doug was here to talk to, someone other than herself to make the decision. It had only been three months since she'd last seen him, but it felt like three years. Would he get leave again before she had the baby? God, she hoped so.

15

Hilda had spoken again to Dora, and, after hearing that hell and damnation weren't preached, she decided to let Ellen go to the Baptist church. So far her daughter had seemed to love it, and now went on and on about Jesus – how he loved us all, how we're his flock – but Hilda barely listened. Ellen was happy and as long as she remained that way it was fine: however, at the least sign of her being upset, she'd stop her going.

Hilda continued to feel unwell, the housework neglected, until on Saturday night, four weeks later, she woke in the night, groaning as pain knifed through her stomach.

No, no, she begged inwardly; please, don't let me lose my baby. She sat up, clutching her stomach as another pain shot through her, this one more agonising than the last. Unable to stifle it, she screamed, and then screamed again.

'Oh . . . oh no! No, not my baby! Oh God, save my baby!'

Ellen stumbled into the room, crying in the darkness: 'Mum! Mum, what's wrong?'

'Get . . . get Mabel.'

'Wh . . . what?'

With gritted teeth as pain struck again, Hilda was able only to grind out, 'Go . . . Mabel.'

Ellen ran out, but too frightened to move, Hilda remained bending forward, her arms around her stomach, holding on, her mind trying to deny what was happening. She couldn't be losing her baby, she couldn't. She was over three months – past what was always considered the dangerous time. It had to be all right – it had to.

Hilda had no idea how long she sat there, one pain gripping her, then another, and another, until at last, Mabel rushed into the room.

'Oh . . . oh, Mabel,' she groaned.

She was aware that Mabel was fumbling for the bedside light, and, as the dim illumination spread across the bed, Hilda screamed again as she felt something slither from her body.

'No! No! Please, Jesus, not my baby!'

'Lay down, Hilda, let me look,' Mabel urged.

Hilda lay back as Mabel gently pulled back the blankets. She knew what her friend would find, but still couldn't hold back a cry of anguish when Mabel spoke.

'Hilda, I'm so sorry.'

Tears spurted then, and she was dimly aware of Mabel's arms around her, trying to comfort her, but there was no comfort. Why had she cried out to God, to Jesus? Why had she been mad enough to think there was a supreme being who would save her baby? Perhaps she had taken in some of the stuff that Ellen had been spouting, but it was rubbish, all rubbish. In anguish she ripped the crucifix from her neck, flinging it to the far side of the room.

'Come on, love, let's see if I can get you cleaned up, and maybe you should see a doctor.'

'No, no, I don't want a doctor. It's too late, Mabel, my . . . my baby is dead.'

With a sigh of sadness, Mabel left the room, while Hilda continued to cry until she felt she was drowning in her own tears.

When Mabel came back she was carrying a bowl of water and a towel under her arm along with a newspaper. She placed the bowl by the bed, saying softly, 'Come on, leave this to me, and I'll need to change your sheet.'

It was only then that Hilda became aware that she was lying in her own blood, and . . . and: 'Oh, Mabel . . .'

'I know, love, I know,' she murmured, swiftly removing something and wrapping it in newspaper.

Hilda couldn't bear it. She knew it was her baby,

her son or daughter, and she cried, 'I want to see it.'

'No, darlin', no,' Mabel said. 'There's nothing to see. It . . . it's tiny and isn't properly formed. I'll take it away,' she added, rushing from the room.

Hilda closed her eyes in despair, wrapped in misery and hardly aware of Mabel returning, of being moved gently first one way then the other as the sheet was removed and her body bathed.

'Try to get some sleep, love. I'll stay with you.'

Mabel's voice had reached her, but Hilda said, 'No, no, I just want to be on my own. Leave me, Mabel, I'll be all right.'

'All right, if you're sure, but I guessed what was happening and left Ellen in my place. I'll keep her with me overnight.'

Hilda nodded, too heartsick to care. Her body felt empty, her baby gone, and when Mabel left she curled again into a ball of anguish.

Mabel locked up for Hilda and then sadly went up to her own flat. She too had once miscarried, remembered well her own grief and her heart went out to Hilda. It had surprised her that a miscarriage had been so painful, and, like Hilda, the heartbreak of losing her baby had been over-whelming. That had been eighteen months after having Billy, and since then there had been no more pregnancies. Not that she minded now. Billy was nearly thirteen, only a year younger than his brother, but he'd been a difficult baby, squalling and demanding so much attention that she had hardly any time left for Percy. He was the same now, a holy terror, but Percy was a joy. There were odd occasions that she longed for a daughter and it wasn't too late. It was the same for Hilda. She and Doug could try again, but that would be of little comfort to Hilda at the moment.

'Is my mum all right?' Ellen said, running up to her worriedly.

'Sit down, love,' Mabel urged.

'No, no, tell me!'

'I'm afraid your mum's lost the baby.'

'Lost it! How?'

'It's just something that happens and nobody really knows why.'

'Is . . . is she all right?'

'Yes, but it may take her a while to get over it. Naturally she's very sad, and she wants to be on her own for a bit. I told her you'd sleep here tonight, but it'll have to be the sofa, I'm afraid.'

Ellen looked close to tears, and it was only then that Percy spoke. 'She can have my bed,' he said. 'I'll sleep on the sofa.'

Mabel smiled at him gratefully. When Ellen had come banging on the door, it had woken both her and Percy. 'Thanks, love,' she said. 'I'll get you some blankets.'

Mabel went to fetch them from the cupboard, and, peeping into Billy's room, she saw that he was still asleep. Nothing seemed to disturb him, and if she didn't know better she'd have described it as the sleep of an innocent. Innocent! Huh, not Billy, the little sod was always up to mischief.

What a night, Mabel thought as she returned to bed. Poor Hilda, and it didn't seem right to leave her downstairs on her own. She'd pop down first thing in the morning, but for now, it was time that they all got some sleep.

Ellen was up early after a restless night's sleep. She wanted to see her mum – to make sure she was all right. There was no sign of Mabel, but Percy was stretched out on the sofa, blankets in a tangle around him as he said groggily, 'My mum's gone downstairs.'

Without a word Ellen ran through the kitchen and down the iron stairs, almost falling inside the back door to find Mabel in the kitchen. 'Is . . . is my mum all right?'

'She's only just woken up and looks fine.'

Ellen ran to her mother's room, halting momentarily. She didn't look fine, she looked awful.

'Mum . . .' Ellen choked.

Her head turned, her eyes dull and voice reedy,

151

'Don't worry, I'm all right, just . . . just a bit tired, that's all.'

Ellen scrambled onto the bed, placing an arm around her mother, and they lay quietly, but then Mabel appeared carrying a tray.

'I've made you some tea, Hilda, and do you think you could manage this bit of toast?'

'No, I'm not hungry.'

Mabel didn't argue, only saying brusquely, 'Right, Ellen, you eat it. I'll get a bowl of water and sort your mum out. Go into the living room, there's a good girl.'

'But . . .'

'You can come back to see your mum after I've given her a wash. Now go on, there's a good girl.'

Ellen reluctantly did as she was told, but she'd only just finished the toast when the back door flew open and Percy almost fell into the room in his haste. 'Where's my mum?'

'She'd giving mine a wash.'

Percy dashed past her and Ellen followed, hovering behind him on the threshold of her mother's bedroom.

'Percy!' Mabel protested. 'Get out of here.'

'Mum, guess what? Dad's here.'

'Jack? My Jack's here?' she parroted.

'Mabel, go. I'll be all right,' Hilda said.

'But . . . but you need . . .'

'I can manage, and, anyway, I've got Ellen.'

'Well, if you're sure . . .' Mabel said.

'I'm sure – now just go.'

Mabel hurried out, while Ellen just stood there, unsure of what to do. She saw the bowl of water beside the bed, tinged red, her eyes widening.

'It's all right, nothing to worry about, but go and pour it away.'

Ellen managed it, spilling only a little, and then went back to her mum. 'What do you want me to do now?'

'Nothing,' she said, her mother's tone lacklustre. 'I'll call you if I need anything.'

'I'll tell Lucy I won't be going to church today.'

There was no answer, her mum's eyes already closing. Ellen saw something glinting on the floor and crept across the room to pick it up. It was her mum's cross and chain. She'd give it back to her later, but for now she left quietly, going through the kitchen and out of the back door, calling out, 'Lucy! Lucy!'

It wasn't Lucy who responded, it was Dora. 'Lucy isn't dressed yet. Is something wrong, Ellen?'

'I can't come to church today. My . . . my mum lost the baby.'

'Oh, how awful for her. I'm so sorry, my dear. Don't worry, I know you can't come to church, but tell your mother we'll all pray for her swift recovery.'

'Thank you,' Ellen choked as her eyes filled with tears.

'You can pray for her too, Ellen. You don't have to be in church for the Lord to hear your prayers.'

'Yes . . . yes, I will.'

'Good girl, and if there's anything I can do, anything your mother needs, let me know.'

Ellen thanked her, still tearful when she went back inside. She had been to church quite a few times now and last week had seen a baptism. Before the lady had been immersed in water she had talked about her spiritual conversion, of being born again. The lady had looked so happy, as though something wonderful had happened to her, but despite being told about it, Ellen still didn't understand. How could you be born again?

It was an hour before her mum called her, and Ellen rushed to her bedroom, relieved to see she was sitting up and looking a little better.

'Are you all right, Mum?'

'My throat's parched. Will you make me a cup of tea?'

'Yes, and I found this on the floor,' Ellen said, holding out the necklace. 'The chain's broken but maybe Percy will be able to fix it.'

'Keep it. I don't want it.'

'What? I can have it?'

'That's what I said.'

'Thanks, Mum, and . . . and I told Dora I wouldn't be going to church today. She said to tell you that she'll ask everyone to pray for you to get better.'

'Tell her not to bother. I prayed to God, to Jesus, to save my baby and a fat lot of good it did.'

'I . . . I'll make your tea,' Ellen said unable to think of anything else to say. She liked going to church, but there were so many questions, so many things she still didn't understand. Why hadn't her mum's prayers been answered – or the ones to bring Socks back?

16

Hilda recovered quickly, at least in body, but the loss of her baby weighed her down. There were times when she longed for the comfort of her mother's arms and the grief of losing her parents would resurface to add to her misery. There were also times when she reached automatically for her mother's necklace, only to find it wasn't there. Ellen was wearing it now, and Hilda didn't feel she could ask her to give it back.

For her daughter's sake, Hilda made an effort, but her smiles were forced, and her heart heavy. In September it was Mabel who finally came to the rescue, persuading her to take a job with her in a factory on the other side of the Common.

Ellen was still going to church and as she continued to enjoy it, Hilda didn't have the heart to stop her. Not only that, Dora was so reliable that she'd approached the woman to ask if she'd look after Ellen after school. It cost her five shillings a week, but it was worth it for peace of mind, and the arrangement was working well. The work at the engineering factory was hard, but at least Hilda felt she was doing something important for the war effort.

It was now Friday; her week's work over as Hilda knocked on Dora's door. 'Hello, and has Ellen behaved herself?'

'Yes, she's been as good as gold. Ellen, your mum's here.'

Hilda handed over five bob, admiring Dora's blonde curls. 'Your hair looks nice. Have you had a perm?'

'No, but I've had it in curlers all day. Cyril's coming home tonight and he likes me to look nice.'

Ellen appeared then and they both said their goodbyes to Dora. As they walked next door, Ellen asked, 'Mum, what's for dinner?'

'A bit of Spam and mashed potatoes,' Hilda told her. Though a little hungry, she wasn't looking forward to the pink, tinned meat that had now become a regular part of their diet. She flopped tiredly onto a chair, kicking her shoes off with relief. 'Put the kettle on the gas, Ellen. I could murder a cup of tea.'

'You look worn out, Mum.'

'I am, but at least I've got the weekend off.'

As her daughter made the tea, Hilda closed her

eyes, only to open them moments later when Mabel burst into the room, her face white with panic.

'Hilda, Percy's gone.'

'Gone! Gone where?'

'I came home to find Billy on his own and a note on the table from Percy. He said he's gone to join up, but I don't know where. He ain't been the same since his dad went back after those two weeks' leave. Oh, Hilda, what am I gonna do?'

'Calm down, love. I know Percy's big for his age, but he isn't fourteen till next week and doesn't look old enough to join up. They'll probably take one look at him and send him home with a flea in his ear.'

'I hope you're right, but I know Percy's fed up. He wants to leave school now, but they won't let him go until Christmas. He hates it, *and* having to keep an eye on Billy. The little sod drives him mad, me too, but I never thought Percy would try this.'

Billy appeared then, and Hilda hid a smile. There was no doubt that Billy was a little sod, but his cheeky grin was irresistible. With dark curly hair, green eyes and a sprinkle of freckles across his nose, he took after his mother in looks. He said, 'Panic over, Mum. Percy's just turned up.'

Mabel's eyes lit up, and pushing Billy ahead of her she hurried out, calling, 'See you later, Hilda.'

There was no doubt that Percy was Mabel's favourite, and Hilda often wondered if that was why Billy was so naughty; perhaps bad behaviour was the only way to get his mother's attention. In front of Billy, Mabel would go on and on about how good Percy was, but she never offered a word of praise to her younger son.

'Here you are, Mum,' Ellen said as she handed her a cup of tea.

'Thanks, darling, you're a good girl,' Hilda said and meant it. She still grieved the loss of her baby, but with a daughter she was proud of, Hilda knew that somehow she had to count her blessings.

Mabel was just thankful to see Percy. She wasn't angry, just relieved. 'Please, love, don't ever do that again. I nearly had a fit when I saw your note.'

'I told him not to go. I told him you'd be upset.'

'Shut up, Billy. I'm not talking to you,' Mabel snapped, her eyes never leaving Percy. He was so like his father, tall, with brown hair and eyes to match. It was bad enough that Jack was in the army, that he was back at the front and she feared for him every single day, without her son joining up too. 'I suppose the recruiting station turned you away.'

'They laughed at me . . . told me to come back when I'm a man.'

'That was a bit cruel, but they're right.'

'I'll be fourteen next week and as soon as I leave school, I'll try again.'

'You'll still be too young, sweetheart. I know you want to be a soldier just like your dad, but there are other things you can do to help the war effort. Like me, you could get a job in an engineering factory and it's important work.'

'Yeah, I suppose so,' Percy said, 'but it ain't the same.'

Mabel knew she would still have the worry of Billy when Percy started work, and though she didn't want to give up her job, her younger son couldn't be trusted on his own. The thought of losing two quid a week in pay caused a surge of anger. If Billy was more like his older brother it wouldn't be a problem, but Billy was a bloody menace, always running off, always nicking things whenever he got the chance, his reputation down the market notorious. If only his father was here to sort him out, but there was no telling when Jack would be home on leave again.

'I'm sorry, Mum,' placated Percy, obviously unaware that her anger wasn't directed at him.

'It's all right, son, but as I said, don't ever do that to me again. Now the two of you can get cleaned up while I make a start on our dinner. You go first, Billy.'

'Ain't you gonna give Percy a hiding?'

'No. Now do as you're told and have a wash.'

'That's not fair. You gave me a hiding yesterday and I only nicked an apple off a stall.'

'And how many times have I got to belt you before you stop thieving?'

With a mutinous look on his face, yet knowing better than to argue, Billy left the room. Mabel heaved a sigh of exasperation, doubting she'd ever be able to knock any sense into her younger son. It had always been the same, Percy the good one, Billy the bad. She smiled at Percy now, thankful that she had at least one son she could be proud of.

When dinner was ready, Hilda called Ellen to the table, but they had eaten only a few mouthfuls before the air raid siren sounded. Bombing raids were infrequent now and Clapham still remained mostly untouched, but despite this Hilda insisted they went to the nearby underground station for shelter.

'Grab your gas mask, Ellen, and let's go.'

'Do we have to? Can't we stay here?'

'After what happened to your grandparents, I'm not going to risk it. Now don't argue and get a move on,' Hilda ordered as she rushed to pick up the bag that contained their papers, along with her own gas mask.

Outside they joined up with Mabel and the boys, and soon Dora and Lucy appeared too.

'I hope Cyril doesn't get caught up in the air raid,' Dora said worriedly. 'Do get a move on, Lucy.'

If bombs fell on Clapham, Hilda knew she'd never be able to forgive herself for bringing Ellen back to danger, but as Gertie had sold the small-holding soon after they left, writing to say she was off to enlist in the ATS, there was no chance of going back to Somerset.

Hilda still hadn't answered Gertie's letter and wondered where she was now – unaware that it wouldn't be long before she got her answer.

17

Gertie stood on the doorstep, straightening her shoulders and tugging down the jacket of her brown uniform. She had been surprised at how quickly she'd been able to sell the smallholding, the nearest farmer taking it on along with the animals. He had taken Bertie on too, and she still missed her little dog. Ellen had written just in time to thank her for sending the books, but soon after that Gertie had left Somerset behind.

With her training over, this was the first chance she'd had to travel to London, but now Gertie hesitated before ringing the doorbell. She'd sent a letter with a return address, but Hilda hadn't replied. Did that mean she wanted her to stay away? Or would she be pleased to see her? The December morning was chilly; the cold wind swirled around her legs as Gertie finally found the courage to ring the bell.

It was Ellen who opened the door, her eyes lighting up with pleasure. 'Gertie!'

'Hello, darling, and look at you. You're almost grown up.'

'I'm thirteen now.'

'I know, and I'm sorry it's late, but I've brought your present.'

Ellen smiled with delight as she took the package, and Gertie was struck by the change in her. She had small, burgeoning breasts, but other than that she looked gangly and coltish now, with long, thin legs; her dark hair was cut short and framed her pretty face.

'Mum, Gertie's here,' Ellen called as she reached out a hand to take Gertie's, pulling her inside.

They crossed the small hall into the living room, Hilda saying when she saw Gertie, 'Well, look what the cat dragged in.'

Gertie had been holding her breath, but there was no trace of animosity in Hilda's tone. Relieved, she said, 'This is my first leave and I wanted to bring Ellen her birthday present.'

'It seems funny to see you in a skirt,' Hilda commented.

'Don't you like it?' Gertie asked, removing her peaked hat.

'It's all right, but I can't say the same for those shoes.'

Gertie looked down at her shiny, black lace-ups, hating the way the just-below-knee-length skirt showed her fat ankles and chunky legs. 'Yes, well, they aren't the most flattering.'

'Sit down, Gertie.'

'All right, but I can't stay long.'

'Oh, thanks, Gertie,' Ellen said smiling with delight as she unwrapped the book. 'Look, Mum, it's tips on gardening.'

'Very nice,' Hilda said dryly. 'Anyway, Gertie, how are you enjoying life in the ATS?'

'What does ATS stand for?' asked Ellen.

'Auxiliary Territorial Service,' Gertie told her, 'and I love it. I'm a driver now but, after Ned, learning to drive a car took some getting used to. I also had to learn all about what's under the bonnet – the carburettor and cam shaft to name a couple of things.'

'Sounds like double Dutch to me. I'm working in an engineering factory making parts for military vehicles, but I don't know what they are.'

'You didn't answer my letter and I've been a bit worried about you. Is everything all right?'

'Mum lost the baby,' Ellen said.

'Baby! What baby?'

'I came back to London to find myself pregnant, but . . . but I miscarried.'

'I'm so sorry. It must have been dreadful.'

'Doug wrote to say that he was dead chuffed I was having a baby, but then I had to write again to say I'd lost it. I haven't had a letter from him since then and dread to think how he took it.'

'I'm sure he'll be more concerned about you,' Gertie said consolingly.

Hilda's eyes suddenly welled with tears. 'Yeah, maybe, but can we talk about something else?'

Gertie fumbled for something to say and turned to Ellen, asking, 'What happened to your hair? It's very short now.'

'Nits,' Ellen told her.

'Oh, dear,' Gertie murmured.

'She picked them up not long after starting school,' Hilda said. 'I have to use a steel comb regularly now and it's less painful when it's that length.'

'They weren't half itchy,' Ellen complained.

'I bet,' Gertie said, then turning to Hilda again, 'I've got another bit of news. My father died last month.'

'Did he? I'm sorry to hear that.'

'Hilda, there's no need to pretend. I know how you felt about my father and I don't blame you.'

'Yeah, well, despite everything, he was still your dad.'

'I hadn't seen him for years, and though we had an awful relationship I must admit I did shed a tear. Not only that, despite everything he said, all the vitriol thrown at me, he still left me as his heir.'

'What? That great big house is yours now?'

'Yes, and a fair bit of money, but I don't ever

want to live in that place again. If it survives this war, I'll sell it.'

'You'll be stinking rich.'

'Maybe, but money can't buy you happiness,' Gertie said sadly.

'Only those who have got a few bob come out with that cherry.'

'Yes, I suppose so. Anyway, where's Socks?'

'He went off soon after we got here.'

'I looked and looked for him,' Ellen said, 'but he never came back.'

'What a shame. I miss Bertie so know you must miss Socks too.'

'I do, but Mum won't let me have another cat.'

'I have enough of a problem finding enough meat for us, without having to feed an animal too. Now go and fill the kettle. I expect Gertie will want a cup of tea.'

'No, it's all right; in fact, I've got to go now,' Gertie said as she glanced at her watch.

'What, already? You've only just got here.'

'This is the first chance I've had to make an appointment to see my father's solicitor and it's at two o'clock. I don't know how long I'll be with him, and I'm due back on base at five.'

'It's Saturday. Haven't you got the weekend off?'

'I'm afraid there's no nine to five in the army, Hilda. It doesn't work like that and I'm on duty tonight.'

Ellen ran up to Gertie, throwing thin arms around her waist. 'Will you come again soon?'

'I don't know, darling. I'm based in England at the moment, but I could be sent abroad at any time.'

Hilda stood up too. 'It's been nice to see you, Gertie.'

'Do you mean that?'

'Yeah, I mean it.'

Gertie knew that she daren't touch Hilda, that this fragile thread of friendship could still be easily broken. 'Thanks, Hilda, but I really must go now.'

Hilda and Ellen walked her to the door, saying goodbye, and Gertie lifted a hand to wave as she walked away. They still felt like her family and it had been nice to see them, but somehow the visit had emphasised how her life had already moved forward. She had made a few new friends in the ATS, one a bit special, but it was early days yet and she had at last learned to be cautious.

'It was lovely to see Gertie,' Ellen said. 'I love my book and I think she looks nice in her uniform.'

'She was only here for about ten minutes, but, yes, it was nice to see her.'

'It's only me,' Mabel called. 'Did I just see a woman in uniform leaving?'

'If you had your nose pinned to the window, yes,' Hilda said. 'It was Gertie.'

'I was just looking outside to see what the weather was like,' Mabel protested. 'I'm off to the shops and thought you might need a few things too.'

'I do, but it'll probably be a waste of time trying to find anything. Are you coming, Ellen?'

'Can I go to play with Lucy?'

'I suppose so,' Hilda agreed, thinking her daughter was more in Dora's place than their own. Ellen was taking Bible lessons too now, and, though it irritated Hilda when she went on and on about the church and Jesus, her daughter was happy and that was all that mattered.

'Are you coming or not?' Mabel asked impatiently.

'Yeah, sorry, I was miles away. I'll just get my coat.'

The three of them left, pausing at Dora's while Ellen knocked on the door, and, as soon as Lucy let her in, they walked swiftly on in an attempt to keep warm.

'After what you told me when you came back from Somerset, Hilda, I'm surprised you kept in touch with Gertie.'

'I didn't answer her letters, but I'm sorry for that now.'

'Don't be daft. You should have sent her off with a flea in her ear!'

'Ellen was so pleased to see her.'

'I still think you should tell her to get lost.'

'No, Mabel. I've had lots of time to think about it now. Gertie hasn't had much of a life and has only known years of unhappiness. She was living like a recluse, and if I hadn't asked her to put us up, none of it would have happened.'

'That doesn't make it right.'

'Look, I don't like Gertie's preferences and find them abhorrent, but in a way I understand why her feelings were misplaced. We were with her for a long time, hardly saw anyone, and only had each other, along with Ellen for company. If there had been more people around, Gertie might have met someone of her own type, and I hope she does that now.'

'Yeah, it would get her off your back.'

Hilda knew that Mabel would never approve of Gertie, few people did. It would always be hard for Gertie, and even if she did meet someone it would have to be a relationship that remained hidden. Would Gertie ever find happiness? Hilda didn't know, but they went back a long way and, despite what had happened, she hoped Gertie would.

18

Ellen turned over in bed and burrowed under the blankets, unwilling to get up and face the cold. Christmas was over, and Ellen wasn't happy. Her mum had put up a few decorations, but now that she'd learned the meaning of the celebrations, Ellen thought they should have done more. Her mum refused to pray before dinner too, and despite Dora telling her not to give up – that she should go on talking to her mother about the church and Jesus – Ellen felt that no matter how hard she tried, her mum was never going to listen.

She had asked the pastor why her mum's prayer to save the baby hadn't been answered. He'd said it was to do with faith, that you had to believe in the Lord, trust in him to answer your prayers and he would. The pastor had then gone on to say that we don't always get what we ask for, and if that happens we have to accept God's will, leaving Ellen more confused than ever.

Ellen burrowed down further. She had faith, she believed in Jesus, but he still didn't answer her prayers. She had begged Jesus to bring her dad home for Christmas, but it hadn't worked. Maybe it was because she still hadn't felt that strange born-again thing they talked about in church? She would have to try harder, and, clutching the crucifix, Ellen closed her eyes, praying and hoping Jesus was listening.

Hilda looked at the scant Christmas decorations and decided to take them down. They were only just into the New Year, yet she wasn't superstitious, and what a New Year it had been. Mabel had somehow got hold of a bottle of gin, probably from Harry, and when the kids were in bed they had seen 1944 in together, both getting tipsy and both sorry for it the next morning. Still, it had been a laugh and Hilda was a little happier now, the loss of her baby growing easier with the passing of time.

Queues for food were growing ever longer, and these days if Hilda saw one she just joined it without even knowing what the shop had just got in until word passed down the line. She longed to see Doug. He had been upset to hear that she'd lost the baby, but more concerned about her recovery, and though his letters were sometimes infrequent, at least he was alive. With so many women losing their husbands and sons, at least Hilda knew she had that to be thankful for. It was early on a Saturday morning and, as Ellen was still in bed, Hilda dragged a chair forward, deciding to get on with it. She had almost finished and was reaching for the last chain when Ellen appeared.

'Mum, what are you doing?'

'Ain't it obvious?'

'Be careful,' Ellen cautioned, running forward to grab the back of the chair as it wobbled.

'There, done it,' Hilda said as the last chain floated down and she stepped cautiously onto the floor.

There was a knock on the door now and Ellen said, 'I'll get it.'

'No, you're still in your pyjamas,' Hilda protested. She crossed the hall to open it, her knees almost caving when she saw the young man standing on the step.

'Sorry, missus,' he said, thrusting the envelope forward and then turning to hurry back to his bicycle.

'Oh, no . . . no!' Hilda cried as she stared at the envelope.

'Mum, what is it? What's wrong?'

'I . . . I can't. I can't open it,' she sobbed, staggering back to the living room and collapsing onto a chair.

* * *

Ellen had never seen her mother like this, her whole body shaking, something falling from her hand and fluttering to the floor. Ellen ran to pick it up, her stomach turning a somersault. A telegram! Her eyes flew to her mother again, frightened by what she saw.

'Mum, are you all right? You look like you're going to faint.'

'Get . . . get Mabel.'

Heart racing, Ellen pounded up the back stairs, bursting into Mabel's kitchen, Percy the first person she saw.

'My . . . my mum . . . telegram . . . Mabel.'

'Oh shit,' he said. 'Mum! Mum!'

'Blimey, what's all the fuss about?'

'It's Ellen. She said they've got a telegram.'

In her haste, Mabel shoved Percy aside to hurry after Ellen, saying, 'What did the telegram say?'

'I . . . I don't know,' but as they rushed into the living room, Ellen saw that her mother had it clutched in her hand again – but this time it was open.

'Mabel . . . Oh Mabel,' she cried. 'It's Doug. His ship's been sunk.'

'Don't give up, love. He may have been rescued.'

With a glimmer of hope, Ellen looked at her mother, only for it to die when she sobbed, 'The . . . the telegram said his ship went down with all hands lost.'

Ellen felt dizzy, pinpricks of light dancing before her eyes.

'No, no, not my dad!' she squealed, before sinking into a black void.

When Hilda saw her daughter collapsing onto the floor, she did her best to stand up, but felt as though her heart had been torn in two. Doug, her handsome, lovely Doug . . . the thought of never seeing him again more than she could bear.

'It's all right, I'll see to her,' Mabel said, gently pushing Hilda back onto the chair.

Hilda didn't argue. In fact, she doubted her legs would support her as her whole body continued to shake with shock. She was aware that Ellen was coming round, that Mabel was helping her up. Hilda knew why her daughter had fainted. She had done the same thing when her parents had died, but this time her own pain was so overwhelming, so consuming, that she felt unable to comfort her.

Locked in her own grief, sobs began to rack Hilda's body. She was unaware of time passing until she realised that somehow Mabel had managed to get her to her feet, one step slowly following another as she was led into her bedroom.

'Lie down,' Mabel urged. 'Don't worry about Ellen. I'll take her to my place, settle her with the boys and then come back.'

'No . . . no . . . I just want to be on my own.'

'Oh, Hilda, I'm so sorry.'

Hilda was barely aware of Mabel's hand as she gently stroked her hair, or when she later left the room. Doug, her man, the love of her life, was dead. She would never see him again, never be held in his arms, and she didn't know how she was going to face life without him. *Why?* Hilda's mind screamed. *Why me? First my parents, then my baby . . . and now this!*

Mabel did her best to comfort Ellen, but the girl was distraught. Percy was white-faced as he stood watching them, Ellen clinging to her. Oh, it was dreadful, dreadful, and Mabel felt so helpless. Like all women with loved ones away, she dreaded getting a telegram, knowing that, like Hilda, she'd find it unbearable.

'What's the matter with her?' Billy asked as, having just got out of bed, he strolled into the room.

'There's been a bit of bad news. Percy, take him through to the kitchen and tell him.'

'What for?' Billy complained.

'Just do it,' Mabel snapped.

Mabel heard the whispers, surprised when Billy appeared again, this time to say, 'Ellen, I'm sorry to hear about your dad.'

Ellen's arms tightened around Mabel, her sobs

176

increasing again. It had been nice of Billy to say that, but his sympathy had made Ellen worse.

'Come on, darling. You've got to be strong for your mum's sake.'

Ellen burrowed even closer and Mabel cursed her ineffectual, daft words. How could a thirteen-year-old girl be strong when she'd just heard that her dad was dead? Like Hilda, Mabel wasn't much for religion, but Ellen had recently taken to going to church so perhaps Dora could help.

'Percy, run next door and get Dora.'

Ellen continued to cling to her, but at last Percy came back, Dora with him, the woman saying, 'Percy told me and I'm so sorry, Ellen. I can see how upset you are, but lean on Jesus and he'll give you comfort. He loves you as he loves us all, and your father is with him in heaven now.'

Mabel felt Ellen stiffen, her eyes red and swollen as she choked, 'If Jesus loves me he wouldn't have let my dad die. He . . . he wouldn't have taken him away from me.'

'It's this war, Ellen, this war that's taken your father away from you, not Jesus.'

'He should have stopped it then. The . . . the pastor said that Jesus can do anything, move mountains, and that if we believe in him, we can do anything too. Well, I did believe and I prayed to him but instead of bringing my dad home, he . . . he's dead!'

'Mabel, I think I'll ask our pastor to come and talk to Ellen.'

'No! No, I don't want to see him,' Ellen cried, unaware that she was mimicking the actions her mother had once made as she ripped the chain from her neck and threw it across the room. 'This – this is supposed to be Jesus on the cross, but there is no Jesus! Religion is all a load of rubbish.'

'Oh, Ellen, you don't mean that.'

'Yes, I do. Go away! Go away and leave me alone.'

'Dora, I think it might be for the best,' Mabel urged.

Sighing, Dora left, but not before saying, 'Ellen, when you're up to it, we'll talk again.'

'I . . . I want my mum,' Ellen then said, pulling away from Mabel. 'I'm going to see my mum.'

'Ellen, no! Wait,' Mabel called, running after her.

When Hilda heard her daughter and Mabel, she feigned sleep. She didn't want to see them, didn't want to see anyone. She just wanted to be alone, to lick her wounds in private, as Gertie had once said. However, unlike Gertie's, Hilda didn't think her wounds would ever heal. She felt as though her heart had been ripped from her body and all that remained of her was a shell. The pain of having a miscarriage had been horrendous, but it was nothing compared to the agony of losing Doug and at this moment she'd have welcomed death.

'Come on, Ellen,' said Mabel. 'Your mum's asleep and maybe it's the best thing for her.'

'No,' Ellen said, and then Hilda was aware of the bed dipping, of her daughter climbing up beside her, arms wrapping around her body. She sobbed, turning to cling to Ellen, barely aware of Mabel creeping from the room.

19

Ellen was heartbroken by her father's death and longed for the comfort of her mum's arms again, but her mother seemed to be locked in a world of her own. Mabel had tried, but hadn't been successful in rousing her, only able to shake her head sadly and say that her mum was sure to get better given time. It was Mabel whom Ellen clung to, Mabel who held her so many times when she cried.

Now Ellen was back at school, but she was really worried about her mum. She hardly moved from her chair and Ellen would come home to find the housework untouched, her mum smelling, with her body and hair unwashed. She tried to look after her, managed to cook easy things, and, though Mabel was at work she often found the time to make enough stew for them all to eat, yet her mother barely touched it.

The Luftwaffe had returned, the warning siren

wailing frequently these days, and it was the only sound that brought her mother to life. Though bombs rained down on London again, Clapham still remained hardly touched, yet her mum would rally enough at the sound of the siren to insist that they went to shelter in the underground station.

The bombing raids went on and on, into February, and at last Ellen could see that her mum was a little better, though she was still distant and remote. The air raid sounded once more and wearily Ellen got up, dressed quickly and picked up her gas mask, blinking with tiredness as she went into the hall.

'I was about to call you,' her mother said.

Ellen could see that her mum's eyes were red and swollen, giving away the fact that she had been crying again. 'Are you all right, Mum?'

'Not really, but we . . . we've got to get to the shelter.'

'Can't we stay here? Can't we give the underground station a miss for once?'

'No, no!' she cried. 'You're all I've got left and I'm not risking it.'

When they went outside there was no sign of Mabel or Dora and, though the blackout was in force, a full moon cast an eerie glow on the frost-covered pavements and rooftops. A bombers' moon, Mabel's son, Percy, called it, and Ellen shivered at the thought of how much damage the Luftwaffe might cause that night somewhere in or on the outskirts of London.

'I've forgotten me fags,' said her mother suddenly.

'Do you want me to run back for them?' Ellen offered.

'It's too dangerous.'

'Mum, you know this area has hardly been hit.'

'There's always a first time and I can always cadge a couple off Mabel,' she said as they turned the corner, and moments later they joined other people streaming below. The Shelter Marshal was there, the 'SM' painted on the front of his helmet visible as he tried to keep order. Ignoring him, Hilda found them a free bunk.

As usual, Ellen climbed onto the top one, while her mother sat below, and soon Mabel turned up with her boys, followed by Dora and Lucy. Ellen barely acknowledged Lucy, but nonetheless she came running over to climb up beside her.

'You were quick to get down here,' Lucy said.

'A few minutes and then I want you settled in your own bunk,' Dora called.

'All right, Mum,' Lucy agreed before turning to Ellen again. 'Why won't you walk with me to school now?'

With her head down, Ellen just shrugged. She still liked Lucy, but now that she wasn't going to church, she felt awkward in her company. She didn't want to hear about God, Jesus, or his love for his flock. Dora had tried talking to her again, saying that Jesus wasn't there for their earthly needs; that it was man who caused war and unnecessary deaths. Jesus was there for their spiritual needs, Dora insisted, for their souls' growth and comfort. Her words hadn't helped. There was no comfort, there was no one there when, like her mother, Ellen cried at night.

'Please tell me,' Lucy urged.

'It's because I don't want to hear you going on and on about Jesus.'

'I won't any more. I thought it might help, but my mum said that you aren't ready to listen yet.'

'She's right.'

'Can't we still be friends?'

'Yes, but don't ask me to come to church with you.'

'All right, but lots of people have asked how you are and we miss you in Bible class.'

Deep down, Ellen missed church too, the friends she had made, the congregation and the feeling of belonging. Yet she couldn't go back, not now when she no longer believed in anything she'd been taught.

Dora's voice rang out again.

'Lucy, come on now.'

'I'd best go. Can we walk to school together in the morning?'

Ellen only nodded, saying nothing as Lucy jumped down from the bunk. She lay down, closing her eyes, but soon the sound of Mabel and Dora's voices began to drift up to her as they sat with her mother on the bunk below. 'Another broken night's sleep,' Mabel complained, 'but at least Berlin's getting it too.'

'Hilda, how are you?' Dora asked.

'I still can't believe that Doug's gone. In Somerset I yearned to come back to London, but now I feel this place is cursed. First I lost my parents, then my baby, and now . . . now Doug.'

There was a pause before Mabel spoke. 'Hilda, this has been burning a hole in my pocket. I've been holding on to it until I thought the time was right and now I wonder if either you or Ellen would like it back.'

'Oh, Mabel! It's my mother's necklace.'

'Yes, love.'

'I . . . I think I'd like to wear it again.'

'I'm sure Ellen won't mind,' Mabel said, then raising her voice, she called: 'Ain't that right, Ellen?'

'Put a sock in it,' someone yelled. 'I've got work in the morning.'

'Yeah, so have I, and my boy, but we ain't complaining,' Mabel shouted back.

Mabel's loud voice echoed in the tunnel and it was followed by a few titters of laughter.

'Yeah, well, I suppose I should get some sleep, too. Are you going to be all right, Hilda?'

Ellen didn't hear her mother's reply, and soon, other than the occasional cough from nearby bunks, all became quiet. She tried to sleep, turning this way and that, but, as her mother began to cry softly, Ellen found it impossible. She was about to climb down when someone, a woman, walked over to crouch down in front of her mother. Ellen strained her ears to hear the woman's quiet words.

'I'm sorry to disturb you,' she said, 'but I heard you crying and felt compelled to come and talk to you.'

'I . . . I'm all right.'

'No, you're not, and though this is going to sound strange, when I heard you crying, I had a sort of vision.'

There were a few sniffs, and then Ellen thought her mother's voice sounded stronger as she said, 'Leave me alone. Go away.'

'But I have to tell you about my vision. You see, I saw a man, a sailor. He was on some sort of raft, holding his back. I . . . I feel that it's your husband.'

There was a pause, but then sounding forceful, more like her old self, Hilda snapped, 'Look, lady, I don't know what your game is, or who's been gossiping about me, but if it's money you're after, you can forget it. I'm not mug enough to fall for this sort of mumbo jumbo.'

'I don't want money. It's as I said – I felt compelled to talk to you.'

'Well, feel compelled to bugger off again!'

'I'll go, but you see I usually see spirits, souls that have passed over. But this time it was different. I feel that your husband is still alive, that he survived and is coming home to you,' said the woman, before turning to walk away.

Ellen sat up. Alive! The woman had said her dad was alive!

'Mum, who was that?' she hissed eagerly.

'She was nobody. A nutter.'

'But she said Dad's coming home.'

'She was talking a load of rubbish. Your dad's dead. You know that, I know that. Now please, go to sleep.'

Ellen felt the sting of tears and closed her eyes against her mother's words. If only that woman hadn't been a nutter. If only it was true and her dad really was coming home.

20

After a restless night in the underground station, it was six o'clock before people began to stir. Ellen woke, surprised to find that at some point she must have fallen asleep, and stretched, about to climb off the bunk, when Mabel bustled over.

'Hilda, who was that woman I saw talking to you last night?'

'I don't know. I've never seen her before, but she was nobody, a daft cow who talked a load of rubbish.'

'She said that my dad's coming home,' Ellen said.

'What?' Mabel exclaimed. 'But how can she possibly know that?'

'She said she had a vision,' answered Ellen.

'Ellen, I told you, the woman was off her head.'

'Hilda, you shouldn't just dismiss it,' Mabel said. 'There are people around who can do strange things. Take old Mrs Porter. She can read the tea leaves and I'm told she's ever so good.'

'It's a load of tosh and probably a scam to make money, that's all.'

'She only charges sixpence,' Mabel protested, but then, seeing Billy strolling towards her, she shouted: 'You little bugger. Where have you been? You're supposed to be in your bunk.'

'I went to the lav,' he said, wide-eyed with innocence.

'Yeah, that's what you always say, but I don't believe you. Wait till I get you home, and you, Percy, get our stuff and let's go.'

'Come on, Ellen, let's get home too,' Hilda urged.

They were all walking home together when Mabel brought up the subject again, but Dora huffed, her voice strident as she said, 'It's wrong to consult people like that, tarot readers, mediums, and even those who do something that seems as harmless as reading tea leaves.'

'I don't see why,' Mabel protested.

'It warns against it in the Bible.'

'Well, Dora, you're entitled to your opinions, but as for me, I enjoy a bit of fortune telling.'

Ellen listened to them, her head still full of the woman who had spoken to her mum. She wanted to talk to Mabel, to ask her about the people she had said could do strange things, but daren't in front of her mother. Tea leaves. How could anyone read *tea leaves*?

* * *

Unlike Ellen, Hilda was fuming. Someone had been gossiping, had told that woman that Doug was dead, and if she got her hands on them she'd wring their bloody neck. It was nasty, cruel to feed her and God knows who else, false hope. Hilda wasn't a fool and could see what was coming. The woman had spouted her rubbish, and if she'd been daft enough to believe her, the bitch would have offered more information, but this time she'd have asked for money, to cross her hand with silver or something like that.

It annoyed her that Mabel had brought it up again in front of Ellen. She had seen the light of hope in her daughter's eyes after that daft woman had talked about her vision, and then had watched it die again. For the first time, Hilda felt her heart stirring for her daughter and along with that came guilt – guilt that since the news that Doug's ship had gone down, she'd hardly spared Ellen a thought.

They were soon home, Lucy calling to Ellen, 'Give me a knock when you're ready for school.'

'Yes, all right.'

'Hilda, I'll see you when I finish work,' Mabel said.

Hilda nodded, finding that her mind was working again, coming to life. Until now she'd been inside a cocoon of grief, unable to think of anything but Doug's death and feeling that she had died with him. She had to somehow pull herself together and to start with she'd have to go back to work. A war widow's pension wasn't enough to live on and the two quid a week she could earn at the factory would make all the difference.

'Ellen, come here,' Hilda said as soon as they walked into the living room, her arms held out. Ellen looked a bit puzzled, but she walked into them and Hilda held her tightly as she said, 'I'm sorry, love, sorry that I haven't been here for you.'

'It's all right, Mum,' Ellen cried, but clung to her like a limpet.

'There's just the two of us now, but don't worry, we'll be all right. We've got each other and to start with, I'm going back to the factory. That's if you don't mind going to Dora's again after school.'

'I . . . I suppose it'll be all right,' Ellen said, 'but . . . but are you sure you're up to going back to work?'

Hilda felt another surge of guilt. She'd left Ellen to do everything, the housework when she came home from school, the shopping and even the cooking, while she had hardly moved off her chair.

'I'm fine, and from now on things are going to be different. To start with, go and wash the stink of the underground off while I see to our breakfast.'

Ellen looked up at her face, and Hilda managed

a reassuring smile that dropped as soon as her daughter left the room. She would have to bring Ellen up alone now and it wouldn't be easy, but she'd do it, somehow she'd do it. Her daughter was the only thing she had to live for now.

Ellen didn't really want to go to Dora's again after school, but thankfully so far neither she nor Lucy had mentioned church. Despite her mum saying that the woman's vision had been nonsense, Mabel had disagreed, and now Ellen was living in hope. As soon as she had got the chance, she'd spoken to Mabel and asked her about fortune tellers, but had been fobbed off, told that she was too young to worry about such things.

She had then tried some of the older girls at school, but they didn't know anything, just talking about ghosts and scaring her so much that for a while she had burrowed under the blankets at night.

With nobody else to ask, Ellen had been forced to give up and, as the weeks passed, she wrestled with her feelings. She still missed going to church, meeting the friends she'd made, and the joyful singing that somehow made you feel, well, sort of happy inside. Yet how could she go back when they'd deny the only thing that gave her any hope? That woman had said her dad was alive, that he was on a raft and coming home. Ellen clung to those words, the only thing that eased the awful lump of pain she had felt inside since the day the telegram had arrived. The vision had to be real, it just had to. He wasn't dead. Her dad wasn't dead.

21

The air raids had stopped at the end of April, and trips to the underground station became a thing of the past as spring turned to early summer. It had been over five months since the dreadful telegram arrived, but Ellen couldn't remember the last time she'd heard her mum's tinkling laugh. She still tried to cling on to hope that her dad was still alive, but that hope was becoming forlorn and Ellen didn't laugh much either any more.

She often sought solace in the garden, the June evening sun warm as she worked outside, but without proper fertiliser the few vegetables she'd managed to grow looked spindly and sad, as if echoing her feelings.

There was the sound of ringing steps on the iron stairs behind her and, standing up, Ellen brushed her hands on her skirt.

'I'm just popping in to see your mum,' Mabel said.

Ellen followed her inside and Mabel flopped onto a chair, sighing as she said, 'I'm glad I moved away from Battersea, Hilda. They're calling those bombing raids we had earlier in the year the Little Blitz, and loads more houses in Battersea were flattened. Still, with D-day and all that, the war must be ending soon.'

Ellen heard an odd sound, coming closer – a loud droning noise – and ran to the window. 'Mum, what's that?' she cried, pointing at a strange rocket-shaped object with two stubby wings that was shooting low across the sky. It was already going out of sight by the time her mother and Mabel reached the window and all they were in time to see were flames shooting from the tail.

'I don't know what it was, but I don't like the look of it,' said Hilda.

'Nor me,' Mabel agreed.

They remained at the window but, hearing or seeing nothing else, Hilda and Mabel soon returned to their chairs, only to jump up again at the sound of an air raid warning.

'Come on, Ellen! Let's go.'

'I'll get my boys,' Mabel said, hastily leaving to run upstairs.

Fearful of the strange rocket, they all hurried to the underground station where it soon became obvious that many people had seen it. The talk was of nothing else until Ellen's mum turned to her, saying, 'You might as well settle down, Ellen. We could be down here all night.'

Ellen climbed onto a bunk, but her mum was proved wrong when the all-clear sounded two hours later and they made their way home again.

'Maybe it was just a one-off,' Mabel said, 'something being tested by our lot and nothing to do with Hitler.'

'If that's the case, why did the warning siren go off?'

'I dunno, mate, but whatever it was, it didn't do us any harm.'

Mabel proved to be wrong and that night was the beginning of what Hilda could only describe as hell. It wasn't long before they found out about the strange object that had appeared in the sky because, only two weeks later, the pilotless V1 rockets were coming over in their hundreds, soon earning the nickname of doodlebugs. They were terrifying, leaving everyone on constant alert and jumpy. First there was a droning noise and then you held your breath, terrified of hearing the engine cutting out overhead, because when it did, the monstrous thing would drop out of the sky to explode on impact.

The idea of Clapham as a safe haven soon became a thing of the past when a V1 dropped near a pond on the Common. Fortunately no one was hurt and little damage done, but, soon after, one fell closer to them on the South side, this time damaging property. Things grew steadily worse after that, with fifty houses being damaged in Ellerslie Street near Acre Lane, forty in Studley Road, and deaths mounting when seven people died in Kepler Road, and twelve in Station Road.

None of these places were close by, but Hilda's nerves were now at breaking point and she was terrified of letting Ellen out of her sight. Dora and Lucy had already gone, Dora's husband moving them out of London, and, fearful of her daughter being alone after school, Hilda had cut down her hours, doing only part-time work now. She felt the drop in her wages, but there was no way she was going to let Ellen fend for herself if there was a rocket attack.

It was Saturday morning, and Mabel had popped down to see Hilda, no sooner sitting down before she started complaining, 'I can't stand much more of this. A doodlebug fell on Paradise Road yesterday and hit the gasometer. It's a bloody miracle that no one was killed. I wrote to Jack yesterday, but I didn't tell him how bad it is. He'd only worry himself sick. He's in Burma and Gawd knows when he'll be home again.'

Hilda was about to speak when the doorbell rang and when she went to open it her face stretched with surprise. 'Gertie!'

'Sorry, I can't stay long, but I've been worried about you.'

'Come on in.'

When they walked into the living room, Mabel was already on her feet and said, 'I'll be off, Hilda.'

'You don't have to leave on my account,' said Gertie. 'I'm only able to spare half an hour. I drove one of our officers to London, but I've got to pick him up again soon and drive him back to base.'

Mabel had a disapproving look on her face as she looked at Gertie, but despite this Hilda said, 'You don't need to go, Mabel.'

Mabel sat down again, her lips set in a tight line, while Gertie said, 'I was so sorry to hear about Doug. How are you coping?'

'Gertie, how do you think?'

'Yes, sorry, daft question.'

Hilda quickly changed the subject and, noticing Gertie's uniform, she said, 'I see you've gained stripes. What are you, a sergeant?'

'Yes, but I've only just been promoted.'

Just then the siren howled and Mabel jumped to her feet. 'I'll get my boys. See you at the underground station.'

Hilda rushed to the back door too and called Ellen in from the garden, barely aware of her daughter's excitement at seeing Gertie as she dashed around to grab their things. Moments later they were running outside, Gertie shouting, 'Jump in the car.'

'No, no, the underground station is only just round the corner,' Hilda protested.

They legged it, Hilda's heart thumping in her chest. The V1 rockets were terrifying. If you heard the engine cut out, you knew the rocket was going to fall, and the last thing you wanted was to be out in the open. They reached the station, Hilda's panic only easing when they were deep underground.

'We made it,' she said, hugging Ellen to her.

They found somewhere to sit, Gertie looking at her watch and frowning. 'I've got to pick up my officer.'

'You can't drive around London with a rocket attack overhead,' Hilda warned.

'I haven't got any choice; but you have, Hilda. It's madness to stay here. You should get out of London again, or at least arrange for Ellen to be evacuated.'

'No, Mum!' Ellen cried. 'I won't go unless you come too.'

'Hilda, protests or not, you must get her out of here.'

'I won't go! I won't.'

Hilda felt as if Gertie had opened her eyes. Ellen had been like this since she had first suggested sending her away and, not wanting to part with her daughter, she had given in too easily.

'You're right, Gertie. I wish I could go with her,

but I only get a war widow's pension and have to work.'

'I've just had a thought. One of the girls on base has a cottage in Hampshire. I'm sure she'd let you use it for a while, and maybe rent-free, too.'

Hilda's mind began to race. If she didn't have to pay rent for the cottage, she might just be able to manage on her pension. 'If she'll let me have it rent-free, I'd love it.'

'Leave it with me and I'll have a word with Veronica when I get back to base. Now though, V1s or not, I've got to go. If Veronica agrees, I'll get the keys to you as soon as I can.'

'Thanks, Gertie – but I still think you should wait for the all-clear.'

'I can't,' Gertie insisted, then gave Ellen a quick hug before saying goodbye and dashing off.

'I . . . I hope we can go to that cottage, Mum.'

'Yes, me too,' Hilda agreed. In Hampshire they'd be living in the country, something she had vowed never to do again – but London was no longer safe and she welcomed the thought of moving away.

Gertie ran back to the staff car, gunning the engine to life. She wasn't looking forward to driving across London, but her officer would be waiting and there was no way she was going to let the man down.

The noise outside was deafening, the sky glowing

red from fires as she sped away from Clapham. She had hated that Hilda and Ellen were in so much danger, and annoyed too that Ellen hadn't been evacuated. Yes, Hilda had lost Doug and no doubt she'd been in a dreadful state, but even so it was wrong to keep Ellen in London.

'Good, you're back,' the officer said as he climbed into the car. 'Hellish trip, no doubt, but did you manage to see your friend?'

'Yes, sir, but she and her daughter were in a dreadful state, both bundles of nerves,' Gertie told him. She liked this officer – the man was happy to chat – and, taking a deep breath, she decided to ask the favour.

'They need to get out of London and I know of a cottage in Hampshire. The only thing is, if I can get it for them, I'll need to give them the keys. Is there any chance of a day pass tomorrow?'

'I don't see why not, but make sure I've got a decent driver on hand in case I need the car.'

'Yes, sir,' Gertie said, relief flooding through her. Knowing that Hilda and Ellen were safe, she'd sleep easier, both of them constantly on her mind since the V1 attacks had begun.

'How old is the daughter?'

'She's thirteen, sir.'

'She should have been evacuated before this.'

'I know, sir.'

'Marvellous men, those RAF pilots,' he said,

looking up at the sky. 'I was overseas in 1940, but heard how they fought like demons over London against the Luftwaffe. Churchill was right when he called it the Battle of Britain and, if you ask me, one day it'll be seen as the turning point in this war.'

'Do you think there's an end in sight, sir?'

'I think the D-day landings marked the beginning of the end, but we're not there yet.'

They were quiet then, each lost in their own thoughts, as Gertie drove past scenes of devastation that she feared would live with her for ever. So many buildings destroyed, dust, dirt, fires – so many dead, broken bodies – but as they reached the outskirts of London the skies cleared; the V1 attack was now over. Yes, for now, Gertie thought: but unless their troops could find and destroy the launch sites, more were sure to follow.

22

Hilda took Ellen to live in Hampshire and, as Gertie had said, the cottage wasn't much, but at least this time they weren't stuck in the middle of nowhere. They were on the borders of Hampshire and Wiltshire in a nice little village. The girl who owned the cottage had let them have it rent-free, and Hilda would for ever be grateful for that.

Money was tight, though, and it was a struggle to pay the rent on their flat in Clapham, but fearful of being homeless again, Hilda was determined to keep it up. She knew it was silly, that the place might not survive the rocket attacks, but if it did, at least they'd have a home to go back to when the war was finally over.

So far she hadn't found any work. The village was surrounded by farmland and soon Hilda knew she'd have to try the nearest farm, but dreaded the thought of working outdoors again in all weathers. She had hated it in Somerset, but now when Hilda thought back to her time there, she at last acknowledged that she'd played a part in what happened. Gertie had the feelings of a man and, when the hugs had started, Hilda realised now she should have stopped them. Instead, by saying nothing, she'd led Gertie on, given her false hope, and that had been cruel. When things had gone too far, she'd used it as an excuse to return to London, and look what had happened. She'd lost her baby, then Doug, and, not only that, when the bombings started again, followed by rocket attacks, her selfish decision had put Ellen at risk.

'I'm home,' Ellen called, nose bright red from the cold wind outside as she came in. 'What's for dinner? I'm starving.'

Hilda's breath caught in her throat at Ellen's striking resemblance to Doug, her daughter all she had left of him now. It had been selfish not to have her evacuated away from danger, but thanks to Gertie she'd been brought to her senses.

'Hello, pet, we're having egg and chips,' Hilda told her. 'How was school?'

'It was all right.'

As Hilda began to peel potatoes, her mind drifted again. Though she liked Hampshire, she missed Mabel, but her friend had refused her offer to share the cottage. With Percy at work there, Mabel felt unable to leave London, her thoughts only for her eldest son.

Despite feeling safe here, with money tight there had been a moment when Hilda had considered going back to London again, and that had been when news broke that British troops had found and destroyed the V1 launch sites in France. Hilda was glad that she had changed her mind, because in September Germany unleashed an even more terrifying weapon than the V1.

She glanced out of the window, the back garden bleak. It was now November, but when they'd arrived, though a little late for much planting, Ellen had taken it over, her daughter a dab hand at growing vegetables in the lovely, rich soil.

'Mum, when I leave school, I think I can get a job on the farm. I'd be in the dairy, making butter and cheese.'

Last week it had been Ellen's birthday. She was fourteen now, leaving the village school at the end of term, but to Hilda she was still a child. If she had her way, Ellen would continue on at school, but – no doubt because of all they had been through – she hadn't passed the examination that would have allowed her to continue her education. Hilda turned from her task to ask, 'Do you fancy working in a dairy?'

'Not really, but it's better than nothing.'

'Maybe I could get a job there too. The extra money would come in handy.'

'That's probably Sheila,' Ellen said, as the

doorbell rang and she went to answer it. 'I said I'd lend her one of my books.'

Hilda smiled, pleased that Ellen had settled so well and made new friends, but moments later there was an excited shout.

'Mum! Look!'

Hilda spun around, a potato falling from her hand in shock.

'Mabel, Billy, what on earth are you doing here?'

'Can you put us up, Hilda? I can't stand it any more. I had to get out of London, but don't worry, I'll pay me way.'

'Of course I can put you up, but what's happened?'

'Nothing . . . well, not yet . . . but it's them V2s. I'm so scared I'm nearly going out of my mind. Percy made me come here, but I hate leaving him behind.'

'Sit down – you too, Billy – and it looks like you could both do with a cup of tea.'

'Thanks, and what a bloody journey. Now are you sure you've got room for us?'

'Ellen can double up with me, leaving the other two rooms for you and Billy.'

'I don't want to put you out.'

'Mabel, I'm chuffed you're here,' Hilda insisted and she meant it, though she looked doubtfully at Billy. He was a little bugger, but, she mused, a lovable one. Goodness knows though what they'd make of him in the village.

Ellen eyed Billy warily, unhappy that he'd be staying with them. If it had been Percy, she wouldn't have minded. Unlike Billy he was nice, and she would never forget his kindness when her dad had died. Or Lucy – it would have been smashing if it had been Lucy – but Dora and Lucy had moved out of London before them and she wondered where they were now.

'Blimey, how do you stand this dead-and-alive hole?' Billy asked.

'Now then, I warned you,' Mabel said. 'It's good of Hilda to put us up and like it or not, you'll have to make the best of it.'

'Ellen, take Billy upstairs and show him the back bedroom,' her mother said. 'He can sleep in there.'

'Do I have to?'

'Yes, you do.'

'Billy, take our cases with you,' Mabel said.

'Yes, madam,' Billy said affecting a haughty tone. 'But hasn't anyone told you that slavery has been abolished?'

'You cheeky sod,' Mabel snapped. 'One of these days you'll push me too far. Now just do as you're told and take our stuff upstairs.'

'Put your mum's case in the other single bedroom,' Hilda called.

'Yes, madam,' Billy said again as he paused to give a little bow. 'Is there anything else I can do for you while I'm at it? I mean, you could always stick a broom up me arse and I'll sweep the floor.'

'Billy!' Mabel yelled.

Ellen expected her mother to be annoyed, but instead she doubled up with laughter.

'Oh . . . oh, Mabel,' she managed to gasp. 'You can't help but love the cheeky little sod.'

'Love him! I'll bleedin' kill him!' But then Mabel too began to laugh, tears of mirth soon rolling down their cheeks.

Ellen shook her head, bewildered as she led Billy upstairs. It was strange to hear her mum laughing again, but sort of nice too. Perhaps it wouldn't be so bad having Billy here, and, not only that, for the first time she had noticed how good looking he was.

'Billy is so funny,' Hilda said when she had finally managed to stop laughing.

'Yeah, I'll admit that, but don't let him fool you. He may be a looker and a charmer, but he can't pull the wool over my eyes. There's something not right about him, Hilda, something sneaky, and he's been nothing but trouble since the day he was born.'

'He can't be all bad.'

'I hope not, and though I moan about him, I love

the little sod. Percy tries to make him see sense, but Billy just doesn't seem to care about anyone else's feelings but his own.'

'I expect all lads of his age are the same.'

Mabel didn't look convinced so, changing the subject, Hilda asked, 'Has it been rough in London?'

'Hilda, if you thought those V1s were frightening, believe me, they were nothing compared to the V2,' Mabel said, sober now as she continued. 'At first I couldn't understand what was going on. You'd hear a loud bang before the sound of the engine, and Percy said it's because the bloody things can fly faster than the speed of sound. It's all double Dutch to me, but when they hit you hear an almighty explosion, and even at a quarter of a mile away the force of it can shatter your windows or washbasins. I dread to think what would happen if one hit any closer. There's no warning, Hilda, no chance to dive for cover, and one that hit Battersea left a ten-foot crater.'

Hilda could hear a tremor in Mabel's voice and said gently, 'You're safe now.'

'What about my Percy? He wouldn't leave the factory and is still there.'

'Our troops destroyed the V1 launch sites, and I'm sure they'll do the same with the V2s.'

'Things are never gonna be the same, Hilda.'

'What do you mean, love?'

'We grew up in the same street, went to the same school, and when we got married we stayed in the area. We knew nearly everyone around us, family, friends, our neighbours, but that way of life has gone now. Thanks to the bloomin' Luftwaffe we were forced to leave Battersea, as have so many of the folks we knew, and Gawd knows where they are now. Clapham was all right, and I settled down, especially having you living downstairs, but now we've both been forced to leave there too.'

'We'll go back as soon as this rotten war is over. Now come on, buck up and give me a hand with getting our dinner,' Hilda urged in an attempt to cheer her friend up. Like her, Mabel must feel as if she'd been forced from pillar to post, but at least they were safe here with a roof over their heads, however temporary. 'I'm afraid it's only fresh egg and chips though.'

'Eggs! Real eggs?'

'Most of the locals keep chickens so, yes, real ones.'

'Blimey, what a treat,' Mabel said, smiling again. 'I think I'm gonna like it here.'

Billy looked around the small room and then flung his case on the bed. He wandered over to the tiny leaded window, his heart sinking. All he could see were a few cottages with fields behind, and doubted there'd be any rich pickings around here. He hated leaving London, his mates and the few bob they made. If his mum found out what he got up to, she'd go barmy, despite the fact that she bought stuff from Harry that was obviously nicked. What a joke. Harry had the right idea and, as he'd told Billy on the sly, he was making money while the going was good.

He turned from the window, asking Ellen, 'What do you get up to around here?'

'The school's nice, but I'll be leaving soon. I like walking, exploring the woods and things like that.'

Billy shook his head in disgust. Woods, what good was exploring woods? There had to be a way of making a few bob and tomorrow he'd make a start on finding it. For now, he followed Ellen to the opposite room, and, after leaving his mother's case, they went back downstairs.

'Wash your hands, you two,' Hilda said. 'Dinner won't be long.'

Billy stared at the eggs in a bowl, gobsmacked. Real eggs! Bloody hell, in London he could make a bomb selling them. But he wasn't in London, he was stuck here, and once again his heart sank.

They had all eaten their dinner and sat back, replete, Mabel saying, 'That was smashing, Hilda.'

'It wasn't much. Mind you, there's still more

fresh produce here than in London. With nearly everyone growing vegetables, us too, they aren't in short supply, nor are chickens and eggs. There aren't long queues at the village shop either and that's a treat in itself.'

'No queues! It must be like living in a different world here.'

'It is, Mabel, and this time, I don't miss London.'

'Nor me,' Ellen said, 'well, except for Lucy.'

'Have you heard from Dora?' Hilda asked Mabel.

'No, not a word so I couldn't write to tell her I was leaving.'

'What about Jack? Have you heard from him?'

'Yes, and he's still in Burma, fighting alongside the Gurkhas. He's got nothing but praise for them but, as usual, his letters are heavily censored.'

'Yes, Doug's were too,' Hilda said, a surge of grief knotting her stomach.

'You've had a rough time of it, Hilda,' said Mabel, as though sensing her feelings.

Hilda nodded, and then put her hand into her apron pocket, feeling for the cross and chain. She wanted to wear it again, to bring it into the open, so pulling it out she held it up.

'Ellen, when you ripped this off, Mabel wasn't sure what to do with it so gave it to me for safe-keeping. I should give it back to you, but if you don't mind, I . . . I'd like to keep it.'

'Yes, keep it. I don't want it.'

Billy shoved back his chair. 'Mum, I'm going for a scout around.'

'Oh, I dunno about that.'

'It's all right, Mabel. He can't come to any harm around here – well, other than getting lost.'

'I'll go with him,' Ellen offered.

Billy put his coat on, saying abruptly, 'Right then, if you're coming, get a move on.'

'Give me a chance to put my coat on too!'

'All right, keep yer hair on.'

Ellen marched out ahead of Billy and, shaking her head, Mabel said, 'Oh dear, I reckon sparks might fly between those two.'

'You could be right,' Hilda agreed. But what sort of sparks? So far Ellen had never given her a moment of worry, but with Billy in such close proximity she'd have to keep an eye on her daughter. No, she was being silly. Ellen was still only fourteen, far too young to be thinking about boys, Hilda decided, comforted by the thought.

'I hope that lad behaves himself,' Mabel said.

'There isn't much he can get up to around here,' Hilda told her, unaware that Billy had already scrambled over a wall into the grounds of the nearby manor house, while Ellen was frantically calling him back.

23

By the end of January the following year, the change in Billy was already remarkable. When he'd jumped over the manor house wall, Billy had discovered stables, horses, and been instantly smitten. Instead of getting into trouble as his mother had expected, he'd found a mentor in the head groom, an old man who was so desperate for help that he'd taken Billy under his wing.

Billy now worked at the stables, loving it so much that he even went in on his days off, spending more time there than in the cottage, which, Ellen tried to assure herself, suited her just fine.

It was Friday, freezing outside, snow that had fallen during the night thick on the ground. Billy was up at the crack of dawn and had already left by the time Ellen got up to find her mother and Mabel talking about him.

'I'd never have believed it,' Mabel was saying.

'Who'd have thought my Billy would be happy to get out of bed at six in the morning, let alone going out in this weather? Mind you, he might seem like a different lad now, but he's still got that selfish streak. I asked him to write to his dad and you'd think he'd be worried about him, but no, he couldn't be bothered. The only thing he seems to care about is horses.'

Yes, Ellen thought, Billy was so potty about horses that he never spared her a glance.

'Good morning,' she said.

They both turned, Mabel saying, 'Hello, Ellen, you're up then. It's nice that you haven't got work today.'

'Yes, but I've got to go in this weekend,' she said, dreading the thought. When they'd left school, she and her best friend Sheila had both found jobs working in the dairy. Ellen didn't like it, hated the task of churning milk into butter and, much to the farmer's wife's annoyance, she still hadn't mastered the art of forming the freshly made butter into nice neat little shapes with wooden paddles. The smell of cream, of cheese-making, made her feel sick, and then there was endless cleaning too, along with scalding the pails.

'It's a shame there weren't any more vacancies, but to be honest, now you're here, Mabel, the extra money you put into the pot makes all the difference and I can just about manage without finding a job. All there would have been is farm work and I really don't fancy that.'

'Me neither, but it's easier for me. I've got the money Jack allows me, plus Percy stumps up a fair bit of his wages, and now Billy's working too – not that he earns much.'

'I don't either,' Ellen complained.

'I'll get your breakfast. Will a couple of bits of toast do?'

'Yes, Mum, that's fine and I'll have it with jam.'

'There's only a bit in the jar, enough for you, but I'll have to see if Mrs Jones will sell us another one.'

'She makes nice jam,' Mabel said. 'I'm going to the village shop to see if there's any letters. I'll stop at her cottage on the way.'

'I'll go,' Ellen offered.

'Bless you, love, but it's enough to freeze your socks off out there.'

'I don't mind.'

'All right, though wrap up warm,' Mabel warned.

Ellen smiled. Having Mabel living with them was like having two mothers; both caring, but at least Mabel didn't treat her like a child.

After breakfast, Ellen stepped outside into the biting cold and at first hurried along, but then, struck by how pretty everything looked, she slowed. The skeletal branches of the trees, heavy with snow, looked lovely, the hedgerows too, and the fields a blanket of white that stretched far into the distance.

The church spire could be seen in the distance, but she hadn't been inside. It wasn't a Baptist church and Ellen didn't know what it would be like, how the service would be conducted, or what sort of hymns they sang – yet sometimes on Sundays, when she saw villagers heading in that direction, she felt a pull to join them.

A man was walking along the lane towards her, and Ellen's eyes narrowed. There was something familiar about him, but with his head down as he trudged along, she was unable to see his face. He drew closer, looking up, and Ellen felt her head spinning. A ghost! She was looking at a ghost, but one that was solid and nothing like the ethereal image she'd imagined.

'Ellen, is that you?'

It wasn't a ghost, it was real, and she screamed with joy. 'Dad! Oh, Dad! They . . . they told us that you were dead.'

'They told you wrong. As you can see, I'm alive and kicking.'

Ellen flung herself into his arms. Her dad! He wasn't dead – he was here!

'Let's go and see your mum,' he said, gently pulling away to take her hand. 'I would have been here yesterday, but I had a right job finding you.

I knocked and knocked on the door of that down-stairs flat and then asked around, but nobody had a clue where you were. Somebody told me that Mabel's son worked at a local factory and still lived upstairs, so I hung around until he came home from work. Thankfully he had your address, but I've been stuck at a station all night and have only just managed to get here.'

'Oh, I can't wait to see Mum's face.'

'Nor me. In fact, all I've dreamed about is seeing both your faces again.'

Soon they were at the cottage, and Ellen quietly opened the door, urging her dad ahead of her. For a moment there was just a frozen tableau, the colour draining from her mother's face, but then, like a wax dummy coming to life, she jumped to her feet.

'Doug! Oh, Doug!'

'Hello, darling.'

The next minute Ellen saw her mother in his arms, sobbing uncontrollably, her words barely coherent. 'They . . . they told me you . . . you went down with your ship.'

'I know, love. It's a long story, but I'm here now.'

Ellen saw that Mabel had tears in her eyes too, both of them smiling as they watched the scene. It's like a miracle, Ellen thought, but then was struck by another. 'Mabel, that woman was right.'

'What woman?'

'Don't you remember? It was when we were sheltering in the underground. She told Mum about a vision, that she'd seen Dad on a raft and he was coming home.'

Though still clinging to him like a limpet, Hilda turned her head, eyes alight with happiness. 'Yes, she was right, and I'll never pooh-pooh people like her again.'

It was some time before they settled, and Hilda couldn't take her eyes off Doug. She still couldn't believe it, still felt she was dreaming as she handed him a cup of tea.

'Doug, what happened to you? Why didn't you write to tell me that you survived?'

'As I said, it's a long story.'

'I'd still like to hear it.'

'All right, but to make sense of it I'll have to start at the beginning. It's true that my ship went down. It was struck by a torpedo when we were in the South Atlantic and when a second one hit we began to list to starboard. It was pandemonium: fires, explosions, the fight to lower boats. By then we were listing so badly that it was impossible and, with no other choice, we began to scramble over the sides. My one thought as I plunged into the sea among debris and oil was to get as far away from the ship as possible.'

'Oh, Doug,' Hilda gasped.

'I ain't much of a swimmer and thought I was a goner, but thankfully I managed to grab hold of a piece of debris that was floating past. I don't know what it was, but it was wooden and floating so I scrambled onto it and paddled like mad.'

'That woman said you were on a raft,' Mabel said.

'What?'

'Sorry, Doug, I shouldn't have interrupted you.'

'That's all right. Anyway, where was I? Oh, yes, I was paddling like mad to get away. After a while my arms were screaming with pain and I had to stop, looking back to see a scene that was like something out of Dante's hell. There were men in the water, some surrounded by ignited fuel, screaming, shouting, and others still on board, clinging on for dear life as the ship went down, bow first.'

'It must have been awful,' Hilda murmured.

'It was, but it got worse. I was about to paddle back to see if I could pick anyone up when the U-boat surfaced.'

For a moment Doug closed his eyes, his mouth tight with anger when he spoke again. 'The bastards opened fire, gunning down the men in the water, and me, well, I got one in the back and another in the head.'

'Oh, no!' Hilda exclaimed.

'Yeah, well, as you can see, neither killed me.

I don't know how many days I drifted, or in which direction as I floated in and out of consciousness. When I was picked up by an American ship, it seems I was in a bad way, but I don't remember it, only really coming to when I was taken to a navy hospital in Trinidad.'

'But if you were rescued, why wasn't I told?'

'Nobody recognised me at the hospital. My uniform was in tatters and I didn't have any form of identification on me.'

'But you must have told them who you are.'

'That's just it, I couldn't. The bullet I took in the head must have done something to my memory. It wasn't a bad wound, yet I couldn't remember a thing. I was taken to the operating theatre to remove the bullet from my back and it took a long time to recover from that.'

'Are you all right now?' Hilda asked worriedly.

'My back is never going to be perfect again, and I'm not fit for action.'

'Dad, does this mean you're home for good?' Ellen asked excitedly.

'It depends on the medical board – but probably.'

Hilda could have danced with joy, but she managed to remain seated. There would be so much to sort out, not least her war widow's pension, and she had no idea what would change financially for them. Would Doug still receive army

220

pay? She pushed all this to one side for now as Doug spoke again.

'Anyway, to cut this long story short, thanks to the care I got, my memory slowly came back. I didn't want to remember the ship going down – the crew in the water, the gunning, the slaughter – and the chap who was helping me said that the trauma might have been the root cause of my memory loss. Once I was able to recall it, the rest followed, and, well, here I am.'

Hilda couldn't hold herself back. She wanted to be in Doug's arms again, to feel him, and moved to sit on his lap. 'I still can't believe you're really here.'

'Well, I am, and ain't it about time someone fed me? Three women here and not one of you has offered to cook me something to eat.'

'I'm not a woman, Dad,' Ellen protested.

'Well, by the look of you, you're not far off.'

Despite the horror of Doug's story, Hilda was smiling as she rose to her feet. Her man was home, he was here to stay, and the part of her she thought had died with him came to life again.

24

For Ellen the following weeks were joyous ones. She felt that she not only had her dad back, she had her mother too. Laughter often rang out in the cottage now, though she had noticed that Mabel had become subdued. Billy was still rarely in and, as Ellen could no longer share her mum's bedroom, she was given his room while he slept on the sofa downstairs.

Ellen couldn't get the woman who'd had the vision out of her mind now. Dora had said that anything to do with fortune telling was wrong, against God's teachings, but how could it be? If her mum had believed the woman she wouldn't have suffered for so long thinking that her dad was dead – she'd have known he was coming home. There was so much Ellen wanted to know now, to find out, her curiosity about such things renewed.

In this sleepy village it was impossible to find out much, but Sheila had told her about a woman her mother once went to who read some kind of stones, called runes. The two friends were sneaking off to see her now, her cottage on the outskirts of the village.

Sheila knocked on the ancient-looking door, both girls looking nervously at each other, but then it was opened by what looked like a very, very old woman.

'Yes, me dears, what can I do for you?'

'Er . . . er, we've been told you can tell fortunes,' Ellen stammered.

'Come in, come in,' the woman invited.

The cottage was dim, the walls unpainted grey stone, but a fire burned in the hearth. The old woman sat down in a rocking chair, close to the warmth, her small, dark eyes roaming over them.

'Sit down, but I think you're a bit young to be asking me to cast the runes.'

'We're fourteen, and we're both at work,' Ellen protested. 'We can pay you.'

'I don't want your money. I just want to know what brings you to me.'

'Er, well, you see,' Ellen began nervously, gaining a bit more confidence as she told of the woman who'd had the vision about her dad and how she was now curious about such things.

'So now you seek answers?'

'Well . . . yes. You see, I don't understand. Why

does the church say that things like that are wrong, against God?'

'I'm not a wise woman, just a simple one. I've gone my own way, this way of life my choosing, and I can't speak for the church.'

'Come on, Ellen, we should go,' Sheila urged.

'Wait,' the old woman said, and taking out a small, purple silk bag, she shook it before drawing out some stones. Her eyes seemed strange now, unfocused, as though she was looking at Ellen, but through her as she cast the selection. The stones had strange markings on them, some sort of symbols that Ellen didn't understand, and now the old woman studied them.

'You have travelled, and will travel again. Much is before you: happiness, pain and grief. Your search will continue, until one day you will be given a sign that will at last bring you peace.'

'I . . . I don't understand.'

'When you see the sign you will remember me and my words. The stones have nothing more to say.' And with that she stood up, shuffling across the room to open the door.

Sheila was the first out, barely saying goodbye as she hurried off, and, after thanking the woman, Ellen ran after her.

'What's the matter? Why did you dash off like a scalded cat?'

'There was something about her I didn't like,'

Sheila scowled. 'And, anyway, it was a waste of time. She could tell you're a Londoner, so of course you've travelled, and as for the rest of it, everyone has happiness and pain in their lives; we'll all have to face grief too. That reading could have been for anyone, something I could have told you without casting rune stones.'

'Yes, maybe, but she also said I'd see a sign.'

'If you ask me she didn't see anything in those daft stones and only said that to make you think that she's some sort of mystic.'

Ellen wasn't convinced, her mind still on the old woman as they made their way home. A sign, she had said. What sort of sign?

A few more days passed, and when Ellen woke up on Friday morning, she looked out of the window to see that snow had stopped falling, but it was still cold as she hurriedly dressed to go downstairs. Almost reaching the kitchen, she paused, her ears pricked. Surely she'd misheard? Surely Mabel hadn't said she was going back to London? Ellen remained out of sight, listening.

'Why, Mabel?' her mother asked. 'Surely it's too risky?'

'I feel in the way now and it's for the best.'

'Look, just because Doug's come home, it doesn't mean you're in the way.'

'You need time on your own.'

'We get that. Nowadays you're always popping out to see Mrs Jones, and gone for hours.'

'She likes a bit of company.'

'Come on, Mabel, what's this really about? Have I done something to upset you?'

'Of course you haven't.'

'Then why?'

'I'm too embarrassed to tell you.'

'Don't be daft. We've been friends for years and there's nothing we don't know about each other.'

'All right, I'll tell you the truth. It's hearing you and Doug. My bedroom's next door to yours and as my Jack hasn't been home for such a long time, it's driving me mad with frustration listening to you.'

Ellen knew that if she walked into the room they'd stop talking, so she continued to stand out of sight. What did Mabel mean? Why did sleeping in the next room to her parents drive her mad with frustration?

'Oh, Mabel,' her mother now said, 'now it's me who's embarrassed.'

'You're only doing what's natural, but that bed don't 'arf squeak.'

'Mabel!'

'Look at you. You've gone as red as a beetroot.'

'No wonder I'm blushing. I had no idea that you could hear us making love last night.'

'Now that you know, you'll want your privacy.'

'With Doug's back playing him up, we . . . well . . . we don't do it that often. Anyway, privacy or not, I don't want you going back to London. There's Billy to think about too. He'd go mad if you try to drag him away from those horses.'

'I'm sure the war won't last much longer, and we'd have to go back then. It might as well be now as later.'

'If it's only hearing me and Doug that's brought this on we can soon solve that. You can swap rooms with Ellen.'

Ellen bit on her lower lip. They were talking about lovemaking, but it was something she knew little about. All her mother had ever told her was that she'd been born under a gooseberry bush, which made no sense at all, and other than that all she'd heard were playground whispers when she'd been at school.

'What are you up to, pumpkin?'

Startled, Ellen turned to see her father coming down the stairs. 'Noth . . . nothing,' she blustered. 'I've just got up.'

His eyebrows rose sceptically, but then he smiled. 'Yes, me too.'

'It's about time,' Hilda said as they walked into the room.

'Have a heart,' Doug protested. 'You know my back was bad when I woke up this morning.'

'I wonder why?' Mabel chuckled.

Ellen saw her mother flush, but then she said, 'Ellen, after you've had breakfast I want you to move your things into Mabel's room. You're swapping.'

'Why?'

'Never you mind. Just do as you're told, and Doug, I'll tell you why later.'

'Fair enough. Now, woman, where's me grub?'

'I'll give you woman,' she threatened.

'Lovely. How many?'

'I said woman, not *women*.'

'What a shame. It'd be nice to have a harem.'

'Oh, would it now?' Hilda said, hands on hips and glaring up at him. 'Well, Douglas Stone, you can forget it. This woman is the only one you're getting.'

'Maybe it's just as well. You're enough to handle as it is.'

'Yeah, and last night he did plenty of handling.'

'Mabel!'

'Sorry, love, but you've got to admit it's funny.'

'What's funny?' Doug asked.

'Don't ask,' Hilda insisted. 'Now, sit down, the pair of you, and I'll see to your breakfasts.'

Ellen smiled. Her mother was back on form, her dad joking, and it seemed that Mabel would be staying, though it remained a mystery why she had wanted to leave. Perhaps she could ask Sheila. She might know what lovemaking was.

* * *

Billy was deep in thought as he mucked out a stable. Doug had said that the end of the war was in sight now, and if he was right, Billy knew it meant they'd go back to London. It was funny really, and he hadn't expected to feel like this, but Billy didn't want to go. He loved the horses, and even loved the smell of the stables, finding no distaste at shovelling up horse shit, or manure, as Mr Dunning insisted he called it.

'Well done, Billy,' the old man said as he walked up to him.

'Do you reckon the war will be over soon?'

'Yes, lad, but why the long face?'

'When it is, my mum will want to go back to London.'

Mr Dunning pursed his lips, his eyes thoughtful, and then said, 'When this lot's over, our troops will be coming home, and no doubt looking for jobs again, but I'll have room for a decent stable lad. If you want to stay, the job will still be yours.'

Billy felt a surge of excitement, which quickly deflated. 'Thanks, Mr Dunning, it's good of you to offer, but once my mum and the Stones go back to London, I won't have anywhere to live.'

'I'm sure we can sort some accommodation, and if you like I'll have a chat with your mother. For now, though, get on with your work.'

As the man walked away, Billy jumped in the

air, clicking his heels together, his fist raised to punch the air with delight.

For the rest of the day Billy worked steadily, but when it was time to leave, he almost ran all the way home, saying as he rushed into the cottage, 'Mum, Mr Dunning said that if I want to stay on after the war, he can find me somewhere to live.'

'Has he now? Well, you can forget it. When we go back, I'm not leaving you here.'

'Why not?'

'Billy, you're only fourteen.'

'Mum, please, I'd never find a job working with horses in London.'

'You could try the Young's brewery. They use drays.'

'No, it won't be the same. I want to stay here.'

'Ellen said the same thing when I told her we were leaving Somerset,' Hilda observed, 'but I didn't expect to hear it from you, Billy.'

'I feel the same now,' said Ellen. 'I'd like to stay here too.'

'Well, we can't,' Hilda said. 'This cottage isn't ours and when the war's over we'll have to leave.'

'I like life in the country too.'

'I know, Doug, but what choice have we got? We'll have nowhere to live, no jobs, but at least we've got a home to go back to in London.'

'Yeah,' Mabel agreed, 'and, anyway, my Percy's

in London. Not only that, when Jack comes home I want to be there, waiting for him.'

'All right, Mum, you go,' Billy said, 'but I'll stay.'

'If you think I'm leaving you here, you must be out of your mind.'

'Hold on, Mabel. Surely if Billy is old enough to work, he's old enough to make his own decisions?' Doug said. 'If he's really keen on keeping the job and if Mr Dunning is willing to keep an eye on him, I don't think you should stand in his way.'

Billy smiled gratefully at Doug, but the smile was short-lived as his mother reared to her feet. 'So you'd leave Ellen to fend for herself at the age of fourteen, would you?'

'Well, no, but Billy's a boy.'

'You said it, Doug,' snapped Mabel. 'He's a *boy*, not a man. Not only that, this is my decision, not yours.'

'All right, you have a point. I'm sorry for sticking my nose in,' Doug said, smiling ruefully.

Billy knew he had lost then, and with no appetite now he said, 'I'm going out for a walk.'

'Hold on, what about your dinner?'

'I'm not hungry,' he said, stomping out.

'Billy!' Mabel shouted.

'I'll go after him,' Ellen said, grabbing her coat and running out before her mother could stop her.

* * *

Ellen could see how upset Billy was when she caught up with him and said, 'I'm sorry. I know how you feel.'

'It ain't bleedin' fair. I don't want to go back to soddin' London.'

'Me neither.'

Their eyes met as he said, 'We've got something in common then.'

Ellen flushed, and quickly looked away. Since Billy had arrived she'd been confused by her feelings, but he'd been so wrapped up in his job that he'd hardly spared her a glance.

They turned the corner to see Sheila coming out of her cottage, her younger brother, Colin, with her.

'Hello,' Sheila called.

'Hello,' Ellen called back, thinking how much her friend Sheila reminded her of Lucy, both with blonde, curly hair, blue eyes, their features doll-like.

'She's a bit of all right,' Billy said, brightening as Sheila joined them.

'Hello, Billy,' said eight-year-old Colin as he looked up at Billy adoringly.

Billy had stood up for Colin when a group of boys had been tormenting him and since then he'd become his hero. Colin was small for his age, a target for the bullies, but almost from the day Billy arrived in the village he'd earned a reputation, the country boys out of their depth with a streetwise London kid. Billy seemed older somehow, and the other boys were fascinated by him and the tales of his antics in London.

'Hello, Billy,' said Sheila, smiling softly, doe-eyed as she looked at him.

Ellen felt a pang of jealousy, her voice clipped as she said, 'Come on, Billy. Dinner's ready.'

'You go, I'm not hungry.'

'We've had ours and were just going for a walk. Do you want to join us, Billy?'

'Yeah, why not?'

Ellen was fuming. Sheila had hardly said a word to her, all her focus on Billy. Huh, some friend, fawning over Billy and cutting her out. Turning on her heels, she marched off, slamming the door shut as she stomped into the cottage.

'I can see something's got up your nose, Ellen,' said Hilda, 'but there's no need to slam the door like that.'

'Sorry,' she said shortly.

'What's the matter?'

'Sheila's gone off with Billy.'

'Blimey, don't tell me he's got his eye on a girl instead of a horse,' Doug chuckled.

'He seems a bit young to be interested in girls.'

'Leave it out, Hilda,' Doug protested. 'He's growing up fast, and you've got to admit that Sheila's a lovely-looking girl.'

'Doug, you don't think he'll . . . oh, you know . . . try it on?' Mabel asked worriedly.

'Boys will be boys,' Doug warned.

'Oh, no! What if he gets her into trouble?'

'They're still just kids and I doubt it'll go that far, but don't worry, leave it to me. I'll have a word with the lad.'

'Thanks, Doug.'

'Mabel, what do you mean?' Ellen asked. 'How can Billy get Sheila into trouble?'

Before Mabel could open her mouth, Hilda snapped, 'Haven't you two got any sense? You shouldn't be talking about such things in front of Ellen.'

'Calm down,' Mabel urged. 'Ellen's fourteen too and she's got to find out about the facts of life sometime. Maybe it's time you had a word with her too.'

'I'll do no such thing. Unlike Sheila, my daughter doesn't go chasing after boys. Now if you don't mind, I'd think it's time to change the subject.'

'Please yourself,' Mabel said huffily, 'but if you ask me, you're over-protecting her – as usual.'

'I'll bring my daughter up as I see fit.'

'Come on, you two, there's no need to fall out over this,' Doug said.

Mabel was the first to concede. 'Yeah, you're right, and sorry, Hilda. As usual, I'm sticking my nose in where it isn't wanted.'

'Fine. Now let's have dinner.'

Ellen sat at the table, none of them aware of her thoughts. She still wanted to know what Mabel meant by Billy trying it on with Sheila, but as usual, her questions remained unanswered.

25

'What's wrong with Ellen?' Doug asked. 'She's not the same lately and it's a job to get a word out of her.'

'If you remember, Sheila went off with Billy and I think Ellen feels pushed out.'

'The lad's too busy at the stables to see much of Sheila, and with Billy, horses come first.'

'It's just as well. I still think Sheila's a bit young to be going out with boys, and I don't think Ellen should be told the facts of life, despite what Mabel said. My mother didn't tell me anything and it didn't do me any harm. I reckon talking to young girls about such things will just make them curious and it's better they stay innocent.'

'You'll be lucky. If you ask me that Sheila knows a thing or two and Ellen's probably heard it from her.'

'No, Doug, Sheila's a lovely girl.'

'Surely it's better to hear the truth than the

things I picked up at school. I thought you got a girl pregnant by touching her belly button.'

'I thought you only had to kiss a boy to get in the family way, and you've got to admit, it kept us from misbehaving.'

Doug stood up to pull Hilda into his arms, saying with a wink, 'I dunno about that, but give us a kiss then and we'll go on from there.'

'Behave. Mabel will be up soon.'

'I'm already up.'

'Don't talk like that, it's rude!' Hilda protested, pulling away. 'I know what your problem is, Douglas Stone. You're bored.'

'It's only me,' Mabel called as she walked in. 'I didn't hear Billy get up and I hope he had a bit of breakfast before he left.'

'Yes, he did. I saw the remnants when I got up.'

'I caught the tail end of what you were saying, something about you being bored, Doug.'

'Yeah, I am a bit.'

'What about a bit of decorating? With all of us smoking, the walls are looking a bit yellow in here.'

'I don't think your back is up to it, Doug,' Hilda warned.

'It might be all right. If I remember rightly, I saw a few old cans of paint in the shed. I'll go and have a look.'

'I'm not sure about this,' Hilda said as Doug

went outside. 'Doug tries to hide it but I think his back is getting worse.'

'If he can't manage it, we can take over.'

'It still feels like a miracle to have him back. I thought that woman at the underground station was just making it up about her vision, trying to get money out of me. Gertie once talked about it, saying nothing like that has been proved, but Doug *was* on a raft; he *did* come home,' Hilda said. She felt it was proof enough, but despite that, she doubted Gertie would believe her and would come up with some sort of explanation. She wouldn't tell Gertie, she'd keep it to herself, especially as she now believed that someone really was standing next to her in Somerset, someone unseen. If Gertie hadn't called out, would it have manifested itself? Could it have been her mother?

With no idea that she'd been the subject of discussion when she'd left for work that morning, Ellen made her way to the farm. She heard someone running up behind her and turned to see Sheila.

'Ellen, please, this is silly. If you'd told me you had your eye on Billy, I wouldn't have flirted with him.'

'Flirt with him all you want. I couldn't care less.'

'Then why aren't we friends now?'

Ellen fumbled for an answer, but, unable to find

one, she went on the defensive. 'Don't blame me. Nowadays you prefer Billy's company to mine.'

'That isn't true. Yes, he comes out for the occasional walk, but there's nothing to stop you joining us.'

'No, thanks. I wouldn't want to be in the way.'

'Colin's always with us and you know that. If you ask me, you're jealous.'

'Jealous! Of you and Billy! You must be joking.'

'If you say so, but please, can't we be friends? I admit I like Billy, but all he ever really talks about is horses. I'd have to be a brood mare before he'd show any real interest in me.'

'What's a brood mare?'

'It's a horse used for breeding, one they put with a stallion.'

Ellen frowned. 'Put with a stallion. What do you mean?'

'You know, they mate to have a foal.'

'Mate! What's that?'

'Don't you know anything?'

'Not about horses,' Ellen said. 'It's Billy who's mad about them, not me.'

'So you know how babies are made.'

'Do you?'

'Yes, of course. When you grow up in the country you soon find out. I've seen all sorts of animals mating, wild ones, farm ones.'

'What's that got to do with having babies?'

With a lift of her eyebrows, Sheila told her and Ellen blanched, appalled. 'No, surely our parents aren't like the animals? Surely they don't do that?'

'They do, though I've never seen my mum and dad at it. Have you?'

'Of course not. It sounds disgusting.'

'When you get married and want babies, you'll have to do it too.'

'No, thanks,' Ellen said, at last making the link. So mating was sex, lovemaking, but it didn't sound much like love to her. She had thought it was just kissing, cuddling, something her parents were always doing, but not . . . not *that*.

'Please, can't we be friends again?' Sheila asked. 'You don't have to worry about Billy; he hardly spends any time with me lately.'

'Yes, of course we can,' Ellen said, linking arms with Sheila as they set off for the farm again. If Billy wasn't seeing much of Sheila now, perhaps he was going off her. Maybe he'd notice her at last – but then Ellen flushed. If he did, she'd never be able to look him in the eye, the thought of doing *that* with him disgusting.

26

On a Sunday in early April, the weather turned; the temperature became warmer. It had taken some time, but at last Doug's army pay had been sorted out. They had stopped Hilda's widow's pension and deducted it from Doug's backdated pay, but it had still left them a small amount of savings. Hilda's only worry was that Doug was now waiting to go before the medical board of assessment. They would decide the extent of his disability, and, if necessary, discharge him and award a pension dependent on whether they thought he was capable of doing any kind of work.

'Mabel, a letter for you,' Doug said as he came back from the village shop.

Hilda looked at her husband worriedly, unable to miss the signs of pain etched on his face. Painting this room had proved impossible, and he'd been forced to let her and Mabel finish it while he lay flat on the floor until his back eased. He was getting worse, she was sure of it, but he kept insisting that he was all right, in fact, fine after a little rest.

Mabel took the envelope, a smile on her face. 'Oh, look, it's from Jack.' But as she read the letter her face paled. 'Oh, my God!'

'Mabel, what's wrong?'

'Ja . . . Jack's been wounded. He says he took a bullet in his stomach.'

'He's alive, and managed to write to you,' Doug said. 'Surely that's a good sign?'

Mabel turned the page over, quickly reading the other side. 'He says he was operated on in a field hospital, and though it was touch and go for a while, he . . . he's all right now and . . . and . . . they're shipping him home . . . My Jack's coming home! I'll have to go back to London. I want to be there when he arrives,' Mabel cried, rising quickly to her feet. 'Billy! He'll have to pack, too. I'll run down to the stables to get him. Trains! I'll have to find out what time the train leaves.'

'Mabel, calm down. You don't know when Jack will arrive, and if it's a stomach wound, he could be sent straight to hospital,' Doug warned softly. 'I'll go and tell Billy to come home, and then sort out your travel arrangements.'

'Will you? Oh, thank you, Doug.'

As Doug left the cottage, Ellen ran downstairs.

'I'm going back to Sheila's house,' she called, a book in her hand and not stopping on her way to the door.

'Wait,' Hilda called. 'Mabel and Billy are leaving.'

'Leaving! Why?'

'My Jack's been wounded, and he's coming home.'

'Is he all right?'

'Well, love, he says he is,' Mabel told her, but then paled again. 'Oh, Hilda, I've just had a thought. If Jack's all right he'd be fit for action and they wouldn't be shipping him home. What if he's bad? What if he's really bad?'

'Don't get in a tizzy again. As Doug said, Jack was well enough to write, so look on the bright side. He's coming home and you'll be seeing him again soon.'

'You're right. He's alive and that's all that matters. I'd best go and pack,' Mabel said, looking brighter as she left the room.

Mabel had barely gone out of sight when Ellen said, 'Mum, the talk is that the war will be over soon. We'll go back to London then, won't we?' she asked eagerly.

'Yes, but you've changed your tune. You actually sound keen on the idea.'

'Why shouldn't I be?'

'Ellen, you once said you wanted to stay here.'

A blush rose all the way up from Ellen's neck to her cheeks. 'I . . . I didn't. I was talking about Somerset, how I didn't want to leave there.'

Hilda's eyes narrowed. It was funny that just because Billy might be going back to London, Ellen wanted to go too. The door opened, Billy walking in, and quickly Hilda said, 'Your mum's upstairs.'

'It ain't fair. Just because me dad's come home, I've got to go back to London. I don't know why I can't stay here.'

'Billy, your dad's been wounded. Surely you want to see him?'

'Yeah, I suppose so,' he said, then stomped off upstairs.

Hilda saw the expression on her daughter's face. She looked upset, but all Hilda felt was a surge of relief. If Ellen had a childish crush on Billy, it was just as well he wasn't going to be under the same roof now. It was sure to be a case of out of sight, out of mind, and that suited Hilda just fine.

Ellen chewed on her bottom lip. It had stopped her in her tracks, hearing that Billy was leaving and she felt confused by her feelings. She'd decided that she wasn't interested in Billy, in any boys, so why was she upset? I'm not, she told herself. Good riddance. He was just a smelly boy, coming home stinking of the stables and going on and on about horses. All he cared about was those flaming animals, and hardly spared her a glance.

Only a few minutes later, her father walked in. 'There's a train in two hours so if Mabel gets a move on they should be able to get it.'

'Billy doesn't seem keen on leaving.'

'He took a bit of persuading, only agreeing when Mr Dunning said again that he'd keep his job open.'

'I don't think Mabel will let him come back on his own. Billy was always up to mischief in London, hopping school, nicking things, and she'll want him where she can keep an eye on him.'

Ellen's mind drifted from their conversation. Her mother was right, Billy had been a menace in London and she had kept out of his way as much as possible. His brother, Percy, was different, and she had always liked him. *Yes, but now you like Billy too, but in a different way,* a small voice whispered in the back of her mind. *I don't, I don't,* Ellen argued.

'Mum, is it all right if I go up and say goodbye now?' she asked. 'Sheila's waiting for me and she must be wondering where I am.'

'Yes, all right, and tell Mabel about the train.'

'I've just popped up to say goodbye,' Ellen said

as she walked into the room to find Mabel cramming clothes into a suitcase. 'Dad said there's a train in two hours.'

'We've nearly finished packing, but come here,' Mabel said, holding out her arms. 'Bye, sweetheart. I'm gonna miss you.'

Ellen hugged her, and then, trying to sound offhand, she said, 'Bye, Billy.'

His reply was brusque, 'Yeah, bye.'

Ellen waited a second, but he, too, was packing and didn't even look at her. She turned away and ran downstairs, picked up her book and called, 'I'm going along to Sheila's.'

'You were a long time,' Sheila said. 'I was beginning to think you weren't coming back.'

'Billy and his mum are leaving. I had to wait for him to come back from the stables to say goodbye.'

'Billy! Billy's leaving! What – now?'

'Yes, they're off to the station to catch the London train.'

'Is he coming back?'

'I doubt it.'

Sheila's face fell. 'I'll pop along to your place to say goodbye to him.'

'You're too late, they've gone,' Ellen lied.

'Oh, no, but that means I'll never see him again.'

'No, I suppose not,' Ellen said off-handedly,

cheered by the thought. When they went back to London, *she'd* see Billy again and at last admitted inwardly that she liked him – *really* liked him.

27

At first, they weren't sure whether to believe the rumours that spread rapidly around the village, but on the eighth of May there was an official announcement. It was Victory in Europe – VE day – and, along with the other villagers, Hilda, Doug and Ellen poured onto the narrow cobbled streets, joining in the party atmosphere as people waved flags, danced, laughed and sang.

The celebrations went on for hours, until at last, exhausted but happy, they returned to the cottage, where Hilda kicked off her shoes to rub her aching feet.

'Well, that's it,' Doug said. 'We'll have to go back to London now.'

There was a time when Hilda might have welcomed this, but not now. London had brought her nothing but heartache and, shaking her head, she said, 'It might be victory in Europe, but the war isn't over yet. Until we hear from Veronica that she wants the cottage back, I think we should stay here.'

'Hilda, you know the assessment board discharged me with only a fifty percent pension. It's not enough to live on and we've been dipping into our savings.'

'You could try finding work around here, go back to being a milkman, or one of the farms might take you on.'

'With my back, I won't be able to lift the milk crates, let alone the constant bending to put bottles on doorsteps. It'd be the same on a farm. I couldn't handle the digging or any other heavy work.'

'It won't be any different in London.'

'Yes it will. I'm not keen on going back either, but at least I'll be able to find some sort of light work there, maybe a bench job in a factory.'

'I still think we should wait.'

'Our savings won't last, you know that. We need to go now, before our lads come home and all the jobs are filled.'

Hilda wanted to protest, to find an excuse – any excuse to keep them here.

'What about you, Ellen? Surely you don't want to leave?'

'I don't mind, Mum. I hate working in the dairy and I'm bound to find a better job in London.'

Hilda knew she had lost the argument and her stomach churned, but with nothing further to offer in protest, she said sadly, 'All right then, we'll go back.'

Ellen was up early the next morning and ran along to Sheila's cottage, saying when her friend opened the door, 'We're going back to London and I won't be coming to work. Will you tell them at the farm and that I'll collect my wages later today?'

'Oh, no! First Billy and now you. When are you leaving?'

'Tomorrow morning.'

'I'm going to miss you,' Sheila said sadly, 'but hold on a minute.'

She ran inside, returning with a piece of paper.

'It's my address. I didn't get a chance to say goodbye to Billy when he left, but would you give him this and . . . and ask him to write to me?'

'Yes, all right,' Ellen said as she stuffed the piece of paper into her pocket. She had no intention of passing it on to Billy, but Sheila didn't know that. 'I'd best go. Mum wants my help to give the cottage a thorough clean and then I've got packing to do.'

'If I don't get a move on I'll be late for work. I'll see you later when you come to the farm.'

'Yeah, see you,' Ellen called, and as she walked back home she put her hand into her pocket, crushing the piece of paper with Sheila's address on it into a ball before lobbing it over a hedge and into a field.

Her eyes were drawn to the church in the distance, to the steeple and cross on top. She was still confused by the old woman and the rune stones and always found herself looking for signs. Was the cross the sign? Was she supposed to go to church again?

'Right, Ellen, that's it,' Hilda said as she emptied a pail of water. 'All done, and once you've had a bit of a break, you might as well go to the farm. You won't get a full week's wages, but anything is better than nothing.'

'I'll have a wash first.'

Hilda looked around the room, pleased to see that it looked almost exactly as she'd found it; better, in fact, without a speck of dirt of dust to be seen. She envied Veronica this lovely cottage, a place that she had come to love. She'd been over there, sitting in that chair when Doug had come back to her, the memory a joyful one. In fact, unlike the London flat, there were only happy memories here and she was heartsick at the thought of leaving.

'Cheer up, love,' Doug said. 'At least we've got a home to go back to, and with so many people in London without decent accommodation, we've got that to be thankful for.'

'I know,' she said tiredly.

When Ellen came back from having a wash,

Doug asked, 'What sort of job are you after when we get back to London?'

'I dunno, Dad, maybe work in a flower shop or something like that. It'd be lovely to handle so many different flowers, and to learn how to make lovely bouquets.'

'I can't say I'm surprised,' Hilda said. 'You've always been plant-mad and spend hours working in the garden. Anyway, if you want your wages, you'd best get off to the farm.'

'I'll walk with her,' said Doug.

'Yes, go, and while you're both out it'll give me a chance to put my feet up for a bit. We'll start packing when you come back.'

Hilda's face was downcast as they left. She dreaded the morning, hated the thought of leaving the cottage, and prayed that London wouldn't bring her more heartache.

Ellen was taking in the countryside as they walked to the farm. Yes, she'd miss it, but she was excited at the thought of seeing Billy again. When her dad had asked her what sort of job she hoped to find in London, she'd just blurted out the first thing that sprang to mind, but, thinking about it now, she realised that maybe it wouldn't be so bad working in a flower shop. It wouldn't be quite the same as growing things, but it was better than nothing.

'Do you know, Ellen, when at sea I used to dream of a life in the country, and envied Gertie her smallholding? I can't say I'm looking forward to going back to London, but I'm afraid, needs must.'

'Never mind, Dad. One day I might be rich and then I'd buy you a cottage, just like the one we're leaving. You wouldn't have to work again either, and you could spend all your time living the life of Riley.'

'That sounds good, but take your time. I might have a bad back, but I ain't ready to be put out to pasture yet.'

'Billy liked living here too and I wonder how he's getting on in London.'

'He hasn't been there for five minutes, but his job at the stables will be open if he wants to come back.'

Ellen remembered her mum saying that she doubted Mabel would allow it and was cheered by the thought. Yes, but what if her mum was wrong? What if Billy could persuade Mabel to let him come back?

Doug, too, was deep in thought. He'd told Ellen that he wasn't ready to be put out to pasture, but now wondered if that was all he was fit for. He hid it as best he could from Hilda and his daughter, but the constant pain in his back was grinding him down.

He hadn't wanted Hilda to think him less than a man now and made love to her when he could, but of late had begun to fear that soon it would be beyond him. Afterwards Hilda would fall asleep in his arms, happy, content, while he lay in excruciating agony, unable to sleep until the early hours of the morning. As he stumbled on a stone, a hot rod of pain now shot up Doug's spine and he gasped.

'Dad, are you all right?'

'It was just a twinge,' Doug lied, gritting his teeth as he continued to walk. It was his own fault. He'd been warned, the doctors cautioning against any further damage and Doug knew that if he didn't want to end up a permanent cripple, he would have to tell Hilda that there'd be no more lovemaking.

'Nearly there, Dad.'

Doug would be relieved to stop for a while, and was glad when they reached the farm. He waited outside, watching Ellen as she went to the dairy. It amazed him how grown up she looked now and there were signs that she was going to be a beautiful young woman. Dark hair framed her pretty face, her small nose was sprinkled with freckles and her blue eyes were clear and bright. It wouldn't be long before blokes were sniffing around, but they'd have to get past him first. If he could, he'd give his daughter the world, but with a gammy back what chance did he have of earning a decent wage?

Morose, he took in the view now. It really was a lovely area, the New Forest on the doorstep, and he'd be sorry to leave. The countryside was beautiful, lush, green and the still quietness enough to soothe your soul. Doug grinned – hark at him getting all poetic – and his good humour was restored by the time Ellen returned.

'All set, love?'

'Yes, let's go.'

As they walked back to the cottage, Doug was once again struck by the beautiful countryside. He wasn't looking forward to going back to London, but with the need to earn a living there was no choice.

One day though, no matter what, he'd come back to this area. Doug didn't know how, or when, but somehow, he'd do it.

28

Ellen looked out of the window. They were on the last leg of their journey, sitting on the bus that would take them to Clapham. She had thought London looked awful when they returned from Somerset, but it was even worse now. They had already passed through areas that looked totally destroyed, great swathes of rubble with hardly a building left standing.

As they reached the north side of Clapham, Ellen saw that a row of houses had been flattened opposite the underground station, and others, along with a church, severely damaged. Worse, as they neared Clapham South, it was no longer untouched and she saw ruin after ruin where homes had once stood.

'Doug, the whole of London looks awful and rebuilding is going to take years,' Ellen heard her mother say.

'Yes, but though Hitler may have crushed property, I doubt he's crushed Londoners' spirits.'

'But so many thousands have died.'

Ellen closed her eyes against her mother's words, yet knew they were true, her grandparents among the dead. She had never known her father's parents. They had died in a house fire before she was born, and it suddenly struck Ellen that they were a tiny family, just the three of them now.

Still, Ellen thought, trying to cheer herself up, her dad had come home, he was alive, and once again she recalled the woman who had spoken to her mother about a vision. It still amazed her that anyone could foresee the future, and Ellen wished she had that ability too. If she could, she would know if Billy was going to return to Hampshire, something she was desperate for him not to do.

Hilda rose to her feet to follow Doug along the aisle between the seats, saying impatiently, 'Come on, Ellen, buck yourself up. We're here.'

Doug winced as he pulled out the two suitcases that were stowed behind the conductor. Hilda could see that he was in pain and blamed the long journey. They were all tired, jolted on trains and buses, so it wasn't surprising that Doug's back was playing him up.

Hilda pulled out another case, urged Ellen to take the last one, and as they got off the bus she paused to take in their surroundings. She hadn't wanted to come back to London and now saw nothing to make her change her mind. It had once been a place she loved, where she had been born and bred, yet it brought her nothing but bad memories now. *Mum, keep us safe, please don't let there be any more bad luck,* she inwardly begged, her hand automatically going to her neck to clutch the necklace, but it was under her coat and out of reach.

'Are you coming or what?' Doug said impatiently.

It was unusual for Doug to be snappy, and a sure sign that he was in pain, so, picking up her case again, Hilda forced a smile.

'Yes, let's go, and thank goodness our place is only around the corner.'

Hilda wrinkled her nose as they walked into the downstairs flat. It was dark with the blackout curtains drawn, the smell damp and musty. Doug put the cases down and walked over to the window, pulling the curtains back before throwing it open. Able to see clearly now, Hilda took in the room – the ancient furniture, the yellowing wallpaper – and though the flat had been shut up, there was a thin layer of dust over everything. It looked dismal, depressing, but seeing the pain etched on Doug's face she forced her voice to sound light.

'Right, let's get ourselves sorted out. Ellen, you'll need to run to the shops. We'll need to get some stuff in, but before you do that, pop up to Mabel's and see if she can lend us a bit of tea and milk. A cup of Rosie Lee will perk us all up.'

'I'll just comb my hair.'

'Your hair looks fine. Now scat!'

Ellen pulled a face, but did as she was told while Doug sank onto a chair, saying, 'I'm bushed. I'll have a bit of a rest and then give you a hand.'

'There's no need. Once this place has been aired and dusted it'll be fine.'

'If you say so,' he said, looking around the room doubtfully.

Hilda knew it was the first time he'd been inside, and to his eyes it must look awful. Somehow, though, they had to make the best of it.

'As you said, Doug, there's worse off than us and at least we've got a roof over our heads.'

'I suppose so,' he agreed, but Hilda could see that Doug was far from his usual cheery self.

She picked up two cases and heaved them through to their bedroom, knowing that another job would be to air the linen for their beds. Once again there was a musty smell, so she drew back the blackout curtains, opened the window, and stood grimly looking out onto the street for a moment.

'Hello, it's only me.'

It hadn't been long since she'd seen her, but Hilda had missed Mabel. With a smile on her face at last, she hurried back to the living room.

'Hilda, why didn't you write and tell me you were coming? I'd have aired this place for you and got you in a bit of shopping.'

'It all happened so quickly and we'd have got here before a letter.'

'I wish you'd been here on VE day to join in the knees-up. You should have seen the celebrations.'

'They went a bit mad in the village, too, and even old Mrs Jones had a little bit of a dance.'

'Did she? I'd wish I'd seen that.'

'It wasn't a pretty sight,' Doug said. 'She even lifted her skirt showing off her knee-length bloomers. Talk about passion killers.'

Hilda was glad to see that his humour seemed restored, but he still looked drained and there were dark circles under his eyes. She frowned, asking, 'Where's Ellen? I need her to go to the shops.'

'Billy came home a bit early today and she's still chatting to him, but don't worry, shopping can wait till the morning. I've got enough in for you to have dinner with me, but in the meantime here's some tea, milk and a packet of biscuits.'

'Biscuits?' Hilda said, her brow rising.

'Thanks to Harry.'

'He's still up to his old tricks then?'

'Yes, but he's getting a bit worried. With the war more or less over, he said he'll have to find a new line of business. I told him he's jumping the gun; that the men my Jack served with in Burma are still fighting, let alone our troops in other places outside of Europe. Since VE day they seem to have been forgotten.'

'Thanks for writing to tell me about Jack. How's he doing?'

'He's fine, though as I said in my letter, he lost a few intestines. He's applied to go back on the buses, but we're still waiting to hear. It's all women now, drivers and conductors, so we're not sure how things stand.'

'Once their husbands come home, they'll soon pack the jobs in.'

'That's true,' Mabel agreed and then grinned widely. 'It's good to have you back in London. I know it hasn't been long, but I've missed you.'

'What, even our spats?' Hilda asked.

'Yeah, even them.'

'Thanks for the tea. I could do with a cup and so could Doug.'

'Well, if you're making one,' Mabel said as she sat down. 'I'll have a cup too.'

Hilda walked through to the kitchen, another room that would need a good clean, she thought, lifting the blackout blind over the small window and at the same time thinking that it was about time Ellen showed her face again. Mabel had said she was chatting to Billy, and now Hilda worried that her daughter's interest in the boy would be rekindled.

* * *

Ellen was listening to Billy, gazing at his face as he talked about a job he had found locally.

'I'm a van boy for a department store. It ain't a bad job and it's nice to be out and about, but I'd rather be back in Hampshire working with the horses.'

'Will your mum let you go back?' Ellen asked worriedly.

'She might, but my dad's dead against it. I was gonna run off, go back without telling them, but they'd come after me.'

'What a shame,' Ellen said, trying to sound sincere. 'Why is your dad so against it?'

'He says there's no future in being a stable boy. I told him there's no future in being a van boy either, but that just earned me a clip round the ear. I'd forgotten how strict he is. I'm fourteen, out earning a few bob, but he still treats me like a kid.'

'My parents are the same, especially my mum. Sometimes she treats me like a ten-year-old.'

'With you looking like that, she must be blind.'

Ellen flushed, but covered her embarrassment by saying, 'I won't miss working in the dairy.'

'I think you're mad coming back here.'

'It wasn't my idea.'

'I miss the place, the stables.'

'What about Sheila?' Ellen asked, cursing herself for not being able to hold back the thought.

'She was a bit of all right, but what I really miss are the horses. I suppose I could write to Sheila, and I expect you know her address, but what's the point? Mr Dunning won't keep the job open until I'm old enough to leave home without permission, so I doubt I'll ever see her again.'

Ellen held back a sigh of relief. 'No, I don't suppose I will either.'

'Ellen, your mum wants you,' Mabel said as she walked in. 'There's a lot to do and she needs a hand.'

With reluctance, Ellen stood up. She would rather stay and chat to Billy, but still, they were back now, living downstairs, and she was sure to see lots of him. She smiled at the thought, saying, 'See you later, Billy.'

'Yeah, see you,' he said, giving her a little wink.

Ellen's stomach fluttered. Could that little wink have been a sign that he liked her; that he had noticed her at last?

It's funny, Billy thought, but he'd never really noticed Ellen before. She had just been the girl who had come to live downstairs and who had gone to the same school. Like him, she'd been just a gangly kid, and even in Hampshire he'd hardly clocked that she was growing up. Now, though, seeing her again, he realised that she was a bit tasty – thin, but pretty. Not that he was interested.

He had better things to do than to chase girls, and, anyway, he preferred blondes.

He glanced at the clock. He was meeting Harry later, the two of them off to buy a bit of gear. As he'd suspected, fresh eggs were in big demand, and only a few days after coming back to London he'd made a beeline for Harry. He hadn't been keen on the idea at first, but Billy had talked him round and they now had a few suppliers, blokes who kept chickens on allotments around Wimbledon way who were willing to sell them their eggs for a decent price. They wouldn't make a fortune, but Billy was always on the lookout for other opportunities, finding a good mentor in Harry.

'It's nice to have Hilda back,' his mother said, smiling happily. 'I said they could join us for dinner so I'd best get on with it. Percy will be home soon, and it's about time your dad showed his face.'

'Don't do any dinner for me, Mum. I'm off out soon.'

'Where to?'

'I'm just meeting a mate, that's all.'

'Now that we're back in London, I hope you ain't up to mischief again. If you are, your dad will skin you alive.'

'Mum, I ain't a kid.'

'You're still only fourteen.'

'Yeah, but I'll be fifteen in October and surely that's old enough to leave home?'

'Of course it isn't and if you're going to go on about those stables again, forget it.'

Billy hung his head. He felt an affinity to horses, loved them, and felt a surge of determination. No matter what his mum and dad said, one day he'd go to live in the country again. He'd find a job in a stable and whether there was a future in it or not, it was what he wanted to do.

29

Ellen's hopes were dashed. They had been back in London for over six weeks, but she'd seen little of Billy. She was always finding excuses to go up to Mabel's flat, but Billy was rarely in and, if he was, he hardly spoke to her. She hadn't found a job in a flower shop either, and had wanted to go on looking, but with her mother constantly nagging her to find a job, she had reluctantly found work in a local grocer's shop, taking over from a woman who had given up the job when her husband had been demobilised. He was one of the first to come home when the mass demobilisation of British troops had begun two weeks ago, and, though they had victory in Europe, the war wasn't over yet.

Mabel had said lots of women would give up work when their men came home and she was proved to be right, though many of them were doing so reluctantly. Ellen would stand at the counter, listening to their complaints, and the little food on offer was another thing for them to moan about.

It was nearly midday on Sunday morning, the sun shining through the window when Mabel called through the door, 'It's only me.'

Ellen saw her father fold his newspaper, one passed on to him by Mabel's husband, saying as he struggled to stand up, 'I'm going down the pub.'

'Doug, we haven't got the money for pubs,' her mum complained.

'I was only going to have a half.'

'We need food, not beer.'

'Yeah, yeah, all right, there's no need to nag. Is Jack in, Mabel?'

'Yes, love.'

'Right, I'll go and have a chat with him. At least that costs nothing.'

Ellen felt sorry for her dad. He had hoped to find work, but since their return his back had been so painful that he could hardly move. Bent at the waist, he shuffled slowly out as Ellen looked on sadly.

'He looks rough, Hilda.'

'Don't you think I know that?'

'There's no need to snap.'

'I'm sorry, Mabel, it's just that I'm worried sick. With Doug unable to work and our savings all but gone, money is going to be really tight.'

'When is he due to go before the medical board for reassessment?'

'I don't know.'

'Maybe you should push it. When they see how bad he is now, surely they'll grant him a full pension?'

'I hope so, but in the meantime I'm going to have to tell him that I'll have to get a job.'

'I can lend you a few bob.'

'No, Mabel, though thanks for the offer. If I can get a job, we'll be all right.'

'You're not the only one with worries. Billy was out until all hours last night and I don't know what the little sod was up to. If he's gone back to his old ways and his dad finds out, there'll be murder. Sometimes I wonder if I should have left him in Hampshire.'

'If the job's still open, he could go back.'

'Jack won't allow it, though perhaps I should have a go at persuading him to change his mind.'

Ellen stared aghast at Mabel. No, no, that was the last thing she wanted. If Billy went back to Hampshire, she might never see him again.

When Mabel left to go back upstairs, Hilda sat deep in thought. She dreaded putting her idea to Doug, but if she could find a decent-paying job it would solve their financial problems. Anyway, she decided, it was his fault that they'd been forced to this. He should have told her before – should have said that their lovemaking had made his back worse. Instead he had waited until it was too late and the damage irreparable. Hilda knew she was often short-tempered now, taking her worry out on both Doug and Ellen, but when she thought about their future, it looked so bleak.

'Mum, I'm going to do a bit of work in the garden,' said Ellen.

'If you ask me, it's a waste of time.'

'I've given up on vegetables, but while we were away someone at the factory gave Percy some flower seeds. He sowed them, but didn't thin them out and they won't survive unless some are pulled up. He's a bit heavy-handed so I said I'd show him how to do it.'

Alone now, Hilda looked around the room. There was housework to do, but the old second-hand furniture hardly looked any better, no matter what she did. She'd once hoped to replace it, to re-decorate, but that was impossible now, with even the price of a pot of paint out of reach.

She heard voices, recognising Doug's, and soon after he shuffled in.

'Ellen's in the garden.'

'I know that, Doug,' she said shortly.

'Still stroppy, I see.'

Hilda felt a flare of anger, but took a deep breath. She needed to keep calm, and now said, 'Doug, we can't go on like this. Soon we won't be able to pay the rent, and if we don't want to find ourselves chucked out on the street, I'm going to have to find a job.'

'I don't want my wife working.'

'Talk sense. We haven't any choice.'

'I might get a full pension when I go before the board again.'

'Yes, but that could be months away.'

'We'll just have to manage until then.'

It was no good, she had tried to stay calm, but now Hilda's temper flamed again and she reared to her feet, hands on hips as she yelled, 'Manage on what? The few quid you get barely pays the rent and with our savings nearly gone, it leaves nothing for food.'

'My back might ease and then *I'll* find a job, not you.'

'Might! We can't live on might! Like it or not, there's only one thing for it. Until we find out one way or the other if you're going to get a full pension, I'm going to get a job!'

And on that note Hilda marched out of the room, slamming the door behind her.

Unaware that her parents were rowing, Ellen walked in Mabel's back door.

'Percy, if you're ready, I'll show you how to thin out the seedlings.'

'Yeah, great,' he said eagerly.

'I never thought you'd take to gardening, son.'

'I enjoy it, Dad.'

'It's something he's got in common with Ellen,' Mabel told him. 'She was always in the garden in Hampshire and you should have seen the smashing vegetables she grew.'

'There's not much chance of that here,' Ellen said ruefully. 'The soil's no good, but it might improve if we had a decent bit of fertiliser.'

'Yeah, like horse manure,' Billy said.

Ellen was unable to take her eyes off Billy and fumbled for something to say.

'There isn't much chance of getting horse manure around here.'

'You could always follow behind the brewery dray horses and wait for them to dump a nice pile of shit.'

'Billy!'

'Sorry, Dad.'

'I'm not having you using language like that in front of your mother, or Ellen. You were out late last night. Where were you?'

'Just knocking about, you know, here and there.'

'Who with?'

'A mate and we met a couple of girls.'

'You lying little toad! Girls, my foot. When I came out of the pub I saw you with Harry.'

'That's right, as I said, he's a mate.'

'I won't have you mixing with the likes of him,' Mabel cried.

'I don't know why. We weren't up to anything illegal, and, anyway, Harry's a laugh.'

'A laugh! He's a bleedin' tea leaf.'

'He's not, Mum. He's more a sort of entrepreneur.'

'Entrepreneur, blimey, Billy, where did you get that word from?' Percy asked.

'It's what Harry calls himself and I reckon I can learn a lot from him.'

'That's it!' Mabel yelled. 'I've had enough! Jack, before he gets up to Gawd knows what, I reckon he should go back to Hampshire.'

Ellen's stomach lurched, waiting for Jack's reply.

'Can't you see that's just what he's after? Well, it ain't going to work, son, so you're wasting your time.'

'I don't know what you mean, Dad.'

'The innocent face doesn't wash with me, Billy. You think worrying the life out of your mother is a way to make me give in, but you can think again. You're not helping your case, you're hindering it. All you're doing is showing that you can't be trusted, and until I think you can be, I'm not letting you out of my sight.'

'I didn't mean to worry Mum, honest. It's just that I miss Hampshire, the horses, and I want to go back.'

'Jack, at least let's talk about it,' Mabel urged.

'My mind's made up and it'll be a waste of time.'

Ellen felt a touch on her arm, Percy saying,

'Come on, let's go and get those seedlings sorted out.'

'Yes, go on, Ellen, you don't want to hear all this,' Mabel urged.

Ellen reluctantly followed Percy from the room, hoping Mabel wouldn't be able to persuade her husband to change his mind.

Percy went down the back stairs, thinking that with shortages for manufacturing during the war and so many railings taken to be melted down, it was a wonder the staircase, along with the rest in the street, had remained.

He looked down at the emerging seedlings and saw how crammed in they were. It was just as well Ellen was going to show him how to thin them out or he'd probably have killed the lot. She was a nice girl and it was obvious that she had a huge crush on Billy. Not that his brother had noticed and that was just as well. Billy was no good, causing his mother nothing but worry, and if his dad could be persuaded to let him go back to the stables, Percy would be glad to see the back of him.

'I reckon my mum will talk my dad round and he'll let Billy go back to Hampshire.'

'What! No!'

'It's the best place for him.'

Ellen knelt on the ground, her neck bent and face hidden as she said, 'We'll need to water them first to avoid too much root damage. It would've been better if you'd started the seeds off in trays and then thinned them out, but we should be able to get out the weak-looking ones, leaving room for the others to grow.'

'I'll ask your mum if I can fill a bucket with water.'

Ellen nodded and then stood up, her head still down, but Percy saw a tear running down her cheek and asked softly, 'Are you all right?'

'Oh, Percy, I don't want Billy to go back to Hampshire.'

She looked so unhappy, so vulnerable, and, without thinking, Percy wrapped his arms around her.

'Listen, if Billy stays here and carries on the way he is, he could end up in jail.'

It didn't seem to console Ellen, her head on his chest as she cried. It was the first time Percy had held a girl in his arms, and, feeling her small breasts against him, he felt something happen that had him flushing with embarrassment. Bloody hell, what if Ellen felt it? Abruptly he pushed her away, saying gruffly, 'I'll get that water.'

Thankfully Ellen didn't follow him as he walked into Hilda's kitchen, pausing as he fought to pull himself together, then calling, 'Hilda, can I fill this bucket with water?'

It was Doug who answered, 'Help yourself.'

Percy held the pail under the tap. He'd never thought of Ellen in that way before, seeing her as just a kid, but now knew he'd never be able to look at her in the same light again. How old was she? Yes, fourteen, and it appalled Percy that he now actually fancied someone so young. Yet she would be fifteen soon, in November, and in reality he was only a year older. She was still too young though – too young to even think about for now – but there would come a time when Ellen would be old enough for him to ask her out.

Ellen stayed where she was. If her mother saw her in tears, she'd want to know what was wrong, and Ellen couldn't face her questions. She knew what her mum would say – that this was just a childish crush – but it wasn't. It wasn't! She liked Billy, really liked him, and had hoped that, with Sheila out of the picture, he'd notice her. All right, so far it hadn't happened, but given time, it might.

If Billy went back to Hampshire, Sheila would be there waiting with open arms and Ellen couldn't bear the thought of that. She sniffed, running her forefinger under her nose. She wanted to be the one who was held in Billy's arms, wanted him to kiss *her* – not Sheila.

Percy was gone only a short while, returning with a bucket of water.

'Are you feeling better now?' he asked gruffly, as he began to pour water over the plants.

Ellen nodded, sniffed, and then seeing what he was doing, she said quickly, 'No, don't do it like that or you'll flatten them. Just trickle it.'

'Right,' he said.

Ellen knew they needed a watering can, but they had little in the way of gardening equipment. She wanted to get on with it, to bury her worries by concentrating on the task in hand. Working on her knees with the plants would soothe her raging thoughts, but the water would have to soak in first and that would take a while.

She absentmindedly watched Percy as he now carefully trickled the water, her mind on Billy. His dad had been adamant, and maybe he'd still insist that Billy stayed in London . . . that thought brought her a glimmer of hope.

Later that day, Mabel came downstairs, saying as she walked in, 'I'm sorry about the racket, but it's all sorted now.'

Ellen looked up from the book she was reading as her mother asked, 'What racket?'

'I can't believe you didn't hear us. We've been rowing for hours, but at last Jack's given in. If the job's still open, Billy's going back to Hampshire.'

Ellen's throat constricting, she croaked, 'When?'

'I'll have to write to the head groom, Mr Dunning,

first. Even if the job's still going, there'll be accommodation to sort out. He once said he could find something for Billy.'

'I envy the lad. It was nice in Hampshire.'

'It was, Doug,' agreed Mabel, 'and Billy's so keen to go back that he isn't worried about having anywhere to stay. He said he'd be happy to kip in the stables, but I'm not standing for that. He'll be on tenterhooks now until we get a reply.'

'I don't think he's got anything to worry about. From what I saw, Mr Dunning seemed to think a lot of Billy and I should think he'll welcome him back.'

Ellen wanted to deny her dad's words, her only hope now that he was wrong: that the job had been filled and Billy would have to stay in London.

'If he can't fit him in, Billy's talking about trying other stables,' Mabel said. 'He doesn't care where as long as he can work with horses again.'

It was no good; Ellen couldn't sit there any longer.

'I . . . I'm just going to my room for a minute.'

She saw her mother's questioning look, but ignored it and hurried to her bedroom where she flung herself onto the bed. Ellen's eyes closed, the image of Billy in her mind, his handsome face, dark hair, cheeky grin and green eyes that sparked with mischief. The thought of never seeing him again was unbearable, and Ellen clutched her pillow, fearing that her dream of being held in Billy's arms was over.

30

The letter had come ten days later, and Billy was now so excited about going back to Hampshire that he hardly spared Ellen a glance. She'd been mad to hope that he'd noticed her at last, and her unhappiness sat like a hard knot in her stomach.

She still thought about the old woman and the runes, about the sign that would bring her peace, and she went to the Baptist church again, desperately hoping to find it there. It wasn't the same pastor, but she enjoyed the service, the singing, the warmth of the atmosphere, and remained to talk to a few people when it was over.

'I seem to know your face,' an older woman said. 'I know it's been some time but didn't you used to come here with Mrs Price and her daughter?'

'Yes, that's right.'

'So many people have been scattered, but it's lovely to see you again.'

'I wasn't sure if I should come here again.'

'Why not?' she asked, drawing Ellen to one side. 'What's troubling you, my dear?'

'I was told by an old woman who used rune stones that I would see a sign, but I haven't. I was hoping to find it here. Do you think it's here?'

'This is God's house, not the home of the devil. It's wrong to use rune stones and to consult anyone who casts them.'

'My mother didn't consult anyone, but a woman once approached her and said she'd had a vision. In it she saw that my father hadn't gone down with his ship. He was alive and coming home. She was right too.'

'It is still a form of fortune telling, misguided and against God's teachings.'

'My mother was distressed and the woman was trying to comfort her. Surely that was the Christian thing to do?'

'If she *was* a Christian and the vision came from God, then yes. Was she a Christian?'

'I don't know.'

'Well, my dear, unless we are sure, we shouldn't listen. The devil is wily and comes in many guises to whisper in our ears.'

Ellen couldn't believe the woman at the underground station had been the devil in disguise. 'Thank you for talking to me,' she said, and before the lady could protest Ellen walked off and out of the door. She was still confused and felt it was unfair that the woman, Christian or not, should be condemned just for trying to help her mother.

Going to church hadn't helped. If anything it had turned her away from religion again.

Gradually time passed, and though Ellen still wished Billy hadn't gone back to Hampshire, things were changing around her. To start with, her mother had found a job, and then, in August, came the long-awaited news that the war was officially over.

Once again, as on VE day, there was dancing in the streets, Londoners out in force, but even as Ellen joined in she hadn't been able to help wondering how it was being celebrated in Hampshire. Was Billy dancing with Sheila? Were they a couple now?

Lucy and her family didn't come back to London. Instead a new family moved in next door. They had two very noisy young children who played with a ball in the garden, and when it flew over the wall it wreaked havoc on the flowers that had survived the thinning out. Those still in bloom managed to cheer Ellen up as she regularly dead-headed them, the marigolds giving the best display, but as it was now September the aquilegia was straggly.

Working in the garden at least gave Ellen a chance to get away from the awful atmosphere indoors. Her dad was depressed and morose now that her mother had started full-time work. Ellen knew he was in constant pain and her heart went out to him, but he was no longer the father she knew, one who loved to laugh and joke; yet, as he had once been so active, it was no wonder he was moody.

Her mother now worked in a shop near to Ellen's and they were walking home together one evening when Ellen was snapped out of her reverie by a tug on her arm.

'Ellen, get a move on. When we get home I've got dinner to cook and then a stack of ironing to do.'

'I'll do the ironing,' Ellen offered as she picked up her pace.

'You're a good girl, but it's about time you made some friends. You should be with girls of your own age instead of stuck indoors with us every evening.'

'The only women who come into the shop are housewives and all they do is moan about the continued shortage of food. I wish I'd found a job in a flower shop.'

'What about your old school friends?'

'I haven't seen any of them for ages. Like Lucy, they've probably moved away and haven't come back.'

'Maybe you should go to that Baptist church again. You might meet some nice girls there.'

'I did go, I tried, but no, Mum, it isn't for me.'

'Watcha,' a voice said.

Ellen looked around, smiling when she saw Percy. He still worked in the same factory and he too was on his way home.

'Hello, Percy.'

'How's work?' Hilda said. 'I suppose the production line has changed now the war's over.'

'Yes, it has. To be honest, I'd love a job working outdoors.'

'I thought you liked it in the factory,' said Hilda, surprised.

'I did at first. I felt I was doing something for the war effort, but it's different now.'

'I feel the same. I hate being cooped up in the grocery shop all day.'

'Ellen, it isn't a lot of fun in the ironmonger's and I hate the stink of paraffin, but you don't hear me complaining all the time.'

With Percy walking along beside them it was the ideal opportunity to ask and Ellen changed the subject. 'Has your mum heard from Billy again?'

'She got a letter this morning.'

'What did he have to say?'

'You know Billy, it was mostly about horses.'

'Did . . . did he mention Sheila? She was my friend when we lived there.'

'No, I don't think so, but I only gave the letter a quick scan before I left for work.'

'I was just telling Ellen that she should make new friends,' said Hilda. 'Any ideas, Percy?'

'Sorry, I don't know any girls. I suppose she could come to the pictures with me tonight. I'm going to see Michael Redgrave and John Mills in *The Way to the Stars*.'

'What's it about?' Ellen asked.

'Life on a bomber base during the Battle of Britain.'

'No, thanks, the war's over and I don't want to be reminded of it.'

'I suppose we could go to the Odeon. They're showing an Old Mother Riley film.'

'No, Percy, I don't think either film is suitable for a fourteen-year-old.'

From the expression on her mother's face, Ellen knew it was pointless to argue, and, anyway, she really didn't fancy either film.

'Maybe some other time,' Percy offered.

'We'll see,' her mother said darkly and when they arrived home she ushered Ellen indoors, closing the door firmly behind them. 'I think Percy has got his eye on you, but you're still too young to be going out with boys.'

'Of course he hasn't,' Ellen protested, but then the thought was taken from her mind as they walked into the living room to see they had a visitor.

'Gertie,' she cried, delighted to see her.

* * *

When Gertie had first arrived she couldn't believe the change she saw in Doug. He looked worn down, his back bent with pain, and older than his years. Now she was seeing a change in Ellen too, but a pleasant one, and said, 'Hello, my dear, and look at you, all grown up now.'

'Hello, Gertie,' Hilda said as she flopped onto a chair. 'It's nice to see you, but I wouldn't call Ellen grown up. She isn't even fifteen yet.'

'You look tired,' Gertie said and meant it. Hilda looked awful, with dark rings around her eyes.

'I must admit me feet are throbbing, but as I've been on them all day, it isn't surprising.'

'Doug told me that you're working now.'

'Yeah, in a shop. How long have you been here, Gertie?'

'I only arrived about ten minutes ago.'

'Ellen, I can see your father hasn't offered Gertie anything, so make a pot of tea.'

'I did offer,' Doug protested.

'Yes, he did,' nodded Gertie. 'But knowing you'd be home soon I said I'd wait.'

'I'll do it,' Doug said. 'You two have been at work all day and making tea is all I'm fit for now.'

Gertie watched sadly as he shuffled to the kitchen.

'Hilda, it's awful to see him like this. Can't anything be done?'

'No, the damage is irreparable, but some days are better than others.'

'He was so active and must hate it, along with the fact that you have to be the breadwinner now.'

'I'm not too happy about it either,' Hilda said bitterly. 'He went before the board again, and even in that state they didn't increase his pension.'

'What? But that's dreadful! He should appeal.'

'There's no point. Knowing Doug he didn't make a fuss so it's down to him. He prefers to think he'll improve and will be able to work again.'

'Is that likely to happen?'

'I don't know, and even if it does it'd have to be some sort of light job where he can sit all day. Anyway, enough about us,' Hilda said dismissively. 'I haven't seen you for ages so tell me what you've been up to since you've left the ATS.'

'I haven't been doing anything really. I'm in a rented house in Surrey and just waiting for the sale of my father's house to go through.'

'What? You've sold it already?'

'Yes, and thank goodness for that. I'm just here for a few days to sign papers and finalise things.'

'What will you do after that?'

'I'm not sure yet, but probably buy a place of my own.'

'Gertie, surely you're not going to bury yourself on a smallholding again?'

'No, and, anyway, I don't think Maureen would be keen on the idea.'

Hilda's eyebrows lifted. 'Maureen?'

Gertie glanced at Ellen, then said, 'Yes, my *friend*.'

'Are you happy?'

'I'm ecstatic.'

'Ellen, give me a hand to carry these cups through,' Doug called.

'I'm glad you've met someone,' Hilda said as soon as her daughter was out of earshot. 'I'm pleased for you.'

'Thanks, Hilda. Now tell me, I didn't get a chance to visit you while you were in Veronica's cottage, so how did you find it living there?'

'I loved it, and though you may not believe it, I loved Hampshire too.'

'What, a London girl preferring life in the country? You hated it in Somerset.'

'Your place was too isolated, but the cottage was nice and in a small village. I didn't want to come back to London, and as usual it's brought me nothing but bad luck.'

'What do you mean? What bad luck?'

'You've seen Doug. We came back because he insisted he'd be able to find a job here, but soon after his back got worse. I live in dread of what's going to happen next.'

'Hilda, don't be silly. You can't blame a location for bad luck.'

'Maybe, but we're stuck here now so I'll just have to make the best of it.'

'The best of what?' Ellen asked as she came in, a cup of tea in each hand.

'This place,' Hilda told her. 'Now then, Gertie, I'm not sure what I can rustle up, but you're welcome to stay for dinner.'

'Thanks for the offer, but once I've had this tea I must be off.'

'Don't go yet,' Ellen protested. 'We haven't seen you for ages.'

'I know, but I'm in London for a few more days and I'll come to see you again.'

'Are you staying in your father's house?' Hilda asked.

'No, I can't stand the place. I'm in a small hotel.'

'You can stay here if you like,' Doug said as he held on to the arm of his chair before carefully sitting down. 'It's thanks to you that Hilda and Ellen were safe in Hampshire. You'll always be welcome here, Gertie, but I'm afraid there's only the sofa. It's old, but it's comfortable.'

Gertie was touched. She knew how Doug felt, his suspicions about her – ones that, though he didn't know it, had been accurate enough. Of course, he had nothing to worry about now. She was happy with Maureen, and her feelings for Hilda had at last died. Gertie found she was now seeing Doug in a new light and realised her dislike of him had been down to jealousy. He was a good man, a good husband and father who had fought for his country only to end up on the scrapheap.

'Thanks, Doug, it's kind of you, but Maureen is staying in the hotel too.'

'Maureen?'

'A *friend* of mine.'

He smiled faintly. 'Yeah, right, I get it.'

'When the sale of the house is completed, will you both be staying in London?' Hilda asked.

'I'm not sure where we'll be living yet, but it won't be London. Like me, Maureen prefers the country.'

'Me too,' Doug said wistfully.

Gertie swallowed her tea. 'I'd best be off, but maybe, if you don't mind, I'll bring Maureen to meet you next time.'

'Yes, we'd like that, wouldn't we, Doug?'

'It's fine with me.'

They said their goodbyes, Gertie thoughtful as she left. It had been awful to see them living like that: Doug in pain, Hilda looking worn down, and Ellen hating her job in a shop. She had to do something for them, to ease their burden, and as she was rather well off now it would be simple to write them a cheque. Yet, even as this thought crossed her mind, Gertie knew it wouldn't work. However needy Doug and Hilda might be, they weren't the sort of people who'd accept a handout.

The problem was still on her mind as Gertie

neared the small hotel in Chelsea, and at last an inkling of an idea began to form. The war was over and it was time to move forward – time to start another new chapter in her life. If Doug, Hilda and Ellen could be a part of it, nothing would give her greater pleasure.

So far she and Maureen had idled around doing nothing, but the inactivity was already driving Gertie mad. She needed to do something, to find a new challenge, and the more she thought about it, the surer she was that this plan could work.

31

Only a few days later, on Sunday morning, Gertie called again. Hilda opened the door to see a young woman behind her, a pretty, petite blonde who was the antithesis of Gertie. She looked a little nervous so, smiling, Hilda said, 'It's lovely to see you again, and your friend too. Come on in.'

'Hilda, this is Maureen.'

'Yes, I guessed that, and it's nice to meet you.'

'Hello,' Maureen said shyly.

'Doug, look who's here,' Hilda said as she led them into the living room.

Once again Maureen looked shy as she returned Doug's greeting, her hand clinging to Gertie's. Ellen looked puzzled so Hilda swiftly said, 'Sit down, the pair of you', then kicked herself for using that word. Yet it was true, they were a pair – but that was something she'd rather not explain to Ellen.

'I don't want to get told off again, so this time I'll make a pot of tea straightaway.'

'I'll do it, Dad,' Ellen offered.

'No, it's all right. It won't kill me.'

'You look a little better, Doug.'

'I'm having a good day, Gertie,' he said, back a little straighter as he left the room.

'Has everything been finalised with your father's house now?' Hilda asked.

Gertie pulled a face. 'No, the buyer dropped out and it all fell through. It's going back on the market on Monday.'

'What will you do now?'

'There's nothing we can do until I get another offer.'

'We could still make plans for the business,' said Maureen. 'You know, cost it all out and see if it'd be profitable.'

Hilda's brows shot up. Gertie had only mentioned buying a house.

'What sort of business?'

'It's just an idea really, and I'm not even sure it would work. Maureen, you shouldn't have said anything.'

'But . . . but I thought . . .'

'What's all this about a business?' Doug said as he came back into the room. 'I couldn't help overhearing.'

'All right, I'll tell you,' said Gertie. 'I've seen in Surrey, and elsewhere, that nearly all the gardens have been dug up to grow vegetables.'

'I had a go,' Ellen said, 'but the soil in our garden is useless. Percy planted some flower seeds though and we've had a nice display.'

'Percy? Who's Percy?'

'He's Mabel's son and he's as daft about gardening as Ellen,' explained Hilda. 'Now carry on telling us about this idea of yours.'

'Well, now . . .'

'Sorry to interrupt,' Percy said, as if hearing his name had conjured him up, 'but is it all right if I fill a bucket with water? The garden needs watering.'

'Talk of the devil,' Hilda said ruefully. 'Gertie, this is Percy.'

'Hello there. I hear you like gardening.'

'I love it, not that we've got much of one.'

'Where do you work, Percy?'

'In an engineering factory, but I'd rather work outdoors.'

'Gertie used to have a smallholding and you'd have loved it,' Ellen told him.

'Cor, did you?' he said, sitting down and leaning forward eagerly. 'What did you grow?'

'Mostly fruit and vegetables.'

'Nice, but I like flowers.'

'Gertie, are you going to tell us about this idea of yours or not?' Hilda asked impatiently.

'Percy mentioning flowers leads me into it nicely,' she said. 'You see, that's my idea. We've had so many years of austerity and I think that one day, in the not-too-distant future, people will want a bit of colour in their lives again. What I want to do is to open a plant nursery, to grow flowers, shrubs, trees, and offer them for sale.'

There was silence for a moment, but then Ellen exclaimed, 'I think that's a marvellous idea. I suppose you'll be planting seedlings and, when they're transplanted and a decent size, you'll sell them.'

'Well, that's more or less it.'

'I don't see how it'd work,' Hilda said. 'Why would people buy plants from you? Surely they'd grow their own?'

'A lot of flowers are easy to grow from seed, simple things like marigolds and other cottage garden plants, but others are difficult. There are flowering shrubs, specimen shrubs, rose species, let alone plants that need to be started off under glass. I'd like to specialise in these and I think there'd be a demand.'

'If you ask me, we need food, not flowers.'

'We do now, but I'm talking about what people may want in the future.'

'We grew marigolds, didn't we, Ellen?'

'Yes, Percy, you did,' Hilda said answering for her daughter, 'and didn't you say they need watering?'

'Yeah, right,' he said, taking the hint. 'I'll get on with it.'

'Do that,' Hilda snapped.

Unperturbed, Percy turned to Gertie.

'It was nice to meet you, and good luck with the nursery. If . . . if you're thinking of taking anyone on, I'd love a job.'

'I'm afraid it's nowhere near that stage yet, but if I find I need staff I'll bear you in mind.'

'Really?'

'Yes, really.'

Percy smiled with delight and soon they heard the sound of running water from the kitchen.

'He seems a nice lad,' Gertie said as they heard the back door close.

'Yes, he is,' Doug agreed, 'and you were a bit sharp with him, Hilda.'

'I don't like the way he looks at Ellen. I think he's got his eye on her.'

'She could do worse.'

'Doug,' Hilda said, appalled. 'She's only fourteen.'

'Coming up fifteen.'

'That's still too young.'

'You weren't much older when we first met.'

'I was *seventeen*!'

'Mum, there's no need to argue over this,' Ellen placated. 'I'm not interested in Percy.'

'I should think not.'

Ellen smiled at Gertie. 'It was nice of you to say you'd think about offering him a job though, and I wouldn't mind one too.'

'Goodness, slow down. As I said it's only an idea so far and it might not go any further than that.'

'But, Gertie, I thought . . .' said Maureen.

'That's enough,' Gertie snapped, but, as Maureen then looked tearful, she threw an arm around her. 'Now then, don't get upset. I didn't mean to snap. It's just that I don't want to jump the gun.'

There was something going on, Hilda was sure of it, but Gertie obviously didn't want Maureen to talk about it. Ellen was watching them, looking puzzled again, so to divert her attention, Hilda said: 'Ellen, even if Gertie gets this place up and running you wouldn't be able to work there. It won't be in London.'

'You're right,' Gertie said, removing her arm from around Maureen, 'and, anyway, until I get another buyer for my father's house, my idea will have to be put on the backburner. I have money he left me, and some from the smallholding, but as my plans are long term, it won't be enough.'

'That's a shame,' Doug said. 'It sounds like a good idea and it could work, though I reckon you'd have to offer more than just plants to make a decent profit.'

'I've looked at the figures and know it'll take time to establish and to build up a good supply of plant stock, so any ideas would be welcome, Doug.'

Doug looked thoughtful as he ran a hand around his chin. 'How about selling things like garden tools?'

'What a marvellous idea,' Gertie said.

'Yes, and watering cans, hose pipes, cane

supports, fertiliser,' Ellen suggested eagerly. 'Oh, there are loads of things, even gardening books.'

'Goodness, what a couple of entrepreneurs,' said Gertie. 'Thank you and it's certainly something I'll consider.'

'Do you want another cup of tea?' Hilda asked.

'No, thanks, and we really must go now. We're going back to Surrey and with no idea how long it'll take to find another buyer for my father's house, it could be some time before we're back in London.'

Hilda showed Gertie and Maureen out, chatting for a few minutes on the doorstep before waving goodbye, but when she returned to the living room it was to stand horrified, unable to believe her ears.

'Yeah, well, I suppose you're old enough to know now,' Doug was saying. 'You see, Gertie is different, and she fancies women instead of men.'

'Doug!' Hilda yelled. 'Shut up!'

'It's all right, Mum,' said Ellen. 'I thought there was something funny about Gertie and Maureen and I'm glad Dad told me.'

Hilda glared at Doug, fuming. 'Well, I'm not!'

'Ellen saw them holding hands, saw Gertie's affection for Maureen, and it confused her. What was I supposed to do? Lie to her?' Doug snapped.

'I'm glad you told me the truth, Dad, but I still

don't understand. I mean, what is Gertie? Is she some sort of half-woman, half-man?'

'It's a bit difficult to explain. Gertie's got the body of a woman, but . . . well, I suppose, the feelings of a man.'

'But if she's a woman, why can't she behave like a woman? It seemed funny, odd to see her cuddling Maureen, and now I know why it . . . it makes me feel uncomfortable. I mean, she cuddles me too.'

'That isn't the same,' Hilda snapped. 'Gertie would never look at you in that way.'

'I don't know, Mum. I . . . I'm not sure how I feel about her now.'

'Now you listen to me, my girl. Any affection Gertie has shown is because she sees us as her family, me as a sister and you as her niece.'

'I felt the same way about her, but I don't think I can now.'

'Gertie is still the same person and just because you know about her sexual preferences now, it shouldn't change the way you feel about her. Oh, what am I saying, this is madness! You're too young to understand, too young to be hearing things like this!'

Ellen jumped to her feet and, before Hilda could stop her, she ran outside. Still fuming, Hilda turned on Doug.

'See what you've done!'

'All right, I'm sorry. You're right. I should have kept me mouth shut.'

'It's a bit late for that now! It's hard enough for adults to accept people like Gertie, yet you expect a fourteen-year-old to understand! You must be out of your tiny mind!'

Unaware of the row going on between Hilda and Doug as they made their way home, Maureen said, 'You were right, Gertie. They did accept us.'

'It's a shame that there aren't more people around like Hilda and Doug.'

'We have to be so careful, and it's a wonder nobody found out about us when we were in the ATS.'

'It's more of a wonder that we found each other and even got together. Let's face it, you did play hard to get.'

'I know, Gertie, but to be honest I was nervous. I hated the way I felt, tried to fight it, but every time I saw you it became more and more impossible.'

'Is that why you went out with a couple of the men?'

'Yes, but as I've told you before, I'd been dating men since I was sixteen. It never worked. I just couldn't feel anything for them, hated their kisses, and gained a reputation as being frigid.'

'It still worries me that I'm the first woman you've been with. You won't leave me, will you?'

'Gertie, you know how I feel about you and there'll never be anyone else.'

'What about your family? You must miss them.'

'How many times have I got to tell you? I went to boarding school, forced to stay there during the holidays while my parents travelled. It meant we were never that close and, since meeting you, for the first time in my life I feel truly happy.'

'I am too, very happy – well, except for seeing the dire straits Hilda and Doug are in. I wish I could just write them a cheque, but they'd never accept it.'

'When are you going to tell them?'

'It could be some time before the agents find another buyer for my father's house, and even then we've got to search for the perfect place. I don't want to raise their hopes too soon, but fingers crossed it doesn't take too long.'

'You think a lot of them, don't you?'

'Yes, they're like my family and one day I hope you see them as your family too.'

Maureen nodded, but seeing them as family or not, there was only so much she'd agree to and one part of Gertie's plan had put her back up. She'd bide her time for now – wait until Gertie had the money to go ahead with her plans – then she'd put her foot down.

32

Ellen was chuffed. She had made friends with a girl who lived at the end of the street, and, though Janet was older at seventeen, they got on really well. The only fly in the ointment was that Janet had a lot more freedom than her and went dancing every Saturday night with some of her other mates.

Still, Ellen thought, at least she got out of the house a few evenings a week, if only to sit in Janet's. The atmosphere in her own home was so awful now that she was glad to escape. Her parents bickered constantly, her mother snappy and her father nothing like the laughing and playful man he'd once been.

'Mum, I'm going along to Janet's house.'

'I'm not sure I want you seeing that girl. Her mother's nothing but a tart.'

'You can't blame Janet for that.'

'Maybe not, but the apple doesn't fall far from the tree.'

'Janet's training to be a hairdresser, and she hates it that her mother drinks. When she's fully qualified and can afford it, she's going to leave home.'

'What happened to her father?'

'Janet said he walked out when she was four and she hasn't seen him since.'

'Hilda, if you ask me it sounds like the girl's had a rotten time of it,' said Doug. 'Go on, Ellen, see your friend, but we want you home by nine thirty.'

'Can't I stay out till ten?'

'You heard your father. Nine thirty and no later.'

Ellen knew that if her mum found out that Janet was going to show her how to put make-up on, she'd go potty. It was October and she'd be fifteen next month, but her mum still treated her like a kid and had refused to talk about Gertie again. Ellen still didn't understand, and now every time she thought about Gertie and Maureen, about them kissing each other like her mum and dad kissed, she felt sort of sick.

Now that she knew Janet better, Ellen had decided to talk to her about it. Janet was different, worldly somehow, and a complete contrast to Lucy. Somehow Ellen felt that religion wasn't a subject that would interest her, but maybe they could talk about the runes too, and that woman who'd had the vision.

302

Janet greeted her with a smile. 'Mum's out so we've got the place to ourselves. She'll probably roll home drunk as usual.'

Janet's mum was a brassy, loud-mouthed blonde, so Ellen was relieved that she wasn't in. They settled in the kitchen and as Janet got out her make-up Ellen asked, 'Do you know anything about rune stones and fortune tellers?'

'Not really, but my mum once went to a woman who read tarot cards.'

'What did she tell her?'

'She wasn't told much, nothing concrete, and said it was a waste of money. Booze is more important to my mum so she only went the once. Live for the day, that's what I say, and I don't see the point of worrying about the future.'

It was obviously a closed subject and Ellen hid her disappointment, saying, 'I'm looking forward to learning how to put make-up on.'

'Once you get the hang of it, it's a doddle. I'll show you how I apply mine first, and then you can have a go at copying me.'

Ellen watched, amazed. All her mother had ever done was to apply a bit of powder and lipstick, though she didn't even do that nowadays, whereas Janet was applying a stick-like, thick foundation that made the whole business look a lot more complicated. She wasn't sure she liked the effect and thought Janet looked better without it, but, not wanting to offend her new friend, she said, 'I didn't know you used that stuff.'

'Pan-stick. Yeah, well, I don't during the day, but if I'm going out in the evening, say to a dance, I use it then because it covers up me spots. You're lucky, you've got lovely skin and I don't think you'll need it. We'll just concentrate on your eyes, lips – and how did you get your nails in that state?'

'Gardening. I've been clearing the flowers and digging over the soil.'

'When did you get interested in gardening of all things?'

'During the Blitz my mum took me to live with her friend, Gertie, on her smallholding in Somerset. I learned a lot from her and she was really good to me. I . . . I liked her a lot, but now . . . now that I know what she's like . . .' Ellen trailed off.

'What do you mean?'

Ellen hesitated. She wanted to confide in Janet, ask her opinion and now, finally, plucked up the courage. 'A short while ago, I found out that Gertie . . . well . . . she doesn't like men. She . . . she prefers women.'

'Oh, she's a lesbian.'

'Is that what women like her are called?'

'Don't you know anything? There's men the same, you know, those who prefer their own kind.'

'What!'

'They're called queers, homosexuals.'

'I . . . I didn't know. How did you find out about them?'

'With a mother like mine there ain't much I don't know. She's talked to me like I'm an adult since I was a kid.'

'My mum has never told me anything and I had to find out about the facts of life from a friend. It was my dad who told me about Gertie, and . . . and it makes me feel a bit sick.'

'Has she done anything to hurt you?'

'No, I told you, she's been very good to me, and to my mother.'

'So what's all the fuss about? Each to their own, that's what I say. There's worse around than her and, believe me, I should know.'

'Worse. What do you mean?'

'Grow up, Ellen. What about rapists, murderers, mothers who neglect their kids and pigs who abuse them?' Janet said angrily. 'Gertie and her type aren't hurting anyone, aren't abusing them, unlike . . . unlike one of my so-called uncles.'

'Your uncle? Why, what did he do?'

'I was ten, just a kid, and I'd had a succession of uncles when one of them – my mum's latest – got into my bed one night.'

'At that age, I used to climb in with my mum and dad for a cuddle.'

'Jesus!' Janet exclaimed. 'It wasn't like that.

Bloody hell, do I have to spell it out? He didn't climb in for a cuddle, he . . . he raped me.'

'Oh, Janet, no!'

'Oh, Ellen, yes . . . and from that night on, I never felt like a kid again.'

'What did your mum do when she found out?'

'I didn't tell her. He said he'd come back and kill us if I opened me mouth.'

Ellen had hated thinking about Gertie, but it paled in comparison to this. She had wanted to be treated like a grown up, had wanted to learn about life, but not this . . . not about sick men who raped children.

'Does . . . does your mum know about it now?'

'Yeah, but I sort of sunk into myself at first. After that, when I was around eleven, I became an impossible kid, wild and out of control. Most of the time my mum was too pissed to notice, but one day she brought another bloke back to the house, drunk like her, and when he leered at me, I lost it. I went for him, grabbed a knife . . .'

'Oh, Janet . . .'

Janet's laugh was derisive. 'My mum soon sobered up then. She managed to stop me, and when the geezer left I told her why I did it . . . what had happened when I was ten.'

'What did she say?'

'She was shocked, but other than never bringing blokes back to the house again, nothing much has changed. She's still a piss artist, an alcoholic, and I'll tell you something, Ellen. I hate booze and as long as I live I'll never touch a drop of the stuff.'

'I . . . don't know what to say.'

'I've shocked you. I don't usually talk about it and you'd better keep what I've told you to yourself . . . or else,' Janet warned.

'I won't say a word to anyone, honestly I won't.'

'You'd better not. As I said, I don't usually talk about it, but you got me back up.'

'Did I? How?'

'You was going on about how good Gertie was to you, how you really liked her, but now, just because she's a lesbian, it sounds like you've turned against her. I wish I'd had someone around like her when I was a kid, someone who'd have taken me in and got me away from here.'

'Weren't you evacuated?'

'Don't make me laugh. My mum needs someone to look after her, to put her to bed when she staggers home drunk and to clear up her mess. No, she didn't have me evacuated, 'cos without me, she'd be lost.'

'No wonder you want to leave home.'

'And as soon as I'm earning enough, I will.'

'Janet, I'm sorry.'

'It's me who should be sorry. I keep forgetting that you're just a kid and so I should've kept me mouth shut.'

'Now you sound like my mother. I'm not a kid. I'm nearly fifteen.'

'Compared to me at fifteen you're just a baby. Now, don't get me wrong, I ain't saying there's anything wrong with that. In fact, I wish I'd been so innocent at your age. To be honest, I'm a bit jealous. You've got a mum and dad who care about you . . . who look out for you, which is more than you can say for me. All my mum cares about is where her next drink is coming from and I have to hide most of me wages or she'd leave me without a penny.'

Ellen lowered her eyes. Yes, compared to Janet, she was lucky and realised that now. Janet was right about Gertie too. She *had* been prepared to turn her back on her, had even decided to refuse to see her when she and Maureen came to London again. Now though, she'd welcome them with open arms.

Hilda glanced at the clock.

'Ellen should be home soon, and I still don't like her seeing that girl. Janet may be all right, but I've heard that her mother's on the game.'

'I doubt that. You've seen her and I don't think many men would touch her with a barge pole.'

Yes, Hilda thought, she'd seen Janet's mother. The woman always looked dreadful, her peroxide blonde hair always showing inches of black roots.

She was skinny too, overly thin, her face thick with make-up that did nothing to hide the ravages of the life she led.

'I just hope that Janet doesn't lead Ellen astray.'

'Ellen's a good kid and I don't think we need to worry,' Doug insisted, then, changing the subject, he said, 'I wonder if Gertie has found a buyer for that house yet.'

'I don't know, but if she has no doubt she'll be back in London and we'll find out.'

'She ain't a bad sort and I hope she makes a success of that plant nursery she was going on about.'

'You've changed your tune.'

'What's that supposed to mean?'

'Have you forgotten what you accused me of when you were on leave in Somerset?'

'Bloody hell, typical woman with the memory of an elephant, yet a convenient one. *You* seem to have forgotten that I admitted I was out of order, and that I've been fine with Gertie since then.'

'Yeah, yeah, all right,' Hilda snapped as she rose to her feet. 'I'll make our cocoa.'

'You look tired. I'll do it.'

Hilda glanced in the mirror over the mantelpiece. Yes, she did look tired, her eyes dark-ringed and her face devoid of even a scrap of make-up. Yet, even if she could be bothered to wear it, there was no money for powder and lipstick now, and her voice was sharp as she said, 'Yes, I look tired, but with the hours I put in, what do you expect?'

'Go on, rub it in again. Do you think I like being like this? Do you think I like seeing my wife having to work while all I'm fit for is sitting around doing nothing?'

Hilda flopped back down again and covered her face with her hands.

'I'm sorry, Doug. I don't know what's wrong with me nowadays.'

'I do, and I've known it for some time. It's me, isn't it? I'm less than a man and one who can't even make love to his wife.'

'No, Doug, it isn't that. It's just that I'm feeling a bit worn out, that's all. I'm at work all day and then I have to come home to do the cooking and housework, let alone the washing and ironing.'

'And I can't even help you with that.'

'I know, but do you have to be so miserable all the time, so bitter? And, yes, all right, you can't make love to me, but you could at least show me a bit of affection. You never even hold me now, or kiss me, let alone cross the gap between us in bed.'

'What do you expect? If I showed you a bit of affection, you'd get all excited. Then what? I'd have to leave you all het up and what good would that do?'

Hilda took a deep breath, determined to bring

it out into the open at last – determined to say what was on her mind.

'Doug, there's more than one way to please a woman.'

'You wouldn't be satisfied with that. You've always longed for another baby, but with the way I am now that's never going to happen.'

'We've got Ellen, and one day she'll grow up, get married, and then we'll have grandchildren. All right, we won't have another child of our own, but surely that's something to look forward to? In the meantime I just want to feel close to you again. I love you, and though we can't do the things we used to do before your back gave out, as I said, there's other ways to please each other.'

'And you'd really be happy with that?'

'Of course I would.'

At last he smiled.

'Well, then, I think this calls for an early night.'

'Ooh, yes please,' Hilda said, grinning back at him, chuffed that she had at last brought it out into the open. It might not be perfect, but at least she wouldn't be taut with frustration all the time, and perhaps, just perhaps, their marriage could be a happy one again.

33

Gertie sighed with relief as she signed the papers, the date November 1946. They had found another buyer for her father's house, but it had taken a long time, and, though she had kept in touch by letter with Hilda, it had been over a year since she had seen her.

Hilda had written to tell her that Doug was showing a little improvement, but that he was still unable to work, and it seemed that both she and Ellen were in the same jobs. Gertie suddenly realised with a start that Ellen would be sixteen tomorrow.

While waiting for a buyer for her father's house, she and Maureen had looked at other counties, both falling in love with Dorset. Yet when it came to starting the business, they decided to stay in Surrey – to gain customers they had to be close to a large town with good transport links. With the sale completed and the location settled at last, they could start looking for a decent-sized plot.

Gertie smiled as they left the solicitor's office. 'Right, Maureen, we're all set now.'

'Are you still sure we're doing the right thing? Nothing much has changed since the war ended last year and if anything rationing is worse. Vegetables might be more profitable.'

'At the moment, yes, but I still think there'll come a time when people will look to flowers again. It's going to take some time to grow enough stock, especially trees and shrubs. In the meantime, with the amount of money we have behind us, a profit isn't something we have to worry about for some time yet. First things first, and that means finding a few acres, with decent living accommodation too.'

'Are you going to tell them now?'

'Not yet. I'd like to find a decent plot first.'

'Has it occurred to you that they might not accept?'

'Of course they will. Now come on, I've just remembered that it's Ellen's birthday tomorrow. I don't know how I forgot it, but let's go and find her a nice present, and as I have something for Hilda too, we'll pop round to see them before we leave London.'

Ellen glanced at the clock as she finished serving a customer. Only five minutes to go until closing time, and though she still hated working in the shop, she was happier these days. It had been a long time since she had heard her parents arguing, and despite her dad still being unable to work, he was more like his old self, cracking jokes and making them laugh.

At last Mr Morton turned the sign on the door to 'closed', saying, 'Off you go, Ellen.'

'Thanks,' she said, feeling a shiver of excitement. She would be sixteen tomorrow, though her mum still treated her like a child, still refused to let her go dancing on a Saturday night. Janet had said that for her sixteenth birthday Ellen deserved a treat and had worked out a way to get around the problem. Tomorrow night, they would pretend to go to the pictures, but in reality Janet was taking her dancing, along with three other girls, and Ellen couldn't wait. Janet had been teaching her the jitterbug, and she loved the energetic dance that had become the latest craze since it had been introduced by American servicemen during the war. It was fun, lively, and she just hoped a boy would ask her to dance.

Ellen ran to get her coat from the backroom and left the shop. She saw her mother with her head down against the biting wind as she hurried towards her.

'Hello, Mum.'

'It's bloody freezing. Let's get home.'

They both almost jumped out of their skin when

they heard a toot behind them, and turned to see a car pulling into the kerb.

'Ellen, it's Maureen and Gertie.'

'Jump in,' Gertie called.

'We're only going round the corner.'

Ellen ignored her mother and scrambled into the back of the car.

'Hello, Gertie; hello, Maureen.'

Maureen only smiled, but Gertie said, 'Hello, darling.'

'Come on, Mum. Get in.'

At last Hilda did, asking, 'Is this your car, Gertie?'

'It certainly is and it's so much nicer than public transport. How are you, Hilda?'

'Fine, I'm fine.'

Ellen was hardly listening as Gertie drove off. She had never been in a car before and even being driven round the corner was a treat. It had been so long – ages – since she had seen Gertie, but instead of disgust she felt only delight to see her again. Thanks to Janet she no longer felt so naïve. As time had passed, she had learned a lot from her friend, some things shocking, others sad – especially when Janet said that her experience with that so-called uncle had made her frigid, before going on to explain what that meant.

'As you're in London, I suppose it means you've sold your father's house?' her mother now asked Gertie.

'Yes. It was all signed and sealed today.'

'That's good, and are you still going ahead with your business idea?'

'Probably,' Gertie said shortly, then turned the corner to pull up outside the house. 'Here we are.'

Ellen wished the drive could have been longer, but she'd enjoyed it immensely. She climbed out of the car, but once again was in for a shock. For a moment she thought her eyes were deceiving her, that it couldn't possibly be him, but as he smiled, her heart did a somersault.

'Billy! What are you doing here?'

'I've got today and the rest of the weekend off and thought it was about time I came to see the parents instead of them travelling down to see me. I was just off to meet Percy. Mum said he'd be walking home about now.'

Ellen couldn't take her eyes off Billy. It had been so long since she had seen him and he looked so handsome. He was taller, his dark hair longer, and his green eyes were sparkling with interest as he now focused on the car. Ellen managed to tear her eyes away as her mother got out, she too looking with surprise at Billy.

'Hello, Billy. What are you doing here? Don't tell me you've left the stables.'

'No, I've just come for a short visit.'

Ellen saw Percy strolling down the street and, as Billy left their side to walk up to him, she found her head reeling. After all this time she thought her feelings for Billy had been nothing – a childish crush, as her mother would have said – but now, seeing him once again, they resurfaced. It was only when her mother spoke that she was roused from her daze.

'Come on, all of you, let's get inside.'

Gertie and Maureen followed her mother into the flat, but Ellen found that she couldn't move as Billy and Percy now drew close. The contrast between them was startling, Billy tall, dark, and Percy a pale shadow by his side.

'Well, Ellen, look what the cat dragged in,' Percy said.

'Yes, I know.'

'Did I see that woman getting out of that car? What was her name? Yeah, Gertie, that was it.'

Ellen nodded, finding that she was fixated on Billy again.

'Has she said anything about that plant nursery?' Percy asked.

'Not really, and I told you ages ago not to build your hopes up.'

'What's all this about?' Billy asked.

Percy started to explain, but then Ellen saw her mother appear again, her voice impatient. 'Ellen, it's about time you came inside.'

'Yes, all right. Bye, Billy, and maybe I'll see you again before you go back to Hampshire.'

'You look great, Ellen, and, yes, you can count on seeing me again,' he said, grinning widely.

Ellen's heart skipped a beat and, feeling her face flush, she gave a small wave before hurrying indoors.

Hilda saw her daughter's red cheeks and her lips tightened. It was Billy, of course, and she hoped the lad wouldn't be around for long. It was bad enough that Percy was obviously smitten with Ellen, though thankfully his interest wasn't returned. She wanted more for her daughter than Percy, a lad who worked in a factory – or his brother, who was nothing but a stable boy.

Gertie was talking, asking her something, and Hilda forced her worries to one side for now. 'Sorry, what did you say, Gertie?'

'I was asking if you remember any of the ornaments in my father's house.'

'Not really. I seem to remember my mother telling us to stay out of most of the rooms so we were nearly always in the kitchen or playing in your bedroom.'

'She was probably worried that we'd break things. You know what my father was like so you can't blame her for that. In fact, we almost did once.'

'Did we?'

'It was my fault, but luckily no damage was done.'

318

'Why are you asking me about the ornaments?'

'Along with the furniture and paintings, most have gone to auction. They should fetch a good price, but I thought you might like this,' Gertie said, drawing something out of her bag. 'I'm sure it's something you *will* remember.'

Hilda felt overwhelmed as she took the ornament from Gertie's hand and, as she held the exquisite white porcelain angel, memories of her mother flooded her mind. It had stood on a small hall table on the first floor of her father's house and they had passed it every time they went up to Gertie's bedroom. Once, during a playful rumpus when Gertie had been chasing her down the stairs, it had been knocked over, but thankfully and miraculously it had survived the fall.

'My . . . my mother loved this.'

'Yes, I remember. She was furious that we might have broken it and said that it was the most beautiful thing in my father's house. In fact, if you remember, she said that out of all of his lovely things, it was the one piece she coveted.'

Hilda's brows shot up. 'I don't think she actually used those words.'

'Well, no,' Gertie said with a chuckle.

'The air was blue with her language.'

'I know, but, as you say, she loved that angel.'

'Gertie, I can't take it. It must be worth a lot of money.'

'Actually, it isn't, or it would have been in one of my father's cabinets. I don't think it was to his taste and probably belonged to my mother. Please, Hilda, I'd like you to have it.'

'But if it was your mother's, wouldn't you like to keep it?'

'There was so much stuff in the house and I can't keep it all. I've taken some things and have put them in storage for now, but the rest had to be sold.'

'It's lovely, Mum,' said Ellen as she came to Hilda's side to look at the ornament. 'I can see why Gran liked it.'

'My goodness, Ellen, you're taller than your mother now.'

'Thanks for pointing that out, Gertie. What with Doug being tall, and now Ellen, I'm beginning to feel like a midget.'

'Of course you aren't,' Maureen protested. 'I'm only just over five foot and you're only a little shorter than me.'

'Ta, that makes me feel a bit better.'

'We may be small, but, like me, I bet you can stand up for yourself.'

'Yes, Hilda can do that all right,' Doug said ruefully.

'We've got something for you too, Ellen,' said Gertie. 'It's for your birthday tomorrow, but it isn't from Father's house. It's in the car and I'll give it to you before we leave.'

'Oh, can't I have it now?'

'What do you think, Maureen?'

'Yes, give it to her. It might not fit and we may have to change it before we leave London.'

'All right then. Here, Ellen, take the car keys and you'll find a package in the boot.'

Ellen ran from the room, soon returning to rip open the wrapping. She gasped, her eyes wide with delight. 'Oh, it's lovely!'

'You must have used all your coupons to buy that,' Hilda said as she eyed the lovely blue coat that was cut in the fashionable, square-shouldered military style. Clothes were still rationed, and there were strict rules on the use of materials, even on buttons, with three being the maximum allowed. The cloth looked lovely and Hilda was sure it must have come from a really good shop. New clothes were a luxury now, and most women had to make do and mend, making their own if they could find the material, so this was a real treat for Ellen and she was thrilled for her daughter.

'Ellen, try it on,' Maureen urged.

The coat fitted beautifully and as Ellen spun around her eyes sparkled with delight. 'Gertie, Maureen, thank you, thank you so much.'

'We're just glad you like it and that it fits so well.'

'She looks a treat in it,' Doug said.

'Yes, she does,' Hilda agreed, and though she

didn't want to acknowledge it, her daughter now looked like a young woman and a lovely one at that. She was growing up fast and would soon be demanding more freedom and to go dancing with that flighty girl, Janet. Then it would be boys, courting . . . but then Hilda gave herself a mental shake. There was no need to worry about it yet. Ellen would only be sixteen tomorrow and there'd be plenty of time before she started courting. It would be a long way off, in the future; but when that time came, Hilda would see that anyone unsuitable was sent on their way.

34

On Saturday morning when Ellen woke up, her stomach was churning with excitement. It was her birthday and she was going dancing with Janet that night, but it was the thought of seeing Billy again that was uppermost in her mind.

'You're up early. Happy birthday.'

'Thanks, Mum, and wasn't it nice of Gertie to buy me that coat?'

'Yes, it was, but I'm afraid me and your dad can't match up to something like that. Here, it isn't much, but I hope you like it.'

'Mum, it's lovely,' Ellen said as she unfolded the dark brown skirt. 'When did you make it?'

'I didn't. Mrs Long offered to run it up for me and she's done a really good job.'

'Yes, she has,' Ellen said as she held the skirt to her waist. New clothes were few and far between, but now she not only had a coat, she had a skirt too. 'I love it, Mum.'

'Happy birthday,' her father said as he shuffled into the room.

'Thanks, Dad, and thanks for the skirt.'

'That was down to your mother, not me.'

'Doug, it's from both of us.'

'Is there any tea made?'

'Yes, and it's still hot. You'd best get dressed, Ellen. We've both got work today.'

Ellen pulled a face at the thought, wishing she had Saturdays off instead of a half-day on Wednesdays. Billy was here, upstairs, but stuck in the shop all day, she doubted she'd get a chance to see him.

'I tell you what, Doug, it was smashing of Gertie to give me that ornament,' her mother said as she nodded towards the angel figurine that now stood on the mantelpiece.

'Yes, it was, but don't you think she was a bit cagey about starting up that plant nursery? I could hardly get a word out of her . . . well, except that she'd been looking in the Surrey area.'

'Perhaps she can't find anywhere suitable and has changed her mind.'

'I don't know, maybe, but she'd be mad if she has. I reckon it's a really good idea.'

Ellen thought so too, but now went to get washed and dressed. She was standing at the sink when she heard Mabel's voice, but by the time she was dressed and hurried to the living room, it was to find that she'd gone.

'Did I hear Mabel?'

'She popped down with that,' her mother said, nodding at a small package on the table. 'She said to wish you a happy birthday.'

Inside was a pair of hand-knitted gloves. 'I'll go and thank her,' Ellen said eagerly, glad of the perfect excuse for going upstairs.

She found them eating. Mabel was the first to speak.

'Hello, love. Happy birthday.'

Ellen had to drag her eyes away from Billy. 'I just popped up to thank you for the gloves.'

'You're welcome, and I expect you'll be out celebrating tonight.'

'Yes . . . I'm going out with Janet.'

'That's nice.'

Ellen felt as if a butterfly was fluttering in her tummy when Billy looked at her, a smile on his face as he said, 'I ain't got anything planned for tonight and if you don't mind, I might join you. Percy too, if he fancies it.'

'It depends. Where are you going?'

Ellen was flummoxed. She couldn't say she was going dancing in front of Mabel – if she did, it was sure to get back to her mum.

'Er . . . er, I'm not sure yet. I'll have a word with Janet and tell you later.' And with that, Ellen turned on her heels. 'I must go or I'll be late for work.'

Ellen found that her heart was thumping as she

went back downstairs. When she told Billy about the dance, would he want to come? And if he did, would he dance with her?

'Percy, who is this Janet?' Billy asked after breakfast as he followed Percy to his bedroom.

'She lives at the end of the street.'

'What's she like?'

'She's all right, around my age and a blonde. From what I've heard, she's a bit flighty.'

'I like them blonde, but if you've got your eye on her I'll keep my distance.'

'No, I'm not interested.'

'Mind you, Ellen is looking a bit tasty nowadays. I might go for her instead.'

'No,' Percy said quickly, 'leave Ellen alone.'

'Why should I?'

'What's the point in going after Ellen? She isn't that type of girl, and, anyway, you're going back to Hampshire tomorrow. Haven't you got a girl there?'

'Yes, Sheila, but it's nothing serious, just a village girl who doesn't mind putting it across.'

'What! You . . . you've done it with her?'

'Of course I have.'

'Blimey,' he said, sinking down onto the bed.

'What's the matter, Percy, ain't you had your leg over yet?'

'If you must know, I haven't. What's it like, Billy?'

'Great, and you don't know what you're missing.'

'You're only sixteen and I can't believe you've found it so easy to find a girl that's willing.'

'They ain't all willing and I soon found that out. After that I stuck with Sheila, but I wouldn't mind a change.'

'Don't, Billy. Don't try it on with Ellen.'

'Yeah, yeah, all right, but I tell you what. If you think this Janet might give it up, I'll leave her to you. It's about time you lost your virginity and if you want a few tips, I'd be happy to pass them on.'

'Go on then,' Percy said leaning forward eagerly.

Billy sat down on the opposite single bed. Yes, Percy could have Janet, and anyway, he'd clocked the way Ellen looked at him. Despite telling Percy that he would leave her alone, there was no way he was going to miss out on a girl who looked ripe for the picking.

Ellen was bubbling with excitement as she got ready that night. It hadn't been easy, but she'd managed to have a quick word with Billy and he'd agreed to go along with the ruse that they were going to the pictures. She knew her mother wasn't really happy that both Billy and Percy were going out with them and for a while Ellen thought she'd refuse to let her go but, thanks to her dad, her mum had at last agreed.

With a last look at her hair, Ellen put on her

coat. She still needed to apply some make-up, but as her mother would never allow it, she'd arranged to meet up with Janet at her house. She'd put some on there and then they'd meet up with Percy and Billy on the corner.

'Right, Mum, I'm going now.'

'You look nice, love. That new coat suits you.'

'Thanks, Dad.'

'Don't forget, I want you in by ten thirty and no later.'

'Yes, Mum, I know.'

It didn't take long to get to Janet's house, and as Ellen was let in she saw Janet's mum flopped in a chair, a glass of something in her hand.

'Hello,' she slurred; her hand shook as she lifted the glass to her lips.

'Hello, Mrs Pellmore.'

'Mrs Pellmore, now that's a laugh. How many times have I got to tell you to call me Sylvia? You two off out, are you?'

'Yes, Mum, I told you,' Janet said impatiently. 'Now come on, Ellen, get your make-up on and we can go.'

'That's it, girl,' Janet's mum said. 'Put on some slap and have a good time. Enjoy yourself while you're young, that's what I say.'

'You certainly did,' Janet said bitterly.

Ellen quickly applied her make-up, then asked, 'Do I look all right, Janet?'

'You look fine. Right, Mum, we're off.'

Billy and Percy were waiting on the opposite corner, both leaning nonchalantly against a wall as they approached. Percy was the first to move towards them.

'Hello, Ellen,' he said. 'You look nice.'

'Thanks,' she said.

'What about me?' asked Janet. 'Don't I get a compliment?'

'Er . . . sorry, yes, you look nice too.'

Janet giggled. 'Look at him blushing.'

Billy had a cigarette clenched between his lips, eyes narrowed against the curling smoke, but now he threw it onto the pavement, crushing it underfoot.

'So, you're Janet?'

'Yeah, that's right, and you must be Billy. You don't look anything like your brother.'

'I'm the good-looking one,' Billy said, his smile cheeky.

'Huh, don't kid yourself,' Janet quipped.

'Come on, are we going or what?' Percy asked.

'Yeah, why not,' Billy said, falling in beside Ellen as they walked along.

Janet was a blonde like Sheila and Ellen thought Billy would make a beeline for her. Janet and Percy were walking behind them, while Ellen was desperately trying to think of something to say. Come on, she told herself, say something; don't walk along beside Billy like a dumb idiot.

'Er . . . do you like dancing, Billy?'

'Not really, though I don't mind a bit of a smooch. I don't get a lot of time for dancing and they only hold those daft ones in the village hall.'

'Do you go with Sheila?'

'Sheila? Oh, you mean that girl you were friends with. No, I hardly see her,' he lied. 'Anyway, she ain't a patch on you.'

Ellen grinned happily. 'Can you do the jitterbug?'

'No, though I wouldn't mind giving it a go.'

'I could teach you.'

'What?' he said, eyebrows lifting. 'You can do the jitterbug?'

'Yes, Janet showed me how.'

'Well, I'm game if you are.'

Ellen smiled with pleasure. Billy would be dancing with her, she would be teaching him the jitterbug and, who knows, they could end up dancing a smooch.

The dance hall was buzzing, and at ten o'clock Billy was doing a slow dance with Ellen, unable to miss the scowl on his brother's face as they passed him. Ellen had her head on his shoulder, humming dreamily to the music, and Billy tightened his arms around her. There were quite a few tasty girls there, including Janet, but why bother with them when it was so obvious that Ellen was hot for him?

'Billy,' she said, raising her head to look at him. 'I'm sorry, but I've got to be home by ten thirty.'

'Have you? All right, get your coat and I'll walk you home.'

'You . . . you don't have to leave too.'

'I'm not letting you walk home on your own. Now go on, get your coat.'

Ellen looked delighted as she headed for the cloakroom, and nonchalantly Billy strolled up to his brother.

'I'm taking Ellen home.'

'Right, I'll come with you.'

'No, Percy, don't go. Come and have a dance,' Janet urged as she took his hand to pull him to his feet. 'It's too early to leave.'

'Yeah, go on, dip your boots,' Billy told him. 'Ellen will be fine with me.'

'You won't . . .'

'I said I wouldn't and meant it.'

'Come on, Percy,' Janet cajoled, pulling him onto the dance floor.

Billy was smiling happily as he met Ellen by the cloakroom and, taking her arm, he led her outside. After the heat of the dance hall, the cold hit them, and using this opportunity he flung an arm around Ellen, saying, 'Here, come closer and it'll keep you warm.'

'Thanks, Billy.'

His mind was racing. Where could he take her?

Where would he be able to find a bit of privacy? Unlike Hampshire, he couldn't sneak her into a barn like he did with Sheila, but, as they turned a corner, Billy saw the perfect place. As they drew nearer to the derelict house, Billy gave it a quick scan. The front door was hanging askew and half the roof was missing, but the walls were still standing and he thought quickly before saying, 'Look at that. One of my mates used to live there. Come on . . . let's take a quick look inside.'

'Wh . . . what for?' Ellen asked, but offered no resistance as he put a shoulder to the door and made a gap large enough to pull her inside.

'For this,' Billy said softly, turning in the hall to put his arms around her and bending his head to give her a gentle, unthreatening kiss.

'Oh . . . Billy . . .'

Slowly, while kissing her again, Billy backed up through a door and into what he guessed must have once been a living room. The ceiling was nearly gone and he could hear the crunch of debris underfoot, but was aware of something soft too, perhaps carpet. His eyes at last adjusted to the gloom and he felt a surge of relief. Perfect – just perfect. His kisses deepened while he unbuttoned her coat, hands reaching inside.

Ellen stiffened. 'No . . . no, don't, Billy.'

'It's all right,' he murmured as though gentling a filly. 'I just want to hold you.'

She relaxed, but as his hands moved to her breasts, she tensed again. 'No, Billy. I've got to go home now or I'll be late.'

'It's all right, there's plenty of time,' he said, lowering his lips to hers again. He then kissed her face, her neck and she groaned softly. Billy found his excitement mounting, and this time he ignored Ellen's small protest as he urged her onto the floor.

'Oh, Billy, no, don't,' she said as his hand moved up her leg.

'It's all right, I won't hurt you,' he murmured, gently stroking her mound.

At Ellen's soft moan of pleasure, Billy's arousal reached fever pitch. He had to have her, had to be inside her, and with one hand he managed to unfasten his zip. In a swift movement he ripped Ellen's knickers to one side, stifling her cries with his lips, and ignoring the resistance as he forcibly entered her. She writhed, but it was too late now, Billy oblivious to anything as he frantically moved towards a climax.

As Billy rolled off her, Ellen curled into a ball, tears running down her cheeks.

'What's wrong with you? Sheila didn't make all this fuss the first time I had it off with her.'

Ellen couldn't bear it. Why? Why had she let it happen? Oh, she knew why. She had loved his kisses, the way he made her feel; a surge of something growing inside, a longing for something else, something more. She had pressed herself against him, allowed herself to be pulled to the floor, but had only become really frightened when he had pulled her knickers to one side. Oh, the pain, but it had been too late and he wouldn't stop.

'For Gawd's sake, Ellen, you were asking for it and let's face it, you didn't say no.'

She shook her head, still sobbing.

'Flaming hell, I never took you for a cry baby. I'd have gone for Janet if I'd known you'd carry on like this. You were ready for it, and now you're making all this fuss over a bit of fun. Now are you coming or what? I thought you didn't want to be late home.'

His words were like a dash of cold water and Ellen struggled to her feet, feeling sore and bruised. She hated herself, hated Billy now, and she stumbled outside, shoulders slumped. She didn't wait to see if Billy was following her, her one thought to get home.

Billy called out, but she didn't look back, her feet moving one in front of the other, eyes on the pavement, until at last she turned into her street. It was only then that Ellen froze, her heart beginning to thump with fear. She couldn't say anything, couldn't tell her parents. They would go mad, absolutely potty, and she dreaded to think what they'd do.

Ellen knew that somehow she had to pull herself together – had to act as if nothing had happened. She took a deep breath and then looked down at her coat, aware then that it was still unbuttoned, but in the dim street light it was almost impossible to see if it looked all right. She fastened the buttons, brushed it down with her hands, and then patted her hair. Did it show? Would they notice anything? Would they be able to tell?

Outside the door, Ellen took another deep breath, forcing her voice to sound light as she went inside, calling, 'I'm back.'

The living room was empty, her mother's voice coming from the kitchen.

'Put the bolt across the door, love. Your dad's just gone to bed and I'm off too. Did you have a good time?'

'Yes, lovely,' Ellen called, and turning back to bolt the front door, she held her breath. If the gods were on her side, she might just make it, and now she almost ran through the living room.

'I'm going to bed too. Night, Mum.'

'Night, love.'

Ellen dashed into her bedroom and closed the door, leaning back against it as she heaved a sigh of relief. She had done it. She'd got to her room without being seen. She switched on the light, and gasped. Her new coat was filthy, covered in dirt and dust. How was she going to explain it away?

She'd fallen over, that might work, she'd say she tripped and fell.

Slowly Ellen undressed, feeling sick when she saw blood on her inner thighs. She felt disgusted with herself, wanted to wash the smell away, to wash all signs of Billy away. She had heard her mother go to bed, so, throwing a nightdress over her head, Ellen sneaked to the bathroom. Oh, how she would love to immerse herself in water, to scrub her body from head to toe, but she was only allowed one bath a week, and that in her mother's leftover few inches of water.

A glance in the mirror showed the make-up, smudged, her cheeks streaked with black mascara. Ellen blanched, horrified that her mother might have seen it. She had wanted Billy to think her pretty, but now she hated the make-up, wishing she could be an innocent child again as she frantically scrubbed it off. How could what happened be called lovemaking? Yes, it had been nice to start with, but then it had been painful, horrible.

At last, still sore, but feeling marginally better, Ellen returned to her room, and, turning off the light, she climbed into bed, shivering with cold as she pulled the blankets up to her chin. She closed her eyes, longing for sleep, for forgetfulness, but it was no good.

Behind closed lids, tears welled as she re-lived what had happened, and the things Billy had said that crushed her. He was seeing Sheila, had done it with her. She'd been stupid, an idiot, thinking herself in love with Billy, thinking that he might be falling for her too, but no, to Billy, it had just been a bit of fun.

Oh, God, I hate myself, Ellen cried inwardly, and it was a long time before her tortured mind at last escaped into sleep.

35

Ellen didn't see Billy again. She knew he had left, that he'd gone back to Hampshire early that morning, but she had remained in bed, curled up in a ball of self-hatred and disgust.

At ten o'clock the bedroom door opened.

'Ellen, it's about time you got up,' said her mother. 'I could do with a hand with the house-work and I've got a stack of ironing to do.'

'Yes, all right, I'm getting up now.'

'Look at your coat. What happened? It's filthy.'

'I tripped over on the way home last night.'

'You'd better hope a sponge down will get these stains off. You've only had it for five minutes and it's in this state already.'

'I know, I'm sorry, Mum.'

'I suppose accidents happen. Did you hurt yourself?'

'No, I'm fine.'

Thankfully her mother left, but Ellen knew that

somehow she'd have to pull herself together or there'd be more questions. She wanted to run, to flee, but there was no escape and somehow she had to act normally. Yet she didn't feel normal – she felt that the last vestiges of her childhood had gone, her eyes well and truly opened now. Billy had flippantly taken a part of her, a part that could never be replaced. She was tainted, ruined.

'It's about time, and you needn't think I'm seeing to your breakfast now,' her mother said when Ellen finally showed her face. 'You can get your own and then you can hang the washing up.'

'I . . . I'll do the ironing too if you like.'

'No, it's quicker if I do it.'

After eating a bowl of cereal, Ellen picked up the bucket of washing, despondently going to peg it out, only to find Percy digging the garden.

'Hello, Ellen, did you get home all right last night?'

'Yes,' she said shortly, but then had a thought. 'Percy, if my mum mentions that I fell over last night, don't look surprised.'

'You fell over? How did you do that?'

'I tripped,' she lied. 'My new coat's in a bit of a state and she isn't too pleased about it.'

'Billy didn't mention it.'

'Why should he? It was only a trip and I . . . I didn't hurt myself.'

'Ellen, are you telling me the truth? I know what

Billy's like and if he did anything to you, touched you, I'll flaming well kill him.'

'I don't know what you mean,' Ellen said, hiding her face as she pegged washing on the line. 'Billy walked me home, that's all. Anyway, I don't know why you're digging the garden again. I've already done it.'

'I know, but it won't hurt to give it another go and I've found loads more rubble,' he said, nodding to a small pile and then to a bucket, 'and I've got that too.'

'What is it?'

'Horse manure. When Billy said jokingly about walking behind the dray horses, I decided it was actually a good idea. I collected that lot yesterday.'

Ellen somehow managed to force a small smile. Her mum hadn't noticed a difference in her, and neither had Percy, but there was a difference, a big one, and it weighed heavily on her mind.

'What's the matter with Ellen?' Doug asked later that day when his daughter had disappeared into the garden again. 'She's been as quiet as a mouse.'

Hilda sighed. She had guessed what was wrong with Ellen, and now said, 'I think she's upset because Billy's gone back to Hampshire.'

'Yeah, well, he is a good-looking lad.'

'She can do better than the likes of him.'

'If you say so,' Doug said, then opened his Sunday newspaper again.

Ellen was sixteen now and Hilda knew she wouldn't be able to hold her back for much longer, but she still didn't like her knocking around with the likes of that Janet. Ellen was still innocent, but could you say the same about Janet? With a mother like that, she doubted it, and she didn't want Ellen tainted by the likes of her. Now if it had been Sheila, the nice girl Ellen had been friends with in Hampshire, Hilda wouldn't have minded. She was a nice girl who, unlike Janet, didn't walk around with make-up plastered all over her face.

'Mum, I think I'll pop down to see Janet,' Ellen said as she came back inside. 'It's too cold to do anything else in the garden.'

'What again? You were out with her last night.'

'I know, but we won't be going out again tonight. We'll just be sitting indoors talking about this and that.'

'Yeah, go on, love, off you go,' Doug urged.

'I think she should stay in.'

'What for? She doesn't want to be stuck in here with us.'

Hilda glared at Doug, but he seemed oblivious to her anger as Ellen went out.

'I don't like her seeing that girl.'

'She's the only friend that Ellen's made since we came back to London and I don't see any harm in her. All right, her mum might not be up to much, but as I've said before, Janet seems a nice girl.'

'I blame the war. We were stuck in Somerset all that time and Ellen lost touch with her school friends, then we went to Hampshire, and by the time we settled back in London most of the girls she used to know had moved away.'

'Well, then, you should be pleased that she's found a friend in Janet.'

'I suppose so,' Hilda said, yet still plagued with doubt.

Ellen hurried along to the end of the street. She couldn't keep it to herself any longer. She needed to talk to someone, to unburden the self-loathing that still swamped her. Not only that, she knew the facts of life and a persistent thought was now terrifying her.

'Can I come in, Janet? I need to talk to you.'

'Yes, but Mum's having a kip on the sofa and I don't want to wake her up. We'll have to talk in my bedroom.'

'That's fine.'

'Right, what's up?' Janet said as she sat on the bed, patting the space beside her.

'I . . . I wanted to talk to you about last night.'

'I had a good time, but blimey, that Percy. When I let him walk me home, he had arms like a bleedin' octopus.'

342

'Percy! Percy tried it on with you?'

'Yeah well, 'cos me mum's like she is, blokes around here think I'm the same – easy – but I ain't and a swift knee in the right place soon sorts them out. Not that I had to resort to that with Percy. How did you get on with Billy? Now that's what I call a good-looking bloke.'

'He . . . he tried it on with me too.'

Janet shrugged. 'That doesn't surprise me. It's something blokes always do, but no doubt you put him straight.'

'I wish I had. Oh . . . oh Janet,' Ellen wailed, tears filling her eyes.

'No! Don't tell me you let him go all the way?'

'Ye . . . yes.'

'Gawd, you soppy cow.'

'What . . . what if I . . . I'm pregnant?'

Janet chewed her lower lip for a moment, then said, 'Well, I've heard it never happens the first time, so you should be all right. It was the first time, wasn't it?'

'Of course it was.'

'That's all right then. You should be OK.'

'It . . . it was horrible.'

'You don't have to tell me that. My mum says it can be great, but if you ask me she's too pissed to know what's going on or she wouldn't think that.'

'I should have stopped Billy, but I didn't. I hate myself.'

'It's no good feeling like that. All right, you've lost your virginity, but it ain't the end of the world. I don't suppose you're the first girl to give it up before marriage, and you certainly won't be the last.'

'Who'd want to marry me now?'

'Leave it out. It ain't the be all and end all. You can lose your virginity riding a horse, and, if you have to, just fake that it's your first time.'

'I don't know what I'm worried about. I didn't like it and I don't think I ever want to get married now.'

'Me neither, but you ain't had such a bad experience as me. You'll get over it, and no doubt, like most girls, you meet a bloke, fall in love, and hey presto, you'll end up married with children. As you like that Billy so much, you could even end up marrying him.'

'No, thanks. I never want to set eyes on him again.'

'Fair enough, but come on, cheer up. Billy got you all worked up and all right, it went too far, but in future you'll know better.'

'In future, I'm gonna stick to plants.'

'You're saying that now, but one day, as I said, you'll meet someone else who'll turn your head.'

'*You* haven't.'

'Don't judge yourself on me. What happened when I was a kid put me off men for life, at least I thought so. Now though, I rather like Percy.'

'Percy! I thought you said he tried it on.'

'Yeah, but he was ever so apologetic. I like him, Ellen. He's soft, gentle, and for the first time I've met a bloke who doesn't make me feel threatened. I actually think that one day I could do it with Percy, to overcome these fears, but we'll just have to see how it goes.'

'You're seeing him again?'

'He hasn't actually asked, but I'll say yes if he does. In fact, maybe you could give him a gentle hint, you know, shove him in my direction.'

'Yes, all right.'

'Do you feel a bit better now?'

Ellen examined her feelings. Yes, she did feel a bit better, especially now she knew she wouldn't be having a baby. Janet had put things into perspective, and talking to her had helped. She had been a naïve fool, led by the way Billy had made her feel, by the strange sensations that had, at first, been nice. 'Yes, I do feel better, and thanks, Janet.'

'What are friends for?'

'You . . . you won't tell anyone, will you?'

'Ellen, of course I won't. I know girls are fond of a bit of gossip, but I wouldn't pass on something like this.'

There was a shout from along the hall.

'Janet, are you there? I don't feel well.'

'Blast it, that's me mum. She came home drunk from the pub at lunchtime and I've already had to clear up a load of vomit. I hope she's not going to be sick again.'

'I'd better go,' Ellen said, 'that is, unless I can do anything to help?'

'It's all right. I'm used to handling her on my own, and, anyway, they are times when she can turn a bit nasty. You're better off out of it.'

Ellen felt sorry for Janet. Because of her mum, she had an awful life, but she rarely complained, taking it all on the chin. It was nice that she liked Percy, and if Ellen could nudge him towards her, she would. Janet was right – Percy was nice, and might be the perfect boyfriend for Janet.

Ellen strolled home. She had thought Billy perfect, but he had taken her virginity without a moment's thought. *Stop it! Stop thinking about it*, she chided herself. It had happened, and there was nothing she could do now to change things. She had to somehow let it go, to get on with her life, but, oh, if only it were that easy.

36

Percy had been collecting manure whenever he got the chance and was now digging it in, but the ground was so hard at this time of year, making it almost impossible. It was nearly Christmas, and he looked up as Ellen came into the garden. It seemed to Percy that she had changed since her birthday. She seemed harder somehow, more like her friend Janet.

'Hello, Percy.'

'Watcha. It's flaming freezing out here but I wanted to get the last of this done.'

'It'll be worth it and I can't wait for the spring to start planting.'

'Yeah, me too.'

'With nothing to do in the garden, I've joined the library. I've found a few books to read about plants and cultivation.'

'That's a good idea. I might do the same.'

'Wouldn't you rather take Janet out?'

'Not this again. I've told you. She ain't my type.'

'She's really nice, Percy, and honestly, she's nothing like her mum.'

'So you said, but I'm still not interested.'

'She really likes you.'

Percy leaned on the shovel. 'Look, will you stop going on and on about Janet?'

'I beg your pardon,' Ellen said sarcastically. 'All I've been doing is trying to set you up with a nice girl, but I can see now that I've been wasting my time.'

'You have. Just leave it alone.'

'Fine, I will,' Ellen said, and with that she stomped back inside.

Percy shook his head. Ellen had a shock coming, and, as she was so keen on Billy, he was glad he wasn't going to be the one breaking the news. Since the letter had arrived yesterday, his mother had been in a right old state, and so far she had been so upset, so ashamed, that she hadn't even confided in Hilda. There was nothing left to do in the garden now, but he dreaded going upstairs. Would his mother be crying again? God, he could kill Billy.

'Are you all right, Mum?' he asked, annoyed that his dad had obviously skedaddled off to the pub, leaving her alone.

'Yes, but I still can't get over it. Billy's too young to take on the responsibility.'

'He should have thought about that before he knocked the girl up.'

'Don't talk like that, it sounds so crude. I'm so ashamed of him, but I'm going to see Hilda. She's got to know sometime, so it might as well be now.'

Percy said nothing as his mother left the room. Ellen was going to find out now, and he wondered how she'd take it.

Hilda was ironing, Ellen polishing the furniture and Doug reading when Mabel walked in.

'I've had some dreadful news,' she said. 'It . . . it's Billy.'

'Has he had an accident? Is he all right?' Hilda asked.

'He . . . he's got a girl up the spout.'

'What! Oh, Mabel.'

'I know, and now he's got to marry her.'

'Marry her? But he's only sixteen!'

'Don't you think I know that? Oh, sorry, Hilda, I didn't mean to shout, it's just that I'm in a right old state.'

'What does Jack say about it?'

'He said that Billy's made his bed and now he'll have to lie in it.'

'Can't you refuse permission? Can't you say no?' Hilda suggested. 'What do you think, Doug?'

'There isn't just Billy to think about, there's the

girl too. How would we feel if it was Ellen and the boy refused to marry her?'

'You can't compare Ellen to this girl. If you ask me, she sounds like a tart.'

'Hilda, you know her,' Mabel said. 'She was Ellen's friend when we all lived in Hampshire. Her name is Sheila. Sheila Erdington.'

'Sheila! But she seemed like such a nice girl. How far gone is she?'

'Three months now and that means Sheila was already pregnant when Billy came to see us last month, not that either of them realised that. It . . . it's due in July.'

Ellen suddenly rose to her feet and dashed from the room. Hilda could guess why. She'd had a crush on Billy, but he was well and truly out of reach now. Good, Hilda thought, but then, as Mabel began to cry, she berated herself, concentrating on her friend again.

'I know it's awful, and Billy seems too young, but it's not the end of the world. All right, he's getting married, but it might be the making of him, and, not only that, you'll have a lovely grandchild.'

'Hilda, I know what Billy's like, selfish through and through, and if anything I feel sorry for the girl. I dread to think what sort of husband Billy will be, or father, and I don't even trust him not to run off. If not now, then as soon as he finds out how hard it's going to be to support a wife and child. I told Jack we should refuse permission, suggested that instead we could offer to support the girl and her baby, but he won't stand for it. We're going to Hampshire tomorrow to sign the papers.'

Hilda didn't know what else to say. Doug was right. If Ellen had got herself into trouble, she'd insist the boy married her, but of course she was lucky and didn't have to worry about that. Ellen was still innocent, untouched, and she'd see that her daughter stayed that way until it was time for her to walk down the aisle. And that would be years away yet.

Ellen had convinced herself that she hated Billy, but now had to face the truth. Despite what had happened, she still couldn't get him out of her mind, and the thought of Sheila having his baby made her feel sick inside.

'Are you all right, Ellen?'

It was only then that she saw Percy. It was cold in the garden, but he was sitting on the bottom stair.

'Yes,' she lied. 'Why shouldn't I be?'

'Because you must have heard about Billy.'

'I've heard. So what? I couldn't care less.'

'You don't have to pretend with me. I know how you feel about him.'

'Do you? Then you'll know I hate him,' Ellen said defensively.

'He's hardly been back to London since he went to work in the stables again, and other than that weekend when we all went to that dance, you've hardly seen him. If you couldn't care less that he's got that girl pregnant, why say you hate him?'

Ellen floundered, but then found a good excuse for her outburst. 'Because the girl you're talking about is Sheila, and she used to be my friend. She . . . she's a nice girl . . . at least I thought she was.'

'Nice or not, it wouldn't bother Billy. From what he told me he's tried it on with loads of girls.'

'You're one to talk. Janet told me you tried it on with her.'

Percy turned the colour of beetroot as he spluttered, 'That's different. Janet, well, she's . . . she's . . . a . . .'

'Don't say it,' Ellen warned. 'Despite what you might have heard, Janet isn't easy, or a tart. She doesn't allow liberties and you must know that.'

'I must admit she wouldn't stand for it.'

'Doesn't that tell you something?'

He shrugged. 'I just thought she was playing hard to get.'

'God, you make me sick. You try it on, get knocked back, but still label the girl a tart.'

'I know you're upset about Billy, but don't take

it out on me. All right, I'm wrong about Janet. Are you happy now?'

'Ecstatic,' she snapped. 'And for your information, I'm not a bit upset about Billy. He and Sheila deserve each other.'

It had been a shock for Hilda to hear that Billy had got Sheila pregnant, a girl the same age as Ellen. Of course she blamed Billy. He was a handsome lad, enough to turn any girl's head, but it would be Sheila who'd bear the brunt of the gossip. If they didn't get married quickly the girl would be labelled a tart and how awful for her mother. Mrs Erdington had seemed a nice woman, a homely sort, but she'd be dying with shame now.

For the first time since returning to London, Hilda was glad they'd left Hampshire. With Billy living in the same cottage anything could have happened . . . but no, she was being silly. She trusted her daughter and wouldn't have had anything to worry about.

'Right, Ellen, now that Mabel's gone and you've shown your face again, we'd better get on with the housework.'

'Why the long face, pumpkin?' asked Doug.

Ellen blinked rapidly, then, choking back a sob, she fled the room, and shortly after they heard the sound of her bedroom door slamming.

'Surely calling her pumpkin ain't that bad?'

'That isn't why she's upset. It was hearing that Billy's getting married. She had a crush on him and seeing him again recently must have set it off again. I was glad to see the back of him when he went back to Hampshire.'

'Maybe you should go and have a word with her. Tell her that there's plenty more fish in the sea, that kind of thing.'

'No, Doug. Least said, soonest mended, that's the saying, and though Ellen's upset now, it was nothing serious. As I said, a silly crush and she'll soon get over it.'

'If you say so,' Doug agreed, and went back to his newspaper.

Hilda went through to the kitchen. She'd leave Ellen for now, let her have a cry and get it out of her system. She was too good for a boy like Billy who was destined for nothing but working in a stable, earning hardly enough to support himself, let alone a wife and child. No, Hilda thought, Ellen could do far better than him – and she'd make sure of that.

37

By the end of January the following year, everyone had had enough of the freezing temperatures. It was 1947, the coldest winter in living memory and there was even news that the sea had frozen over in Margate.

By February, worse had come. Clement Attlee had already nationalised coal mining, setting up the National Coal Board, so they were all shocked when he announced an emergency, he said, of the utmost gravity. Because of the power shortages, everyone would have to conserve fuel and some factories would close, while others would only open for three days a week. On top of that, rationing was at an all-time high and Hilda was at the end of her tether. With hardly any coal, they, like many people, had taken to going to bed after dinner, she and Doug snuggling up together for warmth.

'Are you getting up?' Doug asked Hilda as she stirred beside him.

'Yes, but stay there and I'll bring you a cup of tea.'

'I'll get up too.'

'We've only got a bit of coal and I'd rather save that for later. You'll be warmer in bed.'

'This weather is sure to break soon.'

'I hope so,' Hilda said as she grabbed a pair of Doug's old, and many times darned socks, pulling them on before shoving her feet into slippers, the soles so thin now that they offered little protection from the freezing lino.

'When you've made the tea, are you coming back to bed?'

'No, I'll keep warm by doing a bit of housework,' Hilda said, hurrying to the kitchen. She turned the tap on, hoping the pipes hadn't frozen again and thankful when she was able to fill the kettle with water. She would have to use old tea leaves again and her mood was low. It was bad enough putting up with this – with battling the cold and hunger – but on top of that she was worried sick about Ellen. Her daughter was so quiet and nowadays, other than going to work, she hardly left the house, usually the first into bed after dinner too. All right, Ellen had a crush on Billy, but this was bloody ridiculous and she should have been over it by now.

Maybe she was barking up the wrong tree, Hilda thought as, shivering, she waited for the kettle to boil. Maybe Ellen had fallen out with Janet. As she rarely went out now, that explanation made more sense.

When there was a loud knock on the front door, Hilda went to answer it, wondering who was calling this early on a Sunday morning.

'Gertie! Maureen!'

'Hello, my dear,' Gertie said. 'Can we come in?'

'Of course you can, though you'll have to excuse my nightclothes. It's warmer in bed and I've only just got up.'

Gertie eyed the hearth. 'Haven't you got any coal left?'

'A little bit, but I was saving it for later. Now you're here I'll light the fire. Sit down, the pair of you.'

Neither took off their coats and Hilda didn't blame them as she knelt down, screwing newspaper into a tight ball, laying it in the grate and placing a few sticks of wood on top. 'The kettle's already on and I'll make you a cup of tea when I've done this.'

'Where's Doug?'

'He's still in bed, Ellen too. I'll get them up.'

'That's good. We want to talk to all of you.'

'What about?'

'A proposition, but I'm not saying anything until you're all together.'

Impatiently Hilda laid a few pieces of precious

coal on the fire. 'Right, that's done,' she said, before hastening to the bedroom. 'Doug, get up. Gertie's here and wants to talk to us.'

'I heard her voice,' Doug said, already putting on a shirt.

When Hilda opened her daughter's door, Ellen had her back to her, but when told to get up, she said, 'All right. I'm coming.'

Maybe this would do it, Hilda thought. Maybe seeing Gertie again would lift Ellen's spirits . . . and just what was this proposition she'd mentioned?

Ellen didn't want to get up. She wanted to stay where she was, trying to shut it out and wishing as she did every day that she could just die, so afraid that death would be welcome. Gertie was here with Maureen, but Ellen wanted to stay in bed, to hide away; but there'd be no hiding it soon.

Reluctantly she got up, throwing on a couple of old, baggy jumpers that the freezing weather had given her an excuse to wear.

'Ellen, there you are,' Gertie said as soon as she saw her, but then frowned. 'Are you all right, dear?'

'Yes, I'm fine, just a bit tired, that's all.'

'It's the struggle to keep warm, that's what does it,' Maureen said.

It was Maureen's sympathetic smile that gave Ellen a tiny bit of hope. If she told them now, while Gertie and Maureen were here, maybe, just maybe, they'd be able to offer her some support. Gertie had always been so kind to her, and surely she wouldn't be as shocked as her parents were going to be.

'It . . . it isn't that,' she began hesitantly, head low and unable to look at her mother. 'I . . . I'm pregnant.'

There was a stunned silence, followed by an awful wail from her mother. 'No, no, Ellen, you can't be!'

'Of course she isn't.' This from her father. 'She's probably run down, anaemic or something.'

'Yes, Doug, that's it,' Hilda said clutching eagerly on to his words. 'Of course you aren't pregnant, Ellen. Whatever gave you that idea?'

'I . . . I am, Mum.'

'You haven't been with a boy. You can't be!'

'I have, but . . . but only once.'

Ellen wasn't ready for the blow, the slap across the face so hard it left her reeling as her mother spat, 'A tart . . . you're nothing but a tart!'

'Don't, Hilda, don't!'

Her father was ignored and Ellen cringed as her mother's hand lifted again. Gertie stood up quickly, putting herself as a barrier between them, saying, 'Hilda, stop it, this isn't solving anything.'

'Solved! How can it be solved?' Hilda shouted, pushing Gertie to one side to glare at Ellen again. 'Who was it? You'll have to marry him!'

'I . . . I can't.'

'What do you mean, can't? You'll marry him, my girl, whether you like it or not. Now who was it?'

'Bi . . . Billy.'

'Don't lie to me. You haven't seen Billy since your birthday last year. It can't be his!'

'It . . . it is.'

As her mother glared at her, Ellen could almost see her brain ticking over before she cried, 'But that means you must be over three months gone, and worse, Billy is now married!'

'Ellen, you poor thing,' Gertie murmured.

'She doesn't deserve sympathy! Don't you realise what this means, Gertie? She'll be an unmarried mother and I'll never be able to hold my head up around here again! Doug, do something! Say something!'

'It's no good losing your rag. It's happened, it's done and we'll just have to work something out.'

'Like what?'

'Hilda, I know you're upset, but please listen,' urged Gertie. 'Maureen and I may be able to help.'

'How can you help? How can anybody help!'

'You've just said you'll never be able to hold your head up around here again – well, you may not have to. You see, we came here to offer you all jobs and, not only that, accommodation too. It's taken us some time, but we've found the perfect

360

place for our plant nursery. There's a great deal to do, not least clearing the ground, and I think Doug's idea of a shop is a brilliant one. Now I know you don't like working outdoors, Hilda, but you've had experience of working in a shop, whereas I haven't got a clue. You could take it on, both you and Doug.'

'What good would I be in a shop?' Doug asked.

'You could man the till, and when it's quiet you could learn how to handle and transplant young stock. It's a sitting-down job that isn't too taxing.'

'I dunno, Gertie. I think I'd be more of a handicap than a help.'

'Of course you wouldn't. If you have a bad day when you have to lie flat, it won't be the end of the world, and let me tell you, I'd cut your wages accordingly.'

'You're forgetting that the government introduced the National Insurance Act last year.'

'Yes, Doug, but you have to build up a fair few stamps before you'd get sick pay.'

'Yeah, I know. I'm only joking, Gertie, and as for cutting my pay, I'd expect no less.'

'How can you joke at a time like this?' Hilda shouted. 'Ellen's just told us she's pregnant!'

'I must admit I wasn't expecting this when I came to talk to you, but I'd still like to take Ellen on too. There'll be loads of things to do, some light, some heavy, but we've already decided to take on a man to help with the heavy jobs. We were thinking about Percy, the lad who lives upstairs.'

'What!' cried Hilda. 'No, you can't. He's Billy's brother!'

'Oh dear, right then, we'll find someone else.'

With a sob, Ellen fled the room. It was bad enough that she was pregnant, but now she'd probably ruined Percy's chances too. He'd have loved a job in the plant nursery, and for him it would have been a dream come true, but because of her, it wasn't going to happen. Then her own unhappiness swamped her again and Ellen flung herself across her bed, crying as though her heart would break.

'Maybe I should go after Ellen, but to be honest, I don't think I could keep my hands off of her. How could she do this? How could she do this to me?' Hilda moaned.

'Now then, I know you're upset, and it's understandable, but surely this is worse for Ellen?' Gertie cajoled. 'She now faces the prospect of being an unmarried mother and it isn't going to be easy for her.'

'Don't you think I know that, but it's her flaming fault.'

'You've always kept Ellen so sheltered, so innocent, and I expect this boy took advantage of that. I doubt she understood what could happen . . . what could be the consequences.'

'So you're saying it's down to me.'

'No, Hilda, I'm just trying to make you see that Ellen isn't a bad girl, and if you remember she said it only happened once. Can't you imagine what she's been going through? How terrified she must have been and what it must have taken for her to tell you? Put yourself in her shoes.'

Hilda raked her fingers through her hair. It was all right for Gertie to talk, she didn't have a sixteen-year-old daughter who was having a baby. When Ellen blurted it out, she had almost collapsed in shock. Billy! If she got her hands on him she'd kill him!

'We've got something else to think about,' Doug warned. 'We'll have to tell Jack and Mabel.'

'Maybe we should go now,' Gertie offered. 'We'll come back this evening and perhaps by then you'll have had a chance to talk things through and to think about my offer.'

'I don't know about Hilda, but I don't need to think about it,' said Doug. 'I'm all for it. I hate living in London and being cooped up in here all day. If you're prepared to risk taking me on, I'll do my best not to let you down.'

'What about you, Hilda?' Gertie asked.

'I don't know! My daughter's just told me that she's pregnant and my head's all over the place. I can't think about anything else.'

'Of course you can't, and I understand that, but

just let me say the accommodation is a nice, rent-free cottage not far from the nursery so consider that too. Goodbye for now, and as I said, we'll call back later.'

Hilda managed to return their goodbyes and show them out, but her head was spinning and she didn't know if she was coming or going. Ellen . . . Ellen was pregnant!

'Gertie, that was awful,' Maureen said as they drove away.

'I know. Poor Ellen was in a dreadful state.'

'Hilda was too.'

'She's always been over-protective, and Ellen her perfect daughter. The shock must have been dreadful.'

'I know you're very fond of them, that you see them as your family, but are you absolutely sure this is the right thing to do? It's already a risk taking Doug on, but now you're talking about a pregnant girl too.'

'I'm aware of that, but I still want to help them.'

'Surely there are other ways? Ellen won't be able to do much in the latter months of pregnancy, and with a baby she won't be able to look after it *and* work too. It seems to me that the only one who'll be fit to do a full day's work is Hilda.'

'I thought you liked them.'

'I'm just trying to be practical, and letting them

live in the cottage rent-free when only one member of the family can really pull their weight doesn't make economic sense.'

'I told you. Money isn't an issue.'

'All right, I know you're well off now, but you're only young. If you just let money run down the drain it won't last for ever, and that's what they'll be, Gertie, a drain on your finances.'

'No, they won't. Hilda and Doug will run the shop, and I feel sure that eventually it'll make a profit. That just leaves Ellen and, even with a baby, there'll be loads she can do. In fact, when you think about it, we both hate housework and cooking, so perhaps she could take on the role of our housekeeper.'

'You've got an answer for everything, but at least I was able to talk you out of us all sharing the same accommodation. We'll be living in the big house, but that's only right. The cottage may be tiny in comparison, but at the end of the day, Gertie, they are just staff.'

'No, Maureen, they aren't. They're my family and how many times have I got to tell you that? I gave in to you about sharing the house, but I won't have you looking down your nose at them.'

'All right, I'm sorry, and I will make an effort with them, really I will. All I hope is that you're not making a big financial mistake.'

'Stop worrying. It'll be fine, but it's a shame

about Percy. I rather liked him. What he lacks in experience he makes up for in enthusiasm, but there's no chance of offering him the job now.'

'Well, Hilda, what do you think?' Doug asked.

'I said I don't know! I told you, I'm too shocked about Ellen to think about anything else.'

'I'm shocked to the core too, but at least Gertie has come up with a chance for us to get away from here. You're the one who's worried about the gossips, but if we move quickly we'll be gone before the tongues start wagging.'

'Don't you get it? It'll be the same wherever we live. When her stomach bulges we can hardly hide the fact that Ellen's having a baby, or the fact that she's single.'

'We could come up with some sort of story, say she's been widowed or something.'

'What, with a baby at sixteen? Don't be daft.'

'We could always pretend she's older.'

Yes, that could work, Hilda thought, though not around here. In a new area it might be possible.

'All right, we'll try that.'

'So we're taking the jobs?'

'Yes, we'll take them, but now I've got to go and speak to Mabel.'

'That boy shouldn't get off scot-free. He should at least be made to support Ellen and the baby.'

'With what, Doug? Billy only works in a stable

and he's already got a wife with a child on the way.'

'Then Mabel and Jack should stump up something.'

Hilda agreed, but money was the last thing on her mind at the moment. Head down with misery, she went upstairs to Mabel's flat. It had happened again. London had brought her bad luck and unhappiness: the only glimmer of light was that they'd be getting out of it again. This time, no matter what, she was never, ever, coming back.

38

'What? Oh, no, Hilda, no!'

'The little shit!' Jack shouted. 'That's it, I've had enough. He's no son of mine now. I'm finished with him.'

'Ellen . . . Ellen's having Billy's baby. I . . . I just can't seem to take it in.'

'I know, Mabel. I feel the same.'

'What are we gonna do?' Mabel wailed.

'What can we do?' Hilda said tiredly, her emotions so shot that she could still hardly think clearly. 'Billy's a married man now, with a child on the way.'

'But, Hilda, don't you see what this means? When Ellen has her baby, they'll be half sisters or brothers.'

Hilda's jaw dropped. 'I hadn't thought of that. It's getting worse and worse.'

'And they'll only be a couple of months apart in age too,' Mabel wailed.

Percy found his teeth grinding. Billy . . . Billy had taken Ellen down and he was almost overwhelmed with fury. He knew he wasn't a fighter; since seeing men returning home from the front, crippled and maimed, he'd abhorred war and any violence, yet at this moment, if Billy had been standing in front of him, he'd have throttled the bastard. That word set off another train of thought. Billy couldn't marry Ellen and that's what her child would be – through no fault of its own, it would be born a bastard.

Ellen must be going out of her mind. She was only sixteen, but soon to be an unmarried mother. Percy knew what her life would be like living around here, the subject of disdain and gossip. When it was older, the poor kid would go through hell too; the biddies around here were narrow-minded and cruel.

'If only Billy hadn't got Sheila pregnant,' his mother cried. 'If only he hadn't married her, but it's done now and . . . and he can't marry Ellen too.'

'Yes, and thanks to him it's my Ellen who'll now have to carry the stigma of being an unmarried mother, struggling to bring her child up alone.'

'The little shit will have to support her,' Jack snapped.

'How?' Mabel wailed. 'With what? You know he earns sod all.'

'Then it'll have to be up to us. Ellen's child will be our grandson or granddaughter too, or haven't you thought about that?'

'Oh, Hilda,' Mabel cried, her eyes filling with tears. 'Ellen's having our grandchild, and a shared grandchild with you would have made me the happiest woman in the world, but . . . but not like this.'

Percy hated to see his mother in this state, but hearing her words an idea struck him, one that he pondered on for a while. There would have to be one stipulation, or they could forget it. Yet would Ellen agree? It was the perfect solution, but would she see it that way? He wasn't stupid, knew that Ellen had never been interested in him, but despite this, and the fact that she was having his brother's baby, Percy knew his feelings for her remained the same and always would. Taking a deep breath, he said, 'Mum, I'll marry Ellen.'

'What?'

'I said, I'll marry her.'

'But . . . but Percy, she's having Billy's child.'

'Nobody needs to know the baby's his, and my only condition is that he never finds out. I'll bring the baby up as my own, and I don't want Billy to have anything to do with it.'

All three of them stared at him, but it was his father who finally spoke.

'Are you out of your mind? Why should you

mop up Billy's mistakes? You're only young and have your whole life ahead of you.'

Percy fought for an answer, and the only one he could come up with quickly shot into his mind. 'I begged him, Dad. I begged Billy not to try it on with Ellen and he promised he wouldn't. I know what he's like, shouldn't have trusted him, and . . . and now I feel responsible for what happened.'

'You can't blame yourself for what your brother did. You ain't his keeper, and you ain't getting lumbered with a wife and kid because of him.'

'What about my daughter? If you ask me, she's the one who's been lumbered, but don't worry, Jack,' Hilda said sarcastically, 'there's no need for Percy to marry Ellen. We'll be all right. My friend Gertie has offered us a way out, a job and home in Surrey. We'll move there, and pretend that Ellen is older and widowed, as Doug suggested.'

'What? Gertie's got her plant nursery?'

'Yes, she called round to tell us about it. That . . . that's when Ellen told us that she was pregnant. The jobs are a godsend and it means we can get away from here before the tongues start wagging.'

Percy had hoped that Gertie would offer him a job too and now said desperately, 'That's great, but the offer still stands. I'd be happy to marry her, honest I would.'

'No, Percy,' said Jack. 'Your mum and I will do

what we can to give Ellen financial support, but that's as far as it goes.'

'This is my decision, Dad, not yours.'

'You ain't a man yet and I'm telling you you're off your head.'

'I'm older than Billy and he's married,' Percy snapped, then softened his voice as he turned to Hilda. 'At least let me put it to Ellen.'

'I don't know, Percy. Your father is against it and to be honest I'm not sure how I feel. So much has happened in such a short time and I need to clear my head. Leave it for now and we'll talk again later.'

'Yes, and by then me and Mabel will have talked some sense into our son.'

'You won't talk me out of it, Dad,' Percy said, yet knew Hilda was right. The air was taut with tension and feelings were running high. Surely when his parents, as well as Hilda and Doug, had time to think about it, they'd see the sense of his offer. At least he hoped so.

'Well, what did they say?' Doug asked.

'Like us, they're shocked, but they did offer some financial support.'

'I should think so too.'

'Has Ellen showed her face again?'

'No, she's still in her room.'

Hilda sat down, emotionally exhausted, but her

372

mind refused to stop working. Percy's offer had left her reeling and she wasn't sure how she felt about it, but now, as it finally sunk in, she decided that it could be the perfect solution. They'd all move to Surrey, a respectable family, with their married daughter and son-in-law having their first child. Percy would be able to work at the plant nursery too, supporting Ellen, and instead of having to live a life of pretence and lies, they'd be able to hold their heads high. 'Doug, something else came up.'

'Oh yeah . . . what?'

'Percy has offered to marry Ellen.'

'You're kidding. Why would he do that?'

'Apparently he asked Billy not to try anything on with Ellen, and he agreed. Now, because he trusted his brother and left Ellen alone with him, he feels responsible for what happened.'

'He can't take the blame for what Billy did.'

'That's what Jack told him, but Percy still wants to marry her. I've always known that he had his eye on Ellen, but she's never shown him an ounce of interest. I think that's the real truth of the matter.'

'Leave it out. He may like Ellen, more than like her, but he'd be taking on soiled goods and another man's child at that. I can't see Jack and Mabel allowing it.'

'It should be his decision, not theirs. All Percy

asks is that Billy is never told that he's the baby's father.'

'Hilda, it takes two to make a baby, and Ellen didn't say that Billy raped her. Whether we like it or not, the child is his.'

'I doubt the soppy cow even knew what was happening until it was too late, but you can bet your life Billy did. After all, he'd already got another girl pregnant, so he was hardly a virgin.'

'Forget it, Mum. I'm not marrying Percy.'

Hilda swung around, only aware then that her daughter was standing in the doorway. 'Oh, so you'd rather be a burden on me and your dad for the rest of your life, would you? Well, forget it, my girl, you'll marry Percy and that's that.'

'Hilda, stop it. You can't force Ellen to marry him if she doesn't want to.'

'Who else is going to take her on? As you so bluntly put it, she's soiled goods now, and not only that, she's having a child, one that will be born a bastard unless she marries Percy.'

'I don't want to be a burden to you. I . . . I'll find a way to support myself.'

'With a baby to look after, how do you think you'll be able to do that?'

'I'll talk to Gertie; ask if, when the baby's born, I can bring it to work. That way I'll still be bringing in a wage.'

'You think you've got it all worked out, but how

can you work in a nursery, outdoors in all weathers, with a baby alongside you?'

'I don't know, but I'm not going to marry Percy.'

Hilda glared at her daughter, yet she couldn't now fail to see the change in her. The innocence had gone from Ellen's eyes and she seemed older somehow, assertive. Hilda was at the end of her tether and couldn't take any more. She rose to her feet, saying as she left the room, 'Doug, I give up. You talk some sense into her. I'm freezing and I'm going for a lie down.'

In bed, Hilda clutched the blankets around her. All the dreams she had cherished for her daughter were dead now. There'd be no lovely white wedding, no perfect husband for Ellen, one who would take her away from poverty. There was just this now, Ellen's only choice Percy, or the prospect of being an unmarried mother.

Groaning, Hilda buried her head in the pillow. She and Doug had talked about grandchildren and she had looked forward to that, but not this way . . . no, not this way. Yet, even as this thought crossed her mind, Hilda found herself thinking about the baby. Would it be a boy or a girl? Whatever happened she knew she'd love it, that Doug would love it too, but if Ellen wouldn't marry Percy they were going to have to spend years struggling to support their daughter. Years and years of the same grinding poverty stretched ahead, of hard work with little to show for it, but at least, Hilda decided, a little cheered by the thought, there'd be a baby, a grandchild to love.

'Dad, I'm sorry, and I know Mum's upset, but I can't marry Percy.'

'She's just trying to do the best thing for you. You'd have a husband and the baby would have a father.'

'It's got a father.'

'Yes, but one who can't support you. All Percy asks is that Billy is never told that he's the baby's father.'

'Yes, I heard, but I don't see why.'

'In the circumstances I can guess. If the truth got out he'd look a fool.'

'He'll be the baby's uncle, not its father, and, well, it seems a bit sick that he wants to marry me and pretend differently.'

'You shouldn't think like that. Percy must like you a lot to offer to do this, and I reckon if you make the effort, the pair of you could be happy.'

'How? I . . . I'd have to sleep with him, and I can't, Dad, I can't face it. When . . . when it happened with Billy it was all right at first, but then I . . . I didn't like it.'

'Oh, blimey, I don't feel right talking to you about this. Go and tell your mother how you feel. She'll explain things to you.'

'She never has before and she's in no mood to do it now.'

'Look, this is a bit difficult for me, but I can tell you that for a woman it hurts the first time. After that, well, it's all right.'

'Really?'

'I've never had any complaints,' he said, then reddened. 'I never thought I'd be talking about such things with my own daughter and, if you don't mind, anything else you need to know will have to come from your mother. Now, let's get back to Percy and if you really don't want to marry him, I'll support your decision. All I ask is that you think about it, weigh it all up, you know, the pros and the cons. Then, if you still feel the same, we'll face your mother together.'

'Dad, thank you. I know I've let you down, that I've let Mum down, but . . . but I didn't mean to, honest I didn't. It . . . it just sort of happened.'

'I know, pumpkin, I know. Your mum's in shock, but she'll come round, you'll see.'

'I don't think so. She called me a tart, and . . . and she hates me now.'

'Don't be daft. She just said that in the heat of the moment, that's all. Your mum loves you, we both do, and no matter what, you're still our little girl.'

'I wish I was. I wish I could wind the clock back and be a little girl again.'

377

'We all wish that at times – that we could go back and change things – but we can't, pet. We've just got to make the best of it and live with the mistakes we've made.'

'I'm going back to my room, Dad. Like you said, I've got a lot to think about and it's freezing in here.'

'Let me know what decision you come to.'

Ellen too wrapped herself in blankets, going over and over all that had been said. Despite all her parents' arguments, she still didn't think she could face marrying Percy. Yes, he was nice, but she felt nothing for him, well, other than friendship. Yet look where feelings had got her. *Oh Billy, Billy*, her mind cried. *I'm having your baby and you don't even know.*

Slowly, Ellen came to a decision, her mind at last made up. She would tell her parents first, but then she'd have to face Percy. It was only right that he heard it from her, but would he understand? She hoped so – hoped that he'd be content with friendship. Then somehow she had to move forward, putting Billy out of her mind once and for all.

39

It was chaos, everything moving so swiftly. With the cottage unfurnished, Hilda wasn't happy that they had to take all their old stuff that was already ancient and second-hand when they had moved into this downstairs flat.

Still, Hilda thought as she sealed the last box, at least they were moving now. They'd be leaving London, a place that had brought her nothing but misery, and once again Hilda was adamant in her mind that she would never come back. Of course Mabel was still there, upstairs, the two of them remaining friends, despite everything and the rows that had raged. In fact, they were even more linked now with a shared grandchild on the way.

Gertie had been so kind, wonderful to Ellen, and Hilda wondered what time they'd arrive at the cottage. Gertie had wanted to drive down that morning to give them a lift, but Hilda had felt that Gertie was doing enough and insisted that they'd be fine travelling by train.

'The van's almost packed. Are you ready?' Doug asked as he poked his head into the room.

'Yes, all set,' she said. The room stripped of furniture looked empty, bleak, and just for a moment Hilda looked out of the window, thankful that it was the last time she'd look out onto a London street. Until the war she'd never been out of Battersea, but now she'd lived in Somerset, Clapham, Hampshire and now Surrey. Would it be their last move? Would they finally settle?

When they'd told Gertie that they wanted to accept her offer, she had taken them to see the plant nursery, the cottage and the nearest village, which had the funny name of Christmas Pie. They'd be in a lovely setting just outside Guildford and on a place called the Hogs Back. Unlike here, the views from the cottage window were wonderful; though close to the town, they would be set high up with an unobstructed vista of the beautiful countryside that stretched for miles.

'I saw the van, are you off?'

'Yes, Mabel, we're going now.'

'I'm gonna miss you so much.'

'I'll miss you too, but it's an easy train journey to Guildford, as I've told you. You and Jack are welcome to visit us whenever you like.'

'I know, but it isn't the same as having you living

downstairs. If it's all right with you, and if Percy doesn't do his nut, me and Jack will come to see you all next weekend.'

'Don't worry about Percy. I'm sure he's over it now.'

'I don't know about that.'

'Stop worrying. I have, and you've got to do the same. Percy is still young and he'll come round. You were only trying to do what you thought was right for him and now the dust has settled, he'll understand that.'

'Yeah, maybe.'

'It's time to go,' Doug urged.

'Right, see you next weekend, Mabel.'

'It'll be down to how Percy feels about it.'

'Just come; after all, he can hardly stop you.'

'All right, we'll do that, and even if it causes another big row, as you said, we were only trying to do what was right for him.'

Hilda gave Mabel a hug; she was sure it would all work out. Yes, there had been rows, big ones, but it was over now. She wouldn't cry. There was no need – Mabel and Jack she was sure would be frequent visitors.

With a last look around the room, Hilda picked up her handbag. Soon, though Guildford wasn't miles away, London would be behind her, and then their luck was sure to change. There'd be no more heartache, just, she hoped, contentment.

* * *

Hilda smiled as she opened the door to Lavender Cottage, delighted to see a fire burning in the range. Gertie had been there to meet them at Guildford station, but she must have come to the cottage first.

'Gertie, thank you.'

'Until you find your way around, I've stocked you up with enough food for the weekend. There's a kettle and things to make some tea, but I'm off because I've got a few things to sort out before I go to the station again. See you later.'

Doug closed the door behind Gertie, the warmth of the room enveloping them. Hopefully, Hilda thought, the removal van would arrive shortly, but in the meantime a cup of tea was just what they needed.

There was a tap on the door and, thinking that Gertie had come back for some reason, Hilda opened it to see a young woman holding a tray.

'Er . . . Hello.'

'Hello,' she greeted in return. 'My name's Valerie, but call me Val. I live just down the lane in Mayflower Cottage. I saw you arriving and thought you might like this. It's only tea and biscuits but it'll tide you over until your things arrive.'

'It's very kind of you,' Hilda said as she looked at the slender, pretty young woman, her long, golden hair hanging over her shoulders in rippling waves. 'Would you like to come in?'

'Just for a tick then,' she said, stepping inside.

'That's Doug, my husband, and I'm Hilda.'

'Hello, Doug. Now where can I put this tray?'

'Here, lay it on the window seat,' he suggested.

Val put it down, then looked around. 'It looks so different now, fresh and lovely.'

'It's been re-decorated,' Hilda said. 'Did you know the last people who lived here?'

'Yes, old Mr and Mrs Green. There's something about this cottage, a warm feeling, and they both loved it. Sadly, when Mrs Green died, her husband soon followed. He was lost without her, and just sort of faded away. We kept an eye on him as much as we could but, though I know it might sound fanciful, I think he died of a broken heart.'

'The poor man,' Hilda said.

'Yes, but he's with his wife now and happy again.'

There was the rattle of cups, Doug saying as he poured tea from the pot, 'It was good of you to bring us this and it'll go down a treat.'

Val cocked her head to one side as she looked at him. 'You've got a lot of pain in your back, haven't you?'

'Well, yes, but how do you know about my back?'

'I sort of sensed it,' she said off-handedly. 'Anyway, I'd best be off. It's nice to have a family living here again, and if you need anything else, just give me a knock. Bye for now.'

'Well, love, the natives seem friendly,' Doug said as Hilda closed the door behind Val.

'She was a bit odd. I mean, how could she have sensed that you've got a bad back?'

'She probably just saw that I was moving awkwardly, that's all.'

'What about that comment about Mr Green being happy now that he's with his wife?'

'Surely that's what we all say when someone dies.'

'I don't, and what about her saying this cottage has got a nice feel about it?'

'Now then, Hilda, you made the same comment when Gertie drove us down to see it. Val is just a nice young woman who was kind enough to bring us this tea and make us welcome.'

'Yes, yes, I suppose so,' Hilda said, yet despite agreeing, she still felt the young woman was odd. There was something about Val that reminded Hilda of the woman who had spoken of her vision. It was their eyes, she thought, as if they were able to see things that most other people couldn't. Once again a shiver ran up her spine, but then Doug spoke again and the moment passed.

'That sounds like the van,' he said, crossing the room to open the door. 'Yes,' he called back over his shoulder, 'it's here.'

'That was quick,' Hilda said as she gave herself

a mental shake. There was enough to do without worrying about their new neighbour, and she now stood ready to direct where the furniture should be placed.

The removal men were quick and efficient and it wasn't long before everything was unloaded. They even put the beds together, and Hilda felt awful that she hadn't been able to give them a large tip.

Now, after all the activity, it was just the two of them again, but at least they had chairs to sit on and Hilda looked around the living room with satisfaction. Strangely, the old furniture looked all right in the cottage, fitting somehow.

'Leave it,' Doug said as Hilda began to open boxes. 'You can't manage all this unpacking on your own. They'll be here soon to give us a hand.'

'I can make a start.'

'Do you know what, Hilda, this place reminds me of Hampshire. When we left there I vowed I'd return one day, but this'll do me.'

'Yes, it'll do me too,' Hilda agreed as she carefully lifted the porcelain angel out of the box to unwrap it. With a smile, she placed it on the tall mantelpiece above the range.

'Considering that you don't believe in God and all that, I'm surprised that you love that thing so much,' Doug said.

'Since that woman had that vision about you coming home, I don't know what I believe in any more. There must be something, Doug, and a long time ago I had a funny feeling that someone was standing beside me. It scared the life out of me, but nowadays I like to think it was my mum,' Hilda told him, and when she thought about her mother, her hand as usual went to the cross and chain she still wore around her neck.

'I don't believe in all that stuff, but your mum was a good sort, your dad too. I wonder what they'd have made of this cottage.'

'They were Londoners born and bred and even during the Blitz there was no way they'd leave Battersea . . .' Hilda paused. Yes, and the Blitz had killed her parents. Well, she was away from London now, starting a new life and leaving all her unhappiness behind. She gazed at the angel and there was something about the ornament that drew her. It hadn't had this effect on her before, and it was silly, fanciful really, but it was almost as if the angel was watching over them.

Stop it, Hilda chided herself. It was daft to think that, and anyway, she had enough to do without standing there gazing at a statue. Yet she couldn't help wondering. Are there angels? Do they really exist?

40

'Nearly there,' Ellen said. 'Aren't telephones wonderful? I rang Gertie from the hotel to tell her what time we'd be arriving and she said she'd be waiting for us at the station.'

'Perhaps one day everyone will have telephones.'

'I doubt that. Only businesses and rich people can afford them.'

'I can't wait to start work on Monday.'

'No wonder Gertie was so keen to take you on.'

'It was good of her to pay for our week in Brighton.'

'Yes, but the weather was rotten.'

'It wasn't that bad for the end of March, and the hotel was nice.'

Ellen nodded her agreement, her thoughts drifting as she watched the passing scenery. They'd asked for single beds and got them, but it felt strange in the hotel room and she'd been nervous at first. She needn't have worried. Percy had kept to his agreement of a platonic marriage until after the baby was born, but Ellen wondered if she would ever be able to lie in his arms, to have him touching her, doing *that* to her. Oh, she liked Percy – how could anyone fail to like Percy – but she didn't love him and doubted she ever would.

'Come on, we're here,' he said as the train drew into the station, standing up to grab their cases from the rack overhead.

There was a cloud of steam from the engine as they climbed from the carriage, but as soon as it cleared Ellen saw Gertie and Maureen at the end of the platform, both their faces lighting up in a smile. Ellen hurried towards them, wrapping them both in a hug.

'Thanks for meeting us.'

'It's lovely to see you,' Gertie said. 'Your parents have arrived and when I left them they were waiting for the furniture van to show up.'

'Did you enjoy yourself in Brighton?' Maureen asked.

'Yes, it was lovely.'

'Percy, do get a move on,' Gertie called brusquely.

Ellen hid a smile as he joined them and they all then walked to the car. Gertie sounded bossy as usual, but she didn't mind. Once he started work in the plant nursery, Percy would have to get used to it too, but she doubted he'd complain. He'd be doing something he loved, and that had been a large factor in her decision to marry him. A love of plants, of growing things, was something they had in common and it had weighed heavily that because of her he would lose his chance to work at the nursery.

'I sure your mother will be glad to see you. She's certainly going to need a hand with all the unpacking,' Maureen said.

'Do you know, I was only thinking on the way back that it's the first time I've been anywhere without her.'

'I know you're very young, but you're a married woman now,' Gertie chuckled, 'and she could hardly join you on your honeymoon.'

Ellen hadn't wanted to be a burden to her parents, or to force them to live a lie, and that too had gone a long way in her decision; but when they'd told Percy's parents they were getting married, she hadn't been prepared for the awful rows that had followed. However, as Percy put their luggage in the boot and they climbed into the car, Ellen's thoughts were snapped back to the present when Gertie spoke.

'I'm glad you liked Brighton, but what about the hotel? Was it all right?'

'It was lovely and I can't thank you enough.'

'Yeah, me too, Gertie,' Percy agreed.

Ellen gazed out of the window with interest. Guildford was a town she looked forward to exploring, but soon they were on the outskirts, driving up a steep hill and onto the Hogs Back. The scenery was breathtaking and just a short way along Gertie turned off to drive down a small country lane, Lavender Cottage soon coming into view.

Smoke was spiralling from the chimney as though signalling a welcome and, moments later, as if they'd been looking out for the car, Ellen's parents appeared on the doorstep. With her father's arm around her mother's shoulder, somehow it all looked just right, and when both their hands lifted to wave, Ellen was the first out of the car.

'Hello, you got here then?' her mother said.

'Well, Mum, we aren't an optical illusion.'

'Very funny. Now did you have a nice time?' Hilda asked, looking at her keenly.

'Yes, lovely, thanks.'

'Well, come on then, all of you. Let's get inside out of the cold.'

'Sorry, Hilda, we can't stop,' Gertie called as she opened the boot for Percy to take out the cases. 'We've got a lot to do, but if it's all right, we'll pop back this evening.'

'That's fine, and thanks for picking these two up from the station.'

'It was no trouble,' Gertie called, and moments later the car drove off again, Maureen waving at them from the passenger window.

'This is nice,' Percy said as they walked inside.

'It'll be a darn sight better when we get these boxes cleared. Oh, and Percy, I saw your mum before we left. She said they'd pop down next weekend to see us.'

Percy's lips thinned. 'She said that, did she? I'm still not sure that I want to see them.'

'Now, Percy, I know they were against this marriage, but they're still your parents. We've buried the hatchet and you should too.'

'I can't forget how much persuasion it took for you to convince them to come to the registry office.'

Ellen touched his arm. 'Percy, I told you that your mum gave me a big hug after the service, your dad too, but by then you had walked off with the hump.'

Percy's eyelids were hooded, an expression Ellen had come to recognise when he was thinking about something. She could understand why Mabel and Jack hadn't wanted Percy to marry her, and the rows had been dreadful. She hadn't wanted to come between Percy and his parents, had almost changed her mind, but he'd been adamant, telling them that if they didn't agree, they'd never see him again.

'Percy, give them a chance,' Hilda urged. 'They came round eventually and your mum isn't only my friend, she's family now. It wouldn't be right to keep them away.'

'Yeah, yeah, all right.'

'Good, I'm glad that's settled,' Doug said. 'Now I expect these two want a cup of tea before we tackle any more boxes.'

'Yes, and I'd better take that tray back to Val.'

'Who's Val?' Ellen asked.

'A nice young woman who lives in the next cottage, at least I think she's nice. There was something a bit odd about her.'

'Take no notice of your mother. Val was just a thoughtful neighbour who kindly brought us tea and biscuits when we first arrived.'

'I'd like to meet her. Leave the tray for now, Mum. It'll give me an excuse to pop along there later.'

'Fine, and, Percy, there's enough clutter in here so take those suitcases up to your room.'

As he went upstairs, Ellen followed him, saying, 'I might as well unpack them, Mum. It's mostly dirty washing anyway so there won't be much to hang up.'

'When you come back down the tea should be ready.'

Ellen was pleased to see two single beds when she walked into the room. With money tight it had been the perfect excuse not to buy a double and

Percy's mum had agreed that he could bring his own bed. There wasn't much of a gap between them, but at least they'd still be sleeping separately.

'It's a smashing view,' Percy said, looking out of the tiny window.

'Percy, come on, unpack your case.'

'Yes, madam,' he said with a small bow.

Ellen's heart jumped. For a brief moment, his action had reminded her of Billy, and, as though in agreement, for the first time she felt a tiny flutter in her tummy.

'What is it? What's the matter?'

'Oh . . . oh . . . the baby moved.'

'Blimey, you've gone all pale. Here, sit down,' he said, hastily moving a suitcase on the bed to one side.

'There's no need. I'm fine. Oh, Percy, it moved, my baby moved.'

'*Our* baby, Ellen.'

'Yes, yes, of course,' she agreed, yet deep down Ellen wondered if she would ever be able to think of the baby as Percy's. Billy might never know the truth, but she did, yet for her baby's sake it had to be a secret that would never be revealed.

'Let's leave the rest until tomorrow,' Hilda said as she sank, exhausted, onto a chair. They'd had a scratch dinner and it was now after eight in the evening. With four of them in the room, she had to admit it seemed a little cramped, but with both Ellen and Percy earning soon, eventually they'd want a place of their own. Of course it wouldn't be easy, and they'd have furniture to buy, as well as all the paraphernalia needed for the baby. Hilda smiled softly, sure it would be some time before they could afford it, and happy with that. Now that the shock of her daughter's pregnancy had diminished – now that she was married to Percy and their respectability was intact – she found herself looking forward to having her first grandchild.

'You look knackered,' Doug said as he held out a weak cup of tea – at least the fourth pot he'd made since they'd arrived.

Hilda knew she'd have to keep an eye on their ration or there'd be none left. Still, at least it made Doug feel useful and, once Percy had put boxes on the table so that Doug didn't have to bend down, he'd even managed to unpack a few. Since Gertie's offer of a job and accommodation to go with it, Doug seemed to have taken on a new lease of life. His back was still bad, and she knew it always would be, but he seemed to stand straighter somehow, as though the thought of being a wage earner had made him feel like a man again.

'It's only us,' Gertie called as she poked her head inside the door.

'Come on in,' Hilda said, her welcome warm.

'It looks so cosy in here,' Maureen said.

'Here, sit by the fire. There's room for three on the sofa,' Percy urged, moving to perch on the arm beside Ellen. 'I can't wait to start work on Monday; in fact, if I'm not needed for any more unpacking here, I wouldn't mind starting tomorrow.'

'Goodness, you're keen,' Gertie said.

'I've been reading up, Ellen has too, and we know loads about soil improvement, along with propagating and grafting, among other things.'

'Do you now? Well, that's good, but before we even think about stock we need to get the ground ready and a greenhouse set up. I've got a rotavator and I'll show you how to use it, Percy; and yes, you can start tomorrow if you like.'

'Great,' he said.

They chatted for a while, Gertie going over their plans for the nursery again and of course the shop.

'We're going to be busy with the grounds so, if you don't mind, Hilda, we'll leave setting up to you and Doug. We've had the outbuilding cleared, but you'll need to sort out the fittings. After that you'll need to buy in gardening equipment and anything else you think might sell.'

'Buying isn't something I've tackled before and with the shortages I'm not sure what I'll find. I'll try some wholesalers and maybe local craftsmen who can give us a good price.'

'I knew I could rely on you.'

'There isn't much I can do yet,' Doug said worriedly.

'Yes, there is,' Hilda insisted. 'For a start you can plan the layout of the shop, the shelving we'll need, and that's something I wouldn't be able to get my head around.'

Ellen was obviously unable to stifle a yawn and said apologetically, 'Sorry, but I'm bushed.'

'Yes, of course you are,' Gertie said. 'After such a long day, you all must be so we'll go now. Percy, we'll see you in the morning.'

'I'll be there bright and early.'

They all said their goodbyes, and it was only then that Hilda thought about Val's tray and tea things again. It was too late to take them back now, she decided, so it would have to wait until the morning.

Ellen yawned again and Hilda looked worriedly at her daughter. Yes, she did look tired, and suddenly, Hilda felt a flutter of fear. She had felt worn out and tired when she'd miscarried, but surely Ellen would be fine? She was over four months gone now, past the dangerous stage and the baby was due in August. Still, to be on the safe side she'd insist that her daughter rested tomorrow.

Stop worrying, Hilda chided herself. They were out of London now, and nothing would go wrong. Ellen would be fine, they'd all be fine and, comforted by that thought she said, 'I don't know about the rest of you, but I wouldn't mind an early night.'

'That's fine with me,' Doug agreed.

'Yes, us too,' Ellen said, she and Percy saying goodnight and going upstairs.

Hilda looked blearily at Doug. 'Go on up, love. I'll just bank down the fire and then I'll join you.'

He nodded, a pained expression on his face as he stood up, and Hilda saw that his back was bent as he went upstairs. Of course, with the unpacking he'd insisted on doing, Hilda wasn't surprised, but it didn't bode well for working in the shop. She'd just have to keep an eye on him, insist that when he was in too much pain he took the day off.

Alone now, Hilda banked down the fire, pausing before going upstairs as the calm atmosphere of the cottage seemed to wrap itself around her. She looked at the angel, smiling as she whispered, 'Goodnight. Keep watching over us.'

Hilda then chuckled. Hark at her, talking to a statue. If Doug heard her he'd say she was losing her mind. It was this place, this cottage. From the moment they had stepped over the threshold it had seemed to welcome them, and she felt a wave of contentment. They were going to be happy here, all of them, their future at last looking bright.

41

Ellen didn't know what the time was when she awoke the next morning, but turned over to see that Percy was already up and getting dressed. In the dim light his back was towards her, but she could see the outline of his broad, bare shoulders. Embarrassed, she looked away, asking, 'What time is it?'

'I dunno, but from the racket the birds are making it must be past dawn. We could do with a clock in here, but they're as good as an alarm. There I was thinking it'd be peaceful in the country, but they make more noise than London traffic.'

'It was the same in Somerset, and Hampshire. Still, at least I can't hear a cockerel, so that's something.'

'You needn't get up. Stay there and I'll fetch you a cup of tea before I go to work.'

'No, it's all right. Anyway, you'll need breakfast before you leave.'

Percy was dressed now and they heard a noise downstairs. 'It sounds like someone is already up.'

'It's probably my mum.'

Percy fished for his shoes and put them on. He bent to tie the laces, then said, 'You looked worn out when we came to bed so if you'd rather lie in for a while, I'm sure she'll sort me out something to eat.'

'Stop worrying, I'm fine now,' Ellen told him, unable to help thinking how nice it was that Percy was always so attentive and concerned about her. It wasn't any wonder that Janet liked him and Ellen still felt guilty that she'd been the one to marry him.

'Percy, it was bad enough telling Janet that you weren't interested in her, but then later I had to tell her that we were getting married. She really did like you.'

'Yeah, so you said, but at least she didn't twig that you're pregnant.'

'I'm not so sure. She went on and on about us being too young for marriage, and as she knew about Billy, I think she was suspicious.'

'There's no point in worrying about it. We've left London now and I doubt you'll see her again.'

'But I'd like to. Surely we'll go back now and then to see your parents?'

'I dunno . . . maybe. Now are you sure you don't want me to fetch you a cup of tea?'

'I'm sure.'

'Right, see you downstairs then.'

For a few minutes Ellen remained snuggled under

the blankets, her thoughts drifting. When the awful truth dawned that she was pregnant, she'd hardly seen Janet. Instead, with the perfect excuse of the coal shortage, she had hidden away in her room nearly every evening and in desperation had turned to God again, praying for help. There had been no answer, yet if a heavenly Father existed, she'd turned away from him and perhaps that was why her prayers had remained unanswered. Yet had they? Percy had come to the rescue, married her, and though it wasn't really a true marriage, perhaps one day it could be. Maybe she would grow to love him, and, at this thought, Ellen threw back the blankets. She couldn't leave everything to her mother. Percy was her husband and it was time to cook his breakfast.

It was gone ten o'clock before the last of the unpacking was done and the cupboards sorted.

'Right, Ellen, if you're not going to do it, I'm taking that tray back to Valerie,' said Hilda.

'No, I'll go,' Ellen insisted, finding that she was looking forward to meeting their new neighbour.

As Ellen carried the tray along the small garden path, she saw that the small, wooden gate ahead had blown open, the catch loose. It would be something for Percy to fix later and she wondered how he was getting on at the nursery. It was still cold, but there were signs of spring in the front garden, shoots emerging on some of the small shrubs. A few early daffodils were in bloom, and other bulbs were poking their head out of the soil. She saw weeds, lots of weeds, and itched to pull them out, but first of all she had to take this tray along to Valerie.

It was only a little way along the lane to Mayflower Cottage and Ellen floundered, wondering how she was going to knock on the door with the tray in her hands. No sooner had the thought crossed her mind than the door was flung open.

'Hello, and thanks for bringing that back, though I'm not sure who you are.'

'You met my mum and dad. I'm Ellen, their daughter,' she said, gazing with amazement at Val's wonderful, golden hair. How did she manage to make those waves, or were they natural, she wondered, wishing she too had hair like that.

'Will you be living in Lavender Cottage too?'

'Yes . . . and my husband.'

'Well, I never. It'll be lovely to have someone of around my own age close by. If you can spare the time, come on in.'

'Thanks,' Ellen said, thinking that Val looked a lot older than her, probably in her mid-twenties.

'Take your coat off and sit down,' Val urged, taking the tray. 'It'll be nice to have a chat.'

Ellen did just that, but as she held her coat over her arm now, Val spoke again.

'Like me, you're pregnant. It's nice we've got something in common.'

Ellen looked down with a start, sure that though she was now four months pregnant, her baggy jumper hid her tummy.

'How do you know I'm pregnant? Did my mother tell you?'

'No, she didn't mention it, but I can always tell. It's something in the face that gives it away.'

Ellen sat on the chintz-covered sofa and, as a wayward spring poked her, she shifted sideways. Val sat opposite, close to the range, then said, 'I used the last of my tea earlier this morning, but I've got some homemade apple juice. Would you like some?'

'No, I'm fine, thanks.'

'Is your husband going to be working around here?'

'Percy, yes, he's working at a nearby plant nursery. A friend of the family is starting it up, but it'll be a while yet before it opens.'

'That'll be Grange House and grounds. I saw it had been sold.'

There was a pause in the conversation so, filling the gap, Ellen asked, 'What does your husband do?'

'My Bob works on Elmwood Farm. He was off out early this morning to do the milking, but as it's Sunday he'll be home by twelve.'

'Will this be your first child?'

'Yes, and I'm not sure if I want a boy or a girl. What about you?'

'I don't really mind,' Ellen said. 'Mine's due in August. What about yours?'

'Maybe late August or early September, but lovely that we'll both be having them around the same time. I tell you what. My old mum showed me a way of finding out what sex the baby will be. Do you want to give it a go?'

'Er . . . I'm not sure. What would you have to do?'

Val lifted a wooden box from the mantelpiece and, sitting down again, she rummaged inside, pulling out a length of ribbon with a long, wooden pendulum on the end.

'All I have to do is to hold this over your tummy. I'll ask if your baby is a girl, and if it rotates in a circle from left to right, the answer is yes.'

'What if it's a boy?'

'Silly, if it's a boy the answer is no and it won't move.'

'Surely that can't work?' Ellen said doubtfully.

'We won't know unless we give it a try. Go on, lie down.'

Despite herself, Ellen found that she was intrigued and lay on the sofa, her head propped up on a cushion.

'This seems silly,' she said, giggling.

'It won't work if you don't take it seriously,' Val warned as she wrapped the ends of the ribbon around her forefinger. She then dangled the pendulum over Ellen's stomach. 'We just need to wait until it's still and settled before I ask the question.'

Ellen had composed herself now and waited until at last, satisfied, Val asked, 'Is this baby a girl?'

At first there was no movement, but then slowly but surely the pendulum began to circle from left to right, gaining momentum, going faster and faster.

'My, that was strong,' Val said. 'You're definitely having a girl.'

'It was you, it had to be. You made the pendulum move.'

'Now why would I do that? If you had a boy I'd look proper silly.'

'Well, yes, there is that.'

'Swap places and try it on me.'

Ellen took the pendulum, but felt silly as she mimicked Val's actions. She found it difficult to keep the pendulum still, sure then that Val had somehow held it in a way to make it circle, but nevertheless she asked, 'Is this baby a girl?'

Nothing changed, no definite circle, and, grinning, Val said, 'I reckon I must be having a boy.'

Sceptically, Ellen said, 'I wouldn't bank on it.'

'We'll just have to wait and see,' Val said as she sat up again, patting the seat beside her, 'but I'm looking forward to saying "I told you so".'

'You said your mother showed you how to do it,' Ellen said as she returned the pendulum. 'Does she live around here?'

'No, bless her, she died four years ago. This was her cottage, and, as my dad passed on when I was a baby, it came to me.' Val paused, her eyes saddening. 'My mum was a wonderful woman and she taught me a lot. She could even do healing.'

'Healing? What do you mean? Was she a nurse or something?'

Val chuckled. 'No, nothing like that. Mum was a spiritual healer and could sense things with her hands. People used to come from Guildford Town, Christmas Pie, and they all said they could feel the heat radiating from her palms. She managed to help so many of them, but of course there were those that she couldn't and it always saddened her.'

'Can you do this healing?'

'No, I haven't inherited my mother's gifts. I can sometimes sense pain, but that's all and occasionally I get feelings about things.'

'What do you mean by gifts?'

'I don't think I should tell you. You already think I'm daft.'

'No, no, of course I don't,' Ellen protested. 'Some of the things you've said sound a bit strange to me, but that doesn't make you daft. A woman once told my mum about a vision she'd had, and I went to see an old lady who used rune stones. Is that what you mean by gifts?'

'Could be, there are all sorts. We've all got them, but most people spend their lives ignoring them.'

'When the old lady cast the stones she told me I'd see a sign that would bring me peace. Do you know what she meant?'

'Goodness me, I've no idea. I've never even seen rune stones,' Val said as she rose to her feet.

Ellen felt it was a signal for her to leave, and not wanting to outstay her welcome she stood up too.

'I'd best get back. We've finished the unpacking, but there's a stack of washing waiting to go in soak.'

'If you get the chance, pop along to see me tomorrow,' Val suggested.

'Thanks, I'll do that.'

'That's good because I have a feeling you and I are going to become good friends. Well, bye for now.'

Ellen walked the short distance back to Lavender Cottage, intrigued by Val. She had talked about spiritual healing, gifts, and that thing with the pendulum was odd too. It had to be a game and surely it couldn't work? Yet even as this thought crossed her mind, Ellen wondered if she really was going to have a baby girl.

42

By April, with so much to do setting up the shop, Hilda found herself tired, but other than worrying about Doug, she was still really happy. He was doing his best, had planned the shop's layout, but there was little now he could do. He'd had to stand back while the carpenters put up shelving and she could see he was growing frustrated with the handicap of his back.

With the men working inside, they were both standing outside the shop and watching the newly delivered greenhouse going up. Hilda smiled, saying, 'Look at Gertie. She calls it supervising, but from here it looks more like she's shouting orders as usual.'

'It's just her way,' Doug said as they continued to watch the activity. Percy was mucking in, but Ellen was standing back. 'Ellen's getting a bit fed up. In her condition, there isn't much she can do at the moment.'

'There'll be plenty for her to get on with once the stock plants start arriving.'

'If Gertie doesn't get a move on with ordering them, there won't be much in the way of profit this year.'

'From what Ellen said, there'll be some for sale, but most will be kept for base stock and used for propagating. It seems Gertie isn't worried about making a profit yet.'

'That just leaves the shop and I can't see the tools and things you've ordered attracting many customers.'

'Gertie knows that and she's prepared to take a loss on the shop too.'

Doug pursed his lips, quiet then as they continued to watch the greenhouse going up, but then he said, 'I might have an idea.'

'What sort of idea?'

'Let me give it a bit more thought first,' he said, then turned to go back inside. 'To start with, where are those seed catalogues?'

'Under the desk, but what do you want them for? We've already ordered seeds and a display rack.'

Doug didn't answer and, shaking her head, Hilda followed him inside. No doubt Doug would tell her when he was good and ready. Some tools had been ordered from local craftsmen but until they and the other bits and pieces she'd ordered had been delivered, all they could do was to wait. She saw that the carpenters had nearly finished the shelving, and hopefully by the end of May they'd be ready to open.

Ellen knew she wouldn't be allowed to do anything, and her frustration was mounting. They were all over-protecting her, with Gertie refusing to let her help with preparing the ground. The greenhouse was up now, the work done, the men gone, and, as they stood admiring it, Ellen said, 'Gertie, are you going to order plant stock now?'

'With some of the ground prepared and the greenhouse up, yes. I'll get on to it later.'

'I'll be glad when they arrive, but until then I'm doing nothing to justify my wages. I might as well stay at home.'

'Don't be silly. You've done a lot in helping me to plan the grounds, and I could do with your input when it comes to placing the orders. It was all fruit and vegetables on the smallholding, but you know far more about flowers, shrubs, and trees than me.'

'Gertie, that isn't true. I know you've been reading up on them.'

'Yes, a bit, but I don't feel confident enough to tackle it on my own and need someone to chew over ideas with. It's funny really, but before you married Percy we were thinking about offering you a job as our housekeeper. Like me, Maureen doesn't like housework or cooking, but that all changed as soon as she saw the house. She fell in love with it on sight, and now likes nothing better than staying at home to keep it nice. She's even learning to cook and shows no interest in developing the plant nursery. So you see, my dear, your help is now going to be invaluable to me.'

'Really?'

'Yes, really. Now I don't know about you, but I could do with a hot drink. What about you, Percy?' Gertie called. 'Would you like a cup of coffee?'

'I won't say no,' he said. 'I'll just check that all the windows fit properly first.'

'Righto,' Gertie said before marching off.

Ellen didn't follow her immediately, but instead wandered up to Percy, saying, 'Did you hear that? Gertie wants my help with ordering stock.'

'Yes, and I can see you're chuffed.'

'I am, and as I'm not even allowed to dig in a bit of fertiliser, at least I'll feel that I'm doing something.'

'You're five months gone now. Of course you can't do digging.'

'Now you sound as bad as Gertie and my mother. I'm not ill, I'm pregnant.'

'I don't know anything about having babies so all I can do is follow their lead. If I let you help me with manual work your mother would have my guts for garters, let alone Gertie. It's bad enough having one mother-in-law, but sometimes it feels like I've got two.'

'You poor thing. Is it that bad?'

Percy grinned. 'Now you're being sarcastic.'

'Talking of mothers-in-law brings me to mine. I love Mabel and I'm glad you've patched things up with her and your dad.'

'With you and your mum nagging me I didn't have a lot of choice.'

'I don't nag. It was just a bit of gentle persuasion, that's all.'

'If you say so,' he said sceptically as his eyes roamed over the greenhouse again. 'Anyway, I'd best get on with checking those windows.'

'I'll see you in the shop,' Ellen said as she walked away. She was comfortable with Percy now, but as they lived in the same house, slept in the same room and both worked at the smallholding, it wasn't surprising. He was still keeping to his promise, but on the odd occasion he would give her a brief hug or a chaste kiss on the cheek. Ellen bit on her lower lip. She liked Percy, was sort of fond of him, but still dreaded the time when she would have to allow his lovemaking.

Not yet, it would be ages yet, Ellen thought, forcing her worries to one side. Soon they'd be ordering plant stock and she was looking forward to wading through what was on offer. In her mind she was already picturing wisteria, and a show-piece entrance of it dripping from arched trellises. Buddleias, she'd suggest those, and roses of all varieties – in fact, plants for every season.

Gertie went to check on the carpenters as soon as she went into the shop, pleased to see how well things were progressing. Hilda was sweeping up behind them, and Doug was sitting at the desk, scribbling on bits of paper.

'Hello, Doug, and what are you up to?'

'I'm working on an idea.'

'What sort of idea?' Gertie asked as Ellen now walked in to join them.

'I'm not really ready to talk about it yet. It still needs more costing to see if it's viable.'

'Tell me anyway, and, Hilda, make us all a cup of coffee.'

'Yes, madam.'

'I'll make it, Mum.'

'No, Ellen. I was told to do it,' she said, walking off to the tiny sectioned-off staff area.

Gertie lifted her eyebrows, but then perched on the edge of the desk, saying brusquely, 'Well, Doug, what have you got in mind?'

'Annuals,' he said, pointing to the seed cata-logue. 'It'll bulk up the other stock on offer. So far I've worked out the price of seeds, along with trays and soil. I think there'd be a decent profit.'

'It's a bit late to think about annuals.'

'If we start them off in the greenhouse we can force them on.'

'Maybe, but I can't see many people wanting to buy them.'

'A lot of men from around here work in London and, not only that, many women are still working too. Their lives are busier now, with less time to spend on gardening. Ready-made plants might be just what they need.'

Gertie turned it over in her mind. She didn't really want to sell annuals, felt they were a waste of time and effort, and not only that, for some time yet, making a profit wasn't an issue.

'Well, Gertie, what do you think?'

She looked at Doug, saw the appeal in his eyes, and with Ellen straining at the bit for more to do, maybe it *was* a good idea. Both Doug and Ellen could work together sowing the seeds, both sitting down, and they could do the same when it came to transplanting.

Gertie knew little about pregnancy, but Hilda had lost a baby and perhaps it was something that ran in the family. She certainly didn't want to risk the same thing happening to Ellen and her mind was almost made up when she said, 'Well . . . I suppose we could use the trays again so they wouldn't be wasted, but show me your figures.'

Doug eagerly shoved them forward, pointing out

his calculations. Gertie studied them, soon working out that the only real costs would be in manpower. With Doug and Ellen doing most of the work she wouldn't have to take on more staff, so that wasn't a problem, and when it came to transplanting, perhaps she could drag Maureen from the house for a few hours a day to muck in too. There would be a limit to how much they could handle, but it would keep Doug and Ellen happy and occupied, that was the main thing. Doug especially needed to feel that he was contributing something to the success of the business and if the annuals made a profit, he would certainly feel he was useful.

'All right, Doug, you've got my go ahead.'

'Go ahead for what?' Hilda asked as she carried in a large tray of tin mugs, pausing to give the carpenters their drinks first.

Gertie waited until Hilda drew closer and, taking a mug from the tray, she said, 'To sell annuals – but be warned, it's going to keep both Ellen and Doug busy so you won't get much help in the shop from now on.'

'Me! Why will it keep me busy?' Ellen asked.

'Surely you don't want your father to tackle this alone? It's a really good idea, but it's going to involve a lot of work.'

'Yes, I suppose it will,' Ellen agreed, 'but I thought I was going to help you to select plant stock?'

'There'll be time enough for that too.'

414

'All right then, I'm game.'

Gertie turned to Hilda. 'What about you? How do you feel about it?'

'It doesn't sound like I've got a lot of choice, but are you sure you can manage it, Doug?'

'It isn't exactly hard labour, so yes, I think I'll be all right.'

'I'll get a nice long work bench set up, and find some decent-height chairs so you won't be bent over. Percy can fill the seed trays with soil, and when they're ready, he can put them in the greenhouse.'

'Gertie, I'm quite capable of doing that,' Ellen protested.

'Yes, maybe, but we don't want you exerting yourself.'

'For goodness' sake, you're as bad as my mother. I keep telling her – and you – that I'm fine.'

'You should be thankful that Gertie's looking after you,' Hilda snapped. 'You wouldn't find another boss who'd be as thoughtful.'

'Don't call me that,' Gertie protested. 'I don't want you to think of me as your boss. We're just one big happy family. And you, Hilda, can stop calling me madam. It sounds ridiculous.'

'With the way you give out orders, what do you expect? You're not in the army now, but it's a wonder you don't expect us to salute you.'

Gertie knew Hilda was right and wanted to

smile, but instead she forced a look of annoyance. 'Only you would have the nerve to talk to me like that, Hilda.'

Hilda flushed; her manner unusually contrite. 'I'm sorry, Gertie. You've been so good to us, giving us all jobs and a lovely home. I'm grateful, really I am, and I won't talk to you like that again.'

Unable to hold it back now, Gertie laughed. 'Hilda, stop it. This doesn't sound like you at all, and if you must know, I wouldn't change you for the world. I know I come over as bossy and need someone like you to bring me down a peg or two.'

Hilda smiled, her manner back to normal as she said, 'That's just as well 'cos I ain't likely to change now.'

'Good, and as for being grateful, let's get one thing straight. I didn't take you on out of pity. I took you all on because I wanted people working for me that I love and trust.'

'Oh, sod it,' said Hilda. 'That means I'll have to bring back those scissors I nicked yesterday. They're nice and sharp too.'

'Very funny,' Gertie said, grinning as she lifted her mug to finish the coffee. 'Right, Doug, you can get on with ordering what you need in the way of seeds and things, but I'm off now. Maureen will be back soon and I think you're all going to love what she's bringing with her.'

'Why? What is it?' Ellen asked.

'She went to buy a puppy,' Gertie said, seeing the smile that lit up Ellen's face. Since Socks, Ellen hadn't had a pet, and while in Somerset she had loved Bertie. Not that this puppy was a Jack Russell, instead it was a favourite breed of Maureen's, but one that Ellen was sure to love.

Maureen had been right in saying that paying them all a wage would be a drag on her finances, but Gertie wouldn't have it any other way. She really did see them as her family – the family she had never had – and soon, in August, Ellen would be bringing another member into the fold.

43

Ellen was holding Percy's hand as they set off on a walk to explore more of the area, something they both enjoyed. They passed Val's cottage and Ellen wished she could see more of her, but, working all day, six days a week, that only left Sundays and Percy liked them to spend it together.

Val still intrigued Ellen, but as there hadn't been many opportunities to chat, she knew little more about the spiritual gifts. It was a subject she and Percy had never discussed, but now she wondered what he thought about it.

'Percy, do you believe in fortune tellers or anything like that?'

'I can't say I've given it much thought.'

'Do you believe in God?'

'In a way, but I'm not one for churches, hymns, praying and I just can't see God as a man sitting on a throne surrounded by angels.'

'Yes, but you said you believe in a way. What way?'

'I look at nature. It's so perfect, so ordered, unless man mucks it up, and I can't believe it all came about by chance. There must have been some sort of huge, unimaginable force to create all this, but our minds just can't comprehend it.'

Percy wasn't much of a talker, more a doer, and Ellen was surprised at the depth of his thinking.

'So are you saying that because we can't understand the enormity of this force, we've reduced it to a place called heaven and a God sitting on a throne?'

'Something like that, but look, there's a magpie in that tree. It's a beauty. Just like you,' he said, squeezing her hand.

'All right, I'll take the hint. You've had enough of this deep conversation, but thanks for the compliment,' Ellen said, smiling warmly. Percy was so sweet, so nice, and she enjoyed his company, yet she still couldn't feel anything for him other than a deepening friendship. He deserved more, deserved a wife who could truly love him, but much as she tried, Ellen still dreaded the time when he would want a full marriage.

'Gertie, take your feet off the sofa.'

'Sorry, ma'am,' Gertie said. 'Honestly, I never thought I'd see the day when you'd become all houseproud.'

'You know that from the moment I saw this place, I fell in love with it.'

'I'll admit the Georgian architecture is lovely, but it's our home, Maureen, not a showpiece.'

'I like it to look nice.'

'Nice, yes, but there isn't even a cushion out of place. Instead of mucking in with the nursery, you spend most of your time in here.'

'That's not fair. I've been helping out with the transplanting and enjoyed it too. It was nice to work alongside Ellen and Doug. I got to know them better and I feel closer to them now.'

'I'm glad, but since then you've hardly done a thing. I need you working outside so I think it's time we found a housekeeper. Now that Ellen's married she won't want the job, but we can find someone else.'

'No, Gertie. I don't want a strange woman around poking into our things, and as we only use one bedroom it won't take her long to figure it out. If you can't do without me working outside, couldn't you take someone on to do that instead?' Maureen appealed, looking close to tears.

Gertie stood up and pulled Maureen into her arms. 'There's no need to get upset.'

'But don't you see; this is just what I mean. When we're in this house it's the only time we have any privacy and you wouldn't be able to hold me like this with a strange woman around.'

'Point taken. All right, I'll take someone else on

to work outside, but I was going to do that anyway. Ellen won't be able to work for much longer.'

'I envy her. I love you, Gertie, but I'll never be able to have a baby. We'll never have children.'

Gertie tensed with fear. She knew why Maureen had wanted the puppy, a sort of replacement, but this was the first time she'd brought it into the open like this. If Maureen yearned for a child, what would she do? Would she leave her, find a man who could give her what she needed? Gertie crushed Maureen to her, the thought unbearable.

Hilda smiled at Doug. 'Well, love, only three months to go now and we'll have our first grandchild.'

'Without a spare room, it's going to be a squash to fit a baby in.'

'The cot will fit in their bedroom.'

'It won't be in a cot for ever. Maybe it's time they found their own place.'

Hilda shook her head against the idea. 'They can't afford it yet. Perhaps in a year or so.'

'A year or so! They can't wait that long.'

'Hello, we're back.'

'Hello, love,' Hilda said, pleased to see her daughter looking so happy. The marriage had worked out better than she'd dared to hope and it was clear to see that Percy thought the world of Ellen. A happy future stretched ahead of them, and one day she was sure there'd be more children, yet for now she was content to wait for the first one. She looked up at the angel and as always had a strange feeling that it was watching over them.

Hilda sighed. She had so much to be thankful for now, but in truth most of it was down to Gertie. In fact, Gertie had been a true guardian angel, one who had brought them here, to this wonderful cottage.

Their lives were already so different, all working together now, all happy, and the events in London becoming just unhappy memories. Oh Mum, Hilda thought, clutching the necklace. Don't let anything go wrong again, keep us happy and safe. The thought crossed her mind again and she berated herself for being silly. Of course it hadn't been her mother who had stood, unseen beside her all that time ago. Or had it?

44

'I know Ellen had to stop work, Percy, but I miss having her around,' Gertie said.

'It's just as well you put your foot down or she'd have carried on working right into labour.'

'Yes, I know, but I expect she's still complaining.'

'A bit,' Percy said as his eyes swept around the grounds. They had come a long way since March, and it was now August. In just five months the nursery had taken shape. Gertie and Ellen had ordered stock, some being sold, but most were held back for propagating. Young trees had been ordered too, including fruit trees, but, with limited space, not as many as they would have liked.

Gertie had taken advice from a Ministry of Food inspector and, though reluctant at first, she had given over a large portion of the grounds to growing vegetables. There were still food shortages, and until they eased Gertie would sell what vegetables she grew to the Ministry at a fixed price.

Another man, Harold, had been taken on, an experienced gardener, and the vegetable plots continued to thrive. It was interesting to learn about growing them, but Percy still looked forward to the time when they could concentrate solely on flowers.

Maureen was walking towards them and Percy grinned. The Labrador puppy had put on a lot of growth, looking gangly now, and spotting them it bounded forward, tail wagging and tongue lolling as it reached them to bounce excitedly around Gertie.

'You daft lump,' Gertie cajoled as the dog reared up, planting both front paws on her chest.

'Goldie, get down,' Maureen ordered, but as usual the dog ignored her.

'Down!' Gertie commanded.

This time Goldie obeyed and Maureen frowned, saying, 'Why won't she do that for me?'

'You're not firm enough, that's why.'

Percy hid a smile. When it came to firmness, Gertie had that in abundance, but he was used to her now. Underneath her brusque exterior he knew she had a heart of gold and not for one minute had he regretted coming to work for her.

'How's Ellen?' Maureen asked.

'She's fine, but fed up with being at home.'

'The baby will be here soon and then she'll have plenty to do.'

'Right, enough idle chatter,' Gertie said. 'Percy, check that the greenhouse is well ventilated and then make sure the outside plants aren't showing any sign of pests, especially the roses. I've picked up another load of horse manure from the stables. Harold can tell you what he needs for the vegetable plots, and the rest can be bagged up for sale in the shop.'

Percy nodded, head down now as he walked towards the greenhouse. The mention of stables had brought Billy to mind and his teeth were clenched. Sheila had given birth to a boy in July, his parents coming to see them to break the news. Percy had seen the look on Ellen's face, and for the rest of that weekend she'd been quiet. Until then, Ellen had seemed happy and he'd convinced himself that she was growing fond of him, but after that doubts had set in. Did she still want Billy? Despite what his brother had done, did Ellen still yearn after him?

The greenhouse was humid as Percy walked inside and he quickly opened more windows. The last thing they wanted was mould on the young stock and to make sure they were all right he checked them row by row, his mind still turning. Ellen was carrying Billy's child, and what if the baby served as a constant reminder that his brother had been first – what if it looked like Billy?

Sweat beaded his brow as at last Percy walked

outside, fighting his feelings. Seeing Doug looking at a plot of roses, he tried to distract his mind and asked, 'Is there a problem?'

'I'm not inspecting them, just stretching my legs.'

'Is your back playing up?'

'It's fine; in fact, it's better than it's been for a long time. What are you up to?'

'I've got to check plants for pests and then bag up some horse manure for sale in the shop.'

'Can I give you a hand?'

'No, thanks, and anyway, if Hilda saw you doing any bending or lifting, she'd skin you alive.'

'You've got that right, but what the eye doesn't see . . .'

'It's up to you, but if your back's feeling better the last thing you need is to strain it.'

'I suppose I'll just have to stick to sitting at the till, or propagating.'

'If you ask me, building up stock is the most important thing and you're doing that.'

Doug smiled. 'You've missed your vocation, son. You should have been a diplomat. Oh, well, I'd best get back to the shop.'

Percy inspected the roses, thinking that if it wasn't for his doubts about Ellen and the baby, he'd be a perfectly happy man. He got on well with Doug and Hilda; and though he didn't mind living with them in the cottage, one day he hoped that he and Ellen would find a place of their own.

He had dreamed of a full marriage once Ellen had the baby, children of his own, but now began to wonder if Ellen would ever see him as anything more than a friend.

'Not long now, Ellen,' Val said as the two of them sat in her back garden. 'Our babies are nearly due.'

'I hope you have yours first,' Ellen said.

'I doubt it. Your tummy looks lower and I think that's a sign.'

'Is it? I don't feel any different – well, except for my bladder.'

'My Bob can't wait and the daft bugger suggested that I could move things along by going for a run around the village.'

Ellen chuckled. 'Run! I can hardly walk, especially in this heat.'

'Yes, that's what I told Bob. Mind you, I expect Percy feels the same.'

Ellen feared the changes the birth of her baby would bring. Percy had been wonderful, she couldn't deny that, but she still only thought of him as a friend. One thing still marred her happiness, and that was the thought of having to be a proper wife to Percy, something she dreaded and worried about in equal measures.

'What's up, Ellen?'

'Oh, nothing,' she lied. 'I'm just a bit nervous about having the baby, that's all.'

'There's no need. You'll be fine, the baby will be fine and you'll be in safe hands with Mrs Ainsworth from the village. She's brought loads of babies into the world.'

'Is that another one of your feelings?'

Val shrugged. 'I just know you're going to be all right.'

'I think you're wrong about everyone having spiritual gifts. I haven't got any.'

'My mum used to say they need developing, but I must admit that as much as I tried, I never could do healing. She told me that her mother, my grandmother, could foresee the future, rather like that woman you told me about who had that vision about your dad.'

'I used to go to church yet they preached against things like that. I was once told that it was an abomination in God's eyes, yet there were spiritual things happening in the congregation.'

'My mother had a natural gift for healing and she helped a lot of people. Surely that can't be wrong?'

'I don't see how it can be and, to be honest, I'm not sure what I believe in now. There are so many religions, all preaching different things. How are we supposed to know which is the right one?'

'I've no idea. My mum taught me right from

wrong, encouraged me to help people and that's all that matters to me. I believe in God, but in my own way.'

'You sound like Percy and, as I asked him, what sort of way?'

'I think we each have to find our own path. Yours once led you to the church, but mine didn't. When the time is right you'll find your path again, but until then it's not up to me to lead you where you may not be meant to go.'

'I know you're twenty-five, but when you talk like that you seem so much older. You sound, oh, I don't know, wise, I suppose.'

'It was my mum who was wise, not me. I still miss her, especially now . . . with . . . with my baby close to being born.'

Ellen had never seen Val like this before, vulnerable, her eyes glistening with tears.

'There I was going on about being nervous, but you must be too.'

Val sniffed then nodded. 'I am a bit.'

'Well, let's hope you're first then, and if you are, I promise I'll be here to hold your hand.'

'No, I won't be first.'

'It doesn't matter; even if I've just had my baby, when you go into labour I'll get here somehow, even if Percy has to carry me.'

'You . . . you'd do that?'

'Of course I will.'

A smile at last broke through. 'Ellen, I'm so glad you moved into Lavender Cottage.'

'So am I, and soon we'll know if that pendulum was right.'

'A girl for you and a boy for me. It'll be nice, they'll be able to play together, grow up together, and . . .'

The colour had drained from Val's face, and nervously Ellen asked, 'What is it? You didn't finish what you were going to say. And what?'

'It . . . it was nothing . . . nothing. The baby kicked hard and it took me by surprise, that's all.'

'Are you all right now?'

'Yes, I'm fine.'

'What were you going to say then?'

'I can't remember now,' Val said dismissively and then glanced at her watch. 'My goodness, look at the time. I'd better make a start on Bob's dinner.'

Ellen frowned. Val wasn't meeting her eyes, and she was sure that she was hiding something. 'Tell me the truth. Did you have one of your feelings?'

'No, no, I told you, it was just the baby kicking. Now I must get on, but I'll see you tomorrow.'

'Yes, all right,' Ellen said as she reluctantly left. She was still sure that Val had felt something, that she was hiding something. But what?

45

Over a week passed and on Sunday Hilda was relishing her day off. She did some housework, lovingly dusted the angel ornament, and, though she knew it was probably foolish, she still felt that it somehow looked over them.

'Thank you,' she whispered before placing it back on the mantelpiece.

It was eleven o'clock now and, needing a break, Hilda picked up her knitting before going into the garden to sit next to Ellen. The sky was blue, bees buzzed among the flowers and she sighed happily, soon feeling lethargic; the knitting sitting un-attended in her lap.

'You look hot, Mum. You should have let me help.'

'No, love, your ankles are swollen and you need to rest.'

'I'm going in to get a glass of orange juice. Do you want one?'

'You stay there. I'll get it.'

'It's all right. My back's aching and I need to stretch it out.'

Hilda watched Ellen as she walked inside, one hand resting in the small of her back. The baby would be born soon and Hilda smiled with pleasure at the thought, her grandson or granddaughter a summer baby. Ellen had told her about Val and the pendulum, how it had forecast a girl, but to her it sounded like nonsense. She had thought Val a bit strange from the start, but despite this Hilda had to admit that she liked their neighbour. Val might come out with some strange things now and then, but she was always pleasant, always smiling, and she and Ellen had become fast friends.

'Here you are,' Ellen said as she held out a glass of juice.

'Thanks, pet. How are you feeling now? Does your back still ache?'

'No, it's eased off. It's always the same if I sit too long.'

'I've almost finished this now,' Hilda said, picking up her knitting. 'It'll just need sewing together and then you can give it to Val.'

'It's good of you, Mum. I know she appreciates it that you've been knitting for both of us.'

'The poor girl lost her mother when she was only twenty-one, and, anyway, with the amount of old jumpers and cardigans I managed to find at the jumble sale to unravel, I've got plenty of wool.'

'Hello, it's only me. I thought you'd be out here.'

'Talk of the devil,' Hilda quipped as she turned to see Val, her tummy huge like Ellen's and her movements cumbersome.

'I had a funny feeling and just popped along to see if I'm right,' Val said, her eyes on Ellen.

'Right about what?' Hilda asked.

'I thought Ellen might be in labour.'

'No, I'm fine, so for once your feelings are wrong.'

'Are you sure?'

'I think I'd know if the baby was coming.'

'Yes, I suppose so,' Val said doubtfully.

'All I've got is a backache.'

'I thought you said it had eased,' Hilda said sharply.

'It had, but it's back again now.'

'Hilda, where's Percy?' Val asked.

'He's gone to the pub with Doug for a lunchtime drink.'

'Right, I'll send my Bob to get them, and on his way he can call in on Mrs Ainsworth. She'll be needed soon.'

'I don't need Mrs Ainsworth. I told you, it's only a backache,' Ellen protested, but then bent forward, clutching her tummy. 'Oh . . . oh . . . I've got a pain in my stomach now.'

'I knew it. You *are* in labour.'

Hilda rose swiftly to her feet. 'Come on, Ellen, let's get you inside.'

'Mum, I'm scared.'

'Don't be, Ellen, you'll be fine,' Val said. 'I'm off to tell Bob now, and Mrs Ainsworth will soon be here.'

As Val waddled off, Hilda held Ellen's arm and inside she urged her upstairs. Half way up, there was another wail, Ellen standing frozen as her waters broke.

'Oh, Mum!'

'It's all right, it's perfectly normal,' Hilda said. Her daughter looked wide-eyed, so frightened, and for a moment Hilda almost panicked too. What if something went wrong? This was her daughter, her only child. She was sixteen, hardly more than a child herself and about to give birth.

Despite her fears, Hilda knew she had to hold herself together and now sought for something to give her strength. *Please, please let her be all right. Please, angel, watch over Ellen, keep her safe,* Hilda inwardly begged, and this time, for once, she didn't berate herself for being foolish.

Ellen gave birth to a baby daughter at nine thirty that evening. She was exhausted, but held the baby tenderly, love shining in her eyes. 'Mum, she's so tiny.'

'Born on the twenty-seventh of August, tiny but perfect. You'll have to think of a name now.'

'I already have. I'm going to call her Sarah.'

'My mother's name? Oh, Ellen, that's lovely.'

There was a mist of tears in her mum's eyes, but then Ellen looked away as Mrs Ainsworth came in, all bustling efficiency again.

'Right, my dear, let's get you cleaned up and then we can bring Sarah's daddy up to see her.'

Ellen tried to smile, but it was difficult. It should be Billy looking at his baby daughter, sharing the love she felt, the bond. Instead it would be Percy, and how could he feel the same? How could he feel this overwhelming love for a child that wasn't his own? It wasn't right, wasn't fair that her daughter would never know her real father and a father's love. Regret now swamped her. She shouldn't have done it – shouldn't have agreed that Percy pass Sarah off as his own.

'Here, I'll take her.'

Ellen gently passed Sarah to her mother, saw how lovingly she held her, and felt a little better. Sarah might never know her father, but she had grandparents who would love her as much as she herself did. She lay back on the pillows, too tired to think about it any more. Her daughter had come safely into the world, just as Val had said and, for now, that was all that mattered.

Unaware of Ellen's thoughts, Percy was still pacing. He had heard Ellen's screams – screams that seemed to go on and on until at last there was the small cry of a baby. Since then, nothing!

'Doug, what the hell's going on up there? Why is it taking so long?'

No sooner had Percy asked the question than Hilda appeared, with a wide smile on her face.

'Well, Doug, we've got a granddaughter.'

'A girl, that's nice. What about Ellen? Is she all right?'

'She's fine.'

Mrs Ainsworth came downstairs now, a smile on her face.

'Congratulations, Percy, you've got a beautiful baby girl. You can go on up to see her now.'

'What about me?' Doug protested.

'Let Ellen and Percy have a little time on their own first,' Hilda said.

Percy found his heart thumping in his chest. A girl, Ellen had had a daughter – but what if she looked like Billy? He found Ellen looking at the baby, but she looked up as he nervously approached the bed. Her smile was radiant and, despite the exhaustion etched on her face, he had never seen her looking more beautiful. For a moment words caught in his throat, but then he managed to stammer, 'How . . . how are you?'

'I'm fine,' she said, 'but look, Percy, isn't she lovely?'

Gingerly he sat on the side of the bed and, as Ellen pulled the swaddling to one side, Percy gazed at the baby. She was tiny, her face screwed up and cute little lips puckered as though about to cry. He couldn't see anyone in her, not Ellen, not Billy; in fact, he thought with a smile, if anything she looked like a sweet, red-faced little monkey.

'I've called her Sarah, after my grandmother. I hope you don't mind?'

'Of course I don't,' he said, reaching out to stroke the baby's tiny, outstretched palm, amazed when her fingers curled around his. Percy felt a sudden surge of protection that was so strong it almost took his breath away. It was a magical moment, and though she was his niece, Percy at last knew that he would be able to see Sarah as more than that, much more.

'Hello, sweetheart,' he said, smiling softly. 'I'm your daddy and I'm gonna love you to bits.'

There was a choking sob and, surprised, he saw that Ellen was in tears. 'What is it? What's wrong?'

With a watery smile, Ellen said, 'Nothing . . . nothing at all. Everything is just perfect.'

As Sarah let go of his finger, Percy leaned forward to kiss Ellen's cheek and then for a while the two of them just gazed at the baby, until at last Percy said, 'I'd better tell your dad he can come up.'

'Yes, and no doubt my mum will be with him. We'll have to watch it, Percy, or the pair of them will take this baby over.'

'Maybe it's time to find a place of our own.'

Ellen was quiet for a moment, but then said, 'Yes, I'd like that, but don't say anything to Mum and Dad yet.'

'Don't worry, I won't, and anyway, it might take us a while to find something we can afford, a place that's close to the nursery,' Percy said, then reached out to gently touch the baby's cheek. 'I won't be long, but it's time for you to meet your granddad.'

Ellen was smiling as she watched Percy leaving the room. She'd been silly, worrying about nothing. As soon as Percy saw the baby, it was obvious he was smitten and she was sure now that his love would grow. When she'd seen the look on his face, the amazement when Sarah clutched his finger, something had stirred in her heart. Percy had committed himself to taking care of her and Sarah, and deserved more than a wife who couldn't love him.

Could she? Could she open her heart to Percy? He was such a good man, but she had only seen him as a pale shadow compared to his brother. She'd been blinded by Billy's looks, had ignored his nature, but now knew how stupid she had been.

Yes, Ellen decided, she would try – try to love Percy – and as she liked him so much, surely that was a start.

46

Ellen recovered well and was up and about when, less than a week later, on Sunday, there was a knock on the door. Percy went to answer, but, hearing a voice, Ellen tensed. No, no, she didn't want to see him. She wanted to flee the room, but it was too late and Billy was already walking in. Sheila was behind him, a baby in her arms, followed by Mabel and Jack. Ellen knew this would happen one day, a time when they would all meet up together, but not like this, not without advance warning.

'Billy insisted on joining us,' Mabel said, her eyes wide with anxiety.

'What's going on?' asked Billy, frowning. 'Why shouldn't I come to see my brother and new niece? It's about time Percy met his nephew too.'

Percy was the one who answered, yet Ellen could hear the strain in his voice.

'There's nothing wrong, Billy. It's just that it's

been so long since we've seen you that it came as a surprise.'

Ellen could see the tightness in her mother's face as she said, 'Yes, it is a surprise, but sit down all of you.'

The tension in the room was palpable, but thankfully Mabel broke through it as she said, 'Come on then, Ellen, let me see my new granddaughter.'

'Here she is,' Ellen said, placing Sarah in Mabel's arms.

'Oh, look, Jack, isn't she gorgeous?'

'Yeah, a doll,' Jack agreed.

Ellen was trembling as Billy now looked at Sarah, her stomach churning when he said, 'I see she's got dark hair, just like my nipper.'

'You're forgetting that Ellen has dark hair too, and Sarah's is more like hers, thick with a wave in it.'

'Yeah, and it's lucky she didn't inherit her dad's thin, mousy hair.'

'There's nothing wrong with Percy's hair,' Mabel said indignantly.

Ellen felt the same indignation, but also a huge surge of relief. It was obvious by his comment that Billy hadn't worked it out, hadn't considered the dates, and so far didn't suspect anything.

'Ain't it about time you looked at my boy, Percy? You'll see that Freddie takes after me, a real chip off the old block.'

Ellen knew she had to keep up the pretence and now joined Percy as he went to take a look at Billy's son. Sheila looked up them, saying quietly, 'Hello, Ellen.'

'He . . . hello, Sheila, it's nice to see you again,' she managed, looking down at the baby.

'Yeah, you're right, Billy,' said Percy. 'He does look like you.'

Billy strolled over, wrinkling his nose. 'Sheila, Freddie stinks. Get off your fat arse and change his nappy.'

'Billy, watch your language,' Jack snapped.

Ellen turned to see that he looked livid, Mabel distressed, and her parents' faces were strained too.

'I . . . I'll make us all a drink,' she said.

'No, I'll do it,' her dad insisted.

With reluctance, Ellen sat down again, but then said, 'Mabel, are you all right with Sarah? Do you want me to take her?'

'No, darling, this is the first time I've had a chance to hold her and I want to make the most of it.'

'Mum's got two grandchildren now, but I beat you to it, Percy. Just like I beat you to everything,' Billy said, a sly look on his face as he glanced at Ellen.

'That's enough, Billy. What does it matter which baby came first? I love Freddie and this one too. They're both gorgeous.'

441

Ellen knew that Mabel hadn't seen Billy's sly look – that she hadn't cottoned on to his innuendo – but Percy had, and his fists clenched in anger. Had Billy worked it out? Oh, please, no, and unable to stand it any more, Ellen rose to her feet, just wanting to get out of the room.

'I . . . I'll give Dad a hand with the tea,' she spluttered.

'Don't let him get to you,' her mother whispered, joining Ellen as she walked to the kitchen. 'Mabel has always favoured Percy and Billy knows that. I don't think he suspects anything, it's just that he's jealous.'

'Hilda, after what he did to Ellen, I still feel like wringing his bloody neck.'

'I feel the same, Doug, but somehow we've got to get through this.'

Ellen found that the next hour wasn't easy, but at least it served to show Billy's true colours. The way he spoke to Sheila was awful, and she jumped to do his bidding, but mostly he just talked about himself.

'I'm doing well in the stables, but I want a promotion and know how to go about it. Mr Dunning is getting a bit past it now so I reckon I can point out a few of his lapses on the sly, spread a few whispers, and with any luck it'll ensure he gets put out to pasture.'

'Billy, he's been very good to you,' Mabel said. 'How can you do that to him?'

With a shrug, Billy said, 'Needs must. With Mr Dunning out of the way I'll go up a rung, and who knows, one day it might be me who's head groom.'

'Billy's always at the stables,' Sheila said.

'What's to come home for? Look at the state of you, and that brat's always squalling.'

'That's enough, Billy!' said Jack, his face dark with anger. 'You'll never change. You're selfish through and through, and I'm not sitting here listening to you talk to your wife like that.'

'Yes, Jack, come on, I've heard enough of this too,' Doug said. 'Let's you and I go for a stroll outside.'

'Billy, now look what you've done,' wailed Mabel. 'Hilda, I . . . I'm sorry. When they come back from their walk, we'll go.'

'What did I say?' asked Billy. 'What's all the fuss about?'

Nobody answered him, but Percy sat on the arm of Mabel's chair and placed an arm around her shoulders. 'It's all right, Mum, don't get upset. You don't have to apologise for Billy and you can come down again next weekend.'

Ellen looked at Billy but, unlike Percy, he showed no concern for his mother. She just wanted him to go, to see the back of him, but only moments later there was a frantic knock on the door and Bob almost fell into the room.

'Val's gone into labour,' he gasped. 'Ellen, I'm off to get Mrs Ainsworth but she insisted I come here first.'

Ellen jumped to her feet. 'Sorry, but I've got to go. Val needs me.'

'I didn't know you had company. It's all right, Ellen, I'll tell Val you can't make it.'

'Mum . . . Percy?' Ellen appealed.

'Just go, love,' Percy said.

'What about Sarah?'

'If she needs a feed, Percy can bring her along to you.'

'Thanks, Mum,' Ellen said, calling a quick general goodbye before hurrying out after Bob. 'Go on, don't wait for me, just go and get Mrs Ainsworth.'

He was off, running down the lane, while Ellen hurried to Mayflower Cottage where she found Val sitting in a chair, her eyes wide with fear. Ellen's heart went out to her. When she had gone into labour her mother had been there to help, to calm her, but Val had nobody until Mrs Ainsworth arrived.

'Come on, let's get you up to bed,' she said softly.

'Ellen, thank God you're here.'

'How often are the pains coming?'

'I woke up about three this morning and they weren't too bad. I didn't want to disturb Mrs Ainsworth that early, or you, so I hung on, but now my waters have broken and they're coming thick and fast . . . Oh . . . ohh,' she cried, doubling over as Ellen led her towards the stairs.

Ellen held her while waiting for it to pass, but Val had barely got onto the bed when another pain hit her. So far Val hadn't wanted to push, and Ellen just hoped Mrs Ainsworth would arrive before she did. If she had gone into labour at three in the morning, that was only six hours ago. Her own labour had lasted much longer and surely Val couldn't be that close to giving birth?

As she sat with Val, Ellen found that her thoughts turned to Billy. There had been a moment of fear when he had looked at Sarah, but it had passed. He'd seen her – had thought her his niece – and though later there had been that sly innuendo, she now felt her mother was right and there was nothing to worry about.

Billy had no idea that Sarah was Freddie's half sister. It was a terrible secret to keep, but Ellen felt as though her eyes had been well and truly opened now and it was better than the alternative. Billy might be handsome, but he was vain, nasty, an awful father and husband, the total opposite to Percy in character.

It was over now, the secret safe, and they could all get on with their lives. Sarah would grow up accepting Percy as her father and, unlike Billy, he'd be a good one, a loving one. She doubted they'd ever see much of Billy, and that was just fine with her, sure that Percy and her parents felt the same.

'Oh . . . Ohh, Ellen. I didn't realise it would be as bad as this. Why didn't you tell me?'

'I didn't want to frighten you, but honestly, once the baby is born you'll soon forget it.'

'Forget it! You must be joking and if Bob wants to come near me again I'll cut off his bloody John Thomas!'

Ellen smiled, but then another pain gripped Val and she cried out in anguish. 'No . . . no . . . I can't stand this any more, I just can't. When is it going to stop?'

'Hold on, it'll pass soon,' Ellen said, hiding her worry and wishing that Mrs Ainsworth would hurry up and get here.

At last there was the sound of footsteps on the stairs, the woman bustling into the room just as Val cried, 'Ellen, the baby must be coming. I want to push.'

'Well, my dear, you cut it a bit fine, didn't you?' Mrs Ainsworth said, but her manner was calm. 'Let's get you sorted out then.'

Ellen slumped with relief, but Val was still clutching her hand, refusing to let go, so she remained where she was. Only a week ago she had given birth to Sarah, and though the memory of the pain had dimmed, her heart went out to Val.

She was screaming now, red-faced in her effort to force the baby from her body.

'That's it,' Mrs Ainsworth said when there was a small pause, but then she urged again: 'Push again, Valerie. Come on, push. Good girl, I can see the head.'

'Head!' Val yelled. 'It feels more like a bloody great melon.'

'Right, that's it. Don't push for a moment, Valerie.'

'Don't push! You must be joking!'

Only moments later there was a small cry, and now the expression on Val's face turned to one of wonder.

'Is he all right, Mrs Ainsworth? Is my baby all right?'

'The baby is fine, but it's not a *he*, Valerie. You have a lovely little girl.'

'So much for the pendulum,' Ellen said, grinning widely.

The baby was placed in Val's arms and her smile one of wonder. 'Oh . . . look, Ellen. She's beautiful.'

The door flew open, Bob white-faced and his hair standing up where he'd been raking his fingers through it.

'Valerie! Val, are you all right?'

'Now then, you can't come in yet,' Mrs Ainsworth told him as she hurried to usher him out. 'Your wife is fine and you have a daughter, but please go downstairs until I call you.'

'Sod that. I want to see me wife,' he argued, pushing past the woman.

'Well, really!' Mrs Ainsworth huffed.

Ellen moved out of Bob's way and he took her place.

'Look, Bob,' Val said. 'This is your daughter and isn't she lovely?'

There was a choking sound, Bob's voice cracking as he said, 'She's so tiny. Is she all right?'

'She's fine.'

'A daughter – and there I was expecting a son.'

'Are you disappointed?'

He sniffed, wiping tears from his cheeks. 'No, and anyway, we've got plenty of time to have a boy.'

'After what I've just been through, you'll be lucky.'

'Can I hold her?'

'Of course you can.'

'Valerie,' Mrs Ainsworth said brusquely. 'I don't usually let the father in until the afterbirth has been sorted out, but this time I had no choice. However, I must insist that your husband leaves now.'

'Yes, all right, I'm going,' Bob said, but not before leaning over to kiss Valerie on the cheek.

'I'll go too,' Ellen said. 'You're worn out and need to rest now.'

'I won't argue with that, but, thanks, Ellen, thanks for being here.'

As they went downstairs, Bob said, 'I'll add my thanks to Val's. It was good that you were there. I know how scared she was and I hated leaving her while I went to fetch Mrs Ainsworth.'

'There's no need to thank me, and if it's all right, I'll pop along again later.'

'Yes, of course it is,' he said, his eyes still shining with tears as Ellen left.

She walked back to the cottage, hoping that Billy and the others would have left by now. Yes, they'd gone, and smiling, she announced, 'Val had a girl too.'

'That was quick,' said Hilda. 'I expected you to be gone for hours. I was glad to see the back of Billy, and your dad was too. He's a nasty piece of work. Anyway, love, you're just in time because Sarah needs a feed.'

Ellen took her daughter from her mother's arms. 'Where's Dad and Percy?'

'They're in the garden and Percy's doing a bit of weeding. With working with plants all week you'd think he'd be sick of it. Of course, it might be that he just needed to take his mind off Billy. He wanted to throttle him, your dad too.'

Ellen smiled down on Sarah. 'Bob was over the moon, and when he first saw the baby he broke down in tears.'

'Your dad was the same when I had you.'

'Was he? I didn't know that.'

'I think it takes a lot of men that way.'

Ellen doubted Billy would have been like that when his son was born. The only person Billy cared about was himself. She put Sarah to her breast, thankful now that she'd married Percy, and hoping she could be a true wife to him at last.

47

Val had called her baby Pauline and, when everyone else was at work during the week, Val and Ellen spent hours together every day. They were both new mums, both learning, yet it soon became obvious that Pauline was the more robust of the two babies, putting on more weight than Sarah. Ellen's mother told her not to worry, saying that Pauline had simply been born a heavier baby and that Sarah would soon catch up.

It was now close to the end of November, but, as much as Ellen had wanted to be a true wife to Percy, she just couldn't. The first time he'd tried to make love to her she had frozen, then fought, pushing him off. Percy had been so hurt, but she'd found an excuse, blaming it on their lack of privacy – that with her parents just next door, she hadn't been able to relax.

She'd been the same the next time he tried, fighting him off, using the same excuse, but in truth

Ellen was beginning to fear that she was frigid. Had Billy taken more than just her virginity? Had he destroyed something else within her too? She wanted to confide in someone, yet couldn't go to Val. Val thought Sarah was Percy's child and to confess that her marriage was still unconsummated would mean revealing the secret. That only left her mother, but sex was a subject that had never been discussed and she doubted it would be any different now.

Ellen was gazing into the fire when her mother came in, rubbing her hands together and heading straight for the fire.

'I've hung the nappies up but it's so cold out there and I think there's a threat of rain. We might have to dry them indoors.' Hilda then sat down, holding her hands out to the flames. 'What's the matter? Why the long face?'

'It's nothing, Mum.'

'You haven't been yourself lately, so something's upsetting you.'

'There's nothing. I'm fine.'

'It's your birthday tomorrow, and that should cheer you up. Percy's got a surprise for you.'

'Has he? What sort of surprise?'

'Now then, it won't be one if I tell you. I'm sure you'll like it – but I don't.'

'Why? What's wrong with it?'

'Oh, nothing, I suppose. It's just going to change things.'

'I don't like the sound of that. What sort of things?'

When her mother shook her head, Ellen urged, 'Come on, Mum, you can't leave me up in the air like this.'

'All right, I'll tell you, but you'll have to pretend you didn't know. Percy has found a cottage on the other side of the Hogs Back, a place of your own.'

'What! Oh, no!'

'I thought you'd be pleased.'

'But . . . but we'll be alone and . . . and that means . . .'

'Means what, Ellen?'

'Noth . . . nothing. It's nothing.'

'Don't give me that. I've just told you that you're getting a home of your own, but instead of being happy you look, oh, I dunno, sort of frightened.' Hilda's eyes then narrowed. 'Percy! Is that it! My God, I can't believe it of him, but if he's hurting you I'll have his guts for garters.'

'No, Mum. He hasn't hurt me. It isn't that.'

'What is it then?'

Ellen hesitated, but then haltingly she said, 'When we're in our own place, I won't have any more excuses. I'll have to make love to him.'

'I don't understand. What's wrong with that?'

'We . . . we haven't yet and . . . and I don't think I can.'

'I can't believe this. You've telling me you've never let Percy make love to you?'

'He . . . he agreed to wait until after I'd had the baby.'

'He must think a lot of you to go along with that, but hold on, you had Sarah in August so what's stopping him now?'

'I . . . I just can't do it.'

'Now listen, Ellen, you need to put yourself in Percy's shoes. He married you, took on another man's baby, and from what you've said, he's kept to his side of the bargain. A man has his needs, and it's been wonderful of him to wait this long, but now the least you can do is be a proper wife to him.'

'I've told you, I can't. Maybe . . . maybe it's because I don't love him.'

'For goodness' sake, you aren't the only woman who's married a man she doesn't love. Some women marry for money, others perhaps to escape an unhappy home life. In fact, there are a host of reasons, but it doesn't stop them from sleeping with their husbands. All right, I won't deny that sex is wonderful with the man you love, but without love it can still be enjoyable.'

'How do you know, Mum? Don't you love Dad?'

'Of course I do, but I know someone who didn't love her husband when she married him. Now don't ask who, because it was told to me in confidence.

Suffice to say, she grew to love him, just as you might grow to love Percy.'

'Mabel! I think you're talking about Mabel.'

'I'm not saying. I just hope it's made you see sense.'

'Mum. I'm fond of Percy, but that . . . that time with Billy, I didn't like it. I felt dirty, soiled and disgusted with myself. I . . . I think it might have made me frigid.'

'Nonsense. Look, I know you denied it, but I still think Billy forced you, so of course you didn't like it. I should have told you the facts of life, warned you, and I still blame myself that you got into trouble.'

'No, Mum, it wasn't your fault. I wasn't that naïve, but I *was* a fool. I thought myself in love with Billy and let him go too far.'

'Love, huh! I doubt that. It was more like a crush mixed with lust.'

Ellen flushed. 'Mum, I can't believe you're talking to me like this. You never have before.'

'You're seventeen tomorrow, a married woman with a baby and you've had to grow up fast. As for Percy, liking someone first then growing to love them is different and lasting. You said you're fond of Percy and that's a good foundation for a happy marriage, but if you don't sort yourself out you could lose him. With keeping him waiting this long it's a wonder he hasn't looked elsewhere.'

'What! You mean another woman?'

'Well, you don't want him, so what do you expect?'

'I don't like the thought of him going off with someone else.'

'If that's the case, you must think more of Percy than you realise. Take my advice, Ellen. If you don't want Percy to stray or to leave you, the bedroom is the most important room in the house.'

Ellen flushed. 'Mum!'

'I'm only telling you for your own good. I don't like the thought of you moving out, and I'll miss both you and Sarah, but if you want this marriage to work, you've got to make a fresh start.'

'I . . . I know.'

'Goodness, Ellen, look at the time. Your father and Percy will be back from the pub soon and looking for their Sunday dinner. Get the cauliflower sorted while I turn the roast potatoes.'

'Mum, thanks, I'm glad I plucked up the courage to talk to you,' Ellen said as she laid Sarah in her pram.

'Don't say that, Ellen. I should be the one you naturally come to with your problems.'

'I was too embarrassed, Mum, but I won't be in future.'

'I'm glad, but it's down to me that you felt like that. I tried to keep you a child, didn't want you to grow up, that's the problem. Huh, some mother I've been.'

'You're a wonderful mother and I wouldn't swap you for the world.'

'Thanks, and in my own defence I can only say I did my best. You don't get lessons in being a parent and I just followed on from my own mother's example. When I think about it, I couldn't have spoken to her either, at least not about things like that. Still, it's a lesson learned and you'll know better with Sarah.'

The door opened, Percy calling, 'We're back,' then sniffing the air. 'Cor, that smells good enough to eat.'

Ellen looked at her husband, at the smile on his face, and it hit her then. The thought of him leaving her, of being with another woman really did make her feel sick inside. She'd been so wrapped up in her pregnancy, then in Sarah, that she had taken Percy for granted. He was always there, always the same, even-tempered and kind, and somehow it must have crept up on her. Her mother was right. Maybe she *did* love him.

'How's my girl?' he asked, looking in the pram.

Ellen impulsively stood behind Percy. She had never yet instigated a show of affection, but now wrapped her arms around his waist. 'She's fine.'

Percy turned around, a look of bemusement on his face. 'What's all this then?'

'I can give my husband a cuddle if I want, can't I? In fact, I wouldn't mind a kiss.'

His eyes widened, and Ellen felt a surge of guilt. She had never done this before either, never offered to kiss him, and saw his eyes shine with delight before he lowered his lips to hers.

'If you two don't mind, I'm trying to sort this dinner out, and Ellen, what about that cauliflower?'

'Sorry, Mum. I just felt like giving Percy a kiss,' she said, grinning widely when her mother gave her a knowing wink. It was going to be all right, her marriage was going to be all right, and now she looked forward to the future with happiness instead of fear.

48

Ellen had been right to look forward to the future. Though it was about a twenty-minute walk from her parents, and on the other side of the Hogs Back, she had fallen in love with the cottage Percy had found on sight; but, best of all, she had found that she could now give herself willingly to her husband, to find that she revelled in his love-making. It had been fumbling and awkward at first, but they now found joy in each other's bodies.

Together they had watched Sarah grow, had laughed when she first went on all fours to crawl, but so far she hadn't managed to walk. Mostly, though, Sarah was a quiet, contented baby, happy to just sit on the rug playing with the wooden toys her grandfather had made.

When Val arrived at midday, Ellen let her in, the two tots placed side by side on the hearthrug and chuckling to see each other.

'I know you moved in here ten months ago and I should be used to it by now,' Val mused as Ellen passed her a glass of apple juice, 'but I still miss having you living down the road.'

'It isn't the same, that's for sure.'

Val grinned. 'I should be used to this room too, but it still looks stuffed full of furniture.'

'Yes, I know,' Ellen agreed. It not only looked stuffed full, it looked out of place, but nevertheless she loved it. Among other things, Gertie had given them a lovely, long, red velvet sofa with ornate legs, along with a fireside chair, and a beauti-fully carved mahogany sideboard. There were side tables too, and lovely lamps, the furniture more suited to a large drawing room than a cottage parlour.

'Look, Ellen, look,' Val said excitedly. 'Pauline's up on her feet again.'

Sarah was sitting on the rug, flapping her arms as Pauline clung to the edge of the chair before taking one, then two tottering steps towards her mother. She then sank down, but Val swept her up into her arms, crying, 'You clever girl. Just over twelve months old and walking.'

Ellen smiled at the scene. Pauline was so like her mother with her blonde hair – though her eyes were blue, not grey. In contrast, Sarah was dark, her eyes brown and her smile impish. Ellen had feared for a while that her daughter was starting to look like Billy, but instead she now bore a distinct resemblance to her father, something he loved pointing out.

'Did you see that, Sarah? Pauline walked. She beat you to it, and now you should try too.'

Val put Pauline down next to Sarah, and both chuckled as though they understood every word, but it was Pauline who clung to the chair and struggled to her feet again.

'Oh, dear, there'll be no stopping her now,' Val said. 'I think I'm going to need a playpen, especially in my condition.'

'Condition! What condition? Val, don't tell me you're pregnant again!'

'Yes, I am, but I wanted to be sure before I told you.'

'That's wonderful and I bet Bob's chuffed.'

'Yes, but this time he wants a boy. I told him it's nothing to do with me and he'll have to take what we get.'

'The pendulum was wrong so it's no good trying that again.'

'I know, and I must admit I was shocked when Mrs Ainsworth told me I had a girl.'

'I don't suppose you'll be using her this time. My dad said that thanks to Nye Bevan we've now got this wonderful National Health Service.'

'I haven't thought that far ahead, but I think I'd like Mrs Ainsworth to deliver this baby too.'

'You've beat us to it,' Ellen said ruefully. 'We've been trying for a baby, but no luck so far.'

'Don't worry, it'll happen one day.'

'Are you just saying that, or is it one of your feelings?'

'I suppose it's a feeling because somehow I just know you'll have another baby.'

'That's good, and I'd like a boy next time too. Any feelings about that?'

'Sorry, no.'

'I was an only child, but I want Sarah to have a brother or sister. I just hope it happens soon.'

'Ellen, for now just cherish Sarah.'

'I do cherish her. What made you say that?'

'No reason really, but tell me, how are things going at the plant nursery?'

Ellen was surprised at the swift change of subject. 'From what I'm told, they've done really well this year. They sold all the stock, including annuals again, but the summer season is nearly over now. No doubt they'll still have vegetables for sale and, as Christmas trees sold really well last year, I expect they'll get them in again, but that won't be until December.'

'Do you miss working there?'

'Yes, sometimes, but with this little madam to look after,' Ellen said, smiling at her daughter, 'I'm happy to stay at home.'

'You always keep the place so nice. Mind you,

with those two dribbling everywhere it's just as well you covered the chair and sofa with these old curtains. Plush red velvet and babies don't mix.'

'Percy's just as bad. He scrubs his hands every day, but working at the nursery means they're always engrained with dirt.'

They continued to watch the children, chatting idly about this and that, but then an hour later both children were getting crotchety and needed a nap. Val picked Pauline up.

'I'd best be off. I'll see you tomorrow at my place.'

'I'll be there around midday,' Ellen said as Val struggled to put her protesting daughter into her pram.

Sarah held out her arms, hating to see Pauline go and her face puckering with distress. Ellen did her best to soothe her daughter when they left, stroking Sarah's hair as her mind wandered. It was nice for Val that she was going to have another baby, and she hoped it wouldn't be long before she fell pregnant again too.

Val said it would happen, but hadn't predicted when. Oh, please let it be soon, she thought. Her mother was right; she had fallen in love with Percy, deeply in love and couldn't wait to see the delight on his face when she could tell him she was having his baby.

'And you, darling,' she said, holding Sarah close, 'you'll have a baby sister or brother.'

Val pushed the pram home, her expression one of sadness. There were times when she hated her feelings, hated what they told her. Maybe she'd been mistaken. It was rare, but she'd been wrong before and there was no sign that anything was amiss. Feeling marginally better, Val stopped outside the village shop.

A lot of things were still rationed, but not bread or flour now, and with only a heel of bread left she needed to buy another loaf. She left the pram outside, finding just one customer ahead of her, the old, wizened woman turning to look at Val as she stepped inside.

'Been to see that friend of yours, have you?'

Used to the fact that everyone in the village knew everyone else's business, Val said, 'Yes, Mrs Norris.'

'I know her husband works up at that nursery, her parents too, but there's talk about those women who own it.'

'Is there? What sort of talk?'

'Now, Valerie, you know I'm not one for passing on gossip, especially of that sort.'

It was obvious that Mrs Norris was itching to tell her, so shrugging, Val said, 'Fine, don't tell me.'

'I suppose you'll find out soon enough, so you

might as well hear it from me,' Mrs Norris said, pausing to lick her lips before continuing. 'Well, now, according to Mrs Oliphant, whose daughter is a friend of a friend of the girl who was taken on at the nursery at the beginning of the year, those two women aren't just spinsters as we thought.'

'Oh, are they married then?'

'No, it isn't that, and if you ask me it's disgusting, that's what it is.'

'You've lost me, Mrs Norris. What's disgusting?'

'The girl who works for them now, told this friend of a friend of Mrs Oliphant's daughter, that she's seen things.'

'What sort of things?'

Mrs Norris sniffed, her lips curling in distaste. 'She's seen that big woman, her that always wears trousers, cuddling the other one, and not only that, kissing her too.'

Val frowned, but before she could gather her thoughts, the shopkeeper, Mrs Short, put her pennyworth in too.

'Yes, Valerie, and it wasn't just friendly affection. They were kissing each other on the lips.'

'What! No, surely not?'

'That's what we've heard, Valerie,' Mrs Norris said. 'Now, I think you should warn your friend. Once her husband and parents find out, they won't want to work for the likes of them, and if people around here have their way, those women will be drummed out of the village. Now then, Mrs Short, how much do I owe you?'

Val walked out of the shop in a daze, her loaf of bread forgotten as she gripped the handle of the pram. She knew little about that type of thing between two women, but the thought of it turned her stomach. Yet it couldn't be true, it just couldn't. From what Ellen had told her, she had known the big woman – Gertie was it – from childhood and she seemed really fond of her. Ellen would never condone something like that going on, and neither would her parents.

She would have to tell them – warn them about the gossip that was spreading round the village. If she did that, maybe it could be nipped in the bud before the villagers started to take any action. Her mouth set in a grim line, Val turned the pram around, heading back to Ellen's cottage.

Ellen opened her door, surprised to see Val again.

'Hello, did you forget something?'

'No, but I've just heard some awful gossip. I had to come back to warn you.'

Ellen paled. Warn her about what? Surely nobody had found out that Sarah wasn't Percy's child?

'What's being said?'

'Pauline's asleep so I'll leave her outside,' Val said, then stepped over the threshold. 'The gossip's about your friends, them that own the nursery.'

Ellen's first reaction was one of relief that it wasn't about her and said, 'I suppose you mean Gertie and Maureen?'

'Yes, and it isn't very nice, Ellen. There's talk that they aren't . . . well . . . just friends. Now don't get upset, because I'm sure it isn't true, but a girl who works there said she's seen them kissing each other.'

'That's rubbish,' Ellen snapped, instinctively lying to protect them.

'The trouble is the villagers are up in arms about it. If they don't want to be hounded out, they'll need to do something to stop the gossip.'

'Hound them out? But that's awful. Gertie and Maureen haven't harmed anyone and I don't see why they should have to defend themselves.'

'I know, but I still think they need to be told.'

Ellen was relieved when Val didn't stay. She still couldn't believe that the village would try to hound Gertie and Maureen out and that was bad enough, but if they succeeded it would mean that Percy and her parents would lose their jobs too. She had to do something, quickly warn Gertie, and to do that she'd have to go to the nursery.

49

At the nursery, Gertie was watching Nancy as she wheeled a barrow of manure along to Harold. The girl worked hard, there was no doubt of that, but she was over-familiar, and Gertie saw her now as a rival.

'What's up, Gertie?' Maureen asked as she walked to her side with the dog. 'You look a bit grim.'

Gertie leaned down to make a fuss of Goldie, her face hidden. 'It's Nancy. I'm still not sure about her.'

'Not this again. You've no need to be jealous. Nancy is just friendly, that's all.'

'If you say so, but I bet you don't get out of the gates without her contriving to bump into you.'

'Now you sound paranoid.'

Nancy was heading back to the mound of fertiliser now, her head turning in their direction and instinctively Gertie threw an arm around Maureen.

'Stop it,' she snapped. 'We agreed there'd be no

displays of affection outside of the house, but you seem to have forgotten that. I know what you're doing, but you don't have to lay claim to me. Nancy isn't interested in me in that way.'

'I'm not so sure.'

'For goodness' sake, if it's worrying you that much, get rid of Nancy. Give her the sack,' Maureen said in exasperation.

'I might just do that.'

'Fine, now if you don't mind, before Goldie pulls my arm out of its socket, I'm taking her for a walk.'

Gertie watched as Goldie almost dragged Maureen off, but then turned to find that Nancy was nowhere in sight. Her lips thinned. Nancy had abandoned her work and, as she'd suspected, she was probably off to intercept Maureen before she left the grounds. That's it, Gertie thought, she'd had enough. The girl would have to go, and now she headed in the direction of the gates too, determined to sack the girl.

Sarah was asleep, but, anxious to get to the nursery, Ellen laid her gently in the pram, pleased when her daughter didn't stir. She left the cottage, shortly turning into the lane that would lead her up to the main road that crossed the Hogs Back, the nursery on the other side.

It was a lovely September day, the countryside

beautiful, and Ellen noticed that some trees were starting to turn, their leaves tinged with brown, a sure sign that autumn was upon them. Time had flown, with Sarah having her first birthday in August, and now in a few months it would be Christmas again. She wanted to try her hand at cooking the dinner this time and hoped her mother would agree to come to their cottage, perhaps Mabel and Jack too, all celebrating another wonderful year.

Thinking about Jack and Mabel inevitably brought Billy to mind and Ellen hoped that he and Sheila would celebrate their Christmas in Hampshire. She didn't want to see him again, her feelings for him well and truly dead. Percy may not have Billy's looks, but she had come to love his face: the softness in his eyes and the curve of his mouth when he smiled. More, she had come to love the man, his gentle personality, the way he treasured both her and Sarah.

Ellen was close to the top of the hill now, her thoughts still on Percy. He loved his job too, his enthusiasm never waning, but now she shivered. Val had said that Gertie and Maureen could be hounded out, but surely there was some way to stop the gossip? If they were forced to leave, what would they do? Their homes, their livelihood, were at risk, her parents' too.

With her mind searching for a way to solve the

problem, Ellen stepped out onto the main road, too distracted to see the danger.

Maureen had picked up her pace when she saw Nancy heading towards her and managed to get out of the gates without being intercepted. Though she had denied it, Maureen knew that Gertie had reason to be jealous. She had done nothing to encourage it, but Nancy had made her feelings obvious since they had worked together on the spring transplanting. Maureen had of course turned her down, and since then did her best to avoid the girl, but it wasn't always possible.

Gertie was understandably suspicious and had started to be overly affectionate in front of Nancy, making it obvious that they were a couple. Maureen knew it annoyed Nancy and, fearing the girl would become vindictive, she had tried to discourage Gertie, but it hadn't worked.

It was getting Maureen down, the juggling, trying to be nice to Nancy without giving her ideas, trying to hide it all from Gertie, and though she hated the thought of anyone losing their job over her, she'd be relieved if Nancy got the sack.

She continued to walk and, unwilling to go back to the nursery just yet, Maureen decided that she'd go across the Hogs Back to see Ellen and her baby. Sarah was adorable, so cute, and, as she hadn't been to the cottage since last week, it would be lovely to see her. Goldie had finished her frolicking to forage among the hedgerows, but now she called her.

'Come on, Goldie, come here.'

The dog trotted to her side and, clipping on the lead again, Maureen stepped out, the walk to the Hogs Back from here only a short one.

The lorry driver was in shock, totally unable to deal with the hysterical woman who was screaming like a banshee as she flung herself on the ground beside the smashed and crushed pram.

A car and a tractor had pulled up now, both the drivers rushing over to the scene. Stuttering, the lorry driver said, 'I . . . I didn't see her, or . . . or the pram. She . . . she came out of nowhere.'

'There's a house over there,' said the car driver, pointing. 'I'll see if they've got a telephone to ring for an ambulance.'

With that he rushed off, while the tractor driver crouched down beside the screaming woman.

'Get her out! Oh, please, get my baby out!' Ellen begged.

The man was pale as he abruptly stood up, saying, 'I think we should wait until an ambulance arrives.'

'No! No! Get her out. Sarah! Sarah!'

Someone else appeared now, running out into the road, a woman with a dog, her eyes wide with horror.

'Ellen! Oh, Ellen!' she cried.

'Maureen! Help me! Please help me.'

The lorry driver ran a hand over his face, and at last his feet moved as he staggered over to the pram. One look and nausea rose in his throat, almost choking him until somehow he forced it down. There was nothing he could do, nothing anyone could do, and as he looked into the pram again, this time there was no forcing the nausea away. He staggered away again, throwing up on the side of the road, knowing that what he had seen would haunt him for ever.

50

Ellen awoke to find herself in a strange room, and at first blinked with confusion; but then in an awful rush it all came back to her. The lorry, the horrendous noise as it hit the pram, taking it from her hands and sending it flying, only to land in front of the lorry again. The scream of brakes . . . the wheels . . . the sickening crunch.

'Sarah! Sarah!' she screamed.

Two women rushed into the room, both in uniforms. Nurses, Ellen thought, her voice high in appeal. 'Where is she? Where's my baby?'

'Nurse Davies, get Doctor Mason.'

As one of the nurses rushed out, Ellen tried again. 'Please, please. I want to see my baby!'

'You must calm down or the doctor will have to sedate you again,' the woman soothed.

A man came into the room, the nurse moving aside as he approached the bed. There was something in his eyes, sympathy, and Ellen felt a jolt in her stomach.

'No . . . no . . .' she groaned, dreading his words.

'Mrs Johnson,' he said gently. 'I'm so sorry, but I have to tell you that there was nothing we could do to save your baby.'

'No!' Ellen screeched. 'Sarah can't be dead . . . she can't! Give me my baby! I want my baby!'

'Nurse, hold her arm, please.'

Ellen writhed, but the grip was vice-like and then she felt the prick as a needle penetrated her skin.

'Don't . . . don't,' she sobbed.

The nurse gently urged her to lie down, the pillows soft beneath her head.

'Sarah . . . Sarah,' Ellen sobbed, but then her body felt heavy and she felt that she was sinking into an abyss as her eyes closed.

Hilda almost staggered into the cottage ahead of Doug, and the first thing her eyes focused on was the angel. A surge of anger shot through her body and her feet were firm now as she marched across the room to grab it from the mantelpiece. She held it aloft for a second, her eyes blazing with hate, and then with all the force she could muster she smashed it onto the floor.

'Mad! I was mad to think that you were watching over us!'

'Hilda, don't. It's only an ornament and this isn't helping,' Doug said.

'Help! There is no help! She's dead! Sarah's dead!'

The door flew open, Val crying, 'Someone knocked on my door to tell me there's been a dreadful accident. Oh, tell me it isn't true.'

Hilda was thankful that it was Doug who answered, his voice a croak. 'It's true.'

'No . . . no, not Sarah! And Ellen, what about Ellen? Is she all right?'

'Ellen wasn't hurt,' Doug told her, 'but she's in hospital. She had to be sedated.'

'Will . . . will I be able to go to see her?'

'I don't think so, not at the moment, but she may be allowed home tomorrow.'

Hilda doubted it, fearing for her daughter after being told by a nurse that Ellen was almost out of her mind with grief. There were pieces of white porcelain scattered across the floor but, when she looked down, Hilda saw that the head remained intact, the eyes she felt gazing up at her mockingly. She lifted her foot and stamped on the head, satisfied to hear the crunch as it shattered. A sob escaped her lips. Sarah's head had been crushed too, her injuries so bad that they hadn't even been allowed to see her tiny, broken body.

All her anger spent, Hilda sank onto her knees among the broken pieces of porcelain, uncaring when a shard dug deeply into her leg. Sarah, their beautiful Sarah was dead, and Ellen so over-whelmed, so stricken with grief that she'd had to be sedated.

Percy sat by Ellen's side, feeling utterly helpless. In a way he dreaded her waking up, knowing she would have to face the loss of Sarah all over again. The police had told him what had happened, that Ellen had stepped out onto the main road in front of a lorry, the driver helpless to stop in time.

Percy shifted in his chair, his throat parched. It was now after seven in the evening, but there was no way he was going to leave Ellen's side. Hilda and Doug had gone home earlier, but he guessed they'd be back soon and, as the thought crossed his mind, the door opened.

'Percy, can I come in?'

He looked round, but it was Gertie hovering in the doorway and he croaked, 'Yes.'

'I had to come back to see if there's anything we can do. Has she woken up yet?'

'Once, but she was so hysterical that they had to sedate her again.'

'Have you been sitting there since we left?'

'I don't want to leave her.'

'I thought you might need this,' a nurse said as she came into the room to hand Percy a cup and saucer.

'Thanks, I do,' and, though it was red-hot, he

gulped the tea down. The nurse left and he turned to Gertie, asking, 'How's Maureen?'

'She's still in a bit of a state so I made her stay at home this time. I can't imagine how awful it must have been for her to come across such a scene, but in a way I'm glad she did. At least Ellen had someone there she knew, and Maureen was able to stay with her until the ambulance arrived.'

There was a soft groan, and Percy looked at Ellen worriedly. Was she waking up? The door opened again, and this time it was Hilda and Doug who came in, just in time to see Ellen's eyes open.

She blinked, unfocused at first, but then, seeing her mother, she suddenly struggled to sit up, crying, 'Mum . . . Oh, Mum . . .'

Hilda rushed to gather Ellen into her arms, and hearing her heartrending sobs, Percy stood up; tears filled his eyes too. He had loved Sarah as though she was his own child; he couldn't bear it that she had died, and so horrifically, the thought of her suffering more than he could stand. Sarah's cute, innocent face rose in his mind; her impish smile, the way she held out her arms for him to pick her up, the way she nuzzled her face into his neck.

Percy turned, tears blinding him as he found himself walking into Gertie's outstretched arms.

51

Ellen had been allowed home after forty-eight hours, but was unable to face seeing anyone other than Percy and her parents. She knew that arrangements were being made for the funeral, but the thought of it was more than she could bear. It was her fault! She had pushed the pram into the road. She had killed her beautiful daughter.

The vicar had been to see them, had talked about the service, of hymns, but she had screamed at him to go away. What good were prayers? What good were hymns? Sarah was gone – because of her carelessness, her beautiful baby was gone.

'Ellen, try to eat this,' her mother urged, holding out a sandwich.

'No, I'm not hungry.'

'You've hardly eaten for days. Please, at least try.'

Ellen turned her head away, too racked with guilt to face the thought of food. All she wanted was to die – she deserved to die and would welcome it. Maybe in death she could be with Sarah again, and only that thought offered her a crumb of comfort. She closed her eyes, hardly aware that her mother had gone to open the door.

'Sorry, Val, Ellen still doesn't want to see anyone.'

'Please, let me come in.'

'Val's here, Ellen. She wants to see you.'

Wearily Ellen opened her eyes, about to protest, but it was too late; Val was in the room, moving quickly to crouch in front of her.

'Ellen, I'm so sorry.'

'You knew, didn't you? Why didn't you warn me?'

'How could I? Yes, I had a strange feeling, but that was all.'

Ellen stumbled to her feet. She had worked it out; Val's strange behaviour when they were both pregnant, then the advice to cherish Sarah. She couldn't stand the sight of Val, couldn't bear it that somehow she had known that Sarah was going to die and, pushing her friend aside, she fled upstairs.

'Val, what's this about a feeling?' Hilda asked. 'Don't you think that Ellen's been through enough without you coming here to upset her?'

'I thought I'd fobbed her off – that she'd forgotten,' Val choked, her eyes brimming with tears.

'Forgotten what?'

'It's difficult to explain, but I'd hoped I was wrong, that my feelings were off because of my first pregnancy.'

'You aren't making any sense,' Hilda snapped. 'What did you feel?'

'We were talking about our children growing up together, of going to school together, and at that moment I somehow knew that Sarah wouldn't make it to school age.'

'Oh, my God,' Hilda gasped.

'How could I tell Ellen that? How could I warn her when I had no way of knowing when, or if it would really happen? I hate these feelings, loathe them, and just wish they'd go away.'

'I can understand that, but you should go now. I need to see if Ellen's all right.'

Tearfully, Val said, 'All right, but . . . but tell her I'm sorry.'

When Val left, for a moment Hilda stood motionless. It all sounded mad to her – impossible – but after what that strange woman had predicted on the underground platform all those years ago, it wasn't something she could just dismiss.

*   *   *

'I dread the funeral,' Maureen sobbed. 'I'm having nightmares, re-living the scene, seeing Sarah crushed in the pram. It was awful . . . awful . . .'

'I know, darling,' Gertie soothed. It seemed dreadful to think that she'd been arguing with Nancy, giving her the sack, when just up the hill such a terrible tragedy was taking place.

Maureen was still in a state, unable to stop talking about the accident, but maybe that was for the best. At least she was letting it out, whereas poor Ellen had withdrawn into herself, and, from what Hilda said, the only time she'd shown any sign of animation was when she had screamed at the vicar.

Gertie had closed the nursery, at least until after the funeral, and maybe for longer. Ellen needed her mother, and there was no way of knowing for how long. Percy and Doug were reeling with grief too, and for the time being she and Harold would be there to keep an eye on the plant stock.

She didn't regret sacking Nancy, and was still shocked by the girl's vindictiveness. Nancy had taken great delight in saying that she'd been spreading rumours about them, but thank goodness Gertie had been quick-thinking with her reply. She had turned the tables, telling Nancy that unless the gossip was stopped, Nancy's mother, and others, would be told just why she'd been sacked. The girl had looked horrified, and Gertie just hoped it had worked. Yet what did it matter now? In the light of this terrible tragedy, everything else had faded into insignificance.

'Ellen was hysterical, screaming, and I felt so helpless,' Maureen wailed.

'You were there, and though it was horrendous for you, at least Ellen wasn't alone,' Gertie said, repeating assurances that she had given Maureen over and over again.

'Are . . . are you going to try to see Ellen again today?'

'Yes, but I doubt she's up to it yet.'

'I'm sorry, Gertie. I know she's like a daughter to you and you must feel, well, excluded.'

'Nonsense, and, anyway, it doesn't matter how I feel. All that matters at the moment is Ellen and that she gets the help she needs. If you can't face the thought of the funeral, imagine how she's feeling, and no doubt it's the same for Percy, Hilda and Doug.'

Maureen hung her head, but then she said, 'I've been so selfish, too wrapped up in myself and know that now. You're right, what I'm going through is nothing compared to Ellen and her family. Not only that, you're short-staffed now and I haven't lifted a finger to help you with the nursery. Tell me what needs doing today and I'll muck in.'

'That's my girl,' Gertie said, hugging Maureen.

'I knew you'd snap out of it. You just needed a bit of time, that's all.'

'We've ordered the flowers,' Doug said as he and Percy walked into the cottage.

'I'm sorry I've had to leave it all to you,' Hilda said. 'I . . . I just couldn't face it.'

'Where's Ellen?' Percy asked.

'She's upstairs and I still can't get her to eat anything.'

Hilda and Doug came to the cottage every day, and Percy was thankful to see them. He knew he couldn't cope with Ellen, that he was helpless in the face of her grief. She had turned away from him, an unspoken gulf between them that he felt unable to bridge.

'Percy, you try,' Hilda urged. 'She won't get up, but you could take this sandwich and a cup of tea up to her.'

'All right,' he said reluctantly, 'but I doubt it'll do any good.'

'I just wish we could get her to talk. Something's eating at her, I'm sure it is, but I can hardly get a word out of her.'

'Hilda, you heard the doctor,' Doug said. 'He didn't seem overly worried, only saying that Ellen's grief has to take its natural course.'

Percy went upstairs, thankful that at least all the funeral arrangements were in place now. Both he and Doug had broken down in the funeral parlour, and had done the same when they went to the vicar again. The man had been kind, understanding that Ellen had screamed at him, and had gently taken them through the service, unperturbed that the selection of hymns had been left to him.

Ellen was lying on the bed, her back towards him when Percy walked in.

'Ellen, your mum asked me to bring this up,' he said softly. 'You've got to eat something.'

'I . . . I don't want it.'

'At least drink this tea.'

She didn't answer, only shaking her head.

'Ellen, she's worried about you. We're all worried about you. If you don't eat you'll make yourself ill.'

At last there was a response.

'I don't care. I just want to die, Percy. I deserve to die!'

Percy swiftly put the tray down and sat on the side of the bed. He reached out to stroke Ellen's hair, saying, 'Of course you don't.'

She pushed his hand away, sitting up, her voice bordering on a scream. 'I do! I do! Don't you see! I . . . I killed Sarah. I killed my baby.'

At last it was out in the open, and somehow Percy managed to push his own feelings aside as he made himself say, 'It wasn't your fault. It was an accident, a dreadful accident.'

'It *was* my fault. I didn't look . . . didn't check

485

to see that the road was clear. I pushed my baby into the path of a lorry! I killed her!'

'Ellen, what's wrong?' Hilda said as she rushed into the room. 'I could hear you shouting from downstairs.'

'I killed my baby! I killed Sarah!' Ellen yelled, and then, as though a dam had burst, tears spurted from her eyes, running unchecked down her cheeks.

'Percy, leave her to me,' Hilda ordered.

Helpless, Percy didn't argue, and Ellen's sobs echoed in his head as he left the room. He hadn't passed on what the police had told him about the accident, but Hilda had guessed that something was eating at Ellen. It was eating at him too, anger that he was trying to fight, rearing its ugly head again. Ellen *should* have been more careful – *should* have made sure the road was safe. If she had, Sarah wouldn't have died.

'I've managed to calm her down,' Hilda said when she came downstairs half an hour later, her eyes flicking round the room. 'Where's Percy?'

'Search me. When you sent him down here he just carried on walking and out of the front door. Now are you going to tell me what's going on?'

Hilda told him, watching Doug's eyes widen. 'Yes, I was shocked too, and at first I couldn't believe that Ellen had been so careless, but then I managed to keep her talking and found out why.

Ellen was on her way to see Gertie. She was worried about her, and us, our jobs at the nursery, and with all that on her mind, no wonder she wasn't concentrating on the road.'

'Worried about us. Why?'

When Hilda had finished telling him, Doug asked, 'Does Gertie know about this gossip?'

'I doubt it, but right now I'm more concerned about Ellen. She's riddled with guilt and though I tried to get through to her, I'm frightened. Ellen said she just wants to die and I'm scared, Doug. What if she tries to take her own life?'

'I'll go and talk to her.'

Hilda flopped onto a chair, sick with worry and mentally exhausted. She closed her eyes, wishing she could let go, cry for the loss of her beloved granddaughter, but somehow, for everyone's sake, she had to hold herself together.

It was ten minutes later when Percy returned, his face grim. 'I suppose Ellen told you what happened. How could she, Hilda? How could she have been so careless?'

She then told him why, and of her fears for Ellen, saw him turn pale, and moments later Percy was pounding upstairs.

Percy almost dived into the room, stopping short when he saw Ellen in her father's arms. God, what a complete and utter fool he'd been. Until now he'd had no idea how worried Ellen had been, how distracted she was when she crossed the road. Percy felt sick now – sick that he had turned away from her, leaving Ellen to Hilda, leaving her when she needed him most. No wonder Hilda was so worried. No wonder she feared that Ellen would take her own life.

'Ellen, it wasn't your fault. The accident wasn't your fault.'

'I hope she knows that now, Percy,' Doug said.

Ellen looked up at him, her eyes pools of tears, and as Doug moved away from her he whispered to Percy: 'It's all right. I don't think she'll do anything silly.'

Percy took his place and with a small sob, Ellen threw herself into his arms. 'Oh, Percy . . . Percy.'

Unaware that Doug had crept out of the room, Percy held his wife.

'Ellen, your dad said you won't try to do anything to yourself now. He's right, isn't he? Tell me he's right?'

There was barely a nod, but Percy almost cried out with relief. Ellen was still sobbing and he knew it was going to take time, a long time before their lives would ever be the same again. Somehow they had to get through it, and as yet he didn't know how. He felt so helpless, but at least she was letting him hold her now, the gulf between them at last bridged.

52

The months passed, but Ellen was only a shadow of her former self. Her eighteenth birthday, followed by Christmas, came and went without any celebration and it was now late March, the following year. Ellen managed to function, to keep the house clean, to cook for Percy; but she was still swamped with grief.

Sometimes, when Ellen thought back to the day of Sarah's funeral, most of it remained a daze, but there was something that stuck in her mind, that refused to go away. The vicar had talked of Jesus, of his loving arms welcoming Sarah. Ellen had turned away from the church many years ago, denied its preaching, but there was a deep need within her now – a need to know if there really was an afterlife and that somehow Sarah's soul went on.

The church was just ahead of her now and, hoping the vicar would see her, Ellen headed for the manse. She knocked and waited before the door was opened by a grey-haired woman.

'Can I help you?' she asked kindly.

'Would . . . would it be possible to see the vicar? I . . . I need to talk to him.'

'Come in,' she invited, then pointed to a room on the left. 'Why don't you sit in there while I fetch William?'

'William?'

'Yes, my husband, the vicar. Can I get you anything? A cup of tea?'

'No . . . no thanks.'

Ellen took a seat on the sofa, but only minutes later a soft voice said, 'Hello. Mrs Johnson, isn't it? My wife said you wanted to talk to me.'

'Ye . . . yes, that's right.'

'I know it's early days, only about six months, but how are you coping, my dear?'

'Not . . . not very well.'

'I'm sorry to hear that. Tell me, how can I help?'

'At . . . at my baby's funeral, you talked about Jesus, of him waiting to welcome Sarah into his arms. Do . . . do you really believe in life after death?'

'Of course I do, it's the basis of my faith. Jesus died for us, that our sins might be forgiven, but he rose again and ascended to heaven.'

'But they're just words, words from the Bible. There's no proof, so how can I believe they're true?'

'You must have faith, my dear. Take Jesus into your heart, and he will comfort you.'

The vicar's words were like an echo from the past – they were words that Lucy's mother had used – but they didn't comfort her. Ellen couldn't just rely on faith; she needed proof, needed evidence that there was an afterlife. The vicar was kind, a nice man and Ellen didn't want to be rude, but she just wanted to get out of the manse now.

'Thank you,' she said. 'Thank you for talking to me.' And with that, before the vicar had a chance to protest, Ellen swiftly left the manse.

She wrenched open the door, and almost ran down the path, unable to face the thought of going home to an empty house again. She had shunned Val, the thought of seeing Pauline, who was only a week younger than Sarah, more than she could bear. Yet alone all day for the past six months, she'd had plenty of time to think, slowly beginning to understand the terrible position Val had faced – how awful it must have been for her to know that something was going to happen to Sarah, but not where, or when.

Maybe she could face it now, maybe she could go to see her friend . . . but no, no, Val was having another baby. She couldn't do it, couldn't talk about babies, couldn't face seeing Pauline and how much bigger she must have grown – how much bigger Sarah would have grown. Turning the opposite way, Ellen headed for the nursery.

Maureen was walking the dog when she saw Ellen. She still looked awful, gaunt and pale.

'Hello, are you going to the nursery?'

'Yes. I've been to see the vicar, but it was a waste of time and I didn't feel like going home again just yet.'

Curious, Maureen asked, 'Why did you go to see him?'

'You'll probably think I'm being silly, but I was hoping he could tell me if there really is life after death.'

'I don't think that's silly at all. Was he able to help?'

'No. He just talked about faith, but it isn't faith I need, it's proof.'

Maureen could understand why Ellen felt this need, but how could anyone prove that there was life after death? She had heard of spiritualist churches and, desperate to help, it was the only advice she could think of.

'There's a spiritualist church in the next village,' she said as they fell into step together. 'I think they have guest mediums and one of them might be able to give you the answers you need.'

'Yes, yes, I could try there,' Ellen said eagerly.

'I'll drive you there this evening if you like.'

'Would you? Oh, thanks, Maureen.'

Maureen gulped, hoping she wasn't making a mistake. If Ellen was let down again, how would it affect her? If taking her to the spiritualist church made things worse, she dreaded to think what her parents and Percy would say, let alone Gertie.

When Gertie said she saw Doug, Hilda and Ellen as her family, Maureen had at first been at a loss to understand why. In fact, she had looked down on them, seeing them as lower class with their cockney-sounding accents.

Now though, she felt differently. They were nice people, good people who had never stood in judgement of her relationship with Gertie. Her own parents would be appalled, would probably disown her. As Ellen managed a watery smile, Maureen gave her a comforting hug, finally able to see Ellen and her parents as her family too.

53

That evening, Maureen drove Ellen to the tiny spiritualist church, and it became the first of many visits. Ellen had dared to hope, dared to think she'd find proof of an afterlife, but slowly she became disillusioned. At first, she had sat in anticipation, watching as visiting mediums gave so-called proof to others hoping for a message from their loved ones, but it confused Ellen that the messages were mostly trite.

Despite that, she was here again, hoping that this time it would be different – hoping that this time the medium would come to her.

'I have a woman here,' the medium now said. 'She's showing me a budgerigar, one she loved and I feel she passed over recently. M . . . I think her name began with M . . . perhaps Maud?'

When nobody put up a hand up, the medium tried again, 'Millie then, or Molly? I'm feeling a pain here,' she said, touching her tummy, 'as though she passed over due to a problem in this area.'

At last a hand shot up. 'I had an Aunt Mary. She had a budgie.'

'Yes, Mary, that's it,' the medium said. 'She's nodding her head now. What's that, Mary? Oh . . . right, I'll pass it on to her. It seems your aunt was quite a fussy woman. Is that right?'

'Er . . . maybe. I'm not sure.'

'She's telling me that you should dribble water on your stair carpet before brushing it – that if you do that you'll keep the dust down.'

'But . . . but . . . I haven't got carpet on my stairs.'

'I'm sure there's a hidden meaning there, a parable, and you just have to look for it,' the medium said dismissively, turning from the woman. 'There's someone else trying to come through. I have a man, in uniform, someone who perhaps died during the war?'

Several hands shot up, but Ellen had heard enough. Why would someone who died come back through a medium just to talk about cleaning carpets? The suggestion of a parable seemed meaningless, and it had been the same all those years ago with the rune stones. The old woman had talked about a sign, but that too had been vague, equally meaningless.

Ellen stood up, shuffling past others to get to

the end of the row, but as she crept towards the door a hand touched her arm. She turned to see a woman, her voice a whisper, and Ellen had to strain to hear what she said.

'You're unhappy, my dear, and I can see you haven't found your answers. Please, take this. It's my card and if you want to come to see me, maybe I can help. Come any morning except Sunday and you'll find me in.'

Ellen was beginning to doubt that anyone could help, but she took the card, thrusting it into her coat pocket as she left the building. She longed for Sarah, her baby's death still almost impossible to bear, and her only solace that they might be together again one day. Desolately Ellen walked home. She still so desperately wanted to believe that there was more, that when Sarah died, her spirit, her soul, went somewhere – somewhere better than this, to a place where there was no pain, no unhappiness, only peace and joy.

Percy looked up as Ellen came in. He didn't like her going to the spiritualist church, yet understood her driving need to know that there was life after death. She was too much on her own, that was the problem. Maybe if she returned to the nursery, worked among the plants again, it would help to fill her mind. In the meantime, this quest she was on, this search, seemed to give Ellen a purpose, a reason to get up every day, to get out of the house, and he just hoped she'd find the answers she was looking for.

'Are you all right?' he asked, but could see by the expression on her face that she'd been disappointed again. Inevitably that meant she'd be in tears that night. He hadn't expected that Ellen would turn to him for lovemaking, had thought it would be a long time before she was ready for that, but instead she clung to him nearly every night and he'd come to realise that it was the only time she could forget, if only for a while, that Sarah was dead.

'It was a waste of time,' she said. 'I don't think there's much point in going any more. I might go to see this woman though,' she said, pulling the card out of her pocket. 'She seemed nice and might be able to help me.'

Percy was worried that this search for answers was becoming an obsession.

'Why don't you come back to work? You love working with plants, and we're so busy with transplanting that we could do with a hand.'

'I don't know. I'll think about it.'

'Ellen, while you were out, Val came round. She was hoping to see you. It's been nearly six months, and I know it's still hard, but Val isn't the only woman with a child. You can't avoid them all.'

'Don't you think I know that? It . . . it's just that

Sarah and Pauline were born within a week of each other. I can't face it yet, I just can't. I need more time.'

'All right, love, don't get upset,' Percy said hastily. His parents had been down to see them again last weekend, but as usual it had been a painful visit. Ellen was so quiet and he knew they found it difficult, yet felt powerless to do anything about it. Ellen wasn't just shutting out his parents – she had shut out almost everyone.

'I understand why you don't want to see Val, but I still think you should come back to work.'

Ellen was quiet for a moment, but then she said, 'Tell Gertie I'll start on Monday.'

Percy felt a rush of relief. He was sure it would help Ellen, at least in keeping her mind occupied. Maybe when she was back at the nursery she'd give up this fruitless search for answers – at least he hoped so.

When Percy left for work the next morning, Ellen found herself picking up the woman's card again, as though just looking at it would offer some answers. Amelia Harte – a nice name – and her smile had been so kind. It was Saturday and she'd agreed to go back to work on Monday, so if she wanted to see this woman it would have to be today.

At ten o'clock, hoping it wouldn't be too early,

Ellen made her way to Christmas Pie village. The cottage wasn't hard to find, and nervously Ellen knocked on the door, the woman's welcome warm as she invited her in.

'I'm glad you came,' Amelia said, leading Ellen into a comfortable parlour.

'You . . . you said you may be able to help me.'

'I hope you won't be disappointed, but I have to tell you that I'm not a medium.'

'You're not?'

'I suppose I'm what you would call sensitive, and I dabble a little with palm reading. I saw how unhappy you looked and sensed that you're in deep pain. I too have lost someone and know that sometimes just talking about it can help.'

'I'm sorry, it's kind of you, but I don't need to talk about it.'

'What *do* you need?'

'I . . . I need to know that there's an afterlife.'

'Yes, I felt the same, and like you, I started going to the spiritualist church.'

'Did . . . did you find proof?'

'There was a little evidence, but nothing definitive. In time I slowly came to understand that perhaps it's impossible to prove, yet then again the opposite is true. Those who say there is no afterlife can't prove it either.'

'Yet you still go to the spiritualist church?'

'I've made many friends there, lovely friends,

so yes; and thanks to one of them I found comfort in nature.'

Puzzled, Ellen asked, 'How?'

'Many plants die in winter, but then in spring they come to life again, looking stronger, growing larger, their flowers blooming once more. Then there are butterflies, dragonflies too. They start life as a chrysalis, cocooned, but then suddenly they transform, emerging in a different form, a new and beautiful form. It is renewal, my dear, and I think the same thing happens to us when we die. Our souls leave the cocoon of our body to become a wondrous, spiritual being.'

'It all sounds lovely, but . . . but I can't just accept that. I . . . I need proof.'

The woman leaned forward and took Ellen's hand to gaze at her palm.

'You're so young and I can see by these lines that you've suffered so much. The answers you seek are close to home and it's there you'll find them. In the meantime, if it's any consolation, your future looks bright.'

'Close to home? What do you mean?'

'Just that, my dear,' she said, but then there was a knock on her door. 'Oh dear, it seems someone else has come to see me.'

'I'll go,' Ellen said, 'and . . . and do I owe you anything?'

'Owe me! Oh, you mean money. No, no, of

course not. All I hope is that in some way I've been able to help.'

'Thank you,' Ellen said, and as she left, another woman went in. In a way, she did feel a little comforted, but was still confused. The woman said that her answers lay close to home. But where?

The next morning, Doug saw that Gertie also looked delighted when Percy told her that Ellen wanted to come to work again.

'That's wonderful, Percy. I'm glad you told me this morning because I was just thinking it was time to replace Nancy.'

'I'm surprised you waited this long,' Doug commented.

'After what happened, I must admit I've been a bit nervous.'

'As far as I know, there hasn't been any more gossip.'

'My threat must have done the trick, along with introducing Maureen as my cousin to the vicar.'

'I don't know how you had the nerve,' Doug said, smiling. 'And him a man of the cloth too.'

'It was better to lie than face persecution, and, as there's been no more gossip, word must have spread around the village.'

Yes, and it saved their jobs too, Doug thought as they walked into the shop.

'Hilda, we've got a bit of news. Ellen's coming back to work here on Monday.'

'Oh, that's wonderful,' Hilda said, and for the first time in ages she had a genuine smile on her face and not one just put on for the customers.

'It's great,' nodded Doug. 'And just in time to help me with transplanting the seedlings.'

'You and those flippin' seedlings, you treat them like babies,' Hilda said, but then her voice cracked. 'Oh . . . oh, no. I'll have to be careful I don't say something like that when Ellen's around.'

Doug knew how worried she was about Ellen, and though he was too, he was also concerned about Hilda. She had grown thin, her hair now streaked with grey, and the spark seemed to have gone out of her. When they had moved to Surrey, she'd loved the cottage, could often be heard singing as she pottered around, but those days were gone now.

'Hilda, this is just what Ellen needs, so stop fretting.'

'Yes, Doug's right,' Gertie said. 'Now buck up, Hilda, and make us all a nice cup of tea.'

'Yes, madam,' she quipped.

That's better, Doug thought. Hilda sounded a bit more like her old self now. It was a start and that was something.

Hilda put the kettle onto the small gas ring. She had been so worried about Ellen, but now at last her worries were easing. Work would be the best thing for her daughter, and she'd be there with them every day instead of alone at home.

She only had one concern now, and though Hilda understood how Ellen felt, her heart went out to Val. It had been hard at first when Val called round with Pauline, but then one day the child had toddled up to her, arms out to be picked up and she hadn't been able to resist. Val was six months pregnant now, and seemed vulnerable, alone somehow, and though Hilda had tried, she still hadn't been able to persuade Ellen to see her.

'Need a hand?'

Broken out of her reveries, Hilda said, 'You're actually offering to help? That's a first, Gertie, and I'm honoured.'

'It's nice to hear you being cheeky again.'

'It's been hard, awful. I used to think that London brought me nothing but bad luck, but I was wrong. It doesn't seem to matter where I live, it always follows me. Sometimes I think my family is cursed.'

'Don't be silly, of course you aren't.'

'I hope you're right. I don't think I could stand any more heartache.'

Gertie moved to put an arm around her, and for a moment Hilda leaned on her strength. She had no fear of Gertie's feelings now, knew how happy she was with Maureen, and, feeling stronger, said, 'Get off, you daft cow. I'm supposed to be making a pot of tea. Now make yourself useful and put the mugs on that tray.'

'As you would say, Hilda – yes, madam.'

Hilda was able to smile again. It was still going to be hard for Ellen, but at least working at the nursery she'd have her family around her. Somehow, they all had to move forward, to pick up the pieces, and hopefully this was the beginning.

54

Ellen was glad that she'd returned to work and, as spring turned to summer, she drew pleasure in seeing the trays of plants she and her father had worked on selling well. Amelia Harte had been right, Ellen had also drawn comfort from nature – yet there was still a deep longing within her to know that somehow Sarah lived on, that one day they'd be together again.

Amelia Harte had been wrong, though, in saying that her answers lay close to home – there were still no answers and, as the dreaded day dawned, Ellen curled into a ball, wishing that she hadn't awoken to face it.

'Sarah, oh, Sarah,' she whispered. It was Sarah's birthday and she would have been two years old today. Ellen had never seen her daughter walk, never heard her talk, and the pain of her loss was once again unbearable.

Unable to stifle her sobs, she felt Percy's arm slide around her, and now, knowing he was awake, she turned to him for comfort. He held her, and as his hands ran over her body, Ellen responded, trying to drown her unhappiness in his lovemaking.

All too soon it was over, Percy now saying, 'Why don't you stay home today? I'm sure Gertie will understand.'

'No, no, I don't want to be alone. I'll come to work, but . . . but first, I must go to the cemetery.'

'I'll come with you.'

Ellen wanted to say no – to tell Percy that this time she wanted to be alone when she laid fresh flowers on her daughter's tiny grave – yet she didn't want to hurt him. Every week since Sarah died they had gone together, Percy always with a large pair of scissors to clip the small amount of grass, and she to replace old flowers with new ones.

'All . . . all right,' she said finally.

Percy got ready, all the time keeping an eye on Ellen. They all knew how bad it was going to be for her today, and though Ellen didn't know it, they'd talked about it yesterday. Gertie had said he should follow Ellen's lead. If she wanted to stay at home, that was fine, and if needed, he should stay home with her. Hilda and Doug were going to the cemetery too, Gertie saying that it didn't matter if they were all late for work; that Maureen would open the shop and stay there until they arrived to take over.

'Ready?' Percy asked now.

'I . . . I just need to cut some flowers.'

'We'll do it together,' he said.

They went into the back garden, Ellen's eyes filling with tears as she looked around.

'I wanted roses, but they're nearly finished now. It . . . it'll have to be chrysanthemums.'

'They'll be fine,' he said, cutting some choice blooms.

It was a quiet walk to the cemetery, the day slightly overcast, and when they reached Sarah's grave Ellen appeared all right at first as she knelt to remove the old flowers. Percy handed her the bottle of fresh water, but then stiffened as Ellen suddenly wailed in anguish. Before he could stop her, she flung herself across the grave, crying as though her heart was breaking.

It was then he heard Hilda's voice. 'Oh, darling, come on, get up.'

Together he and Hilda crouched down and managed to get Ellen to her feet, while Doug stood by, watching helplessly, face chalk-white. Ellen ran to him, flinging herself into her father's arms.

'Oh, Dad, I want her back. I want my baby back!'

'I know, pumpkin, I know,' he said, holding her close.

Percy stood watching and, as Hilda held out her hand, he clutched it, until at last he saw Ellen becoming calmer. She moved from her father's arms, bending down to pick up the new flowers she had dropped, and, saying nothing, knelt to arrange them in the vase.

'I . . . I've got some too,' Hilda said, leaving Percy to add yellow dahlias to the arrangement.

At last, Ellen was ready to leave, but as they walked towards the gates, she said, 'I . . . I can't bear to think there's nothing of Sarah now. There has to be more, Percy, there just has to.'

Doug walked with Hilda behind Ellen and Percy, wondering if coming to the cemetery just made things worse. He didn't like it that Ellen had got involved with the spiritualist church and, as far as he was concerned, searching for an afterlife was a waste of time. With all the horrors he had seen during the war, he'd long since given up on believing in God. He had seen men shot, burned, drowning, and many had cried out to God to save them. It hadn't done any good. Despite their pleas, the sea had taken them, just as it had almost taken him.

Hilda had her head down, sniffing as they neared the cemetery gates. Giving her hand a squeeze, he asked, 'Are you all right?'

'How can I be? Seeing Sarah's grave . . . seeing the state Ellen's in brought it all back again. She's only eighteen, Doug, but already Ellen has been through too much.'

'I know, and I wish we could do more to help her.'

'I don't think she's in any state to come to work today.'

'What about you? You don't sound up to it either.'

'I'd rather be doing something than sitting at home.'

'What if Ellen needs you?'

'If she does, then I'll stay with her.'

They caught up with Percy and Ellen, Doug saying, 'We should get to work, but if you need your mum, Ellen, she'll go home with you.'

'No, it's all right. I'll go home to change, but . . . but then I'll come to the nursery.'

'Are you sure?' Percy asked.

Doug saw the concern on his son-in-law's face, and he was glad that Ellen had agreed to marry him, despite his initial reservations. Percy cared deeply for Ellen, and before this dreadful tragedy he knew that his daughter had come to care for him too. If they could get through this, Doug felt they could get through anything, and though this was a dreadful day, so far the signs were still good that their marriage was strong.

Despite saying she'd go to work, Ellen found that she could barely hold herself together, and wanted to be alone to give full vent to her grief. She was holding on, just, and said, 'Percy, I can't face the nursery yet. You go and I might come in later.'

'I don't want to leave you to face this on your own.'

'Look, there's no point in you being here. I've got a splitting headache and I just want to go to bed for a while.'

'I think I should stay.'

'No, please, Percy, just go.'

He looked doubtful, but finally nodded his head. 'All right, but if you're not at work by lunchtime, I'll pop home to see how you are.'

At last he left, and moments later, Ellen broke down, and it was nearly an hour later before her tears were spent. Her eyes were red, sore, and she leaned over the sink to splash them with cold water. She had dreaded this day – a day when there should have been birthday cards on the mantelpiece, presents for Sarah, but instead there was only this awful pain that sat like a rock in her stomach.

It was one of those days when Ellen felt she couldn't go on, when she wished she had the courage to end it all, but how could she do that now? There was something she had to tell Percy, but not now, not today. Her head really was splitting now and all she craved was to escape into sleep before she broke down again.

Ellen climbed into bed, closed her eyes, and at last, at least for a while, she found the peace she sought.

55

It was nearly a week later, on a Sunday morning, when Ellen told Percy.

He looked shocked at first, but then his eyes lit up. 'I can't believe it! Are . . . are you sure?'

'Yes, I'm sure. I wasn't at first, especially as my monthlies have been a bit haywire, but I am now.'

'A baby! We're having a baby? But how . . . when?'

Ellen managed a small smile. 'I should think the how is obvious. As for when, I'm three months pregnant so the baby will be born next year, around March.'

'It'll be 1950 then, Ellen, and our baby born into a new era. Do your parents know?'

'Of course not, I wanted to tell you first.'

Percy hugged her, but then he pulled away a little, asking as he looked down at her face, 'Ellen, is it all right? Are you happy about it?'

'Yes, I'm happy.'

'Come on then, let's go and tell your mum and dad.'

They walked up to the Hogs Back, Ellen's heart thumping and the awful memories returning yet again as they crossed the road. As though in understanding, Percy clutched her hand tightly. It had taken a long time, and though Ellen would never forgive herself for the accident, she knew it was time to move forward. She was having a baby, bringing a new life into the world, and though she would never, ever, forget Sarah, the pain had eased a little.

Soon they were walking towards her parents' cottage, Percy saying, 'I can't wait to see their faces when you tell them.'

Ellen smiled, anticipating their reaction too, and they walked inside to find her mother up to her elbows in flour and her father reading a newspaper. Her mother looked surprised to see them, and strangely, Ellen thought, a little guilty too.

'Ellen, I wasn't expecting you.'

'We've got a bit of news, but you look busy. What are you making?'

Hilda bit on her lower lip, then saying, 'It . . . it's a cake.'

Ellen was puzzled, but then the penny dropped.

'Pauline will be two soon and you're making her a birthday cake.'

'I . . . I'm sorry, love,' Hilda stammered. 'As I said,

I wasn't expecting you and wouldn't have upset you for the world.'

Ellen could see how worried her mother was, the distress in her eyes. Her parents had been through enough, had suffered too when Sarah died, but, so wrapped up in her own pain, she'd hardly spared them a thought. She wanted to change things now, to bring them a little happiness. Ellen smiled gently, and said, 'It's nice you're making a cake for Pauline, Mum.'

'You . . . you don't mind?'

'No, but even nicer, you'll have another one to make in March next year.'

'What do you mean? Why would I be making another birthday cake in Mar . . . ?' Hilda asked, the sentence unfinished as her eyes widened. 'No . . . no . . . you're not . . . ?'

'Yes, Mum, I am. I'm having a baby.'

'Oh . . . oh, Doug. Did you hear that?' Hilda cried, her eyes suddenly brimming with tears.

'Of course I did,' he said, standing up to pull Ellen into his arms. 'Congratulations, pumpkin.'

'Dad, when are you going to stop calling me pumpkin?'

'Sorry, it just sort of slips out,' he said ruefully.

'It's all right, Dad. I'm only kidding. I don't mind really.'

'Good, 'cos as much as I've tried, I ain't likely to stop.' And with that, he released her to turn to

Percy, grabbing his hand and pumping it madly. 'Well done, lad, and congratulations to you too.'

'Thanks, but I'm curious. Where did the nickname pumpkin come from?'

'Yes, tell him, Dad,' Ellen urged. She knew the story, and smiled as she listened to her father.

'When Hilda was carrying Ellen, she was thin, other than her tummy, which got as big as a pumpkin and I used to tease her about it. I suppose you could say the nickname is down to her really, because as soon as she gave birth and held Ellen out to me, she said . . . well, you tell them, Hilda.'

'That's it, blame me,' Hilda said, but she was smiling. 'All I said to him was, "Here Doug, meet Baby Pumpkin." It was meant as a joke, but somehow the nickname stuck.'

'I rather like it. It's cute,' Percy said.

'Now don't you start calling me pumpkin too,' Ellen warned, though glad to hear her parents' laughter. Yes, it was time to move forward and for the first time in over a year she felt a surge of happiness, true happiness. There was one thing she still had to do, and now at last felt strong enough. 'I think I'll go along to see Val. It's time I saw her new baby, and I'd like to tell her the good news.'

'Do you want me to come with you?' Percy asked.

'No, it's lunchtime and Bob is sure to be at the local pub. I'd rather go on my own.'

'Percy, how about you and I go to the pub for

a drink too?' Doug said. 'I think this news calls for a celebratory drink.'

'All right,' Percy agreed. 'I wouldn't say no to a pint.'

They left first, Ellen then turning to her mother. 'I won't be long.'

'Take your time, love. It'll give me a chance to finish this cake, but oh, Ellen, I can't tell you how happy I am. You are too, aren't you?'

'Yes, Mum, I'm happy, though a bit nervous of how Val's going to react when she sees me. I've cut her out, refused to see her, and I wouldn't blame her if she shuts the door in my face.'

'Don't worry, Val won't do that. She understands, and I know she's missed you.'

'Right. I'll see you later,' Ellen said, hoping her mother was right as she walked along to Mayflower Cottage.

Instead of getting on with the cake, Hilda flopped onto a chair, her heart singing with joy. Ellen was having a baby and she hugged herself with happiness. When Mabel and Jack heard about it they'd be overjoyed too. A new life, a new beginning, and now she wondered if Ellen was having a boy or a girl. In a way she hoped it would be a boy – fearing that in some way they would see a girl as a replacement for Sarah. No, she then decided. This new baby would be a child in its own right, and she would love it in that way too, just as she had loved Sarah.

Hilda felt a surge of pain now, the grief still with her at the loss of her granddaughter. Inevitably, as they often did now, her eyes went to the mantelpiece. Her mother had loved the angel and Hilda wished she hadn't smashed it. She'd been devastated, angry, and had used the angel as a scapegoat. It had been a daft thing to do, silly to think an inanimate object was watching over them. Her hand went to her mother's necklace. She had ripped that from her neck in anger once too, but at least she had got it back, and somehow still drew comfort from it.

Hilda stood up. She still had the cake to make and had better get on with it but, as she mixed the fat into the flour, Hilda couldn't help wondering how things were going in Mayflower Cottage. She hoped Ellen wouldn't be too distressed when she saw Pauline and that she'd fall in love with Val's baby boy. Robert, named after his father, was adorable, and Pauline so cute and endearing. She just hoped that, like her, Ellen would find both children hard to resist.

Soon, in six months, Ellen would have another baby to love, and maybe, with her daughter knowing that, it would help.

'Ellen! Oh, Ellen, I can't believe it. Come in. Please come in.'

Val looked so pleased to see her, and any doubts Ellen had were dispelled now as she stepped inside. The first thing she saw, the first thing that her eyes were drawn to, was the hearthrug – the place where Sarah and Pauline had sat playing together. It was empty. She looked around the rest of the room, finding Pauline nowhere in sight.

As though aware of her thoughts, Val said softly, 'Pauline isn't well. She's got a bit of fever and I put her down for a nap. Robert's over there, in his pram.'

'Pauline's all right, isn't she?'

'It's just a cold, and as I said, a bit of a fever, but please, Ellen, sit down. I can't tell you how pleased I am to see you.'

'I'm sorry, Val. I know it's been ages.'

'It doesn't matter. You're here now.'

Ellen drew in a deep breath, and instead of sitting down she went over to the pram, looking down at the baby's face. He was lovely, dark-haired like his father, and softly she said, 'He's beautiful, Val.'

'Thanks,' she said, smiling.

Ellen moved away from the pram to sit down. 'I've got something to tell you, Val. I'm having another baby.'

'You are? That's wonderful and I bet your mum's over the moon.'

'Yes, she is, and it was lovely to see the expression on her face when I broke the news.'

'I can just imagine it. I bet your dad's pleased too, and of course, Percy,' Val said, but then hearing a cry she stiffened. 'That . . . that's Pauline. I might have to get her up.'

'It's all right,' Ellen said. 'Don't worry, I'll be all right.'

'Are . . . are you sure? Your mum said . . .'

'Go, Val, I'll be fine,' Ellen broke in as Pauline cried out again, hoping she was right as Val hurried from the room.

It was a little later when Val returned, Pauline red-faced, crying, and runny-nosed in her arms.

'I . . . I'm sorry, Ellen. I couldn't get her off to sleep again.'

Ellen had dreaded this moment, feared it would be too much, but instead found her heart going out to Pauline. 'Oh, look at her, the poor thing.'

Val sat down, Pauline on her lap, and pulling out a handkerchief, she wiped her daughter's nose. The baby started to cry too, and worriedly, Val said, 'Please, Robbie, not now.'

'I'll see to him,' Ellen said, rising swiftly to her feet and lifting the baby gently into her arms. 'There . . . there,' she soothed.

'He's due for a feed,' Val said. 'Come on, Pauline, you sit down there for a little while.'

With Pauline now on the hearthrug, Val thrust a few toys in front of her and then took the baby from Ellen's arms, opening her blouse to put him to her breast. 'He's such a hungry baby and still needs feeding every two hours. I've forgotten the last time I got a decent night's sleep.'

'I suppose I've got that to look forward to,' Ellen

said, smiling softly at the scene. There was something soothing about watching a baby being fed, and for a time all was quiet in the room. Pauline had stopped crying too, and Ellen looked down at her, the little girl playing with a toy, giggling and chatting away to herself.

'It's not like her,' Val said, frowning as she looked at her daughter. 'She usually demands attention when I'm feeding Robert.'

'Perhaps she's jealous.'

'Yes, I expect so, but this makes a pleasant change.'

Val continued to feed the baby, then moved him to her other breast, and soon Robert was once more sucking contentedly, while Pauline continued to chatter and play in some sort of make-believe game.

Ellen watched Pauline as she held out a toy, but then stiffened. No, no, she was imagining it! She *had* to be imagining it. Swiftly she turned her head to look at Val, but her friend was absorbed in feeding the baby and obviously hadn't heard. Ellen looked back at Pauline, her breath held, but then she slumped. Yes, the child was talking, chattering, but it was just a sort of gibberish really, her words indistinct. She'd imagined it – of course she'd imagined it.

'So, you're done,' Val said, laying Robert against her shoulder to wind him. 'The trouble is he doesn't take enough and I think that's why he needs feeding every two hours.' He burped dutifully and, smiling, Val rose to her feet to lay him in the pram again.

'Right, Ellen, I think it's time I made us both a drink.'

'Me dwink, Mummy,' Pauline appealed, 'and Erra.'

'What did you say?' Val asked.

'Dwink, *please*, Mummy.'

'No, no, I didn't mean that. Oh, never mind. Yes, I'll get you some orange juice.'

'Wait, Val. Please wait,' Ellen appealed. 'Didn't you hear what she said?'

'Yes, something about wanting Erra, but goodness knows what that is.'

'Val, you might think this is mad, but I think she said Sarah.'

'What? No, surely not?' Val said. Her face paled and she went over to crouch in front of her daughter. 'Pauline, you asked for a drink and something else. What is it you want, darling?'

'Erra . . . dwink for Erra too.'

'Oh, my God,' Val gasped.

Ellen could only stare, tears flooding her eyes. Was it possible? Was Pauline able to see Sarah?

'Maybe it's you,' Val said. 'Perhaps seeing you sparked something off in Pauline's memory.'

Val's explanation made sense, but Ellen shook her head. 'No, I think there's more to it than that. You . . . you see I went to see a woman and she told me my answers lay close to home. She was right, well, almost. They were close to home, but not mine – my mother's.'

'What answers?'

'I wanted to know, needed to know, that there's an afterlife.'

'Ellen, I'm sure there is.'

Pauline scrambled to her feet now, toddling over to Ellen, and for a brief moment as just one of the child's hands came to rest on her knee, Ellen felt that there were two. Her heart skipped a beat. Sarah was here, close to her, she could feel it in her soul and tears ran unchecked down her cheeks.

'No cry,' Pauline appealed, holding her arms up.

Ellen lifted her onto her lap, kissing the top of her head. She had rejected this child, dreaded seeing her, but now, thanks to Pauline's innocent eyes, she knew that Sarah lived on.

'Yes, Val, there is an afterlife and now I'm sure too.'

'Erra go now,' Pauline said.

No, no, Ellen thought, but then somewhere deep inside she knew that it was time – that, like her, it was time for her beautiful, beloved daughter to move forward. Softly she said, 'Yes, fly, darling. Fly free until one day, we'll be together again.'

There was a gasp, a choking sound and Ellen looked over Pauline's head to see Val running towards the window. No, no, it had to be a co-incidence, it had to be, Ellen thought as she watched a beautiful butterfly landing on the sill.

Val flung the window open, and spreading its wings again, the butterfly seemed to hesitate for a moment; but then it lifted in flight, soaring outside.

'Did . . . did you see that?' Val asked, eyes wide with wonder. 'You . . . you don't think . . . ?'

Ellen smiled softly and with Pauline in her arms she went over to the window.

'I don't know, Val. Perhaps it was just a coincidence, but it's one that will live with me for the rest of my life.'

'Yes, me too,' Val said, and, as Pauline reached out her arms, Val took her.

Ellen looked out of the window, hoping for a last glimpse of the butterfly. It was there, on a buddleia, wings twitching. A profound feeling of peace filled her, and at that moment she remembered the old woman and the rune stones. This was the sign she had spoken of, Ellen was sure of it, and though some people might think she was living in a world of fantasy, others that she was mad, Ellen didn't care.

What did it matter what other people thought? What she chose to believe, what eased her pain, what gave her comfort and the strength to go on – that was all that mattered. And how could anyone begrudge her that?

The butterfly's wings opened and then it was flying again, soaring away. Fantasy or not, coincidence or not, before it went out of sight for ever, Ellen whispered, 'Goodbye, darling. For now – goodbye.'

Read on for an exclusive chapter of Kitty Neale's
new novel, coming in summer 2010.

Prologue

The argument had raged for two days, but the man couldn't give in – wouldn't give in. His wife had to agree, and once again he urged, 'We've got to do something. All right, I know they were distant relatives, but it was still a shock to hear they died. We're the only family she has left now.'

'*You're* her only family,' his wife snapped. 'I never met them – or their daughter.'

'Like it or not, by marrying me they became your relatives. If this was someone in your family, I wouldn't think twice.'

'That's easy for you to say, but something like this wouldn't have happened in *my* family.'

'There's no need for the high and mighty attitude. We've no idea what happened to her – how she came to be in such a dreadful place, and I for one am not going to judge her.'

'I don't care. I can't do it. You're asking too much of me.'

'And if you expect me to just walk away, you're asking too much of me. I'd never be able to forgive myself – or you.'

'Now you're using emotional blackmail.'

'If you had an ounce of compassion I wouldn't need to.'

'That isn't fair. I do feel sorry for what happened to her, really I do, but . . . but . . .'

He saw the strain on his wife's face, but couldn't stop now. He had to convince her. His voice softened, trying honey this time, 'I'm sorry, darling, that was cruel of me. Of course you're compassionate, in fact its one of the things I love about you. I think that's why I've been taken aback by your attitude. I somehow thought that, like me, you wouldn't be able to just walk away.'

'Please, please, we've been arguing about this for so long and my head is splitting. Let me think. I need time to think.'

He could tell she was weakening and felt a surge of triumph – sure that at last, one final push would do it. He stood up, bent to kiss her, and said before leaving the room, 'All right, darling, I'll leave you to think. You're a wonderful woman, a kind, caring woman, and I feel sure you'll come to the right decision.'

It was two hours later before he got his answer. His wife had agreed, but only in part. She'd been adamant, and he'd been unable to bend her any further. There was only one thing he could do now, but he dreaded it.

The man closed his eyes, the thought of what he was faced with, agonising.

1

Wimbledon, South London, May 1971

It was home, a red bricked facade draped with wisteria, bay windows and warm oak front door that appeared welcoming, yet as Jennifer Lavender pulled out her key, she knew there'd be no such welcome inside. If her father was home it would be different, but he was away again, his job as a sales director often meaning long periods of absence.

With a fixed smile on her face, Jenny walked into the drawing room. 'Hello, Mother, I'm home.'

'I can see that,' Delia Lavender said dismissively before turning her attention back to her son. She was a tall woman, slim, with immaculately groomed auburn hair and hazel eyes that showed concern as she asked him, 'Do you think you can manage to eat something, darling? I could make a shepherds pie.'

'Yes, all right,' Martin said.

To Jenny, her brother didn't look ill, but as usual Martin avoided meeting her eyes. At seventeen years old he had the same colouring as their mother and had come home from college the previous day complaining of a sore throat and headache. As always he was being mollycoddled, but then her mother spoke and Jenny snapped to attention.

'Don't just stand there. Get changed and then you can peel the potatoes.'

Jenny ran upstairs, anxious as ever to please her mother, yet no matter what she did, how hard she tried, she felt the gulf between them. She was confused by her brother's attitude too. They had once been close and she had turned to Martin for sympathy when their father was away, but he had suddenly changed, his manner now as distant as her mothers.

For a moment Jenny looked at her reflection in the mirror, wondering what she had done, and what it was about her that was so unlovable. At fifteen years old she favoured her father in looks, yet lacked his height. Her friends told her she was pretty, but all Jenny saw was pale skin, blonde hair and light blue eyes, her face void of colour.

As so often happened, a wave of loneliness washed over her, but it was something Jenny didn't really understand. She had friends, a family, yet there was this feeling of something missing in her life – something inexplicable.

'Jennifer, do get a move on!'

'Coming,' she called back, hurrying to change out of her school uniform before running downstairs.

'It's about time too,' her mother complained as she stood threading meat into the mincer.

'I got good marks in geography today,' Jenny said, hoping to please her.

'It's a bit late to do well now. If you hadn't failed your eleven plus exam you would be at grammar school like Martin. Instead you're only destined for some sort of menial work.'

'I've done well at typing and could get a job in an office.'

'A typist,' Delia said derisively. 'That's hardly something I can brag about at the tennis club.'

Jenny felt the sting of tears. She knew how appearances were important to her mother, how she valued her social standing, and had felt the pressure. So much so that when the exam papers were put in front of her she had frozen, her mind refusing to work.

'Stop sniffing, it isn't ladylike. I sometimes regret that we didn't send you to a private school, but we've had enough expense in funding Martin's education and his is more important.'

'I'm thirsty,' Martin said as he walked in to pour himself a glass of water.

'You should have called me, darling.'

'Stop fussing, Mother, there's nothing wrong with my legs,' he said, then gulping the water. 'Dad's more away than at home these days, but at least for once he'll be here this weekend.'

'Now then, Martin, you know how hard your father works. The company has expanded into other areas and he's had to recruit a large sales team. Once he has regional managers in place things are sure to be easier.'

'Dad's coming home? When is he arriving?' Jenny asked eagerly.

'He rang this morning and said it'll either be late tonight or early tomorrow morning.'

Jenny's unhappiness faded, to be replaced with joy. Her dad would be home soon and she couldn't wait to see him.

Edward Lavender's eyes were rimmed with tiredness, the strain of such a long drive showing as he at last pulled into the drive. It was after eleven, but as the light was on in the drawing room he knew that Delia was still up.

It had been a long trip, eight weeks away, yet he wasn't looking forward to seeing his wife. The marriage had been fine at first, a son born on their third wedding anniversary, but eighteen months later, from the moment Jennifer had been placed in her arms, Delia had changed from a pliant wife to a petulant, demanding one. He had worked like a dog to provide all she wanted, gained promotions until he was able to buy her the perfect house. Yet it wasn't a home – it was a showplace, with never a thing out of place or a smidgen of dust to be seen anywhere.

There'd been times when Edward had been temped to walk out on Delia, but he could never leave his children, especially Jennifer. Instead he found his needs elsewhere, brief encounters that he paid for; it was less complicated that way.

With a sign Edward climbed out of the car and stretched his cramped muscles before he opened the front door. He knew there would be a cold atmosphere to greet him – along with an even colder wife, but nevertheless as he went into the drawing room, Edward said pleasantly, 'Hello, my dear.'

'So, you're back. I wasn't really expecting you until the morning.'

'I made good time and it was pointless stopping somewhere overnight when I was so close to home.'

'I hope you're not expecting dinner at this time of night.'

'Just a sandwich will do, and perhaps a cup of cocoa.'

Delia exhaled loudly, showing her exasperation, but nevertheless went to the kitchen. Edward had barely sat down when his daughter flew in, her face alight with happiness.

'Dad! Oh, Dad.'

'Hello, darling,' he said, rising quickly and hugging Jennifer to him, thinking as always that she made coming home worthwhile. He'd get some sort of welcome from Martin, but his son was a product of his mother, his emotions held tightly in check.

'How long will you be here?' Jenny asked eagerly.

'Just for the weekend, I'm afraid.'

'Jennifer, what are you doing up at this time of night?' Delia asked sharply as she stormed into the room.'

'I was excited that Dad might be home and couldn't sleep.'

'Go back to bed, *now!*'

'Jenny, do as your mother says,' Edward softly urged. 'I'll still be here in the morning.'

For just a brief moment Jennifer looked mutinous, but then she nodded, 'All right. Goodnight, Dad.'

'Goodnight, darling,' he said, giving her another quick hug.

Delia just stood there, tight lipped. When Jenny left the room she swung around too, heading back to the kitchen.

Delia almost slammed a small saucepan of milk onto the cooker. It was always the same. Edward had arrived home after two months away, but he was no sooner in the door than Jennifer got his attention and affection. She would punish him, Delia decided, just as she'd always punished him; something she had sworn to do from the moment another baby had been forced upon her. She didn't want Jennifer, didn't want another child and Edward had known that.

She took a loaf of bread, cutting two slices, her mind still raging. Oh, she had tried to love Jennifer, but her resentment was high and the maternal instincts she had felt for Martin had been absent from the start. Of course it hadn't helped that Jennifer had been a difficult baby, demanding, and she so tired that if felt she was neglecting her son. Poor Martin had been under two, into everything and needing her attention, something she no longer had the time to give him.

Of course she had made up for it now, her son a wonderful young man who would go far, but Edward would still pay dearly for causing his early neglect.

'I'll eat it in here,' Edward said, taking a seat at the kitchen table.

'Fine,' she said shortly, placing the sandwich and cup of cocoa in front of him.

'As usual, I can see you're pleased to see me,' he drawled sarcastically.

'What do you expect? Unlike Jennifer I didn't even get a kiss on the cheek.'

'If I tried to kiss you, as usual I'd have been rebuffed.'

'You don't know that.'

'No, Delia, I'm not playing your games. You're fond of giving me hope, but then withdrawing it, but I'm not falling for it again. I'm content with the wonderful welcome I received from Jenny.'

'She's sixteen next month, leaves school four weeks later and old enough then to leave home. It's time she was told the truth.'

'No, Delia.'

'If you don't tell her, I will.'

'You'll do no such thing! I know what you're up to. You hope that by telling her she'll *want* to leave home, but I won't stand for it. I don't want her told – ever!'

Delia's jaws ground. Edward didn't know it, but she wasn't finished yet and he'd soon find that out. 'I'm going to bed. Please don't disturb me when you come up.'

'Don't worry, Delia, I know better than to come into your room.'

Without another word, she marched out. Long ago Edward had given her the power to get her own way, and she had made the most of it, insisting amongst other things on separate bedrooms.

She still had that power and would use it. It was time for the truth to come out – time to stop living in a house of secrets.

What's next?

Tell us the name of an author you love

> Kitty Neale | **Go** ▶

and we'll find your next great book.